MICHAEL J. BOWLER

RUNNING THROUGH

I0591125

A DARK PLACE

THE LANCE CHRONICLES 2

Published by Michael J. Bowler, USA stuntshark2.0@gmail.com

Running Through A Dark Place
(The Lance Chronicles 2)
Second Edition Copyright © 2018 by Michael J. Bowler

Cover Art and Interior Formatting by Streetlight Graphics

Print: ISBN: 978-0-9903063-0-6
Mobi: ISBN: 978-0-9903063-1-3
epub: ISBN: 978-0-9903063-2-0

Printed in the United States of America
Second Edition
July 2018

The paraphrasing of "running though a dark place" and the part about children's fears is something I have recalled for years, though in what original form I cannot say. I think it owes its genesis to the novel *Night of the Hunter* and the screenplay of its movie, written by Davis Grubb and James Agee respectively, but not in the exact form I used herein. If so, no intent to plagiarize is intended, but I'm grateful to the originator of those words for they have helped guide my work with children and teens, and kept me mindful that children are not adults and should *never* be treated as such.

As with *Children of the Knight*, this book is dedicated to all of the kids and teens I've worked with over the years, especially those who have run through their own dark place and managed to make it back into the light. Your resilience and fortitude in the face of often-insurmountable odds continues to inspire me each and every day. Oh, and Chris, I left you out of my dedication in *Knight* and apologize for that. You have never left my heart since I met you at age seven, and I hope your life today is amazing. The same goes for all of my "kids" – if you entered my life, even briefly, you touched me deeply and I'll never forget the gift of hope you inspired in me. You're all "my kids," and you're all remarkable. For those of you who are still running through that dark place, don't give up. Ever. The light will come, and there is someone out there to help you. You deserve a second chance, and a third. Never, ever, give up. Hope endures…

FOREWORD

"I wonder if what makes a family a family isn't doing everything right all the time but, instead, giving a second chance to the people you love who do things wrong."

- Jodi Picault

I've always been what you might call a black and white person. As such, in my novels, the good characters are *very, very* good. These characters start out good, and though they may falter, in general terms, they stay good, ultimately emerging from the novel even better than ever. In the same way, my bad characters are examples of pure evil. I have created them to serve a purpose: to foil the noble decency of the "good person."

In that same manner have I long viewed the characters in my own life story. You are my friend or you are my enemy. You are with me or you are against me. With this frame of reference, negotiating my way through a crowd of friends and neighbors becomes quite simple, and easy, too. This one-dimensional, black and white, way of viewing those who surround me, requires less thinking, less analyzing, less patience and commitment, than if I had allowed myself to see the world in shades of gray.

Since meeting Michael Bowler, the author of *Running Through a Dark Place*, however, I have experienced profound personal change in this restricted area of my mind. Michael Bowler, a man whose very existence defines the term humanitarian, believes that human beings are fallible, and as such, they make mistakes. And thus, human beings are entitled to second chances in life. In particular, Bowler's unwavering commitment to the need for a second chance pertains to children. As Bowler sees it, inherent to a child's very nature is the *entitlement* to make mistakes, the right to "mess up" and to be allowed another shot. In other words, the very essence of childhood nullifies a requirement for perfection.

And I assure you, in *Running Through a Dark Place*, Bowler's youthful characters—his colorful Knights of the Round Table—err quite frequently. They mess up, they pay a price, and then newly enlightened adults forgive them, so that they may return to the table to try again. These children, in fact, usually do much better the second time around. Echoes of the sentiment "no matter what transpires, you must never give up on him" resonate from the lips of adults who offer second, and even third chances. The children, themselves, also acknowledge their need for multiple opportunities to get things right. One character spells it out quite clearly, saying, "I'm just a kid...who needs to figure out who he is and what his place is in this crazy world. I messed up, I know that, and I'll do my best not to mess up again. But if I do, stick with me."

The notion of affording second chances, however, permeates the entirety of the novel, extending well beyond the youthful characters' needs for redemption. In *Running Through a Dark Place*, adults need second chances in romantic love.

The corrupt mayor requires a new chance to see the light, as well as the opportunity to change his ways. A world-weary mother needs a chance to reconsider her attitude and react properly. Even the crusade around which the novel's action revolves—the struggle by King Arthur and the youthful Knights of the Round Table to secure equality for children in an adult world—requires a second chance, from an unknown source, to reinvent itself after a tragic event that threatens to derail it.

Closely tied to Bowler's belief that human beings need and deserve second chances, is his firm commitment to the notion that people are actually capable of profound change. It is an optimistic view, and when I saw evidence of it at work in Book I of this series, *Children of the Knight*, where insensitive cops grew big hearts and teachers who expected little to nothing of their students again became impassioned, I was at first uncomfortable and skeptical. But soon I found in my heart a growing seed of hope. In addition, the capability to change applies to former gang members, worthless societal burdens in the eyes of many. "I never had no real choices," one teenaged gang member said, "not till this man came along and showed me how to be good, how to be a man, how to make a difference for other people." In Bowler's eyes, if you possess a soul, you possess the necessary means to change. To see the light. To make good use of that second chance you have been so graciously granted.

By virtue of its very title, *Running Through a Dark Place* is a testament to change and second chances. The process of growing and changing and finding oneself can be dark and terrifying. It holds potential to make a human being feel as if he is scrambling—terrified and alone— through a dimly lit city street, in fear of his life. But Bowler understands that when you have successfully run through the dark place, having been given as many chances as you need to arrive at the light on the other side, you will acquire redemption. You will find what is right.

In conclusion, since familiarizing myself with Michael Bowler the author, as well as Michael Bowler, the person—the selfless volunteer, the man of faith, the committed friend, the unquestionable humanitarian—my world view has changed radically. Or rather, my view of my brothers and sisters, who are struggling to achieve their second chances and find the path to virtue right along beside me, has been forever altered. My mind has been opened to the possibility that, given the faith and the opportunity, even those I considered my enemies, can become my truest friends.

The novel *Running Through a Dark Place* has been instrumental in this profound change in me. In it I saw well defined examples of people taking advantage of second chances. I saw tangible proof that people can change.

Through my connection with Michael Bowler, I have come to believe that today is my second chance to make my own personal change in how I live my life.

I will take this chance.

Mia Kerick, Young Adult Author (Gilford, NH)
The Red Sheet, Love Spell, The Weekend Bucket List, My Crunchy Life

WHAT HAS GONE BEFORE...

IN *CHILDREN OF THE KNIGHT*, the legendary King Arthur appeared in Los Angeles with a mission – to save and empower youth. He started a new Round Table of knights made up exclusively of children and teens. A vision from Merlin led him to Lance, a homeless fourteen-year-old who was destined to lead his Children's Crusade. Arthur trained Lance in swordsmanship and archery, taught the boy discipline and self- control. He came to love Lance beyond measure, and Lance finally found the father he'd longed for growing up as an orphan in "the system."

In turn, Lance taught Arthur the complexities of 21st Century American life. They recruited hundreds of "disposable" youth - gang members looking for something better, homeless kids, gay kids, kids of every race and color – the ones most marginalized by society. These young "knights," under the leadership of Lance and Arthur, won the hearts and minds of Angelenos by rejuvenating poor neighborhoods and jump-starting community activism.

The local politicians resented Arthur's movement for making them look inept, with the mayor, in particular, doing his best to undermine the king. In addition, the head of a major drug cartel determined to destroy Arthur and everything he'd built. When Lance was struck down, the way forward—which moments before had been strong and purposeful—suddenly looked murky. But hope endures, and Lance's fate is not how it appears.

The Lance Chronicles Continue...

THE END OF THE BEGINNING

CHAPTER ONE
WITHOUT LANCE, THE CRUSADE IS DOOMED

O NCE UPON A TIME IN the City of Angels, a boy fell... and the city fell with him.

The cheers rose into the clear night sky, strong and resonant with youthful exuberance. Atop the white mare Llamrei—with the mural of Lance behind him—Arthur's hands enfolded those of Chris, and together they gripped the hilt of Excalibur. The fabled blade pointed heavenward, as though beseeching God for a miracle.

The cheering subsided, slowly and gradually, as the enormity of this night settled over the hundreds of youth and local citizens. Chris's long blond hair was matted with sweat, his soft features streaked with drying tears as his blue eyes tilted upward, along Excalibur's length. Arthur gazed down at the boy and marveled at the resiliency of youth.

Less than twenty minutes prior Chris, and the world, had watched their beloved Lance slip away from them. Arthur's tunic was stained by the blood of his son, a miraculous gift of a boy who had saved the king's life at the cost of his own.

Arthur became aware of the silence around him. He lowered Excalibur and removed it from the small hands of the little boy before him. Sheathing the sword, he gazed out at the crowd. All eyes focused on him, eyes that were expectant, uncertain, eager and sad. Many stared at the amazing mural Arthur's knights had created, a mural celebrating the gift to them all that was his chosen First Knight.

But Arthur knew the road ahead would not be as simple as he'd laid out for his children. Without Lance, how far could the crusade continue without collapsing in upon itself? He recognized the vacuum that losing Lance created, a vacuum impossible to fill with anyone else. Still, he had to push onward. These remarkable youth had already come so far, had accomplished so much, had devoted their very lives to his cause. He *had* to find a path forward.

He turned and glanced over his shoulder at Jenny, the woman who had stolen his heart. She offered a sympathetic smile of support, but it did little to mask her own sorrow. Her soft features were clouded with sadness, and a light breeze wafted her long blonde hair in small wisps across her eyes.

Then Arthur looked at the officials standing on the steps of City Hall. They were eying him with uncertain caution, knowing he had the power over this assembled multitude, and their faces reflected a deep fear that he might use it against them.

But Arthur was a man who believed in using might *for* right, who sought peace and justice over all else. Never would he incite his youth to anarchy, even against so corrupt a mayor as Villagrana, who eyed the king with an expression Arthur couldn't quite discern. Normally the man's face showed nothing but contempt. But now it was different, as though what happened to Lance had somehow broken through the prison walls around his heart and released some of its dormant humanity.

Chris tugged on Arthur's tunic. "What'll we do now, Arthur?"

Arthur looked into those beseeching eyes, and wished for the right words to soothe the child, but they didn't come. Before he could think of any, he heard, "King Arthur."

He looked down at the thin, middle-aged paramedic who had tried, with his partner, to save Lance. The man's face was shadowed as he looked upward. "As the boy's father, I need you to accompany the body, sir."

Chris flinched at the word "body," and Arthur embraced the boy comfortingly, turning to Jenny. "Jenny, would thou remain and guide the children back to their homes?"

"You won't be long, King Arthur," the paramedic said cryptically.

Arthur eyed him, wondering again why the man seemed so familiar, and what he'd been trying to communicate to him mere minutes before about Lance. The man held his gaze a moment, then strode toward his vehicle.

Jenny raised her eyebrows uncertainly, and Arthur shrugged. "Keep them calm, Jenny, until I return. Perhaps Sergeant Ryan may assist you."

She nodded, and then leaned in to kiss him gently on the lips, pulling back and gazing at him with a mix of love and sympathy. "I'll take care of them. Go with Lance."

Arthur slipped down off the back of Llamrei. He reached up for Chris and gently deposited the boy on the pavement, then he assisted Jenny.

Jack stepped forward. "Arthur, I heard what the guy said." The boy looked devastated with grief. "Can I go with you? Please?"

Arthur looked into those wide, sad eyes. He recalled how Jack had said goodbye to Lance, and understood how much the older boy truly loved his son. He placed a hand on Jack's shoulder. "Of course, Sir Jack."

Jenny took Chris's hand and walked him over to where Sergeants Ryan and Gibson stood with Reyna, Esteban and the other silent, expectant knights. As Arthur passed them, Reyna placed a hand lovingly on his arm as a show of comfort.

Everyone stood in reverent silence, and the world watched on live television as the two paramedics loaded the now-covered body onto a stretcher. They hefted it into the back of the paramedic vehicle, its overhead beacon still slashing the night with strobes of blood red light.

The older paramedic instructed the younger to remain behind and assist the wounded until more help arrived. Then the man ushered Jack into the back with Lance. Jack leaped up to sit beside Lance, the double doors slamming shut behind him. Arthur ascended into the passenger seat as the paramedic got behind the wheel.

Jenny watched the vehicle pull away, working its way through the crowd, which parted in waves so the vehicle could navigate its way down Temple Street. Jenny turned to Ryan and Gibson. The two men stood soberly watching the vehicle take Lance's body from the scene, their faces displaying a sense of loss.

Jenny found it oddly touching that two such hardened detectives, who'd no doubt witnessed horrific acts of human brutality over the decades, could have been so moved by one boy. It was yet another testament to the power Lance had over people, the charm, grace and gentle goodness that had won over the entire world.

What will become of us now? she asked herself. *Can Arthur sustain the momentum he's created without Lance at the forefront?*

She honestly didn't know.

Arthur sat within the cramped interior of the emergency vehicle, gazing at, but not really seeing, the vacant expressions of the stunned crowd as he passed through them. Moments ago, he had energized them. Now, once again confronted with the reality of what had transpired, they looked lost and fearful.

Exactly how I feel. Who can possibly replace Lance?

The heaviness of his heart pressed him down into the seat and nearly stopped his breath.

He vaguely noted when the paramedic made a left turn onto Spring Street. So lost was Arthur in thought that he barely registered the U-turn made by the driver, and didn't even notice that the vehicle had stopped in front of the Spring Street entrance to City Hall. Confused, he turned to the driver.

The driver merely whispered, "Hurry, King Arthur, before it's too late," and then popped open the door and dropped down to the street.

Mystified, Arthur flung open his door and alighted to the pavement. He hurried around to the back of the emergency vehicle just as the older man flung open the double doors.

"Quickly," he told Jack, his voice flush with urgency, "help me with the stretcher."

Arthur hesitated a moment, and Jack gazed at the king with an uncertain look. Arthur eyed the paramedic as the man reached in for the back of Lance's stretcher, a vague wisp of memory surfacing.

Something in the voice, in the tonal quality of that voice.

Something…

Rather than search for the recollection, Arthur nodded to Jack and then helped the paramedic drag the stretcher through the open double doors so it rested half in and half out of the vehicle. Jack jumped down to help, his bewildered young face reflected in the yellow of the flashers, the breeze wafting his dark, curly hair in every direction.

The paramedic indicated City Hall and the three of them carried the stretcher down a long walkway. With all the action on the Temple Street side, the interior lobby appeared to be empty when they entered.

Arthur exchanged another perplexed look with Jack as the paramedic glanced around the lobby. To the left was a door marked 'Board of Public Works', and to the right 'City Council Chamber'. The paramedic nodded to the latter.

"In there," he urged, already beginning to walk in that direction. When they had stopped before the ornately carved double doors, Arthur reached out and pulled the handle on the right. The door opened out, and the dimly lit emergency lights illuminated the chamber within. They scuttled through the door with the stretcher, and it closed behind them.

Jack gasped at the grandeur before him. It felt like he was inside of a church. There were enormous high ceilings, benches that looked like pews lining both sides of a long, a tiled walkway with each side flanked by huge marble columns and rounded arches. At the end of the long aisle was the raised dais and seating area where he figured the council members sat for meetings. It looked like huge judge's bench on steroids, with huge black leather chairs behind it for each council member to sit.

He had little time to gawk, however, because the paramedic was ushering them forward. He indicated that they should lay the stretcher down on the floor right in front of the seat of power, as though offering Lance up to these feckless politicians who had failed this city and its children.

As Jack released his hold on the stretcher, he rose to his full six-feet and glared at the opulence around him. Lance was dead. Lance, the most amazing boy in the world, who'd done more for this city than these clowns ever had. His blood began to boil.

"Sir." The feeble light from the night lamps caused the bloodstains on Arthur's tunic to look dark and blotchy. "I still know little of your legal system and procedures, yet this action we have taken seems highly unusual."

Now that they were alone, the middle-aged man with the salt and pepper hair turned on Arthur in anger. "Dammit, Arthur, do you not recognize me yet?"

Jack was taken aback by the man's tone, and so, clearly, was Arthur.

But the king said nothing. He studied the shorter man, squinting in the dimness to see into the man's eyes. His eyes suddenly bulged with astonished recognition.

"Merlin!"

Jack gawked at the small, skinny man with the almost nondescript face, and frail physique *This* was Merlin? *The* Merlin?

The little man looked blustered, "Of course it's me, Arthur!"

Arthur stepped back in shock. He looked stunned, yet somehow not completely surprised.

Jack watched the reunion with deep uncertainty.

Arthur gazed long and hard at the man, his face finally softening. "You look... different. Younger than when last we were together."

"As do you. The mysteries of Avalon are unknown, even to me."

Arthur attempted to embrace the smaller man, but Merlin brushed him off.

"There's no time for this, Arthur," the man snapped, his voice sharp and clipped, his accent similar to Arthur's own. But the tone of his voice was different, Jack noted. It was the tone of a man who'd seen it all, and for whom nothing new could be a surprise.

Except he *did* seem surprised.

"Have you been watching me this entire crusade, Merlin?" Arthur asked sadly. "Did you set it all into motion?"

The man looked about to bust the buttons on his white paramedic shirt. "Of course I did, Arthur. And it all should have gone according to my vision. But no, you had to repeat the same errors of the past!"

Arthur bowed his head, like a scolded schoolboy might to his father after getting suspended. "I know. I failed, Merlin. I have lost my First Knight, my son."

Merlin gesticulated toward the ever-more nervous Jack. "Arthur, this boy discovered what you knew centuries ago, what you should have avoided at all costs. And yet you did not heed your own past experience!"

Arthur glanced quizzically from Merlin to Jack, who just shrugged with confusion.

Merlin released an exasperated sigh, looking at Jack with those piercing gray eyes and seeming to see right through him. "Tell Arthur what you realized, young sir, what you verbalized to Lance in that rather appalling alley where Sir Mark was found."

Jack pulled a startled face, recalling vividly the conversation he'd had with Lance, right before they were kidnapped and everything went to hell. And then he remembered this guy – he was the paramedic who'd come to take Mark away!

Jack cleared his throat. "I, uh, I told Lance that the things we don't say to each other were the most important."

"Exactly!" Merlin exclaimed. "And you knew this, Arthur. You knew. After all the words you left unspoken to Guinevere and Lancelot and Mordred, still you blew it!"

Arthur frowned. "Blew it?"

"Modern street vernacular, Arthur, for 'you failed'."

Jack opened his mouth to come to Arthur's defense, but the older man kept on with his diatribe. "All you needed to tell the boy, Arthur, was that you loved him, that you took great pride in his accomplishments, and all of this would have been avoided." He pointed at the unmoving body on the stretcher beside them.

Arthur bowed his head in shame. "You are correct, Merlin. And it hath cost me everything, has it not? Tell me true."

The older man showed no sympathy whatsoever, which surprised Jack. "If by that you mean was Lance the only one to carry your crusade through to the end, and succeed where no one else could? Yes, Arthur, that is what I mean."

Arthur bowed his head again and Jack reached up to place a comforting hand on the man's shoulder. Arthur turned and cast a grateful look his way.

Jack turned to Merlin and extended a hand. "I'm Sir Jack."

"I know who you are," Merlin snapped. "And no, it cannot be you to lead, either." He must've seen Jack's hurt expression, because he softened a bit. "It was my vision, Sir Jack, which propelled this crusade forward in the beginning. But in that vision, Lance grew to manhood and remained in command. Alas, even you, as good a man as you are, do not have the requisite qualities to see this crusade through to its finish. You know what I'm saying about Lance, do you not, young Jack?"

Jack nodded. He knew, indeed. "Lance was the only one who could talk to everyone, who could be a badass one minute and caring the next. He found something good in everybody. That's why it had to be him, right, Merlin?"

The middle-aged wizard nodded. "The boy possessed leadership abilities coupled with immense compassion and empathy. A once-in-a-generation individual. That's why he was chosen. And that's why he was never slated to die like this, Arthur."

Arthur raised his head and met the older man's gaze. "Then how, Merlin?" He indicated the body at his feet. "How did this happen?"

Merlin blew out a breath, almost like he was spitting. "Call it Fate, the Devil, a cosmic monkey wrench. Call it whatever you choose, Arthur, but the forces of chaos always seek to undo the forces of order and goodness. Had you simply told the boy what he meant to you—"

"I know, Merlin!" Arthur spat, his deep voice echoing off the cavernous ceiling. "Do you not realize what I must live with, the mistakes I must now strive to undo? I loved that boy with all my heart. Torment me no further with my failure!"

"The crusade is doomed, Arthur, unless you act immediately."

"There is for naught that I can do, Merlin! You said so yourself. Without Lance, the crusade is doomed. And he is dead." He paused, his tearful eyes lowering to take in the covered boy at his feet. "My son…is dead."

"No, Arthur. He isn't."

Arthur's head whipped up like a gunshot, and Jack gasped in astonishment.

"What?" Arthur choked, his voice a stunned whisper, his face a mosaic of shock.

Merlin's gaze passed over Jack's beseeching eyes, before diving straight into Arthur's. "The boy yet lives."

CHAPTER TWO
WHERE IS HE?

Jack and Arthur remained a moment in shock. Jack searched the wizard's face for any sign of a cruel joke on the man's part. But Merlin's gaze never wavered.

"Lance... is alive?" Jack spluttered, his heart suddenly pounding with hope.

Merlin nodded solemnly.

"How?" Arthur demanded, throwing his hands outward, indicating the body at his feet. "The boy died in my arms, Merlin. I saw it. I felt it. He's gone."

"We have little time, Arthur, so do not interrupt." Arthur opened his mouth to say something, but a glare from Merlin caused him to shut it quickly. The wizard bent down and pulled the cloth away, revealing Lance's face.

Jack felt his heart lurch at seeing his beloved so peaceful in death. But not death after all?

Arthur gazed at the face of his son with immense sadness. "Lance's body did, in fact, cease to function," Merlin continued. "His wounds were too extensive for me to repair without a countering source of energy. Thus the spirit that animated his body fled. However, his soul remains. For now."

Jack's mouth hung open, his breath coming almost in short gasps.

Arthur looked perplexed. "How?"

"I placed a binding spell on the boy, Arthur, to keep the soul within him. But what I did is so beyond the scope of natural law that the spell may only exist for a short time. If we do not reanimate Lance's body quickly, his soul will move on and you will have lost him forever."

Jack's emotions roiled within him, frustration building at his inability to understand what was going on. "Stop talking in riddles," he said harshly, clenching and unclenching his fists. "If there's some way to save Lance, then why the hell aren't you doing it?"

Merlin eyed the boy with genuine compassion. "It is not so simple, Sir Jack."

"Explain," Arthur commanded, his deep voice firm and leaving no room for argument.

"The cosmos must remain in balance," Merlin explained, as though tutoring pupils in science. "As you know, Arthur, my God- given powers allow me to shift energy, for want of a more satisfactory term, from one entity to another, as long as I maintain balance. That's why my binding spell is so anathema to nature, because I'm using the very air around Lance to force his soul to remain, and to keep oxygen within his brain, but I'm doing nothing to counterbalance that energy."

"Spare me the teacher prattle, Merlin. Can you restore my son or can't you?"

"I can," Merlin said quietly, but firmly. "I can transfer energy into Lance that will repair his body and give him a spirit to reanimate it."

Jack couldn't handle more of this stalling. "So? Do it already!"

Merlin eyed him soberly. "It is not that easy."

Suddenly, Arthur's face looked stricken with horror. "Do you be saying what I think you're saying, Merlin?"

Merlin nodded gravely.

There was a moment of silence. The cavernous room seemed to hold its breath.

"To restore Lance I must remove the spirit, the animating life force, from another human being."

Jack gasped, and Merlin fixed his gaze on him. "Yes, Sir Jack. For Lance to live, someone else must die."

Jack's eyes widened with comprehension, and Arthur cursed quietly beside him.

Out on the Temple Street side of City Hall, Mayor Villagrana and Police Chief Murphy made their way through the crowd to where Jenny stood with Reyna, Esteban, Darnell, Chris, Ryan, Gibson and Justin. Helen waved her cameraman over to capture whatever the mayor had to say. The other knights and citizens milled about aimlessly.

Reyna scowled with disgust at Villagrana.

"Happy now?" she spat, looking mad enough to punch him. Esteban had to forcibly hold her back. "Now that the best boy in the world is dead? If you think we're not coming after you, you're wrong!"

Jenny placed a gentle hand on Reyna's arm, and Chris grabbed the girl's hand lovingly. Just glancing down at the small boy gazing up into her face seemed to calm her, and she settled back against Esteban, streaks of makeup looking like prison bars down her lovely face.

Villagrana's expression surprised Jenny, for it almost appeared compassionate.

"I, uh," he began, suddenly not the smooth talker he usually seemed to be. "I wish to express my deepest condolences on the death of the boy." He paused, took in the faces of everyone around him, noted Helen's camera pointed right at his face, and turned back to Jenny. "While I admit to disagreeing with Arthur and his choices, I never wished to see him or any of these children come to harm. I hope you believe that."

Jenny fought to quell her revulsion. "I accept your condolences, Mr. Mayor, on behalf of the Round Table and King Arthur." She paused, looking into Helen's camera and then back to the mayor. Reaching down, she scooped Chris into her arms and held him up.

"You may think you've won, Mr. Mayor, but you're wrong. The death of that magnificent boy has only strengthened our resolve to get you, and everyone like you, out of office and out of our lives. This boy,"—she shifted Chris so the youngster gazed directly into the embarrassed eyes of the mayor—"and all these others will bring you down. Count on it!"

The knights around Jenny cheered loudly, and Villagrana stepped back. He turned to the police chief, but Murphy merely shrugged. He looked behind him. Sanders, Gale and the other city council members stood in stony-faced silence, gazing at the crowd. When Villagrana turned back, Helen was right there in his face, her microphone thrust under his chin.

"Care to comment on tonight's events, Mr. Mayor?" she asked professionally. "We're still live."

Villagrana eyed the camera. "Thank you, Helen, I would. Ladies and gentlemen of Los Angeles, I stand before you tonight a man saddened, as are you, by the unnecessary death of a fine boy. Rest assured, the assassin of young Lance will be apprehended and brought to justice."

He paused, but no one clapped. "I think I speak for the entire city council when I thank Lance for the goodwill he brought to all Angelenos, and his funeral will, of course, be at city expense, a public tribute to his accomplishments. He will be honored, not just by the remarkable mural behind me, but as a true hero the likes of which Los Angeles is unlikely to see again. I ask everyone watching to give a moment of silence in honor of the fallen Sir Lance."

He bowed his head dramatically, and Reyna cursed beneath her breath at his obvious hypocrisy. Esteban kicked her leg and she dutifully bowed her head. Quiet descended as though from heaven, and it seemed like the whole city fell into a thoughtful reverie.

Merlin gazed soberly at the two men, both of whom stood in speechless silence. Arthur regarded the shattered Jack a moment before turning back to Merlin. "Use me, Merlin," he stated without hesitation. "I will gladly sacrifice myself for my son."

Jack whipped his head up in shock. "No, Arthur, you can't! We need you."

Arthur placed a comforting hand on Jack's shoulder, and their eyes met. "You heard Merlin, Sir Jack," he explained softly, using that tone of voice that had always soothed Jack's soul. "Lance is more important. Without him, all we have accomplished shall be for naught. There is no other way."

He smiled sadly and dropped his hand back to his side. "I am ready, Merlin."

Merlin stood in place, gazing at Arthur with an expression Jack couldn't quite read, but that looked like regret.

"Alas, Arthur, it cannot be you."

"Forsooth, why not?" Arthur exclaimed, almost in anger. "You said it, Merlin, you said Lance is of the greater import. There is no one else I could call upon but myself. I insist!"

Jack watched Merlin's face closely, and the look of regret deepened into one of profound sadness. "Arthur, you lived a full life once before," he patiently explained. "For this crusade, as for any more as might be needed in the future, you are living on what here they call 'borrowed time'. Your sojourn in this era must needs only be a few years, long enough to guide Lance to manhood. Then we both must return to Avalon, to sleep once more."

Jack felt the blood drain from his face at the wizard's words. Arthur, only here for a few more years? What would they do without him?

Arthur's eyes searched Merlin's face for the truth, and he must have seen it for he nodded, and Jack's shoulders slumped with despair.

"Be thou certain, Merlin?" Arthur asked, his voice a desperate whisper.

The wizard nodded heavily. "The volunteer must be someone with a full life force to give. I'm sorry, Arthur."

Arthur slumped down onto the small railing fronting the desks. "Merlin, there be no possible way I could ask anyone to do such a thing."

"That is why what I have done thus far may be for naught, Arthur. But I had to provide the opportunity."

Jack listened to their debate, hearing, but not hearing. His heart and mind were fixed upon Lance at his feet. He knelt down to this astounding boy who had snuck in and stolen his heart right out from under him, vaguely aware that the two men had ceased their conversation. Lance's beautiful face melted his heart anew, and the closed eyes and peaceful expression only strengthened Jack's resolve.

I promised to save you, remember, Lance? It was supposed to be me, not you. And now I'm gonna keep my promise.

Reaching out and clasping Lance's cool hand in his, Jack raised it to his chest and pressed it against his wildly beating heart. Fear clenched his stomach into knots, but he fought it back.

"I volunteer," he whispered, to Lance as much as to Merlin and Arthur.

He heard a startled intake of breath and tilted his head upward to gaze at Arthur's shocked expression.

"Nay, Sir Jack," Arthur blurted. "Ye cannot!"

Jack turned his eyes back to Lance and gently lay the boy's hand down on his chest before rising. "It's the only way, Arthur. You heard him."

"Nay, I forbid it, Sir Jack! Your life is too precious and ye art at but the beginnings of it."

Jack felt himself trembling with fear, and desperate need. He struggled to control his voice. "Arthur, hasn't this whole crusade been about kids like me making our own choices?"

"Aye, but—"

Jack placed a hand on the king's shoulder to quell his protest. "I loved him, Arthur. I was *in* love with him."

Arthur's eyes widened with a new sadness that touched Jack deeply.

"There's nothing I wouldn't do for Lance, Arthur. Do you understand that feeling?"

Arthur nodded. "But we shall find another way, Sir Jack."

Jack smiled, touched by this man's love for him, something he hadn't felt from his own father since early childhood. "There is no other way, is there, Merlin?"

Despite addressing the wizard, Jack kept his eyes fixed on Arthur.

"No, there is not."

Arthur whipped his head. "He is but a boy, Merlin!"

Jack stood as tall and strong as he could, almost as tall as the king. "I'm a man now, Arthur, even if this country doesn't think so."

Arthur's eyes began to well with tears. "And a braver man I have never known, Sir Jack, in either of my lifetimes."

Jack's emotions flooded up into his throat, clogging his speech and tugging tears from behind his eyes. "Thanks, Arthur, for everything. My father thought I was just a worthless queer boy, but I hope I'm more than that."

Arthur's despondent eyes flashed with anger. "You are a gift from God, Sir Jack. I feel so much pride in thee I cannot express but a fraction of it. Other than Lance, there is no one upon this earth I would rather call my son."

Jack almost gagged, feeling such an upsurge of love for this man that he grabbed the king in a tight hug and squeezed. "Thanks… Dad." He pulled back. "Is it okay to call you that?"

A tear dribbled down Arthur's cheek. "You are my son, are you not?"

Jack smiled, his heart pulling tightly against the inside of his chest. "I love you, Arthur."

"And I love you, Jack," Arthur replied, his voice cracking.

Jack blew out a breath filled with every emotion he could imagine.

He was loved.

He had a father who was proud of him.

And he was about to die.

Never would he know the joys of sharing his life with another. But then, how could he have done that anyway when the one boy with whom he'd want to spend his life lay dead at his feet?

At least I can give you a life, Lance. Don't hate me for that. Don't hate yourself.

Jack locked eyes on those of the king. "Arthur, Lance'll be pissed, sorry, really mad about this."

The king nodded sorrowfully.

"I'm gonna write him a note before I…" he stopped and sucked in a breath. "Just keep telling him it was my choice, okay?"

Arthur nodded again, his emotions clearly making speech impossible.

Jack turned to Merlin. "I need to say goodbye to Lance."

The wizard nodded, and turned to scan the desks of the council members. There were fancy pens in even fancier penholders, and pads of paper. Merlin snatched up one of each and held them out to Jack.

With a sigh, realizing those objects represented his last words to Lance on this earth, Jack shuddered a moment as he took them.

"Arthur and I will wait outside," Merlin said, his formerly irritated voice now filled with compassion. "But make haste, Sir Jack, for our time runs short."

Jack nodded, but didn't trust himself to speak.

Merlin took Arthur by the arm and escorted him down the long pathway.

Jack watched in silence as the heavy oaken door opened and then closed, sucking the two men through it. Now there was only he and Lance.

Purposely not looking at the face of his beloved for fear he would lose it, Jack sat himself in one of the luxurious chairs used by the very people who'd allowed the city to decline, who'd allowed Lance to be killed, and kids to become addicted to drugs. The thought of the mayor and these other adults filled him with anger and disgust. Thrusting those feelings aside, Jack put pen to paper and began to write.

Outside the double doors, Arthur paced while Merlin stood stock still, eying the flashing of police and emergency lights drifting in from the Temple Street exit way on the other side of the massive lobby. Arthur stopped his frantic back and forth movements and faced his old mentor. Merlin's gray eyes revealed nothing of the man's emotions, as they seldom did.

"Merlin, are we doing the right thing?"

"To salvage your crusade, yes," Merlin replied in a matter-of-fact tone. "For that brave boy in there…" He just shrugged.

Arthur wanted Merlin to assure him that what he was allowing Jack to do was right, wanted Merlin to have all the answers as he had when Arthur himself was a boy. Yet even then, Merlin was oblique with his knowledge, and his advice. He much preferred that Arthur learn from his own mistakes.

I have already made too many, the king thought to himself, *and they have cost me my Lance. Doth this be yet another, to allow that boy to give up his life thus?*

He stared into the wizard's unblinking eyes, but no answer reflected back at him. As in the past, Merlin would only present choices – it was up to Arthur to choose which one.

Oh Lord, he silently prayed, glancing skyward at the lavish art-deco ceiling overhead, *grant me your wisdom tonight on this, the most painful decision I have yet had to make.*

He paused, as though expecting an answer. Then he lowered his head and resumed pacing.

Jack finished his letter, keeping his head tilted back so his tears would not drown the paper and make it unreadable. Still, some landed on the letter and stained it with his love. He leaned back in the high, leather armchair and scanned the room through blurred vision. How different this messed up city would be if he were here making the laws, or Lance. A slight smile cracked his lips. Maybe Lance *would* sit here one day. Wouldn't that be epic?

Slipping the pen back into its fancy holder, Jack rose from the chair. It squeaked beneath him and the wheels scraped along the floor as he pushed it back. Folding his letter in half, he worked his way back around the massive wooden desk and stopped beside Lance's unmoving form. Tears dripped from his face onto the boy beneath him, some striking the majestic face. Much like he'd done outside, Jack knelt beside Lance and using his thumb gently wiped the tears from his cool, but still amazingly smooth cheek. His brown skin had paled a bit, but not completely.

Jack bent his head, closed his eyes, and planted his lips ever so softly against those of this boy he adored. The lips felt warm, not the iciness of death Jack had expected. Not as warm or soft as the first kiss they'd shared, but proof enough that Lance was still within, just as Merlin had said, awaiting his chance to return. And Jack would give him that chance. It was best for everyone.

Reluctantly, Jack slowly drew back and gazed into the silent, unmoving face of the most incredible boy he'd ever known.

"I love you, Lance," he whispered through his tears. "I'll always love you, no matter where I end up."

Then, knowing time was running out, Jack arose and slipped out his phone. Through his tears, he texted Arthur out in the lobby: 'I'm ready'.

As the door at the other side of the room opened and the two men entered, Jack forced himself to breathe deeply, a futile attempt to calm his pounding heart. He knew he was doing the right thing, but there was no going back here. His mind flashed with images of his all-too-short life, to his realization at a very young age that he was different from other boys, to his deep sense of failure at never making his father happy, to his pervasive feeling of unworthiness, to his feelings of love and acceptance with Arthur and Lance.

You say I'm worthy, Lance, and so does Arthur. So, I guess I must be.

Arthur and Merlin reached him. Jack locked his fear-filled eyes on those of the king, this man who'd been more a father to him than his own ever had, and handed Arthur the letter.

Jack expelled a deep breath and turned to Merlin. "Will it hurt?"

Merlin's eyes offered no false hope. "You will experience the same pain as Lance. His wounds will become yours. I'll do what I can to minimize the discomfort."

"No, it's okay. It'll make me feel closer to him that way."

Arthur nearly gagged, but managed to keep control.

Merlin indicated the floor a couple of feet from Lance's prone body. "Lie here, Sir Jack, parallel to Sir Lance. I shall kneel between you."

Jack cast Arthur one final glance and then complied, stretching out on the cold wood floor beside his beloved. Somehow this seemed right to him, being side-by-side with Lance.

"Arthur, stand away from us until I call for you," Merlin told the king.

Arthur reluctantly stepped to the side, several feet from the two boys, his head bent in sorrow.

Merlin knelt between Jack and Lance. He took Lance's left hand in his and turned to Jack, reaching out for the boy's right. Jack raised it, but then hesitated.

"Merlin, can I, uh, ask you something?"

"Anything," the man replied softly, his hand poised in mid-air. Jack felt almost nauseous, dreading the answer to his question.

"Do you think…" He gulped and shivered. "I'll go to Hell?"

He heard a loud gasp of surprise from Arthur's direction, but kept his eyes fixed on the wizard, searching those eyes for truth.

Merlin looked curiously at him. "What makes you ask that, Sir Jack?"

Jack swallowed fearfully. "It's just that I always been told gay kids like me go to Hell, that God hates us." He paused and searched the man's face. "Is that true?"

Merlin hesitated, and fear shot through Jack. But then the wizard shook his head in disgust. "In many ways, your culture today is as backward as was Arthur's."

Jack was confused. "Was that a no?"

The wizard smiled compassionately. "That was a no. God does not punish us for how we are born, Sir Jack. What we are is God's gift to the world. What we become is our gift to God. And what you have become is the bravest man I have ever known, in all my centuries upon this earth. God will cherish your soul, Sir Jack. Have no fear of that."

Jack exhaled the air he'd been holding in, and the tightness left his body. He was good after all. "Thank you, Merlin."

The older man offered a surprisingly warm and loving smile. "Thank *you*, Sir Jack, for being you."

Jack lifted his right hand and clasped it within the firm grip of Merlin's, and then excruciating pain ripped through his back like a bullet.

The crowd on Temple milled and murmured and glanced everywhere with questioning looks, making Ryan increasingly nervous. This many people, no direction, no focus, no one to lead them. That was a recipe for trouble.

Eyeing the restless teens, Ryan stepped up to Jenny and Reyna. "Any word from Arthur?" he asked quietly, not wanting everyone to overhear their conversation.

Jenny shook her head. "I don't have my phone. Reyna?"

The usually poised collected girl stiffly reached out a hand to Esteban. He understood her silent request and slipped his phone from the pocket of his leather pants. He pushed the side button and the screen lit up. Glancing quickly to see if there were any messages, he found none.

"No," he told the sergeant, his deep voice cutting the uncertain air like a knife.

"Why did he leave with the paramedic?" Ryan asked in the standard detective voice he used when interrogating witnesses.

Jenny shrugged. "He said the man requested he accompany Lance's body."

Ryan frowned, creasing his craggy face even more. "That's not standard procedure. The boy was dead. He should've been taken by the coroner."

He paused as Jenny, Reyna, Esteban and Chris all gazed at him uncertainly.

"Whadda you think it means, Sergeant?" Esteban asked, since he seemed to be the only one in control of his emotions.

Ryan eyed the boy discerningly, a thoughtful expression on his face. "I don't know. Can you call him?"

Esteban glanced over at Jenny, and she nodded, brushing wisps of blond hair away from her eyes.

Esteban speed-dialed Arthur and put the phone on speaker mode. They all heard three rings, and then Reyna's voice came on: "You have reached King Arthur's cell. He is unable—"

Esteban touched the 'end' button and eyed Ryan expectantly.

"Something's wrong," Ryan declared. "Call it a gut instinct. Would you be willing to give me his number? I can have our guys at headquarters triangulate on his phone, find out where he was taken."

Esteban and Reyna exchanged a look, and then both turned to Jenny.

Her brows furrowed with worry. "Do you really think something could have happened to him?"

Ryan nodded, his face deadly serious. "Somebody just tried to kill the man, and failed. Then he gets mysteriously whisked away by a paramedic? Yeah, I do."

Jenny shuddered with fear, nodding toward Esteban. He quickly recited Arthur's number and Ryan tapped it into his own phone.

"Move amongst these kids, will you? Calm 'em, keep 'em from getting out of hand. Assure 'em Arthur will be back soon. I'll get on this trace."

All three of them agreed.

Ryan nodded his thanks and turned back to where Gibson still stood beside Justin. Phone to his ear, the sergeant called Parker Center to start the trace on Arthur's cell.

Jenny directed Reyna and Esteban in two different directions, asking them to alert the other team leaders to move amongst the throng in a calming, reassuring fashion. Then she took Chris's hand and started off into the crowd.

Arthur kept his eyes fixed on both boys, as Merlin, still kneeling between them, seemed almost aglow. Jack groaned in pain a few times, causing the king to grimace sympathetically. He felt the phone in his pocket vibrate, but ignored it. His gaze remained fixed upon these two boys, only one of whom would walk out of this room alive.

After Jack's initial groans and thrashings, the boy lay still. Merlin clasped one hand of each, acting as a sort of conduit, drawing the life force from Jack and sending it into Lance like a blood transfusion. Gradually, the brown of Lance's face deepened, becoming almost flushed. As Arthur watched, Jack's face grew lighter, paler, as life gradually receded from his body.

But the look on the older boy's features was one of peace and joy, as though even now Jack knew that his very essence was flowing into the boy he loved more than anything on earth. Arthur found he could watch no longer, and turned away to swipe at a tear forcing its way out of his eye.

He stood thus, staring into nothingness, for he knew not how long, until he heard Merlin clear his throat.

"Arthur. It is done."

The king whirled around, startled to see Merlin, barely able to stand, weaker than the king had ever seen him, tottering on the brink of collapse. Fearing Merlin would topple, Arthur lurched forward and caught him, just as the older man's knees buckled.

Arthur half-carried, half-led Merlin through the small gates and into the audience chamber, sitting him gently in the first of the wooden pews intended for the general public.

Merlin looked almost devoid of life himself.

"Merlin, are you well?"

The old wizard nodded, his breathing ragged, his shoulders slumped. "That was the most dangerous fashion in which I've ever used my gifts, Arthur, and it has drained me."

Arthur glanced back at the two unmoving boys lying side by side behind him. "And?"

Merlin nodded tiredly. "I was successful." He paused to catch his breath. "Quick, Arthur, carry Lance here, to one of these benches, so he will not see Jack when he awakens."

Arthur felt his heart leap into his throat. He nodded and hurried back to where Lance lay silent and unmoving. No, not unmoving. Arthur's breath hitched as he saw the gentle rise and fall of Lance's chest. His son was breathing!

But then he glanced down at Jack, and his heart lurched. The boy was dead. Clearly and irrevocably, the bruised cheeks already sallow, the blood pooling from beneath him where Lance's wounds had become his own. Yet the boy's face looked handsome and strong, with pure happiness etched into his features.

"Thank you, Sir Jack," Arthur whispered with reverence. "Your name will be honored like no other."

Then Arthur scooped Lance into his arms, realizing how much taller and heavier the boy had become since they'd first met, and lovingly cradled his son, navigating his way through the small gates to lay him out on one of the pews just behind Merlin.

The wizard sat hunched over, still recouping some of the massive energy he'd moments before expended on the boy's behalf.

Arthur placed a grateful hand on the shoulder of his mentor, and then heard Lance groan slightly beneath him.

Arthur watched with awe as the long lashes of his son flicked a few times before slipping open with uncertain hesitation.

Lance looked upward at Arthur's face, his expression scrunched with confusion and wariness. His throat felt dry, as though it hadn't been used in ages. He coughed slightly, expelling air from lungs that he had the oddest feeling shouldn't be working.

"Dad?" he said, hesitant and confused.

Arthur smiled, his face alighting with such a mix of joy and sadness that Lance felt a chill run through him.

"Where am I?" he asked, his wide eyes taking in the high-arched ceiling, the pews on either side of him. He tried to sit quickly, and felt so lightheaded that he nearly collapsed.

But Arthur caught him in his arms, cradling him, easing him into a seated posture against the back of the pew, making certain to shield his view of Jack's lifeless body.

"You're within the city council chambers, Lance."

Lance took a moment to focus on Merlin, and then he remembered. "You were there when Mark died," he whispered, the memory gradually slipping into focus. "And when I…"

His face went ashen, and dread rippled through his entire body. He turned his fearful face to Arthur, who gently brushed his hair from his forehead. Tightness engulfed him. "I got shot, didn't I, Dad?"

Arthur nodded, but said nothing.

Lance reached around with his left hand and felt the bullet hole in his ragged shirt. And the sticky blood. But there was no hole in his skin. He began to panic, his whole body starting to tremble. "And I… died… didn't I?"

Arthur said nothing. He merely indicated Merlin. "This is Merlin, Lance."

Lance's eyes bulged with amazement, and then felt his face go white with fear. "What did you do?" It was but a whisper, for Lance had no more breath with which to speak.

I died, and now…

Merlin eyed him with sympathy. "What do you remember, Lance?"

The question caught Lance off-guard, and he paused. Sinking deep within himself, he considered what he could recall, and told them. He remembered saying goodbye to Jack, and to Arthur. He remembered feeling loved for the first time in his life. And then there had been a momentary blackness – not like someone had turned out the lights, no. This was like a black hole had sucked up every drop of light and left a void.

Lance's face scrunched as he fought to pull up details.

"Then I was standing in a grassy field," he went on cautiously as the images returned to him. "There was a hill right in front of me, covered with grass. And behind it pure light. Not like the sun. Just glowing, perfect light. And Mark was there." He stopped and stared a moment at the men as though fearful of continuing.

Arthur lovingly stroked his hair. "Go on, son."

Lance swallowed, the images flooding in now like a movie. "He stood at the top of the hill, looking at me with that shy little smile he always had. And he held his hand out. He wanted me to go with him. Up the hill and into that light." He paused again, feeling a sense of love and kinship with Mark. "I felt good, Dad, peaceful. And I started walking up the hill toward him."

Lance stopped again, his face suddenly clouding over, another jolt of fear stabbing through him.

"And then?" Merlin prodded quietly.

Lance lifted his eyes and met those of the wizard. "And then he was gone. That black hole thing came back. I don't know for how long. But there was nothing." He chewed his lower lip absently as he pulled the memories from his soul. "And then I was on that hill again. And there was Mark." His eyes widened with sudden remembrance. "And Jack was there, too. They were holding hands and... smiling and... waving goodbye." He stopped suddenly, and turned fear-filled eyes on those of his father. "And then I woke up."

Arthur and Merlin exchanged a look, and something in that look scared Lance, more than he'd ever been scared in his life.

"Where's Jack?" he asked breathlessly.

The two men remained silent, but Lance saw such sadness and pain on their faces that he sat bolt upright as terror stabbed into his heart.

"Dad, where is Jack?"

Both men dropped their eyes, and Lance could see the mix of agony and guilt as they did so. Then Arthur raised his head, his pleading eyes piercing Lance to the core.

"Lance, there was an impossible choice to be made..."

Dread overcame Lance, an intense dread that clamped onto his very soul and seared his heart with horror.

Because he already knew the answer.

"Where *is* he?" Lance screamed, his voice echoing from the cavernous ceilings high above.

Glancing once more at Merlin, Arthur moved to one side so Lance could see behind him. Lance's eyes looked confused as they scanned the area by the city council desks. And then he saw the body. His mouth dropped open with dread, and his heart leapt into his throat. "No..."

He leaped from the bench and half ran, half-staggered across the space, stumbling up the three small steps to Jack's prone, lifeless body. He gazed into the face of this boy who'd been his best friend, and could scarcely breathe.

Jack looked peaceful, despite the drying blood around his lips. Lance felt his own lips, recalling the blood that had been there, but now was gone. With trembling fingers, he lightly caressed Jack's cheek – it was already cool to the touch.

Arthur and Merlin moved to stand behind him.

Lance bounded to his feet and furiously struck Arthur hard in the chest with his fists. "What did you do?" Arthur grabbed him from behind and pinned his flailing arms.

"And you!" Lance shrieked at Merlin, fighting to swing at him. "What did you do?" Tears burst from his eyes, and sorrow poured forth from the depths of his soul.

Jacky...

Arthur just held him as Lance struggled and fought. Arthur battled to keep his voice steady. "Lance, listen to me…"

"You killed him!" Lance shrieked through his tears. "You killed Jacky!"

Merlin moved around in front of Lance. "No, Lance. It was his choice."

"There was no choice!" Lance bellowed, fighting to get free, his hair plastered against his tears as he fought and struggled like a wild animal caught in a trap. "I saved him. I saved my dad. I saved the Round Table. And I died. That was my choice!" He glared at Merlin with fury. "This is all your fault, isn't it?"

Merlin nodded, his expression sad, yet calm. "Guilty as charged, I'm afraid. It was necessary, Lance, or we would not have done it."

"Switch us back!" Lance screamed, still struggling to break free of Arthur's iron grip, his hair flailing about. "I wanna be dead. Bring him back!"

Arthur flinched at Lance's declaration, but he did not loosen his firm hold.

Merlin shook his head sadly. "I no longer have the power, Lance. Much like a battery, I discharged everything to bring you back. It will likely take decades for me to regain it."

"Liar!"

"Lance!" Arthur practically shouted. "He's telling the truth."

Merlin never took his eyes off Lance's face. "It's true, Lance. And even if I did still have the power, Jack's soul has fled his body. He's gone from this world."

The wizard's words struck something deep within Lance, stalling his writhing a moment as he turned to look through his wild hair at Jack. The older boy's face remained peaceful, but the cheeks sagged ever so slightly, the pallor had deepened, the muscular body had shrunk.

Lance's breathing caught a moment in his throat, and his struggles slowed.

Arthur still gripped him hard. "Lance, I need you to remain calm and allow me to explain."

Lance ceased fighting, but his body remained taut as a spring. Arthur released him, and Lance whirled round viciously, his eyes blazing with a fury such as Arthur had never seen.

"Explain what? How you killed someone I loved?"

"No. How someone who loved *you* sacrificed himself *for* you. There was one chance to save you, Lance, a chance provided by Merlin. And Jack took it."

That stopped Lance's anger, caught his fury in a net of uncertainty. "But I didn't want him to. I wanted to save Jack. You should've stopped him!"

"Lance, listen, please," Arthur said, his voice remaining as calm as possible. "Why did you save me from that assassin's bullet?"

Lance's answer was immediate. "Because I love you, Dad."

"And I love you, son, despite my prior reticence at saying such. But tell me, Lance, could anyone have stopped you from saving me?"

"No way."

"Why not?"

"I love you more than I love me."

"Then you understand why I could not stop Jack."

Lance's eyes widened with staggering comprehension.

"He loved you that much. And he believed you more important to our crusade than he himself could ever be. It was his choice, Lance, the bravest choice I've ever seen a man make. But he *was* a man, and he had the freedom to make that choice."

Lance was staggered, wobbly almost, his whole body thrumming with pain and sadness, feeling even more lost than when Mark had died. "He was wrong. I'm not that important."

"Ah, but you are, Lance," Merlin put in, his voice still raspy from his exertion. "You are the key to the entire crusade. Had you died, that would've been the end of everything."

Lance was not convinced. "No. The needs of the whole company, right? No one is indispensable to the cause. Right, Dad? You said it yourself!"

"As a rule, yes," the king responded cautiously. "But in some cases—yours being one of them—the one is essential to the whole. I lost sight of that, Lance. I lost sight of you, and all the others as individuals who require love and praise. It was my error that got you killed. I offered my own life in place of yours, but, alas, it had to come from someone on his first lifetime. Jack did not hesitate. He did not seek to die, but to live on in you and all that you shall yet accomplish."

"For what it's worth, Lance," Merlin put in, his voice filled with admiration, "Jack was the bravest man I've ever had the occasion to meet. You should feel honored to be loved by one such as him."

Arthur held up Jack's letter. "He left this for you. It was his final hope that you not hate him for his decision."

Lance's eyes widened with shock, but he reached out and took the note.

"We shall give you time to say your goodbyes, son, whilst we confer on how best to explain your miraculous return to the other knights, and to the people."

Lance's eyes remained fixed on the folded paper in his trembling hand as the two adults left him alone in the room.

Shaking with sorrow, he opened the note and read it.

'*To My Favorite Badass Boy: Don't be mad at me, Lance. I know how you are and you probably want to kick my ass right now for doing this, but I think my ass has already been kicked enough. LOL Lance, listen to me—this was my choice and mine alone. When I found out there was a way to keep my promise – I did promise to save you – and that the whole crusade, everything we'd worked so hard for, would collapse and die without you, well, the choice was obvious, but not easy. I didn't want to die. But given a choice between me and you, Lance, you would win every time. In case I wasn't clear before, I want you to understand now. I love you, Lance. I'm in love with you, even more than I loved Mark.*

Given a choice to stay with you forever or be a billionaire, you'd win in a heartbeat.'

Lance paused a moment, swiping fresh tears from his face before they stained the paper in his hand.

'*You have no idea how amazing you are. We all spent so much time not saying the things we should have that everything got completely screwed up. So I'm saying it now— you are the most outstanding and special and one-of-a-kind boy I ever met, the kind of boy I dreamed of meeting ever since I figured out I liked boys more than girls. Please, Lance, please, please, please stop hating on yourself for mistakes you think you made. I finally accepted I liked boys and was okay with that. I know you liked it when we kissed and you're afraid it means you're gay and it scares you. Maybe you're gay and maybe not. Just be yourself. Let it be enough. You might fall for some girl one of these days, or you might fall for some guy. But just see where life takes you, that's all I'm saying. Loving you and sharing that one incredible kiss is enough to last me forever. Thank you for that. Don't be depressed that I'm gone. I'll have Mark and we'll take care of each other like we always did.*

You have a world to save, Lance. And maybe along the way, maybe you can make it a little better for gay boys like Mark and me. But you better never get all mopey and give up on the crusade, 'cause if you do, Mark and me'll be back to haunt your ass something fierce. Ha Ha! Stay epic, Lance. You're the best hope us kids ever had. Oh, and find Ricky, the boy we met on the streets. I got a strong feeling about that kid, that he'll be a good friend to you. Okay, I guess I went on enough. Merlin says we don't have much time. Godspeed on your life, Lance. Don't ever change. You're perfect just the way you are. Remember, if someone loves you, that means you're worthy of being loved. And you are most epically worthy, because I now, and for all eternity, love you, Sir Lance, the most amazing boy I ever knew.

Your Buff Man, Jacky'

Tears streamed down Lance's cheeks as he lowered the letter and looked down at Jack's soft, bruised, and peaceful expression.

"I love you too, buff man. And I'll do my best to make you proud of me." He dropped to his knees, sobbing uncontrollably.

In the lobby, Arthur and Merlin paced uneasily back and forth. The wizard still moved slowly, the fatigue of his exertions wearing on him. Even his hair had more gray in it than before he'd performed his miracle.

Suddenly, from the other side of the lobby, Arthur heard Jenny's voice call out, "Arthur!"

He turned abruptly to see Jenny and Ryan hurrying toward him, the clicking of their heels against the hard tile floor echoing around him. Arthur's breath caught in his throat at the sight of them. Jenny looked so lovely, and so afraid, her soft features seemingly carved with uncertainty as she approached.

"Arthur, what are you doing here?"

"How didst you find me, Jenny?" Arthur asked, glancing nervously from her to Ryan. "Is all well with the knights outside?"

"Sergeant Ryan tracked your phone," she explained. "And yeah, the kids are all right, but they need you. Why are you here?"

"Who is this man?" Ryan asked suspiciously, his hand within his coat.

Arthur knew the detective was fingering his weapon. "This... is Merlin."

Jenny sucked in a shocked breath and Ryan squinted suspiciously.

"*The* Merlin?" the detective asked, his aged face crinkled with disbelief. "What happened to the white hair and long beard?"

Merlin shrugged. "Hollywood."

"Something's happened, Arthur," Jenny said quietly. "I know that look. What is it?"

The king and Merlin exchanged a glance before Arthur said, "A miracle, Jenny."

He stepped to the double doors leading into the City Council Chambers and gripped the knob. Jenny moved to his side, and Ryan followed. Arthur turned the knob and quietly pulled the door outward so they could peer into the chamber.

The opening door revealed the rows of pews for the public, the marble columns, and finally the area up front for the council members. Lance knelt beside Jack's body, but the dim lighting convinced Arthur that Jenny hadn't yet recognized him.

Arthur watched as Lance raised his eyes heavenward and clasped his hands in a prayerful gesture.

Jenny gasped.

Ryan expelled a sharp breath, and Arthur eased the door shut.

Both Jenny and Ryan were clearly struck dumb by what they'd seen. Jenny looked like she might faint, and reached out a hand to Arthur. He gripped it and pulled her in close.

"Lance..." she whispered, "...is alive?"

Arthur nodded, his eyes meeting Ryan's over Jenny's shoulder.

He saw in the detective's stunned face a look of someone whose entire worldview had just shifted, suddenly and irrevocably. The man looked literally shell-shocked.

"How?" Jenny managed to ask.

Arthur turned to Merlin, and the wizard explained how and why Lance had returned to them.

Within the chamber, Lance finished his prayer and blessed himself the way he'd seen people do as a child. He hadn't thanked God for bringing him back because, despite what Jack had written, he didn't believe he deserved to be back. And while he'd never cultivated much of a relationship with God until Arthur entered his life, he knew enough not to lie. But he did pray for Jack and Mark, begging God to take care of them and keep them close and not punish them for being gay, something he'd always been told would happen to gay boys.

Still on his knees, Lance clutched Jack's final words in his hands, his eyes fixed on the gentle face of this boy whom he had idolized.

"I don't know if I can ever be happy with you gone, Jacky, especially this way. All I see around me now is darkness and I don't see how I'll ever get out of it. But I'll do my best. For you."

He stood and used the dirty sleeve of his tunic to dry the tears still pooling around his eyes. He gazed again at that face, and a chill ran through him. "You will be honored, Jacky. Trust me on that."

He strode purposefully down the aisle, ignoring the grandeur, uncaring of the surroundings where so many decisions, both good and bad, were made on a daily basis. He had one thought in his mind now – to face his fellow knights and the people of Los Angeles and have them pay homage to Jack for his sacrifice. He felt angry as his footfalls echoed slightly throughout the chamber, angry at Jack, at himself, at the city, hell, at the whole world! He reached the double doors and flung them outward violently.

Arthur, Jenny, Ryan and Merlin reacted with a startled jump of surprise as the doors flew outward and Lance stood gazing fiercely at them. His vibrant eyes blazed with energy and his face reflected a look of resolve.

Momentarily caught off-guard by his sudden appearance, no one said anything. Then Jenny engulfed him in a hug. "Oh, Lance, honey, I'm so happy to see you!"

He hugged her back, but did not respond. His eyes were fixed on Arthur and Merlin. He wanted them to understand he was still not all right with this, with what they had done. "I was okay being dead, Lady Jenny."

She pulled away in shock.

Then Lance turned his gaze on Ryan. The man's expression caught him by surprise. Ryan was staring at him as though Lance had changed his entire life.

Maybe I have, he thought to himself.

Ryan hesitantly extended a hand. Lance eyed it, and then reached out to grasp it.

"Welcome back, Sir Lance," the detective said, his voice raspy and uncertain – a far cry from its usual self-assurance.

Lance released the man's hand. Then he looked his father in the eye.

Arthur met his gaze, and Lance saw the love in those eyes, the silent joy at having him back. He felt guilty for the melancholia surrounding his heart and soul, but he couldn't shake the feeling. The darkness wouldn't go away.

"I'm ready now," he announced.

Arthur exchanged a look with Merlin, and then with Jenny. "I think it best, son, if we go outside and prepare everyone for... your return."

"I'm bringing Jack with me."

Jenny gasped, but Arthur kept his composure. "Very well. Sergeant Ryan can assist you with—"

"I got it, Dad," Lance said firmly, his eyes fixed on his father with determination.

"Lance, Jack is a rather big boy and—"

"I said I got it, Dad. I can carry him." He hoped the tone of voice left no room for argument.

Arthur nodded. "Merlin and I shalt explain to the people. Lady Jenny and Sergeant Ryan shall wait by the glass doors to the street and open them for you at the proper time."

Lance turned to re-enter the chamber.

"Lance," Arthur called out, causing him to turn his head quickly, almost in annoyance. "I love you, son."

Lance's heart skipped a beat, and his face softened. "I love you too, Dad." Then he turned and vanished into the murk of the council chambers.

The adults eyed one another with obvious concern.

Jenny took Arthur's hand in hers. "It's been a shock, Arthur, to him most of all. He needs time."

"The lady is right, Arthur," Merlin agreed, his voice laced with extreme fatigue. "And all of us need to keep a close watch over him."

Arthur's eyebrows shot up questioningly, and Merlin blew out a breath of exasperation.

"Arthur, that boy died before the eyes of the world, and now he has come back. He will be loved and feared in equal measure, worshipped and scorned with equal intensity, unless human nature has substantially changed since our day. He and the world shall never be the same again, and the overwhelming attention will be more than any boy is fit to absorb, even a boy as extraordinary as Lance."

Arthur took in the wizard's words, and understood them. Just based on the media attention Lance had already garnered through the crusade, the king knew for certain that his son would never be free again.

"Did we do the right thing, then, Merlin," he whispered, "in bringing him back?"

Merlin's gray eyes flashed with anger. "You know we did."

"I'll help with him, Arthur," Jenny said. "We all will. We love him, after all."

Arthur smiled sadly, and she returned it. Then the four adults crossed the vastness of the City Hall lobby and stopped before the glass doors leading out onto Temple Street. Arthur turned to Jenny one last time. She raised herself on her toes and kissed him. He smiled, and then he and Merlin stepped through the glass doors.

Reyna, Esteban, and Chris spotted Arthur instantly, and raced up the long flight of steps toward him. The entire crowd gradually realized Arthur had returned, and began to quell their restless talking.

Chris reached the top first and Arthur bent to scoop the boy into his arms. They hugged a moment before Arthur set him back down, but Chris clung to his hand and wouldn't let go. Reyna and Esteban stopped, breathless from their run up so many stairs, and gazed at Arthur questioningly.

"What happened, Arthur?" she asked, her voice quavering with uncertainty. "Why are you here? We thought you went with..." She trailed off, unable to continue.

"Lady Reyna, Sir Esteban," Arthur said, indicating Merlin beside him. "This be my old friend and mentor, Merlin."

Reyna gasped, and even the stoic Esteban made an audible sound of surprise. Chris pulled his face from the folds of Arthur's leather pants to gaze in wonder at the newcomer.

"A pleasure," Merlin said by way of greeting them all, bowing his head slightly in deference to their titles. "I have been watching from the sidelines, as you say today, and have been much impressed with the both of you."

The stunned teens didn't even know what to say in response.

Chris tugged on his black paramedic pants, and Merlin glanced down in surprise. "What about me, Mr. Merlin?" the boy asked. "Did I impress you, too?"

That drew a slight chuckle from the wizard, and he grinned down at the blond boy with the long, shaggy hair and big blue eyes.

"Most assuredly, Sir Christopher," he announced, offering the boy a formal bow.

Chris grinned, but then his soft, youthful face darkened. "Why are you here?"

Reyna cleared her throat. "Is he here because of Lance?"

Momentarily startled by her prescience, Arthur nodded solemnly. "Stand with me," he told his anxious knights, ushering them to either side of himself and Merlin, "and hear something that shall change the world."

Reyna frowned at Esteban, but they complied, keeping Chris wedged in between them. Reyna held one of the little boy's hands and Esteban the other.

Arthur gazed out at the crowd below. He saw Helen, just at the bottom of the steps looking up at him questioningly, her cameraman beside her. The other media personnel were scattered throughout the crowd, regarding him expectantly, every camera aimed his way. He scanned the faces of his knights watching him with need and hope painted onto their eager young faces. He scanned the crowd of Angelenos, also staring at him with anxious wonder. He spotted the mayor and city council members, as well as Sergeant Gibson.

All stood in silence, a silence even deeper and more profound than that which had immediately followed Lance's death. Then Arthur's eyes rose to take in once more the extraordinary mural hanging across the street, and almost lost his breath at the amazing likeness, the lifelike quality to those beautiful green eyes and joyous features of his son.

Glancing once over his shoulder, he spotted Jenny and Ryan poised by the double glass doors, but could not tell if Lance waited behind them.

Arthur turned back to the crowd. "My noble knights, people of Los Angeles, tonight has brought upon us unbearable pain and sorrow, but also a miracle unlike the world has ever seen."

He paused as a murmur of unrest wafted through the throng.

Arthur placed a hand on Merlin's shoulder. "This is my old friend and mentor, the legendary Merlin," he announced, and a collective gasp went up amongst the knights, and some of the people. "While his appearance and exploits have been greatly mythologized over the centuries, he is, nonetheless, a man gifted by God with extraordinary powers."

He let that sink in and the restless murmuring gradually subsided. Even the mayor and other politicians looked stunned into disbelief.

Arthur went on to explain how Merlin's vision brought about the crusade, and the essential nature of Lance to its ultimate success or failure. By now, the crowd stood in open-mouthed fascination, hanging on every word he uttered.

Arthur glanced once more behind him.

Jenny nodded.

Arthur turned back to the crowd. "There is no easy way to prepare you, so I shall simply say it. God, through Merlin, has affected a miracle this night, one that came about at an unimaginable price. But it was a price made by choice, not by force."

He trailed off, unable to continue as images of Jack lying lifeless on the floor flooded his heart and soul.

Obviously speaking for everyone present, Helen called out in confusion, "King Arthur, what are you trying to tell us?"

"I am saying that my son, Sir Lance, yet lives."

The gasp from the crowd was so enormous that it startled Reyna and even Esteban.

Arthur turned to the glass doors as Ryan and Jenny pulled them open. Lance emerged cradling Jack's body in his arms. Though the older boy weighed at least forty pounds more, Lance gave no indication that carrying him was a struggle.

The crowd stood still as statues, stunned and horrified and amazed. There were startled cries of "*Dios mio*," and several women screamed and fainted. Arthur's knights stood speechless with astonishment, and even Helen had her mouth hanging open. Lance strode forward in front of Arthur.

Clutching Chris's hand fiercely in hers, Reyna crushed in against Esteban. His mouth hung open in disbelief, and Chris eyed Lance with suspicion, as though he might be a ghost.

Lance gently, and with great reverence, laid Jack's lifeless body out on the top of the City Hall steps and stood to face the crowd, the front of his green tunic splashed dark red from Jack's blood. He brushed the long hair off his face and gazed upon the enormous mural of himself across the street, tilting his head slightly to marvel at the likeness.

Is that how they see me, he wondered? *All regal and noble-looking like that?*

Whenever he'd looked in a mirror, all he'd ever seen was an okay looking Latino kid with long hair and mad skating skills.

Lance scanned the stunned faces below him. He was shocked to see Mayor Villagrana make the sign of the cross, and even more horrified to see some of the general public, gathered behind his knightly comrades, drop to their knees, hands clasped prayerfully, eyes raised toward him like he was... what? God, or something? It repelled and scared him simultaneously.

He cleared his throat, and fixed his piercing gaze on the people below. They looked up at him in awe, as though he had done something extraordinary. That bred an anger within him that he had to force back down.

Of course they think that, he told himself, *because they don't know.*

"This boy at my feet is the reason I'm standing here with you now. Yes, it was Merlin's power that saved me, but it was Jack who made it happen."

He explained what Arthur and Merlin had told him about how his "death" wasn't supposed to have happened in the first place, and the impossible decisions that had to be made to correct that ill-fated error.

Lance fought to keep his voice steady, fighting back tears. "To all you adults out there, Jack was just a kid. A kid whose family threw him away. But he wasn't just any kid. He—" his voice cracked a moment, and he had to strangle his roiling emotions, "—willingly died so I could live. I gave my life to save my Dad and Jack and everyone else. And I was okay with that. But Jack wasn't. He thought I was more important, so here I am."

He paused again to collect his thoughts, the backs of his eyes burning as he pictured Jack's handsome face and gentle brown eyes. "He shouldn't have done what he did, but he did it out of love. He made a promise to save me, and he kept that promise. So now I hafta do my best to make this city and this state and this country a better place for all kids, especially gay boys like Jack and Mark."

The nearly one thousand youthful knights raised their swords in salute and sent up a loud cheer. Their boisterous support helped to soothe Lance's aching soul.

He turned to Arthur. "Dad, can I borrow Excalibur?"

Without pause, Arthur unsheathed the sword and handed it ove. Lance took the fabled weapon and turned its point to the ground, right beside Jack's prone body.

"Now, I ask that every knight present, and every citizen, take a knee and offer a moment of silence for the greatest hero of our time – Sir Jack the Selfless."

He dropped to one knee before Jack, hands clasped around Excalibur's hilt, his head bent in reverent respect. Arthur immediately did the same, followed by Merlin, Reyna, Esteban, Chris, Ryan, and then, like dominoes falling, every single knight and every single spectator. Even the mayor and city council members, even the police, dropped to one knee in silent respect. All bowed their heads a moment. Not a sound rose into that dark night, not even a whisper.

Fighting back a new wave of tears, Lance rose to his feet, and the hundreds of knights followed suit. But many of the crowd remained down on both knees, their hands clasped reverently in prayer. Lance looked confused and turned to Arthur.

"Dad, why are they still kneeling?"

Arthur and Merlin exchanged a look. Neither man appeared surprised.

"They appear to be praying, Lance," the king responded cautiously.

"Why?" the boy demanded, his eyes wide with sudden worry. Fear shot through him. "I explained everything to them."

The two men didn't respond. Lance stared at them, and then turned to Reyna, who shrugged with uncertainty.

In helpless frustration, Lance called down to Helen, "Lady Helen, ask them why they're praying."

Helen turned to some people behind her and the word went back through the crowd. Lance awaited her answer. A growing dread built up in his gut, and he began to suspect he knew the answer to his own question.

Then someone spoke something quietly to Helen, and she turned to look back up at Lance. "They say you're the Messiah sent by God," she called out, "raised from the dead to save the world."

Lance felt the blood drain from his face. "Dad, make them stop!"

"I cannot, Lance. They have seen this night what they rightly perceive to be a miracle, and will believe of it what they choose."

"No!" the boy shrieked in horror. He whipped back around to face the crowd. "No, everyone, I'm not some messiah from God. I came back, yes, but that was 'cause of Merlin and Jack... Stop, please! *Dejes de orar, por favor!*"

But the crowd heeded him not. In fact, even more of them dropped to their knees, men, women, and children.

Lance was sickened. "Dad, help me..."

Arthur attempted to explain that, while Merlin's power was truly a gift from God, Lance was still the same boy they had all known before. He was human, saved by God for a purpose, but not himself divine.

The crowd barely listened, even when Arthur repeated what he'd said in Spanish. Helplessly, he turned back to Lance, whose mouth hung open in horror.

Ryan urged Arthur to disperse everyone, so the king announced that all knights of the table should return to their homes. Those few who still resided with him would need to wait until his shoulder was tended to. In addition, Ryan explained that the medical personnel would need to examine Lance, and the coroner to remove Jack's body.

The knights hesitated before disbanding, and then Justin's voice rose loudly and clearly into the air. "Long live Lance!"

The knights took up the thunderous chant, over and over again. "Long live Lance! Long live Lance!" and continued to chant it even as they broke apart and took off in different directions.

Lance stared down at them in amazement, astonished by their loyalty to him, and their easy acceptance of his rebirth. Did they need him that much? Had Merlin and Jack been right after all? *Was* he the only one who could lead them?

At that point, the mayor and city council members, Chief Murphy, Gibson, and the emergency medical personnel descended on Lance like a hurricane. He lost track of time and space as they greeted him and slapped him on the back and just touched him reverently, as though fearing he might not be real.

Arthur remained at his side, as did Jenny and Reyna and Esteban, guarding him protectively, clearly fearful of another attack. Lance noted painfully that Chris stayed away from him. The little boy eyed him uncertainly, but Lance saw something in the child's eyes he'd never seen before when it came to him – fear. And that sliced open his heart almost as much as seeing Jack's body zipped into a black plastic bag and loaded into the coroner's van.

As the crowd gradually dispersed, some women remained on their knees, heads bowed, hands clasped tightly in prayer. They would glance shyly upward, see Lance standing with the others, and bless themselves furiously, causing him even greater despair.

Lance felt more exhausted than ever in his life. All this pain, all this drama and emotion had drained him. Not to mention having had nothing to eat all day.

Arthur's shoulder wound was stitched and bandaged. The bullet had passed cleanly through, so only stitches were required. Lance was thoroughly examined, and while his shirt was clearly torn from the bullet ripping through it, his flesh remained undamaged. Despite drying blood on the torn shirt, there was no sign of even the slightest injury. The medical personnel were baffled, apparently hopeful of finding some explanation for the boy's return other than divine intervention.

As Arthur and Jenny led Lance between them down the steps to street level, flanked on either side by Reyna, Esteban, and Chris, Helen stood speaking into her camera. As they passed, her cameraman swung the camera to take in the silent, wearied group.

Lance heard Helen speaking into her microphone.

"Ladies and gentlemen, this night of nights comes to a somber close as we watch King Arthur and company heading back to wherever they reside. We all witnessed live this night a death and a miraculous rebirth, something this reporter will never forget, as I suspect will none of you. There you see, everyone, young Sir Lance, the boy who died and who is now the boy who came back. This is Helen Schaeffer reporting for Channel 7 News."

Lance stared at her in open-mouthed surprise.

Alas, her off-the-cuff moniker soon became known as the nickname heard round the world, and *'the boy who came back'* would follow Lance forever.

CHAPTER THREE

HE WAS MY HERO

WITH THE ENTIRE CITY HAVING witnessed Lance's death and resurrection, Ryan convinced Chief Murphy and the shell-shocked mayor that it might not be safe for Arthur and Lance to be seen on the streets any more that night, and secured police transport for the king and those knights who lived with him. Someone had also called for a horse trailer to bring Llamrei along in the procession.

As the group reached street level, Arthur eyed Mayor Villagrana as the man hovered about, his eyes flicking everywhere at once, but never straying far from Lance. Normally, this man was not wanting for words, but had spoken not once since witnessing Lance's rebirth. He'd only made one fumbling comment to the media about how "what we witnessed here tonight will change us all." And then he stepped out of the spotlight to allow city council members to share their stunned thoughts and feelings.

Villagrana must've felt Arthur's eyes on him because he pulled his own from Lance and looked startled for a moment. Then he bowed his head respectfully, without his usual sneer. Surrounded by police officers as they stood on Temple Street, Arthur, Merlin, Jenny, Lance, Chris, Reyna, Esteban, and Lavern eyed the public still hovering about the scene. Some remained on their knees, while others merely stood in silent awe, their eyes fixed on Lance so intently that he squirmed with discomfort.

"We shall be gone soon, Lance," Arthur whispered into his ear. Ryan strode up and told Arthur he would take the three of them, and police cruisers would drive the rest.

"Thank you, Sergeant Ryan," Arthur said.

Ryan nodded, his steely gaze falling once again to Lance. The boy looked up into that weathered face. The detective's normally hard and stoic features softened slightly, and then he turned back to Arthur.

"I think it would be best for you and your kids to move out of the storm drains, Arthur," he said quietly, causing the king to flinch. "After this, you need to live somewhere more public."

Surprised, Arthur asked the detective how he knew of their hiding place.

"I figured it out last night when I dropped your boys off."

Arthur extended a hand. "Thank you, Sergeant, for all your help."

Ryan shook the king's hand. As he pulled it back, his gaze once more fell on Lance. The boy's face looked sad and lonely and exhausted. "You know, Arthur," Ryan went on, flicking his eyes back to the king, "that nothing'll ever be the same again."

Arthur looked at Lance, and the boy turned his wide eyes up to meet it. Arthur's heart lurched in his chest. He had his son back, yes. But he knew Ryan was right. What Merlin had done would change the world. And Lance must bear the brunt of it. For one, brief, unsettling moment, Arthur considered whether he had given his son a second chance, or condemned him. Jenny took his hand in hers and smiled reassuringly. Arthur nodded to Ryan, and the sergeant led them to his car.

Upon arriving at the primary storm drain entrance, Ryan and the other police cars deposited Arthur and his group along the bank of the L.A. River. Since there had been no rain in months, the concrete riverbed remained dry and forlorn. Reyna had chosen to drive the car towing Llamrei, but Esteban had decided to go with Lavern and Chris in a police cruiser. Once all the black and whites u-turned and drove away from the river, only Ryan remained.

Arthur stepped over to the horse trailer to lead his white mare down the ramp and onto the concrete wall of the riverbed, handing the reins to Chris. Arthur thanked Ryan, who cast one more unreadable look Lance's way before slipping behind the wheel of his four-door sedan and driving off into the night.

Lance stared after the retreating car, his mind numbed, his body barely functioning. As he turned back toward the others, his legs gave way and he started to crumple. But Esteban was there in a flash, grabbing him and holding him tightly against his body.

Arthur and Reyna leapt forward to help, but Esteban shook his head. "I got him."

Lance eyed the circle around him self-consciously, his lids barely able to stay open. "Sorry. Don't know why I'm so tired."

Esteban shook his head in amazement as Arthur stepped forward.

"I shall carry him, Sir Esteban," he said, reaching out for his son.

But Reyna pointed to the king's stitched up shoulder.

"You'll tear out the stitches, Arthur," she admonished, and Jenny agreed.

"I got him," Esteban assured them in his strong, deep voice.

Lance tried to pull away from the older boy, to stand on his own. "I'm okay, Este," he mumbled, his words slurred with fatigue.

"Like hell you are," Esteban said, not loosening his grip. "I'm carrying you."

"You don't gotta carry me, Este," Lance murmured with embarrassment, feebly trying to break away from him.

"I don't gotta do anything. But you're my *carnal*."

Lance's eyes widened with gratitude.

"Now throw your arms around my neck," Esteban said.

Arthur held Jenny's hand as the almost lifeless Lance wrapped his arms around the thick neck of Esteban. Despite the older boy not being any taller, Esteban hefted Lance off the ground, allowing Lance to wrap his legs around his waist. Then Esteban eyed Arthur. "I'm ready."

Reyna chuckled, giving Esteban a little punch on the shoulder. "Show off."

They descended the rocky riverbank to drop onto the ledge below. Reyna stayed beside Esteban in case he needed help with Lance, but Esteban easily slid along the gravelly part and then leaped down to the ledge with ease.

Arthur led Llamrei down the slope and once everyone was safe on the flat surface of the riverbed, he handed the reins to Lavern, asking he and Chris to guide the mare inside. Then he pulled open the huge, iron grate leading into the storm drain system.

By the time Esteban walked passed Arthur, the king saw Lance was already asleep in the boy's arms. He patted Esteban lightly on one shoulder, and Esteban nodded before passing into the darkness.

Once within The Hub, Arthur directed Lavern and Chris to tend to Llamrei, while he pointed out his own bedroll beside the throne for Esteban to deposit Lance.

Esteban restrained a grunt as he carefully squatted down to lay Lance onto the cushioned bedroll. Reyna helped untangle Lance's arms from around Esteban's neck.

Arthur approached with a blanket and covered his sleeping son.

"I thought maybe we might 'a made it work without him," Esteban intoned solemnly. "But we wouldn't have, would we, Arthur?"

"Nay, Sir Este. For a time, yes. But ultimately, no. Lance is the key."

Esteban nodded. "I'm gonna stay tonight, Arthur, with him, if that's okay. I know he's safe here but... I just wanna make sure nothin' else happens to 'im."

Reyna stared at Esteban as though seeing him for the first time, hands to her hips, shaking her head in wonder. "Well if you're gonna guard my baby boy, than I am, too."

"*You'd* sleep on the floor?"

"For him, I'd do anything." Then she grinned and punched him on the arm. "'Sides, it'll be fun. Like a slumber party."

Esteban pulled a confused face. "What the hell's a slumber party?"

Reyna eyed him like he was from another planet.

Jenny threw her arm around Reyna. "Culture clash, Reyna," but it was clear from Esteban's expression that he still didn't get it. Jenny turned to him. "It's a girl thing."

Esteban grunted. "Not any girls I ever knew."

The two ladies shrugged.

Esteban looked at Arthur, but the king's eyes were fixed on the sleeping Lance.

Then everyone prepared to bed down for the night.

Lance dreamed.

He dreamed about dreaming. He saw himself winning the Big Air Final again at the X-Games. But then he saw Jack's bruised and bloodied face as Mr. R's goon beat him up.

Jack, who'd sat and taken it, for him.

And then he was back on the grassy field, with its perfect shades of green and blue.

And that glowing perfection that was the horizon.

And there was Mark, holding hands with Jack. Lance's heart leapt with joy upon seeing Jack alive, strong and toweringly beautiful, just how he would always remember him. The two boys waved goodbye. Lance called out to them to wait, that he wanted to go too. Jack released Mark's hand and strode to Lance, his facial expression unreadable.

Lance gazed up into those eyes. "Please take me with you."

The look of sadness on Jack's face tore into Lance's heart and soul.

"You have to stay, Lance, and make everything right."

And that was when Lance awoke.

His body still felt numb with fatigue, his mind clouded by the dream images of Mark and Jack. And then it all came flooding back, and he sat bolt upright, gazing around him uncertainly. He was in The Hub. Everyone stopped moving about quietly, and turned to look at him.

Lance shook sleep from his fuzzy brain and looked around. He heard the thrumming of the generator powering the scattered lights, and saw Reyna, Jenny, and Esteban sitting together, eating something that smelled like chicken. Chris sat with Lavern, sandwiches halfway to their mouths when they saw him awake. They froze, staring at him with what he interpreted as trepidation.

He reached around and felt his tunic. Torn. Dried blood. He groaned aloud. It was all true.

He was alive.

And Jack was dead.

Reyna hurried over, her makeup still smudged from the crying she'd done.

"Hey, baby boy, how you feeling?" Her smile was generous, but anxious.

Lance saw every set of eyes watching him almost with caution, like he might snap in two at any moment. He hated that feeling. He was not some breakable little toy. He was a boy. And yet he did feel broken, on the inside.

"Jack's still dead, isn't he?" he asked solemnly, his wide eyes orphaned of hope.

Reyna lost her smile. "Yeah."

He deflated, almost collapsing in on himself from lack of food, and deep sorrow. He felt nasty inside and out. He hadn't showered in days, his hair was matted together with dried sweat and blood, his shirt torn and bloody.

Reyna tried for another smile. "Have something to eat, Lance. You must be starved."

He *was* starving, but couldn't even stomach the thought of food right then. Jack was dead. And he shouldn't be.

He caught sight of someone at the back of the group who looked vaguely familiar, but not one of the regular knights. Then he noted Jenny's torn, stained dress and scraped knees, and wondered what had happened to her.

"Where's my Dad?" Fear gripped him like a fist.

Jenny crossed to him, squatting down to feel his forehead. "He's with Helen. So's Merlin. Helen called and said she needed to talk to Art— your dad, so they went to meet her."

"Talk about what? Me?"

Jenny exchanged a look with Reyna, but clearly didn't know how to respond. And that worried Lance even more. Suddenly he heard voices approaching through the tunnels, and moments later Arthur appeared, accompanied by Merlin and Helen.

The king was dressed as he had been the previous night in his tunic and pants, but Merlin had ditched the paramedic garb for a rock band t-shirt, jeans, and skater shoes. Had Lance not felt so morose, he would've laughed. Helen as always, wore a professional looking pantsuit and flat-heeled shoes.

They ceased their conversation when they saw Lance was awake.

Arthur hurriedly approached. "How are you feeling, son?"

Lance shrugged. "What time is it?"

"One in the afternoon," Reyna answered, checking her phone.

Lance's eyes bulged. "Why didn't you wake me?"

Arthur frowned at the tone, but simply answered, "You needed sleep, Lance."

Lance tried to leap to his feet, but his legs felt weak and he stumbled against Arthur, who winced slightly as the boy's hand struck his stitched shoulder.

Rather than feel grateful to Arthur for breaking his fall, Lance pushed himself back. "I got it, Dad."

He noticed Helen approaching, and suddenly felt very self-conscious of his appearance.

Helen stopped in front of him, and Lance suddenly realized he was taller than her. Had he always been, or had he grown over the last few months? She looked as pretty as ever, and he felt embarrassed to be so dirty. And he could smell himself, so he knew she could, too. But she seemed not to care.

Smiling, Helen said, "May I give you a hug, Lance?"

That caught him off-guard, and he stammered, "Uh, I'm like real dirty and nasty, Lady Helen."

Her smile never wavered. "I'm just happy to see you alive."

She opened her arms, and Lance stepped into them, allowing her to hold him close a moment. Then she released him and stepped back and said, "We have a lot to talk about."

Lance glanced over at Arthur, and the king nodded solemnly. "Why don't we all sit and be comfortable," Arthur suggested.

Once chairs or bedrolls were brought in for everyone to sit on, Helen sat beside Arthur and Jenny, while Merlin hovered in the background. The kids gathered in a circle. Lance caught a brief glimpse of the unfamiliar boy—or was it a girl?—the long hair confused him since he didn't have a clear view in the lantern light of the chamber, but the kid still sat at the back of everyone else, as though purposely hiding.

Frowning, Lance sat cross-legged on the bedroll, with Reyna and Esteban seated to his right. Realizing he couldn't get a clear view of the stranger, he waved Chris over to sit beside him, but the little boy held back, eyeing him with doubt. Chris's continued fear of him only heightened Lance's dejection.

"Helen has been telling Merlin and myself of the world-wide response to Lance's... return," Arthur began awkwardly, "which we shall get to momentarily. Firstly, we have an offer of a place to live."

"You mean move out of here?" Lance asked in surprise.

Helen nodded, and then proceeded to explain. It seemed the Celebrity Manor Hotel on Franklin Street in Hollywood would allow Arthur and his knights to move in and rechristen the place 'New Camelot', or whatever they wanted to call it. It was a landmark originally built in the 1920's and modeled after a French Chateau, and looked just like a castle.

She explained that it was owned and operated by the Church of Kabbalogy, which none of the kids had ever heard of. Jenny recognized it from tabloid TV shows she occasionally watched, like TMZ. Mostly Hollywood types frequented the place, but the religion had come under fire for being cultish and weird, so its cachet had tarnished in recent years.

"The bottom line," Helen explained, "is they'll let you move in.

The place is huge and you can use as much of it as you want, and they won't try to shove their beliefs down your throats."

"Whadda they get out of it?" Esteban asked suspiciously.

"Publicity. They get you and Arthur and the boy who came back."

Lance frowned when she said that.

"It'll be in the contract that they can only leave their literature around when you give tours of New Camelot, but no one will proselytize on their behalf," Helen added, purposely avoiding Lance's frown.

"What's prosel— what you said?" Esteban asked, still sounding very distrustful.

"It means trying to push their BS on you," Reyna stated with disgust, shaking her head.

"How does a move from these tunnels sound to you all?" Arthur asked, looking around at everyone.

"Sounds good to me, Arthur," Lavern piped up when no one else did. "Don't wanna be down here when these things flood, do we?"

"Well put, Sir Lavern."

Lance expelled an exasperated breath. "Let's cut the crap, okay?"

Everyone swung their gazes around to him, shock painted on every face.

Lance sighed heavily. "Sorry, but I saw your face before, Dad. What did Lady Helen tell you? About me?"

Arthur frowned, but Helen ignored Lance's tone. "Bottom line, Lance," she said, keeping her voice even, "the only thing being talked about or tweeted about or messaged about is you."

Lance hadn't expected that response. "You mean the whole city?" he asked, the edge gone from his voice.

"The whole world."

His eyes nearly bugged out of his head. "The world?"

"Lance, you... died on live television," she said haltingly, obviously searching for just the right words, "and then you appeared alive again less than an hour later. It's the biggest event since... ever. You're messiah to some and devil to others."

"Devil?"

"A lot of people think the Devil brought you back. Most believe it was God." She paused a moment, and then cleared her throat. "Atheists think it was Hollywood special effects. But there are scattered reports that cults are already forming to... worship you."

Lance gagged, the terror pulling tighter around his heart and soul.

"The videos of your... death and return went viral within minutes," Helen went on. "I'm afraid I started something by calling you *'the boy who came back'*. That nickname is everywhere now. I'm sorry."

Lance nodded, his body numb with fear.

Helen eyed him, and then turned to Arthur. He gestured for her to continue. "Another random posting seems to have gone viral too," she said, casting her eyes toward the anxiously watching Reyna and Esteban, who sat clasping hands. "Someone said you were 'Jesus, Harry Potter, and the Ivory Tower all rolled into one'," she explained, "and now everybody keeps reposting that on your pictures and videos."

Lance felt the blood drain from his face. Jesus? His breathing almost came to a standstill.

"The Ivory Tower?" Esteban asked, as his eyebrows rose questioningly.

"I Googled it," Helen answered, "Originally it's from the Biblical Song of Solomon, though it looks like the one they're talking about is from–"

"The Neverending Story," said a voice from in back, interrupting her.

Lance glanced up and saw the new kid speaking, but it was still too shadowy to discern features. The voice definitely belonged to a boy, however.

"Yes," Helen said with a nod of her head in the direction of the voice. "The book and the movie. I guess it represents—"

"Hope," came the boy-voice from the shadows, and Lance strained harder to see. Who *was* that?

Helen nodded. "Yes, hope." Then she looked squarely at Lance. "Everything's changed, Lance. The world has changed. You changed it, and there's no going back. You are now the most famous person to walk the earth since—"

"Don't say it!" Lance spat, his body trembling with fear. "I'm not Jesus, and I'm not any messiah, or the Devil. I'm just a kid who skates good and..."

He trailed off, unable to continue. Anger and despair and dread all boiled up within him like he was a witches' cauldron, and he glared at his father with such a look that Reyna visibly recoiled.

"You happy now, Dad?" he whispered in a voice of barely controlled rage. "Is this what you wanted? To make me the biggest freak in the world?"

He leapt to his feet and pelted off down one of the side tunnels.

Arthur jumped off his chair. "Lance!" He started forward, but Jenny grabbed his hand.

"Let him be," she admonished gently. "He needs time, especially after all he's been through."

Arthur eyed her, and nodded. He knew well enough that her instincts when it came to children were sound.

"I'm sorry, Arthur," Helen said as she stood, opening her hands in an apologetic gesture. "I didn't mean to upset him. But he needs to understand that he'll likely never have privacy again. He belongs to the whole world now."

Arthur turned and locked eyes with Merlin. He didn't have to say what he was thinking, and Merlin didn't need to use his gift to understand the look. Both men felt the same way. They had done what they'd done to save the crusade.

But what of Lance? Would the boy be able to endure the days and nights ahead? Would he even be able to lead as he was always intended to?

The discussion turned to the business of moving everything to the Manor Hotel as soon as possible, and thus no one noticed the long-haired Latino boy stand up and work his way along the shadowy walls before snatching a lantern from an embedded hook and disappearing down the tunnel that Lance had taken.

Lance ran through the darkness, not caring where he ended up, not caring if he tripped or slipped, not even caring if he became hopelessly lost in this endless labyrinth without light to find his way back. His weakened body finally gave out and he bent over, gasping for breath before collapsing to his knees, the panic attack almost as extreme as those that hit him whenever he thought of Richard and what the man had done to him in that foster home.

He rolled onto his butt, leaning up against the dank, cold concrete wall, drew up his knees and wrapped his arms protectively around them. And then he gazed into the dark and literally saw no light at the end of the tunnel. Was this to be his life from here on out?

Oh, Jacky, I need you now more than ever...

He lowered his head onto his knees and began to cry, softly and despairingly.

Exhaustion, both physical and mental, consumed him and he sat alone, the darkness and drip of water his only companions. He barely noticed the pool of light moving in his direction. Finally, a faint glow drew stronger, penetrating his closed lids like sunlight, and Lance opened his eyes.

Tilting his head upwards, he started, and pushed himself back along the wall a few inches. Someone stood before him, lantern in hand. But the lantern light only illuminated Vans and jeans, and a brown forearm.

"Who are you?" Lance asked, hoping his voice sounded stronger than he felt. He hadn't even heard this person approach.

The arm lifted the lantern slowly, revealing a slightly soiled tank top clinging to a slim, well-defined chest, and then moved higher to reveal the face.

"Ricky!"

The other boy's handsome features broke into a grin, his long, dark hair framing his face and making the grin even more inviting.

"You remember me," he said. Not a question. A statement. And a tone of happiness for having been remembered.

"What are you doing here?"

Ricky shrugged, the lantern shifting slightly and bouncing shadows off the walls. "I joined up this morning, while you were sleeping. You said it was okay, right?"

Lance flashed back to that night, was it only two days ago? He and Jack had met Ricky on the street, and Lance had felt an unexpected kinship with the homeless boy.

"Sure, it's okay."

Ricky smiled again, and Lance found that smile and the boy's innocent face comforting. He eyed Ricky in the shadowy darkness, realizing how similar they were in appearance. Same skin tone, soft smooth features, and long dark-brown, almost black hair. Eerie.

"Mind if I sit?"

Lance shrugged and Ricky took a seat right beside him, setting the lantern down on the damp concrete, and pressed his back up against the wall.

"Ooooh, that's cold," Ricky mumbled, shivering.

For some inexplicable reason, Lance felt an urge to wrap his arm around the boy and pull him in close for warmth, as though Ricky were his brother or something.

How odd, he thought, *for someone I barely know.*

"So, uh, how old are you?" Lance asked, suddenly wanting to ignore everything that happened to him in the last twenty-four hours and focus on this other boy.

"Almost fifteen," Ricky answered. He had a pleasant sounding voice, not super deep like Esteban, but not girly, either. Much like Lance imagined his own voice sounded to others.

Lance nodded. "Me too. So, uh, how'd you, ya know, end up out there?"

Ricky shivered again before lowering his gaze. He laughed bitterly.

"There was this boy my age that I thought was like super amazing and cool and I really admired him," he explained, though his eyes remained on his feet and he seemed reluctant to look into Lance's face as he spoke. "I printed some pix of him from Facebook and stuff because I was too scared to even try to talk to him, you know?"

Lance nodded, though Ricky still didn't make eye contact. "So?"

Ricky exhaled a breath. "So my macho dad found the pix and started calling me a faggot and saying he always knew I was a faggot 'cause I did wrestling."

The word 'faggot' caused Lance to stiffen with fear. His kiss with Jack, and his enjoyment of it, still filled him with dread. He forced those thoughts back down. "You wrestle?"

"Yeah, in eighth and ninth grades. My dad's got that macho Mexican mentality and kept saying it was a 'faggot sport'." He chuckled bitterly. "Like to see him try it."

Lance found it comforting to talk about someone else. He was so tired of himself. "Looks pretty tough to me," he said. "And those high school guys are always buff as hell."

"I know," Ricky agreed. "Like that guy Esteban out there. Man, he's scary."

Lance sniggered, thinking back to the days when *he* was intimidated by Esteban. "I can kick his ass in a sword fight, but I know he'd break me in two on a wrestling mat."

"I could teach you a few moves, if you teach me how to fight like you do, with the sword."

Lance felt a momentary surge of happiness. Something about this boy just made him feel good. He extended a hand. "Deal."

Ricky shook it, and his grip was strong and firm.

"Damn, you got a good grip. Should have no problem with the bigger swords."

Ricky laughed. "Hey, I may look skinny, Lance, but I bet I could kick your ass on the wrestling mat."

Lance's ego took offense, but then he scanned the boy's laughing eyes in the gloom and grinned. "You're on. I'm a lot stronger than I look, too."

"That's what they all say."

The boys laughed together, forgetting for a moment all their personal pain and drama.

Jack's letter came back to Lance then, in that simple, easy moment of peace.

He'll be a good friend to you.

How could Jack have known something like that so quickly, he wondered?

Sitting here with Ricky and feeling as if they'd been best buds their whole lives, Lance realized just how prophetic Jack had been.

The easy laughter settled into an easy calm, and then Ricky said quietly, "I was there last night. At City Hall."

"So who do you say that I am – messiah or devil?"

Ricky met his gaze. "You're just Lance, the coolest guy I ever met."

That stopped Lance cold. Whatever nasty retort he might have made died on his lips. His mouth dropped open in surprise, and he forced it closed.

Ricky lowered his eyes shyly. "I don't got nobody, Lance. No family no more. No friends. No hope. That's why I joined up."

Impulsively, Lance reached out and placed a hand on his shoulder.

Ricky lifted his head in surprise, his eyes wide.

"I lost Mark," Lance said with an exhalation of breath, "and Jack. The others are, well, family. I could really use a friend."

Ricky smiled. And then the smile turned to a grin. "Even one who can kick your ass?"

That brought a grin to Lance's face and he pulled his hand back. "You're the one who's fixing for an ass-whupping, but yeah, even one who *thinks* he can kick my ass." He beamed so widely he almost laughed.

Ricky extended a hand. "Deal."

Lance shook it.

Now Ricky scrunched up his face with a look of disgust. "As your new best friend, Lance, I gotta tell you something."

Lance met his serious gaze questioningly.

"Take a shower, fool. You reek!"

Lance's eyes bulged wide with momentary shock, and then he saw those laughing eyes again and grinned.

"You don't smell so hot yourself, wrestle boy," he said, giving Ricky a playful, but solid shove.

Ricky laughed and shoved him right back. "Yeah, well, at least I don't smell like week old socks I wore for three wrestling matches in a row."

Lance gaped a moment, and then burst into laughter. Ricky joined in and they both made faces to show how bad the other one smelled. Their eyes met, and everything fell into place. They were friends. Just like that.

It took the boys quite some time to wend their way back through the tunnels to The Hub, and when they arrived, all conversation ceased. Helen and Jenny were gone, but everyone else was present. Seeing Ricky with Lance caused Reyna to do a double take.

"This is my friend, Ricky," Lance announced, and Reyna's mouth dropped open.

"We met him this morning," Lavern said with a head nod toward Ricky.

"He's cool," Lance added, throwing an arm across Ricky's shoulders as though daring anyone to contradict him.

"He looks just like you," Reyna exclaimed in an exasperated voice.

Lance glanced at Ricky in the better light within The Hub. Ricky did look crazily like him. He turned back to Reyna and shrugged. "So?"

The girl threw hands to her hips and tilted her head. "You think I'm gonna put up with two of you who're younger and prettier than me?"

Ricky blushed with embarrassment, but Lance chuckled. Reyna's frown switched to a grin, and Ricky relaxed.

"Ricky, meet Reyna, the big sister from hell," Lance announced, waving his arm toward her.

She threw back a look of mock annoyance. "Don't get fresh with me, baby boy, or you'll be sorry."

Esteban stepped forward and extended a hand. "*Carnal de mi carnal es mi carnal.*"

Ricky shook the huge hand. "Thanks, man."

Lance shoved Ricky good-naturedly. "Don't worry – he never smiles."

Esteban grinned at that. "Very funny, little man."

Now Arthur extended a hand to Ricky, who shook it cautiously. "I did not have the occasion this morning to welcome you properly, Ricky."

"Oh, uh, thanks, King Arthur," Ricky stammered, glancing nervously over at Lance for confirmation of the proper protocol.

"Ricky and me met on the streets," Lance offered by way of explanation. "When... Jack and me was looking for Mark."

Arthur nodded, his eyes fixed on Lance's face, clearly searching it for answers, and Lance knew the questions without them being spoken.

"I'm okay, Dad," he said quietly. "I guess. And I'm... I'm sorry about before. I know you didn't want me to be the biggest freak in the world." He searched his father's face for anger, and saw nothing but love.

"I love you, Lance," Arthur said with conviction. "I'll never cease telling you that."

"I love you too, Dad," Lance murmured, glancing shyly into the king's eyes.

Suddenly feeling awkward, especially with Ricky being new, and not wanting to seem feeble or pathetic, he cleared his throat. "So, are we moving to that crazy-ass castle place or what?"

Arthur nodded. "Jenny's uncle is an attorney of the law. She and Helen have gone to him to examine the—what did she call it, Reyna?"

"It's a contract, Arthur," the girl explained.

"Ah, yes, the contract. If all appears satisfactory, we may move in tonight or tomorrow." The king extended his arms around him. "Hence, we have begun packing."

Lance sourly indicated Merlin, sitting on a wooden box apparently lost in thought. "Can't Dumbledore over there, like, wave a wand and move everything in seconds?"

Arthur pulled a confused face. "Dumbledore?"

Merlin strode over, the Megadeth shirt and torn jeans causing Lance to stare again in amazement.

"Dumbledore, Arthur, is a fictitious character," the wizard explained with a disgusted sigh. "Transparently, and I might add very loosely, based upon me."

Arthur nodded. "I see."

"And for your information, Sir Lance," the wizard went on, "I have been drained of my power by bringing back what is known in this era as a 'smart-ass teenager', so no, I cannot wave a magic anything. You shall have to do the heavy lifting yourself."

Lance gaped at him, and Merlin winked. Lance indicated the outfit. "Where did you get all this stuff?"

The wizard looked almost insulted. "This is the style I've adopted since being here in your time."

Lance's mouth fell open.

Merlin eyed him, clearly missing the joke. "I'll have you know I find your heavy metal music rather soothing." Then he slipped an ear bud out from under the black t-shirt and stuck it into his right ear before bowing to Lance and returning to his perch on the large crate.

Lance looked aghast at Arthur, who merely shrugged as if to say, "That's Merlin for you."

Lance exchanged a look of amazement with Ricky before joining the others in gathering up the weapons, clothing, and bedrolls.

Over the next few days, with moving into "New Camelot" and getting settled in, Lance had less time to dwell on his new status as "The Boy Who Came Back." Ricky was a constant presence, a rock for Lance to lean on, always hovering nearby to distract anyone who might upset him.

Every media outlet clamored to interview Lance. Helen, being the contact person, was inundated with requests, but he agreed to talk only with her and only after the funerals for Jack and Mark. For now, the official word was: "Sir Lance is in mourning over the deaths of his friends and will not speak with the media until after their funerals."

As for the news media, the Internet, and every social networking site, there was nothing happening in the world to talk about but Lance and his resurrection. The videos of Lance's death, and his later re-appearance, ran over and over again, always with added commentary from people on the street, theologians, scientists, politicians.

Even the President of the United States made a statement: "What I saw on television last night has left me secure in the belief that God has his hand on our lives and wants this young man to stay with us for a reason. I greatly look forward to meeting the boy who came back in the near future."

Arthur and Jenny and the others, especially Ricky, tried their best to shield Lance from as much of the media onslaught as possible, but it was everywhere. You couldn't turn on a television or computer without Lance being the topic of conversation.

Cults had sprung up overnight, both for and against him. It scared Lance to his core that millions of people seemed to believe he was Jesus returned to earth as a boy and that it meant the end of the world was nigh.

The knowledge that he had become so many things to so many people, and knowing he couldn't possibly live up to half of them, deepened Lance's melancholy over the death of Jack and the prospects for his future. He felt alone and apart from all of his fellow knights, from Arthur and Jenny, even from Chris. The little boy still eyed Lance oddly, and had yet to even hug him since he'd come back.

Upon moving into New Camelot, each boy had his own spacious room on the second floor, the whole of which had been set aside for Arthur's use. Each room sported enormous canopied beds, cavernous closets, and luxurious bathrooms with incredible showers—which Lance had made ample use of upon first arriving.

Everything seemed to be moving in a positive direction for the crusade, except Lance slept in his massive king size bed and missed the comforting presence of Chris beside him. He even missed the dripping water of the storm drains, and was tempted to let his bathroom faucet drip all night long to help him sleep.

He did his best to smile and engage Chris when they weren't busy moving things around, or setting up designated ground floor rooms for the use of New Camelot functions, but the little boy remained apart from him, almost like he was afraid.

Only Ricky could calm Lance's nerves, perhaps because Ricky was new and there had been little between them prior to his return from the dead. Lance felt isolated from everyone else at New Camelot, but with Ricky he felt complete, and almost "normal."

There was an outside area called the Garden Pavilion with a fifty-foot stage for large gatherings and media events, a workout gym, an outdoor area called the Parterre Gardens with enormous French landscaped topiaries, and a massive Renaissance Restaurant that served breakfast, lunch and dinner to hotel guests in a lovely gazebo-like setting, surrounded by the Franklin Gardens and several fountains.

There was also a main dining room with glamorous chandeliers and exquisite flower arrangements. The inside Patio area displayed a hand-painted ceiling of blue sky and lattices with cats and other humorous animals gazing down upon the diners. Lance had never seen anything so opulent as his new home.

To Arthur and Merlin, this chateau and its luxury were astounding. For Reyna, being in such posh digs was nothing new, given the wealth of her family, but to the street kids it was jaw-dropping.

The arrangement Arthur had made allowed him and any of his knights to stay in the hotel and operate all New Camelot business from within. The Church of Kabbalogy would still rent rooms on the upper floors to celebrity guests who wished to stay, but would not interfere with Arthur or his doings. The dining rooms would be open to all. Arthur and his knights would not pay for their food, but renters and regular dinner guests would.

With Arthur's New Camelot being set up by Jenny's uncle as a non-profit, the Church of Kabbalogy would get a tax write-off for everything they donated to the king and his cause, something the struggling religious organization needed. What they also needed was positive publicity, and assisting Arthur in this way, and becoming home to *The Boy Who Came Back* would generate more of that than anything else they could ever do. At least, that was how Helen had explained it to Arthur.

Within days, the Centre had their own sign removed and a new one erected in its stead that proclaimed: 'New Camelot'. Arthur had been given the use of several large meeting and banquet rooms, one of which he designated the Throne Rome, another the Computer Lab, and a third the Training Centre where the weapons would be stowed and knights could hone their skills while visiting New Camelot.

A large computer company offered Arthur as many computers as his Computer Lab could hold, and the king placed Sir Techie in charge of dealing with them and setting up the lab. Jenny designated several large meeting rooms as classrooms for school, which would begin after the funerals. Then the other gang members and disaffected kids could begin their daily trek to New Camelot to begin the eight a.m. to twelve noon home school sessions.

Arthur invited Jenny to move into New Camelot to be closer to him and the knights, but she said she preferred to commute for now, even though Arthur assured her she would have her own room. That had made her blush, but she stuck to her guns.

In the days following Lance's resurrection, donations of money and support for Arthur's crusade poured in. It now seemed everyone wanted to say he or she had something to do with *The Boy Who Came Back*. Since New Camelot did not sport a stable, the Los Angeles Equestrian Center, located near Griffith Park, offered to house Llamrei free of charge in exchange for using Arthur's name in their promotional materials. It amused the king that a company felt they could improve business merely by advertising Llamrei's presence, but he agreed, nonetheless.

Ryan and Gibson dropped by early the following week and marveled at all the progress Arthur and his kids had made in such a short period of time.

Justin, who'd been working all week to help set everything up, offered to show his dad around, proud of what he and the others had already accomplished. Ryan assured Gibson that he would cover the business at hand.

"Can we talk somewhere, Arthur?" Ryan's voice sounded as leathery as his skin. The king exchanged a look with Jenny as they stood within the cavernous lobby, and Arthur nodded.

As they began walking toward the Throne Room, Lance and Ricky bounded down the stairs wearing shorts and tank tops and bragging about who was going to kick whose ass in the Training Centre when they saw Ryan and stopped up short.

Lance hadn't seen the detective since the previous Monday night, right after he'd 'come back'. Now the older man looked at him anew, an uncertain, but slightly amazed look on his face, and eyed Ricky with curiosity.

"How are you, Lance?" he asked, shuffling uncomfortably.

Lance instantly felt on display again, and knew he would likely have to live with that feeling his entire life. "I'm okay, sergeant. And you?"

Ryan cracked a slight smile. "Well, thanks."

He glanced over at Arthur, and Lance caught the look. "What's up, Dad?"

"I do not know. The sergeant only just arrived. Is this something you can say in front of my son?"

"Don't see why not."

Everyone followed Arthur into the enormous Throne Room and he closed the double doors. Arthur's throne had been placed up on a raised platform where normally a live band might perform, with several sizeable chairs spread out on either side. The main floor had folding chairs scattered about, some already in rows facing the throne, others still resting against the wall awaiting deployment.

As they sat, Ryan eyed Ricky with suspicion. Lance patted Ricky on the back.

"This is my friend, Ricky," he announced, as though the detective might challenge him. "He's with me."

Ryan's eyebrows shot up and he turned to Arthur, who merely nodded.

"Autopsy on your boy Jack is complete, except for toxicology, but we won't have those results for several weeks."

Lance's whole body stiffened with tension.

Ricky placed a comforting hand on his shoulder.

Arthur glanced over at Lance protectively, but Lance nodded for Ryan to continue.

The detective cleared his throat awkwardly. "Not to get too graphic, but he died of a single bullet wound to the back. High caliber, armor piercing, likely from a military style sniper weapon."

He glanced at Lance, who sat in open-mouthed shock.

"The, uh, the bullet nicked a lung and lodged near the heart. The boy bled to death." He paused a moment. "Though we all know that wasn't what happened, those are the coroner's findings."

Lance bowed his head, guilt and remorse flooding into his heart. Even Ricky's comforting hand on his shoulder did little to make him feel the least bit right.

"And Mark?" Arthur asked, clearly regretting his decision to allow Lance to sit in on this meeting.

Ryan seemed to shrink into himself even more. "Massive dose of heroin in his system. Like it looked, he O.D.'d."

Lance choked back a sob, refusing to look up, fighting to control the shame boiling up within him.

He was grateful for Ricky's hand on his shoulder, and for Ricky not asking him if he was okay. Such a stupid question, but adults *always* asked it at times like this.

Of course I'm not okay, he wanted to scream, *and I'll never be okay again!*

"Have either of their parents been in contact?" Arthur asked hesitantly, holding Jenny's hand securely in his own.

Ryan shook his head sadly. "Per the mayor's office, both boys will be released to you for burial arrangements, as you requested. A funeral parlor in West Hollywood has offered their services free of charge. Seems the owners are gay and want to pay tribute to these boys, and likely get free publicity in the process."

Arthur glanced at Jenny when Ryan said the last part, and she shrugged. "It's the American way, Arthur."

Now Lance looked up for the first time. "Dad, I wanna put up something in the lobby, a display, something to honor Jack and Mark."

"Of course, son. Any assistance you may need, simply ask."

"I got it. Ricky'll help, won't you?"

Ricky nodded solemnly. "Hell, yeah."

Lance felt Ryan's eyes on him.

"Sorry, Lance," Ryan said when Lance caught him staring. "It's just that you two look so much alike. It's eerie."

Lance nodded, but didn't respond.

Later, as Lance moved about his enormous room, hanging up tunics and pants in the closet and otherwise killing time, Ricky sat on the bed gazing off into space. Lance felt sick about Jack and Mark's parents not wanting to be part of their funeral.

He and Ricky had left the adults and gone to the Training Centre, where Lance taught Ricky some fighting moves with the sword and shield. His "doppelganger," as Reyna had taken to teasingly calling Ricky, learned fast and possessed natural athletic abilities. Both boys got a hot, sweaty workout and managed to burn off some of their pent up emotions.

After they briefly discussed what kind of memorial to honor Jack and Mark, they'd ended up in Lance's room. At Lance's insistence, Ricky had the room right next door and an adjoining door in the middle connected the two. That way they could interact whenever they wanted without disturbing anyone else.

But Lance kept eyeing Ricky as he ambled about his room. His friend looked sad, and Lance knew something was troubling him.

"Hey, ya did good today with the sword," he offered as an icebreaker. "When you gonna teach me some wrestling moves?"

Ricky gave into a slight, mischievous grin. "Whenever you want your ass kicked."

Lance chuckled, but he knew something was wrong. "Tell me."

"What?"

"What's wrong. I can tell."

"Sorry. It's just, you know, Jack and Mark's parents. Made me think of mine."

Lance frowned, and then sat beside Ricky on the bed. "You never told me how you ended up... you know, on the streets."

Ricky shifted uncomfortably. "I told you my dad called me a faggot 'cause 'a that boy I liked?"

Lance nodded, listening intently.

"Well, after that he started throwing every girl my age he could find at me, yelling at me to start dating one of 'em or else."

That piqued Lance's interest. "Did you?"

Ricky laughed bitterly. "Hell no." Then he looked over at Lance quickly. "Not that they weren't pretty and all... it's just 'cause my father wanted it, so I said no. I wouldn't do anything he wanted."

Ricky's temper was flaring, and Lance placed a calming hand on his shoulder.

"Chill, man. Just chill and tell me when it's cool."

Ricky clenched and unclenched his fists. It took him a moment to compose himself.

"It's cool now," he said with an exhalation of breath. "Anyway, he tells me one day we gotta move back to Mexico 'cause the economy over here sucked so bad and we got relatives back there. I told him I didn't wanna go. I don't know no one in Mexico, Lance. Hell, I was born here."

"So what happened?" Lance prodded when Ricky fell silent, remembering the tone of Arthur's voice whenever he wanted Lance to open up to him, and trying hard to match that tone.

Ricky tossed off a cold and heartless laugh. "You know that old joke, Lance, about the kid who comes home from school one day and finds his parents moved away?"

"Holy crap!" Lance blurted. "They just left you?"

Ricky nodded, his eyes tearing up. Frantically, he wiped the moisture away with the sleeve of his tunic. "Left a note. Said the family down there wouldn't put up with a *maricón* like me."

Lance sucked in another breath. Now he was angry, even more than Ricky. What the hell was wrong with people these days? He wanted to scream and shout in frustration, but instead he just whispered, "I'm sorry, man."

Ricky nodded with gratitude, and both boys were too filled with conflicting emotions to speak for a few moments.

"Course, I'd never had sex, Lance, 'fore I hit the streets and found out what I had to do," Ricky whispered, his eyes downcast, his voice filled with pain. "Never even kissed a girl."

Lance's hand rose before he could stop it and landed on Ricky's shoulder. He offered a look of encouragement. "Me, either," he admitted with a sigh. "'Cept Reyna once, but she don't count." He paused. "So. Do you think you might be gay or bi or something?"

Ricky looked terrified for a moment, and then shook his head. "I don't know. Never had a girlfriend. The johns on the street wasn't looking for love, just a boy's ass to—you know." His voice rose an octave. "I hated every minute of it!"

Lance nodded, memories of Richard welling up and threatening to cause another panic attack. He shook it loose.

Then Ricky shivered.

"What's wrong?"

"Nothin'. Just remembered the creepiest guy I met out there, that's all."

"What about him?"

"Guy called himself Dick," Ricky said. "And he was, too. He said I could stay with him and he'd take care of me, but when we got to his place, he started talking crazy, about I looked like his favorite fagboy of all time, and he wanted that boy back."

Ricky paused a moment, and Lance leaned in so close he might have fallen into the other boy's lap. Something about this story scared him.

"He tied my hands to the bed while I was sleeping," Ricky went on, his voice tight with emotion, "and I couldn't get loose. He shoved something into my mouth and…" He trailed off, obviously finding it painful to recount the memory.

Lance was trembling now.

"When he was, you know, doing that to me," Ricky continued, his voice cracking, "and pressing down on me so hard I couldn't even breathe, he kept whispering in my ear, 'You like that, don't you, my little fagboy'. I tried to scream, but—"

Lance froze, face going white "What did he say to you?"

"He kept saying 'you like that, don't you, my little fagboy', but—"

"Oh, God!" Lance exclaimed, throwing his head toward his knees like he was about to vomit.

"What's wrong, Lance? You look like you're gonna be sick."

"What color hair did he...?" Lance whispered to the floor, the world beginning to spin as he fought to control the impending freak out.

"Weird color, like yellow blond or something. Why?"

Lance began hyperventilating, sweat breaking out on his face, memories flooding in and freezing his soul. The sock in his mouth. The weight pressing him into the bed. The searing pain. And those hated words, 'You like that, don't you my little fagboy?'"

Ricky leaped off the bed and knelt before him. "Lance, what's wrong, man?" Ricky felt his forehead and then grabbed his hands. "Lance, man, snap out of it. It's me, Ricky. I'm not gonna hurt you."

Lance raised his terrified eyes, focused on Ricky, and slowly returned to the present. He stared at his friend, glanced down at Ricky's hands clasping his, and squeezed back for all he was worth. The warmth of Ricky's hands in his, the simple humanity of their touch calmed and soothed him.

The panicked look in Ricky's eyes touched Lance more than he could say. His heart rate slowed, breathing returned to normal, and then he gave Ricky's hands one more squeeze of gratitude before letting go.

"Thanks, man. I think I'm okay now."

Once Ricky sat beside him again, Lance told of his rape and near three-year sex-toy status. "It was him, Ricky, the same guy who raped you," he spluttered desperately. "It was Richard. I'm sure of it! Oh God, he's still after me!"

He began to shake again, and this time Ricky wrapped his arms around Lance's shoulders.

"Maybe not," Ricky said with a confidence he clearly didn't feel.

"No, it *was* him. You said he was looking for someone who looked like you, and we look alike. Oh God, Ricky, he's stalking me, and it's not hard to find me since the whole damned world knows where I live!"

Ricky grabbed Lance's hand again and squeezed. "It's okay, man, chill. I got you covered. That sicko comes anywhere near you, I'll kill his ass."

Lance saw real anger in Ricky's face, anger at what Richard had done to both of them.

"I'm sorry, Ricky." He blew out a nervous, embarrassed breath. "I'd take on

Esteban in a fist fight if I had to, even though I'd get my ass kicked. But just thinking about Richard and what he did..." He shivered again. "It's like he's the boogeyman. I just fall apart."

"He's worse than the boogeyman for what he did to you."

Lance observed the painful memories etched across his friend's face, and squeezed Ricky's hand this time. "And to you."

Ricky looked over and their eyes met. Suddenly realizing how close they were, and holding hands, Lance awkwardly let go and turned red with discomfort. They sat in silence for a time, letting their nerves settle and their bodies relax.

Nothing more was said, but Lance's mind kept returning to the boogeyman of his nightmares, and he felt inevitable dread well up within him that he'd not seen the last of Richard Thornton.

The ever-increasing crowds massing outside New Camelot had forced Chief Murphy to assign a round-the-clock contingent of officers to keep order. The Chief had also dropped by that first week to discuss with Arthur the issuance of a Medieval Weapons Carry Permit, so his knights could carry their weapons in public, especially since they wanted to have swords and bows at the funerals the following week.

Lance told Arthur that they would put up the display to honor Jack and Mark after the funerals, because he wanted each boy to have his sword and shield in the casket during the service. Arthur praised the idea, and rather hesitantly asked the boys if they wished to accompany he and Jenny to the mortuary to make the arrangements.

Merlin suggested that Ricky remain behind to "impersonate" Lance. That way the fans and haters outside would believe Lance was still ensconced within New Camelot. Ricky could simply stand at the front door and watch as Arthur and Jenny drove away, with Lance hidden in the back seat.

"Given the resemblance between them, the ruse should work splendidly, if I do say so myself."

Arthur eyed the wizard, now sporting a Black Sabbath t-shirt, and then turned to Lance.

"What be your thoughts, Lance?"

"I want Ricky to come with me." He saw the look of gratitude in his friend's eyes. "But if he's willing to do it, I agree."

Ricky grinned. "You know they'll figure it out 'cause I'm so much hotter than you, Lance."

Despite his dread at picking out coffins for his friends, Lance smiled. "In your dreams."

Ricky turned to the adults. "It's okay, I'll do it."

Reyna faced some drama of her own with the return of her parents from Italy. By this time, of course, they knew all about their daughter's "appalling behavior" while they were gone, and were furious upon their return. They loudly accused her of "cavorting with lowlifes," despite all the good works Arthur and his knights had accomplished, and they forbade her from any more "such associations." When she told them about Esteban, they hit the roof. There was a lot of shouting and cursing in English and Spanish, but Reyna, as always, refused to back down. She vowed to drop out of school and humiliate her parents if they didn't allow her to continue with the crusade.

Finally, after everyone was exhausted from shouting and cussing, they came to an agreement. Reyna could continue her association with "those people" only after school hours, and on weekends, as long as her grades remained high and she didn't miss school. That seemed like an acceptable arrangement to her, so Reyna agreed.

As she left the living room to head upstairs to her own bedroom, she passed Salma, the housekeeper who'd practically raised her, in the hall. Salma winked, and Reyna smiled.

She entered her expansive room and plopped down on her queen-size bed, covered with an archery-themed bed cover, which her mother disdained. Pulling her phone from her pocket, Reyna began texting Esteban about the fight. She knew he'd want every single detail.

The funerals for Jack and Mark would be held at the Community Christian Church in West Hollywood on the second Saturday after Lance's return. It was chosen, in part because it was located on Santa Monica Boulevard, but mainly because it offered itself as a venue. Many of its members were of the local gay community and the church wished to celebrate the heroics of inspirational youth such as Mark, and most especially, Jack. Pastor Tom, who ran the church, had met with Arthur, Jenny, and Lance earlier in the week to make all the arrangements.

Since coming back, Lance had only ventured out of New Camelot on two occasions – to the mortuary and to this church – and both had been in secrecy. Ricky remained at New Camelot, boldly standing at the open front door to the manor and waving goodbye when Arthur and Jenny left in her Prius.

As he did so, Ricky scanned the massive crowds pooling across the street and around the sidewalks, many carrying picket signs. Some sported messages like 'The End is Nigh', others 'The Messiah has Returned', and still others 'Satan's Handiwork' accompanied by a photo of Lance's face taken off the Internet. Ricky worried for his friend's physical safety, and vowed to protect Lance at all costs.

The reaction of the funeral home staff to Lance was an odd standoffishness, as though somehow they thought he ought to be *in* a casket rather than picking one out.

The reaction of Pastor Tom, who ran the Community Christian Church, was altogether different. As Arthur and Jenny entered with Lance, the pastor, tall and thin and middle aged, dropped to both knees in front of the boy and bowed his head reverently.

Lance panicked. "Dad, make him stop."

Arthur looked flummoxed and indecisive, and even Jenny didn't seem to know quite how to respond.

Lance looked at the man on his knees. "Please, sir, don't do that."

The pastor looked up at the boy's horrified expression and smiled. "You have no idea, do you, Sir Lance, how your return has galvanized the faithful worldwide."

Lance shook his head, wanting just to get out of there and go home to New Camelot and hide.

The pastor seemed to understand. "It's all right to be scared. Everyone is when they first realize they've been chosen by God for some task here on earth."

Lance gasped, but the man continued. "You are a living, breathing miracle, Sir Lance, proof of God's hand on our world. Don't let the haters and atheists and non-believers make you feel somehow wrong. You were brought back for a reason, as part of God's plan for us, and I feel blessed and humbled to have you under my roof."

Lance's lower jaw hung open in astonishment as Pastor Tom rose to his full six and a half feet and extended a hand. Lance hesitantly extended his own and the pastor shook it warmly.

Then the man turned to greet Arthur and Jenny, and they settled into a discussion about the service and what they would like to happen.

Lance outlined his ideas, but in the back of his mind he kept seeing the pastor on his knees.

You are proof of God's hand on our world.

For some reason, having that kind of responsibility scared Lance more than death itself and, not for the first time since his return, he felt an odd tug against his soul, as if death wasn't quite finished with him yet.

Since the funerals would mark Lance's first public appearance after "coming back," the area surrounding the church was expected to be a three-ring media circus, with news vans everywhere, helicopters hovering overhead, reporters and TV newscasters peppering a throng of spectators hoping for a glimpse of him.

Feeling it best that he remain out of the spotlight as much as possible, Merlin elected to stay back at the hotel and watch the event on a large flat screen television donated to Arthur by Best Buy, and which now hung on a wall within the Throne Room.

Due to the magnitude of the event, and the small capacity of the church, the service was to be broadcast live on TV and a huge, movie-theatre-sized screen was set up outside the church for the gathered crowd to be part of the service.

Because the gunman had escaped, and the investigation was still ongoing, Chief Murphy provided a phalanx of armed officers to patrol the area and mingle with the crowd.

Ryan and Gibson, accompanied by a motorcade of protective police cruisers, picked up Arthur, Jenny, Lance, Ricky, Chris, and Lavern at New Camelot and personally drove them to the church. Reyna browbeat her parents into loaning her the Escalade—without telling them how often she'd used it in their absence—to bring Esteban, Jaime, Darnell, Justin, Enrique and Luis.

All were dressed in dark clothing, the boys minus sport jackets since they didn't own any, but wearing black shirts and pants. Reyna wore a tight black dress that came down to her knees, and her hair hung loosely about her shoulders, all curls and brown waves.

When Ryan drove into the parking lot, faces of media people pressed in close to the car to see who was inside the darkened windows.

Lance looked out at the strangers floating in and out of his field of vision from the back seat, and shuddered. On the one hand, he kind of understood what he now meant to the world. But on an emotional level, actually having to deal with these crowds and their expectations, hopes and fears regarding him, Lance knew he wasn't ready yet.

He turned to Ricky as Ryan slid the sedan into a pre-arranged parking space closest to the entrance. He knew he must look terrified, because Ricky reached over and grabbed his hand.

"You okay?"

Lance squeezed the hand gratefully. "No, but thanks for having my back."

"Always."

They let go of each other's hand as the door was pulled open and Arthur stood waiting for him to exit. Lance stepped out and blinked at the bright November sun, still warm, even for Southern California. He saw a circle of police officers behind Arthur, batons out, riot gear on, restraining a massive crowd of reporters and citizens alike. Everyone, it seemed, had a camera or phone aimed his way, clicking and recording.

Questions flew at him, praises were shouted, epithets found their way to his ears, and Lance froze by Arthur's side, suddenly desperate to get back into the car with Ricky and flee. Then Ryan was there, flanking Lance on his left, with Arthur still on his right. Both men put a hand to one of Lance's arms and led him forward.

But Lance balked, and turned back for his friend. Ricky was just exiting the vehicle, and the crowd gasped. Both boys were dressed in black pants, white dress shirts, and black jackets. Lance sported a dark red tie, Ricky navy blue. Ricky moved to stand just behind Lance, and the crowd gazed with uncertain amazement at these two boys who looked so much alike.

Lance had his sword in a scabbard attached to his belt, and wore his gold circlet around his head, with Ricky sporting a similar silver circlet Arthur had given him. With their long hair and similar facial features, the eerie resemblance awed the crowd into silence.

Ryan and Arthur took that moment of uncertainty to hustle Lance quickly forward into the church as Jenny stepped to Ricky's side and took his arm to follow.

Lance and Ricky sat in the front pew with Arthur and Jenny and Ryan. Gibson stood in back, keeping watch on the main doors to the church. Behind Lance sat Reyna and Esteban, with Chris and Lavern between them. The rest of the church was filled with Arthur's knights, dressed in their crusader attire and sporting scabbarded swords at their waists. The church was oblong-shaped, very standard, with stained glass windows along both sides and a large wooden cross suspended from chains hanging just behind an altar covered by a white cloth.

The two open caskets sat side by side in front of the altar. Lance, Ricky, and the others had briefly paid their respects as they filed in through the side doors.

Both fallen knights were dressed in the finest tunics Arthur possessed, and each had his sword and shield lying across his chest. Lance nearly lost it as he gazed in at their pasty, almost waxy-looking faces, sunken cheeks and closed eyelids.

They don't look peaceful.

Just dead.

Forever dead.

Pastor Tom's tall, lanky frame, thinning red hair, sharp nose, and dark attire gave him an Ichabod Crane-like appearance. He wore the traditional clerical collar and welcomed everyone to his church, especially all the newcomers and those watching on television. He spoke humbly about not pretending to know the two boys, but how honored he was to have this opportunity before God to allow others to memorialize them here in his church.

There were some passages read from the Bible, most notably the story of Jesus bringing Lazarus back to life. Lance felt every eye in the church on him during that reading, and he squirmed with discomfort. Even Pastor Tom had trouble keeping his eyes off of him as he spoke of the new life Mark and Jack were now partaking of in heaven.

Then it was time for the others to memorialize the fallen boys. Reyna went first. She stepped up to the lectern to one side of the caskets and spoke of the boys' dedication to Arthur and to the cause, and how grateful she was to have worked alongside them.

Esteban took her place as she stepped down, squeezing her hand gently as they passed one another. As always when addressing a crowd, Esteban looked nervous, shifting slightly from side to side. "I said things about Mark that I never really got to make right. Jack, too." He gazed down into the open caskets. "I'm sorry. You'll always be my homeboys." He returned to his seat.

Then Lavern led Chris up front, but the small boy was too short for the podium, so Lavern lifted him up to the microphone. The boy's long blond hair spilled around his shoulders and he looked very grown up in his dark blue suit and cherry red tie. But his face, and his soft blue eyes, begat a terrible sadness as he gazed down at his two friends lying dead beside him.

"Mark and Jack were like brothers to me," he began, his little boy voice echoing off the walls and ceiling. "They always took care 'a me. Mark and me would feed and wash Llamrei and we'd splash more water on us than her."

There were chuckles from some in the congregation, but Chris wasn't smiling. His lower lip quivered, and it was obvious to Lance that he was about to lose it.

"And Jack, he was like Superman, all big and hard and strong. He taught me how to play football. He loved me, and I loved him. I loved both of 'em."

Then he broke down and Lavern cradled him in his arms. With Chris sobbing into his shoulder, Lavern carried him over to Arthur. Arthur held Chris a moment, and then set him down beside Jenny, for it was his turn to speak.

The king, wearing a modern dark gray suit and tie, Excalibur in its sheath at his waist, long hair restrained by his inch-high circular crown, moved to the podium and stood gazing out at the people.

"It is impossible to sum up the lives of two such fine boys in a few of your minutes," he began, his voice strong, but tight with emotion. "I stand corrected. Men. Mark and Jack did willingly step forward to do the work of men, and I have not fought in battle beside better men than them. As king, and as Lady Jenny hath reminded me, surrogate parent, alas I failed Sir Mark, for I did not tend rightly to the needs of his heart and soul. Yet I always looked upon him and saw nothing but greatness. He looked upon himself and saw nothing of value. Ah, my beloved Mark, you were a pearl of great price that I did neglect, and for that you have my eternal regret, and you have my eternal gratitude for being such a treasured gift."

And then his eyes lowered to Jack's unmoving form. "And then there was Sir Jack, a better man than I shall ever be."

There were surprised gasps from the assembled knights.

"He made a promise to my son, when both had been captured by the man who sought to punish *me*. Sir Jack promised to save Sir Lance because he loved my son and believed the world needed Lance more than it needed him. Be that as it may, this world needs countless more men like Jack, men who are self-less and brave and honorable. Godspeed on your journey Sir Jack, and Sir Mark, as you take flight through eternity in the loving embrace of our heavenly Father."

Looking one last time at the open caskets, Arthur returned to his pew. Still crying, Chris threw himself into the king's arms and Arthur gently rocked him back and forth.

The king turned his head to Lance. Lance was looking down, his hands gripping the wooden front of the pew with white-knuckled intensity. He glanced up and met his father's eyes. It was his turn.

Swiping at his eyes with the black sleeve of his jacket, Lance stepped out of the pew, haltingly approaching the bodies of his two best friends, knowing that almost everyone watching today didn't give a rip about them.

No, *he* was the main attraction.

Him.

The Boy Who Came Back.

That angered him, but he fought down the anger. Today was about Mark and Jack, and no way was he gonna let anyone change that.

Taking his place behind the microphone, Lance looked out over the faces gazing up at him, and the cameras whirring away in back. The church felt potent with expectation. Reyna gave him a little smile and Esteban the head nod. And Ricky looked up at him with a soothing strength that encouraged him.

"Growing up, I had no friends. When I first met Mark and Jack I acted like everybody else—I called them fags. I hated on 'em. I even told my Dad they didn't belong in the Round Table. I'm still ashamed of myself for that."

He paused, looked down a moment to collect himself, and then back up.

"I have a secret that I never told anyone but Arthur—my Dad—because it hurt too much. It scared me too much. But one night I told Mark, and you know what he did? He accepted me. He understood me. He became my friend. Just like that. Even after what I said to him. Mark was the first friend I ever had – an amazing, strong, gentle and understanding boy whose only fault was that his heart was too big. He wanted love, but didn't believe he was worthy of it. Neither did Jack."

He wiped away a tear, fighting for control, not wanting to look weak in front of his fellow knights.

"From the moment I met Jack, I idolized him. He was everything I ever wanted to be growing up – tall, handsome, strong, and confident. But he was also gentle, and loving, and the bravest man I'll ever know other than my father. When we got kidnapped, he let himself get beat up for me, to protect me." Another tear worked its way out and rolled down his cheek. "I tried to stop him, but all he wanted was to save my life. He loved me, more than he loved himself. A lot of you people out there think that's nasty, one boy being in love with another. But how many of you so-called straight people out there would step up and die for the one you loved?"

He gazed out at the cameras silently, as though daring anyone to challenge him.

"He made a choice I wish he didn't make, a choice that made him more of a man than anyone in this church or out there watching right now. But he wasn't even a man here in California. Not at seventeen. Not unless he committed a crime. He was the bravest man in this city, but to all of you out there he was just another gay boy. Well, I say the world would be a thousand times better if there were more gay boys like Jack. He was my hero."

He stopped a moment to let that sink in, making eye contact with as many knights as he could. A boy sitting in back suddenly caught his eye and momentarily distracted him. An unfamiliar boy. Big, blond, with chiseled features and penetrating eyes. Something about those eyes distracted Lance. The boy was unknown to him and dressed in regular clothes. Not a knight, and seated by himself, forearms crossed over his chest, gazing up at him with a smirk.

Realizing everyone was awaiting his next words, Lance yanked his gaze from the strange boy and lifted his face directly toward the cameras in back.

"I have a message for Jack and Mark's parents, wherever you are. I hate you."

There were gasps of surprise from the congregation.

"But I thank you, too. I hate you for treating your kids like gum to be scraped off your shoe, but I thank you because if you hadn't scraped them off your shoes and thrown them away, I never would have met the two most incredible friends anyone could have, the two most amazing boys I'll ever know."

Tears sprang from his eyes then, unstoppable and unbidden. He let them dribble down his face while he fought to control his breathing.

"You didn't deserve them. I don't think I did, either, but they loved me anyway. Jack taught me that the things we don't say to one another are the most important. He also taught me that love is given freely, and even when we don't think we're worthy, the person who loves us does, and so we gotta believe it, too."

He stepped from the podium to stand between the two caskets. His blurred vision took in Mark's pale, lifeless face. Then he bent and kissed his friend on the cheek.

"I love you, Mark, even though I was too afraid to tell you when you were alive." Then he repeated the gesture with Jack. "I love you, too, Jack, and I'm happy I got to tell you that before you died. I pray I'll be with you both again one day."

Then he stepped between the two caskets, fighting to control his cascading emotions and moist eyes, and unsheathed his sword, raising it high above his head in salute.

Every knight in the church instantly stood and did the same. With everyone's sword raised to the heavens, Lance called out, "Long live Sir Mark!"

The assembled knights cried in unison, "Long live Sir Mark!"

Then Lance again sent his voice up to the heavens. "Long live Sir Jack!"

The knights repeated the same.

Lance sheathed his sword and began to cry again, hurrying past the caskets and back to his pew. Ricky leaped up and grabbed him, wrapping an arm around his shoulders and easing him back in beside him. Still cradling Chris, Arthur made eye contact with Lance and nodded with pride. Lance's heart lurched and he nodded back.

Pastor Tom ended the service and announced that the caskets would now be transported to the cemetery for burial. He reached reverently into Mark's casket and removed the sword and shield, stepping forward to hand them to Arthur. Then he stepped back to retrieve Jack's weapons, handing these to Lance, who clutched them to his chest. Ricky pulled him in and Lance rested his head on his friend's shoulder, holding the sword and shield as though they were the keys to the universe.

As the knights began to disperse, the camera crews awaited the exit of Arthur and Lance. Lance asked Arthur and Pastor Tom for a final moment alone with Mark and Jack before the caskets were sealed, and they agreed. Arthur squeezed his shoulder lovingly and moved off to gather up the others. Pastor Tom scuttled to the back of the church and let the reporters and camera operators know that Sir Lance wished to be alone with his friends before the journey to the cemetery. Reluctantly, they packed up and exited the building.

Reyna and Ricky hovered near the side door, clearly reluctant to leave him alone. They stood side by side in the shadows, not to eavesdrop, but to be present should he need them.

Lance watched the camera crews exit the church, and Pastor Tom followed them out. The double doors closed and, aside from muted voices coming from the street, a peaceful silence fell over this house of God. He knelt between the caskets and bowed his head in silent prayer.

Then he stood and gazed into Mark's casket.

"I failed you, Mark, when it really mattered. I'm sorry." Then he turned to gaze deeply at Jack's cold, waxy-looking face. "I'm scared, Jacky. I don't know if I... how can I do all this without you? I need you, Jacky, more than ever..."

He broke down in tears, almost crumpling to his knees with sorrow. Reyna and Ricky rushed forward to catch him, but Reyna got there first, grabbing Lance and hugging him to her. Ricky hung back.

"It's okay, baby boy." she said soothingly as Lance sobbed into her shoulder.

Ricky's eyes welled with tears as he watched Lance grieve.

Reyna soothed Lance, stroking his hair and patting him gently on the back.

"Tell me, Lance, did Jack ever give you that kiss I sent?" she whispered into his ear.

Lance pulled away, stunned, his eyes wide and guilty.

"I see he did."

Lance just stared at her. "How did you know, Reyna?"

"You're not like Este and Jaime and those other guys, baby boy. That's what makes you so special. You're badass when you need to be, but you wear your heart on your sleeve the rest of the time. I could see how much you liked Jack." She paused and searched his uncertain green eyes. "Were you in love with him?"

"I don' know. When he kissed me, I felt how much he loved me, and I liked that feeling."

"What's wrong with that?" Reyna asked, gently wiping his tears away.

Lance eyed her, his expression pained. "But Reyna, if I liked it, that means I might be... a fag boy." He could hear Richard's voice even then.

She grabbed him roughly by the shoulders and forced their eyes to meet. "Don't you *ever* use that word, especially on yourself."

"Reyna, I don't wanna be..."

"Gay? Why not? What difference does it make?"

"No one will wanna follow a f— gay boy, you know that. And there's... other stuff too I haven't told you. I don't wanna disappoint my Dad, or you."

"Baby boy, you'd have to go a *long* way to disappoint me, and even longer to disappoint Arthur. First of all, you don't even know you're gay."

Lance blushed.

"But even if you turn out to be, no one will care."

"But Este and—"

"Este won't care. I won't care. No one who knows you will care. We'll follow you to the ends of the earth and back."

Lance's eyes widened in surprise. "Why?"

Reyna put a hand to his chest, right over his heart. "Because of who you are here, inside. Me and Este, we're smart, we can lead a street ops if we need to, but we couldn't do what you do. We've always been too uppity, too hard-edged, too turned off from our feelings. We're getting better, and we're good for each other, but we're learning how to be better from you, Lance. As tough as you are when you need to be, you have more compassion and empathy for people than probably anyone in this city. You're just..."

"Please don't say Jesus, Harry Potter and the Ivory Tower all rolled into one!"

"I wasn't, but whoever posted that wasn't far wrong. You're just the most... *human* person I know. That's why we love you, and that's why we follow you."

Lance threw his arms around her. "I love you, Reyna."

"You better or else," she said into his shoulder.

That drew a smile from Lance as he pulled away from her.

She nodded toward Ricky. "I think Ricky wants to say goodbye to Jack too. I'll see you outside."

She exited the church as Ricky approached. He and Lance locked eyes a moment. Lance felt embarrassed that Ricky had overheard everything.

"I didn't know Jack except that one night we met, Lance," Ricky said with a deep sigh. "But every guy I met out there did, and they thought he was like a god or something—Thor and Wolverine mixed into one. I guess he protected all of 'em, you know, whenever he could. Out on the boulevard, Jack was epic."

"Yeah, he was."

Ricky wrapped an arm around Lance's shoulders and held him in silence for a few moments. Lance didn't pull away. In fact, he slipped his own arm around Ricky's shoulders. Together they gazed into the casket.

A cleared throat startled them and they quickly let go of each other. Lance turned to find Pastor Tom eyeing them with compassion. "I'm sorry to intrude, boys, but it's time to take them to the cemetery."

Lance nodded. He and Ricky made their way to the side exit and out the door, where Ryan and Arthur scuttled them past the screaming crowds and into his car.

The cemetery proved to be another three-ring circus, especially because the media and the general public were not allowed to enter through the main gates. Only the family and the mourners were permitted in, which made Lance feel slightly relieved that he wouldn't have cameras watching him every second while he said his final goodbyes.

An odd feeling had come over him as Ryan steered his car into the cemetery and up along the winding roads, following two hearses bearing the bodies of his friends. It was the same feeling that had come over him at the mortuary looking at all those empty coffins. The graves on either side of the road seemed to call to him, as though beckoning him to join the dead. The feeling persisted even after the cars stopped and he stepped out onto a paved road bisecting rolling hills of grave after grave.

As Ricky stepped from the car beside him, Lance pulled him away from the car before Arthur could get to them. "I feel weird, Ricky, and it's not just 'cause I'm sad, I don't think."

Ricky eyed him uncertainly. "What's wrong?"

Lance shook his head. He didn't know. "It's like those Final Destination movies, you know? I feel like death keeps calling me back." He looked into Ricky's wide brown eyes. "To be with Mark and Jack."

"Are you ready, Lance and Ricky?" Arthur called from the other side of the car.

Lance looked over to see him standing with Jenny and Ryan, eyeing them, but not pushing.

"Be right there, Dad," he said and turned back to Ricky. "I know it's crazy, Ricky, but I felt it last week at the mortuary and I *really* feel it now."

He paused, and lowered his eyes in embarrassment.

"I might need you... to hold my hand." He looked up quickly. "Not, you know... but just to feel someone, a human contact. Something alive. Is that okay?" He looked into Ricky's eyes for disgust or animosity, and only found compassion.

"No problem. Just reach behind my back and I'll know."

Lance smiled with gratitude, and then they joined the adults for the trek uphill to the gravesite.

The two caskets had been laid out side by side. At Lance's insistence, both would share the same grave, so a double-sized hole had been prepared. He had told Arthur when they were making the arrangements, "They belong together," and Arthur agreed.

The caskets sat on rollers in preparation for being lowered into the freshly dug earth. Scanning the mourners, most of whom he recognized as fellow knights who'd been at the service, Lance stiffened upon spotting the same blond boy he'd seen in church. The boy stood at the outer fringes of the crowd, not grieving, just looking stoic.

As Lance spotted him, the blond looked up and right into his eyes. They gazed at one another a long moment before Ricky nudged him, and the spell was broken.

The two boys stood off to one side of the caskets along with Arthur and Jenny, Reyna and Esteban, Chris and Lavern. All watched in silence as Pastor Tom intoned a final graveside prayer over the two closed caskets. Having finished his blessing, the pastor turned to Lance.

With all eyes pinned to him, Lance peeled himself away from Ricky and the others and stepped in front of both caskets. Reaching up to his head, Lance removed the gold circlet and bent down to the coffins of his friends. He gently entwined the circlet through the handle of Jack's casket and then through the handle of Mark's, looping the circlet in through itself so it wouldn't come free when the caskets were lowered, thereby joining his friends together for eternity.

Hair blowing freely in the cool afternoon breeze, Lance began to cry once again as he placed a hand first on Mark's casket and then on Jack's.

After a momentary silence, he raised his head and stepped back to the side with Ricky. As though reading his mind, Ricky unobtrusively slipped his left hand behind Lance's back so Lance could slip his right hand into it. The touch was warm and real and very human. Lance shuddered, the cloying fingers of death gradually pulling away as Ricky's warmth seeped through his skin into his soul.

They watched in silence as the caskets were lowered deep into the earth. Then

Lance and Ricky released each other's hand, removed their boutonnieres, and tossed the flowers into the double grave. Everyone else lined up to do the same.

The boys stood beside Arthur and Jenny and watched the string of mourners file past to toss in their flowers. Lance found his eyes searching for the blond, and to his surprise he saw the boy walking away from the crowd toward the line of parked cars.

He lost sight of the boy as the final two mourners stepped forward, and Lance realized he had no idea who they were. They were a man and a woman, middle aged, the woman heavily made- up and coiffed, the man balding, looking sharp in an expensive tailored suit, and both appearing stricken, sad, and guilty all at the same time. They tossed in their flowers and approached Lance and Arthur.

Arthur glanced at the others, but everyone shrugged. It was obvious no one knew these people. "May we be of service? Did you have the acquaintance of Mark or Jack?"

The woman spoke first, quietly, her voice raspy, as if from years of smoking. "I'm...I'm Jack's mother. Leigh Bennett."

Lance stiffened. Ricky reached behind for his hand, found it, and squeezed firmly.

"And I'm Mark's father," the man said. "Claude Granger."

Arthur stiffened with animosity, but Jenny touched his arm and he quickly regained his composure. "My condolences on the deaths of your sons. They were the most exceptional lads I've ever known, save for my own." He placed a comforting hand on Lance's shoulder.

Both parents nodded sadly, but lifted their tearful eyes to Lance, who bristled with barely contained fury.

"Lance, what you said about us at the funeral was true," Mark's father said, his tone laced with regret and self-recrimination. "I know you don't believe this, but I loved my son. I didn't want him to be gay. But I never wanted him to leave. Looking back now I see how stupid I was to think that way. And weak, like being gay made him not my son or something. I didn't understand it then. And I let my wife send him away." He sighed sadly. "I have to live with that for the rest of my life. If it makes you feel better, I'll never forgive myself for not standing up for my own flesh and blood over the woman I married. You may hate me, but not as much as I hate myself. For what it's worth, I'm glad he found you. Thank you. And thank *you*, King Arthur, for being a better father to my son than I ever was."

Without awaiting a response, he turned to leave.

"Wait," Lance called out, stunned by the confession and, despite his anger, touched by the man's obvious sorrow. "I don't hate you, Mr. Granger. You gave me the first friend I ever had, an amazing friend." He looked the older man straight in the eye. "I don't know if you've been following our crusade, but we got a lot more we wanna accomplish. Us kids need grownups on our side, with us, not against us. Are you in, or out?"

Mark's dad looked surprised by Lance's gesture, and humbled. "Count me in."

"Look for us on the Internet soon. We'll have a website, and a Facebook page."

The man nodded, and offered a shy little smile that almost made Lance gasp with its familiarity, for it was Mark's smile. Then the man turned away, and Lance eyed Jack's mother soberly. She shuffled uncomfortably, forcing herself to meet his steely green eyes.

"Jack was a good boy," she began, grabbing a tissue from her pocketbook and dabbing at her smudged make-up. "I knew he liked other boys even before he did. Mothers know things like that. But I knew my husband, so I said nothing. When Jack finally told me, I begged him to keep it from his father. He was my only child and I loved him. But Jack was brave even then, Lance. He stood up to his father, told him the truth one night. They fought. Taylor... hit him. Hit my son."

Tears rolled down her tortured face, but she ignored them.

"But Jack didn't back down. He was all boy, that one, and already pretty big then. I begged my husband to just let it alone, but he couldn't. I don't know why it bothered him so much that he had to humiliate Jack in front of his coach and the team, but he did. I promise you, Lance, it wasn't my idea to send Jack to one of those conversion places. I fought it, but Taylor always got his way. But not this time, because Jack ran."

Her crying became achingly painful, and Lance felt his emotions rise into his throat. He squeezed Ricky's hand behind his back all the harder.

"I'm so sorry, Lance. I saw him on the news with you, but Taylor forbade me from contacting him. As far as he was concerned, our son was dead. And now he really is."

She broke down then, and Arthur stepped forward to cradle her in his arms.

Lance just stared at her.

When she pulled away from Arthur, she said, "Thank you, Arthur, and thank you Lance, for loving my son when I couldn't."

She turned to leave.

"Mrs. Bennett," Lance called out.

She turned back to face him.

"I ask you the same question I asked Mark's father – are you in or out?"

She looked surprised, but then offered a tragic smile. "I'm in, too."

Lance nodded. "Thank you for the bravest boy I'll ever know."

Tears flowing freely now, she walked slowly away.

Arthur gazed at Lance. "I'm proud of you, son. You handled that with exceptional grace." Lance nodded silently. "Are you ready to return home?"

Lance shook his head, meeting his father's eyes with his own blurry vision. "I'd like to stay till it's finished."

Arthur nodded, and glanced at Ricky.

Ricky looked at Lance. "I'll stay with you, Lance, if you want me to."

Lance smiled gratefully.

"I'll have someone remain behind to drive you both home," Arthur said.

Ryan stepped up immediately. "I'll wait with them. I wanna make sure they get home safely."

"Thank you, Sergeant."

"Gib'll drive you back, Arthur."

The king nodded and turned to Lance. "Whenever you're ready."

Lance released Ricky's hand and hugged his father. "Thanks, Dad. I love you."

"I love you too, son," the king responded.

"I'll wait for you by the car, boys," Ryan said, and followed as Arthur joined the others heading toward their cars. Within minutes, it was only Lance and Ricky left behind. The cemetery fell into an almost preternatural quiet as the last of the car engines died away. The breeze kicked up, blowing Lance's unrestrained hair into his face.

They stood in silence as the gravediggers approached with their shovels and began to fill the graves. Ricky slipped his hand back into Lance's. Lance squeezed it gratefully and watched as the mound of earth grew higher and higher until it covered Mark and Jack forever.

When it was done, Lance tearfully turned to Ricky and said, "Know what I just realized, Ricky?"

The other boy shook his head.

"Today's my birthday," Lance said in a guttural whisper. "Does that suck or what?"

Ricky looked stunned. "Yeah, it does. You know what else sucks? It's my birthday too."

Lance's mouth dropped open. "No way!"

"Way."

Lance blew out an exasperated breath. "Life really bites, Ricky."

"Yeah, it does."

Both stared at the filled graves, gripping each other's hand like they never wanted to let go.

Neither boy noticed the prying eyes fixed on them the entire time.

The blond boy Lance had seen slip away, now stood behind a tree, face inscrutable, narrow brown eyes fixed on Ricky and Lance. He remained in place until the graves were completely filled. When the two boys turned to leave, the blond slunk away into the shadows.

CHAPTER FOUR
ARE YOU SCARED OF ME?

THE FOLLOWING DAY WAS FRIDAY, and Arthur's knights in residence continued to transform the Celebrity Centre into New Camelot in anticipation of the big dedication-hotel-warming party, as Reyna had designated it, scheduled for the following day. Sir Techie and other computer-savvy knights worked feverishly to get the Computer Lab up and running, especially since school was set to begin the following Monday and the kids would need the Internet to do research.

That morning, as Arthur sat with Lance, Ricky, Lavern, and Chris eating breakfast in the spacious dining room—at present there were no hotel guests until the change-over was complete— the king eyed his son and the boy who already seemed an integral part of his team. Lance looked grave, no doubt still mourning the deaths of Jack and Mark. Arthur smiled at Ricky's attempts to draw Lance out by sneaking food from Lance's plate and popping it into his mouth.

At first, Lance didn't notice as he stared vacantly across the expansive room seeing Arthur knew not what. Perhaps nothing. Then Ricky grabbed another sausage, and Lance flung out his hand and snagged Ricky's wrist.

"Got you, fool!" He attempted to mad dog Ricky, but the other boy's disarming grin caused him to laugh and punch Ricky before taking his sausage back and popping it into his mouth. "Think I didn't notice what you was doing?"

And both boys playfully shoved one another. Lavern laughed, but Chris eyed them uncertainly, something that Arthur noted with concern. He made a resolution to talk with Chris later, to see what might be troubling him.

Yes, Arthur realized, Ricky was good for Lance, and vice versa. It seemed that God had sent this boy to them, knowing how desperately Lance needed a friend to get him through the difficult days ahead. Arthur sent a silent prayer of thanks and then cleared his throat.

The tussling boys stopped their horseplay.

"I have been wondering, Lance, about your statement yesterday to Mark's father about a website. Have you been thinking about how the crusade should best go forward?"

"Yeah, Dad, I have," Lance replied, his young voice deeper than before and filling up with excitement. "Everybody's got a website."

"And a Facebook page," Ricky chimed in, and Lance punched him.

"I was gonna say that, fool," Lance chided him with a grin. "And Twitter. Look, Dad, we gotta move this crusade forward, right?" The king nodded. "So Ricky an me have been talking, see, and we gotta use the Internet to get our message out there. We can teach kids the laws of chivalry, the knightly code if they wanna be knighted, and we can start campaigning."

Arthur was thrilled to see Lance so passionate about something. So much so that he didn't even mind the boys calling each other "fool," a word he personally disliked. "Campaigning for what?"

Lance looked straight at his father with those green eyes filled with excitement. "So us kids can have the right to vote, Dad. Just like we always talked about. So we can protect kids like Mark and Jack and make things better."

Arthur sat back with a grin, and stared in awe at this remarkable boy who had become his son.

Now Lance looked confused, and turned to Ricky, who just shrugged. His eyes narrowing with uncertainty, he said, "What, Dad?"

"Pastor Tom was correct. You are a miracle."

Lance blushed and lowered his eyes, but Ricky slapped him hard on the back and grinned. "That's my miracle boy." He laughed, and Lance punched him again.

"It is a magnificent idea, Lance," Arthur went on, his pride in the boy growing ever stronger by the day. "And you two shall take charge of the endeavor."

Lance grinned, and the boys high-fived. Lance glanced at Chris, who sat sipping his orange juice. "You wanna help, little man?"

Chris shrugged noncommittally, causing Lance to frown with disappointment.

Again, Arthur noted Chris's unusual hesitation toward Lance and vowed to talk with the boy at his earliest opportunity.

Later that morning, after Jenny had arrived to help Arthur decorate the Throne

Room, there was a knock at the open door and both adults turned to find Ricky poised uncertainly, as though unsure if he should enter or not.

"Come in, Ricky," Arthur said cheerily. "This is your home now. There be no need for knocking."

Ricky smiled gratefully, and then closed the double doors before approaching. He glanced back over his shoulder at the door, as though expecting to be followed. "I snuck away from Lance for a few, Arthur. Hi, Lady Jenny."

She smiled. Her long blonde hair was tied back in a ponytail and she was dressed in grungy work clothes. "'Morning, Ricky."

Arthur frowned with obvious worry. "What is it, Ricky?"

Ricky sighed and looked up at the much taller man. "Yesterday was Lance's birthday, Arthur. He's fifteen now."

Arthur was shocked, and exchanged a look with an equally surprised Jenny. "How do you know?"

"He remembered at the graveyard," Ricky said flatly.

Arthur sighed. "I had never thought to ask. In this era, does the day of one's birth have great significance?"

"For us kids, yeah, it's kind of a big deal. I know Lance won't feel like any big party or nothing, but maybe we could give him a cake and some presents at the gathering tomorrow?"

"Of course, we shall, Ricky," Arthur affirmed. "I shall put Lady Reyna to the task. Thank you for caring so much for my son."

"He's like my best friend, Arthur," Ricky said shyly. "I know it's crazy but, it's like we been best friends forever."

Arthur smiled, and Jenny nodded in understanding.

Ricky excused himself to hurry back so Lance wouldn't get suspicious.

Arthur immediately pulled out his cell phone and texted Reyna, despite her being in school. She instantly texted back how exciting it would be to have a party for Lance and she'd handle everything. Arthur showed the message to Jenny, and the two adults grinned with pleasure.

For the next hour, Arthur and Jenny continued decorating and setting up the Throne Room.

Lance entered, without Ricky in tow, and approached them.

"You look troubled son," the king said, putting aside the potted plant he was repositioning at Jenny's behest.

Lance shrugged uncertainly. "Just weird feelings, memories. I been sinking into these funks lately."

"Memories never fade, Lance, most notably the good ones. But pain does, in time." He took Lance in his arms and the two stood, Arthur holding him close.

After a moment, Lance pulled away from him and flashed a smile. "Dad, can I ask a favor?"

"Anything, Lance."

"I know you're busy — we all are —but yesterday was Ricky's birthday. He turned fifteen."

Arthur's eyebrows shot up in surprise, and he glanced over at Jenny, but neither of them spoke.

"He's been real good to me, Dad, especially yesterday and, well, I was wondering if we could get him a cake, maybe some presents for the gathering tomorrow? Surprise him?"

"Of course we can, Lance. It is thoughtful of you to so consider his feelings. I shall call Lady Reyna and set her to the task."

"Thanks, Dad."

"Ricky has proven himself an invaluable member of our company, and he's quite devoted to you. That pleases me."

"Do you need me for anything? If you don't, I figured I'd spar with Ricky, work more on his swordsmanship. I want him to be *my* First Knight, you know, like a bodyguard, and I need to get him in shape. Is that ok?"

"Of course, son. The physical exertion shall benefit you both. I am dealing with the more tedious aspects of command, which you, alas, must learn one day. Train him. Teach him well. He shall surely excel with you coaching him."

"Thanks, Dad." Then he left the Throne Room.

Arthur texted Reyna again and explained about the double birthday. She was even more thrilled, commenting that Lance thinking of others before himself was what made him such a great leader.

Arthur agreed, adding the Ricky may prove to have strong leadership qualities, as well. He told Reyna to keep receipts and he would reimburse her later. She scoffed at that. What else did she have all that money for if not to spend it on people she loved? Her parents would just have to deal.

Arthur hung up. "An odd coincidence, do you not think, Jenny? Both boys born the same day and the same year?"

She mulled that over a moment. "I was never so sure about God as you, Arthur, at least not until last week. But it seems like more than a coincidence, more like those two were meant to be together."

Arthur smiled and pulled her in close, gazing deeply into her soft blue eyes. "I quite agree, Lady Jenny." Then he kissed her.

Lance and Ricky sparred off and on with swords and shields, while Lavern and Chris worked on archery practice. The Training Centre was an enormous meeting room from which all the furniture had been removed and where dummy targets now lined one wall. The center area had ample room for sparring, and someone had donated a padded mat for the kids to wrestle on or practice falls and rolls without getting hurt. The weapons and targets looked incongruous beneath sloping crystal chandeliers, surrounded by walls with art-deco copings and fancy wallpaper, but the boys quickly adapted. Finally, unlike in the storm drains, there was real light to practice in.

Ricky's natural athletic abilities allowed him to learn quickly, much to Lance's dismay. The other boy seemed almost to read his mind and know his moves before Lance even made them. Still, Lance had more experience and technique, and managed to disarm Ricky several times. But each time it got harder.

Lavern and Chris stopped firing arrows to watch as the boys' sparring became more intense and exciting.

Finally, Ricky found an opening and the covered point of his blade broke through Lance's defenses, halting near the boy's exposed chest. Panting with exertion, Lance frowned with disgust, but then Ricky made such a gleeful, mocking face that both boys devolved into laughter.

Lavern and Chris clapped at the exciting display, and Lance lightheartedly glared at them.

"Whose side're you on, anyways, me or this fool?"

Lavern grinned and pointed to Ricky, and Ricky gave a dramatic bow, sending all of them to laughing again. All except Chris, who kept eyeing Lance as he had during breakfast.

Lance frowned, and then thought of an idea. "You wanna spar with me, Chris?"

Chris looked nervous and shook his head, causing Lance to start sinking into another funk.

Ricky must've sensed it coming on because he said to Chris, "How 'bout teaching me some of your moves, Chris?"

Chris nodded and ran to the large pantry that had been turned into an armory. This was at Chief Murphy's insistence – he didn't want weapons left around for hotel guests to stumble upon.

Lance gazed sadly at Ricky, who shrugged.

Chris returned with his own sword and shield, and as Lance sadly watched, he taught Ricky some cool moves, including how to drop and roll, tucking the shoulder under so he could land back up on his feet. It was a move Chris had been practicing, and he was quite proud for having mastered it. Ricky knew some drop and roll moves from wrestling, and taught these to Chris. Lavern sat beside Lance and watched the contest in silence.

When the two boys took a rest and sat on the mat with them, Lance tried to high five Chris, but he recoiled from him, and sidled closer to Lavern. Lance felt like he'd been punched in the stomach and looked dejectedly at this boy who used to idolize him.

"What's wrong, Chris?" Ricky asked, glancing over at Lance's hurt expression.

Chris shrugged, and stared at Lance nervously.

"Are you scared of me, Chris?" Lance asked, his voice barely a whisper, his heart pounding with fear.

Please don't say yes...

Chris nodded, and Lance's heart split in two. "I'm sorry, Lance, but you died. I saw it."

Lance felt a desperate need to grab Ricky's hand just then. Those fingers of death clawed at him, clutching at his soul and chilling him to the bone. He fought the feeling, and concentrated on Chris. "And you don't understand how I came back."

Chris shook his head.

Lance took a deep breath, and asked the question he didn't want to ask. "Are you mad at me 'cause of Jack?"

Chris nodded, and melancholy engulfed Lance.

"Would you rather be having Jack alive and Lance dead?" Lavern asked.

Chris looked mortified. "No. I just don' understand, Lance. You died..."

"I know, Chris. I remember it." He shuddered again, and Ricky scooted closer so their bodies could touch, as though he instinctively knew Lance needed some human contact. "But Jack brought me back. I wish he hadn't done that."

Now Ricky blanched. "Don't you say that, Lance. Ever!" He gazed deeply into Lance's surprised eyes a moment before turning to meet Chris's wide-eyed look. "Listen, Chris. I don't understand how this happened either, 'cept, well, maybe God wanted Lance to come home because he loved him just like you do. But then Jack reminded God how much we still needed Lance down here and offered to take his place. So God said yes."

"But why would God do that?"

Ricky shrugged. "I don' know, Chris. Jack believed we needed Lance down here more than we needed him. I guess he talked God into it. But it's still the same Lance, Chris. He's not some ugly-ass zombie or something."

Lance punched Ricky hard and Chris laughed, the tension of the moment broken.

"Well, he *is* ugly-ass, but he's not a zombie," added Ricky with a huge grin that had its desired effect. Lance grinned right back and both Lavern and Chris cracked up.

Then Lance grabbed Ricky in a headlock and down they went, wrestling and rolling around on the mat and laughing. Chris and Lavern laughed again, and then both leaped into the fray and joined Lance in pinning a cackling Ricky to the floor.

"At least my ass isn't as ugly as yours," Lance announced as he sat atop Ricky pinning his arms, with Chris and Lavern holding down his legs.

Ricky laughed and struggled to get up, but then Chris and Lavern started tickling him, causing him to howl with laughter.

"Wow, Lance he's more ticklish than you," Chris chortled with delight.

"Damn straight," Lance said with finality, "and uglier too."

They all laughed and rolled off Ricky, the four boys lying side by side on the mat, panting and giggling like little kids. Chris reached out tentatively and took Lance's hand, squeezing it gently. Lance's eyes welled a little.

"I'm sorry, Lance," Chris whispered.

"No prob, little brother."

Chris beamed, and then leaped to his feet. "I'm gonna go find Arthur and tell him you aren't no ugly-ass zombie."

Before anyone could respond, Chris had run excitedly from the room, leaving the boys laughing hysterically at the thought of Arthur's face when he heard that. Lavern got up and went looking for Chris, to make sure the youngster didn't get lost in the, as yet, unfamiliar floors and corridors of New Camelot.

Lance sat up, hands behind him on the mat and looked at Ricky with gratitude. "Thanks, man. You sure know how to talk to the little ones."

Ricky's face clouded with pain. "I had a little brother, too. He used to love me."

Looking like he might tear up, Ricky shook it off and jumped to his feet, snatching up his sword and shield. "Ready to get your zombie ass whupped?"

Lance jumped up instantly. Grabbing his weapons, he took up a fighting stance. "In your dreams, pretty boy!"

"You think I'm pretty, huh?"

Lance blushed, not quite sure why he'd used that nickname since he'd hated when it was applied to him.

"I am, you know," Ricky went on with a wink. "Pretty badass, that is. You ready to find out how badass?"

"Damn straight. Bring it on!"

They sparred for another twenty minutes with neither one gaining the advantage. Lance was impressed by Ricky's strength and stamina, obviously built up through his wrestling. And the other boy was pretty ripped, too, Lance noticed. Beneath the chain mail, Ricky's white t-shirt clung to his sweaty body and showed nothing but ridges and muscular curves.

He found his old insecurities about his physique creeping back in. Even though he knew, in his mind, that he was at least as built as Ricky, if not more so, somehow in his mind he always came up short against other guys. He shook off the feeling as stupid, and with final thrusts and parries, the boys dropped exhausted onto the mat.

"Not bad for a newbie," Lance said as he fought to catch his breath, punching Ricky on the shoulder.

Ricky grinned through his own panting. "Good enough to stop your weak ass."

Lance laughed and they high fived. Then Lance's phone beeped, signaling an incoming text message. He rolled over to where they'd left their stuff and grabbed his phone. The number displayed was "000000000."

"What the...?" He opened the message. It read: 'Hey Lance, how's it going?'

Ricky moved to Lance's side and gazed at the message, frowning.

Lance tapped in: 'Fine. Who is this?'

A moment later these words appeared: 'Who do you want it to be?'

Lance and Ricky exchanged a look, and Lance thumbed in: 'This isn't funny. Who r u and how did u get my number?'

These words appeared: 'Whatever I want, I get. Again, who do you want me to be? Your boyfriend, Jack?'

Lance blanched, and Ricky reached out to place a hand on his shoulder. Lance thumbed in: 'Not funny! Who the hell r u?'

'That's for me to know and you to find out. For now just call me Jacky. And know that I'm watching you. All the time.'

Lance glanced at Ricky. Something was *very* wrong here.

Fury arose in Lance and he typed, 'Screw you!'

A final text appeared: 'In your dreams, Lance. Ha Ha Ha.' Then nothing more.

Both boys gazed at the phone a moment longer, but nothing new appeared. When Lance tried to call back, a recording indicated he needed to type in a valid number. Ricky frowned with worry, and Lance was scared, too, though he didn't want to show it.

Was this just the beginning? Would he now be harassed as well as worshipped? Was his privacy even here at home a thing of the distant past?

"We need to tell your dad," Ricky said, as Lance lowered the phone to his lap.

"No, Ricky," Lance said with assurance. "Last thing I wanna do is worry him. I got you to protect me, right?"

"Always."

"It's just some jerk prankster," Lance said with a solemn look. "We'll handle it. You and me."

Ricky nodded.

After stowing their weapons and chain mail, they went to visit Sir Techie in the Computer Lab. Once a vast meeting room of some kind, it was now filled with long tables upon which sat a hundred computers. Some were connected, while others were being unboxed and set up by Techie and his assistants. There was debris and packaging material everywhere.

Sir Techie, a sixteen-year-old whose real name was Thuy, sat at one terminal typing something into the keyboard as Lance and Ricky entered. Taking a moment to absorb the vastness of the project, Lance wended their way through tables and boxes to Techie's side, Ricky beside him.

"Morning, Sir Lance," Techie said, eyes never leaving the screen, fingers flying over the keyboard. Lance eyed him in amazement because it took him forever to type anything. "What's up?"

"Sir Techie, somebody's hacked into my phone."

"Some scumbag, you mean," chimed in Ricky as Techie looked up from his typing and frowned.

Lance handed the phone to Sir Techie. "Think you can figure out who?"

"What number comes up?"

Lance opened to the messages. "Just zeroes. See?"

Sir Techie nodded. "Standard routing trick to hide a number. Can I hold on to this for a while? I'll see what I can do."

"Sure."

Ricky grinned mischievously at Sir Techie. "If the guy texts again, tell him to screw off in English and Vietnamese, okay?"

Sir Techie laughed. "You got it."

Lance's face darkened and he indicated the computer. "So how bad is it out there?"

Techie shoved long black bangs from his eyes, and pushed his glasses up along his nose. "How do you mean?"

Lance glanced uncertainly at Ricky. He wasn't really sure he wanted to know. Up to now he'd been avoiding the Internet and the news because everything was about him. But now that he'd gone public at Jack and Mark's funeral, he was curious how the world saw him.

"About me," he whispered.

Techie turned back to the keyboard, clicking open an Internet window. The Google search engine appeared, and Lance watched as Techie typed in "the boy who came back." Lance held his breath. Ricky's comforting presence helped steady his nerves.

Page one of the hits appeared and the boys leaned in to check. There were one hundred twenty two million, eight hundred thirty- six thousand sites, and twelve million, two hundred eighty three thousand, six hundred pages now devoted to Lance. Even as the three boys stared in open-mouthed astonishment, the number kept increasing.

Lance groaned, his heart rate increasing.

As Techie opened random pages, Lance gazed soberly at the enormity of what he'd had become. There were the expected cult pages springing up, either painting him savior or devil. Some cults had taken to wearing tunics and gold circlets around their brows to emulate him. The hater cults put his face in the center of a target and suggested a better shooter take aim next time.

Lance's gut tightened. There were Twilight and Walking Dead parodies with Lance as the undead vampire or zombie figure. There were teen-girl fan sites posting pictures of Lance and proclaiming him hotter than Justin or Harry or Edward or Jacob, with lots of postings attesting to how beautiful he was.

Ricky scoffed at those. "Obviously, those girls are blind," he said, elbowing Lance.

But Lance wouldn't be sucked into the joke. His heart pounded with dismay. This was worse than he imagined. There was every kind of site, from those hawking photos of Lance to ones selling t-shirts with his face emblazoned on them and the words 'The Boy Who Came Back' in bold lettering.

Finally, he couldn't take anymore and shut down the Google window. He stood tautly, almost breathless with shock, as Techie and Ricky looked on.

How could this be right, he asked himself for the umpteenth time? *What could I possibly do for the world to ever make all of this insanity right?*

"Hey," Ricky said, taking hold of his upper arm to steady him.

Lance looked into Ricky's wide, soulful eyes. "I need to get cleaned up."

"Yeah, we both smell like a locker room." Ricky tried for a smile, but Lance wasn't buying in. The boy who came back simply turned away and walked stiffly from the Computer Lab.

Looking fearful, Ricky glanced once at Techie and pointed to Lance's phone before hurrying after his friend.

Jenny and Arthur were talking quietly with Reyna later that afternoon when Lance and Ricky entered the Throne Room. Both had showered and dried their hair, which hung loosely across their shoulders and down their backs. They wore tunics of similar colors and the standard brushed brown leather pants.

The adults and Reyna ceased their conversation when the boys entered, and the sudden cessation was not lost on Lance. Perhaps due to what he'd seen on the Internet, or perhaps because he was becoming more paranoid by the day, Lance decided they had been talking about him behind his back and bristled with indignation.

Ricky must've sensed the coiling of Lance's body because he eased closer and eyed his friend questioningly. Lance eyed him back, annoyed, at first, but then Ricky's soft, caring look melted his anger.

Instead, he merely asked Arthur if there was anything he needed done before the gathering tomorrow.

Arthur glanced at Jenny and Reyna, but they both shrugged.

"No, son," Arthur answered noncommittally. "So how did your new bodyguard perform in combat?"

The question disarmed the remainder of his irritation and he grinned. "He's acceptable."

Ricky threw a mock scowl Lance's way. "I kicked his ass, Arthur, more than a few times."

Reyna laughed at that and Arthur's eyebrows shot up.

Lance gave Ricky a playful shove. "That's not true, Dad. He only got me once."

"Twice," Ricky insisted, shoving Lance right back. "And wait till I teach you wrestling. Man, you'll be on your back 24/7." He laughed.

"In your dreams, fool," Lance retorted. "I'm still stronger than you."

"Says who?"

The adults and Reyna laughed.

Lance heard some indistinct chanting from outside, and froze, the smile gone, the banter lost from thought. "Can't we do anything about those people outside, Dad?"

"Alas, son, according to Chief Murphy they have a right to gather on public sidewalks so long as they do not impede the progress of others. We can only keep them off this property. I'm sorry."

Lance cursed under his breath, causing Jenny to frown. Recalling all the websites he'd seen earlier, Lance looked at the adults with rising anger.

"What's wrong with these people anyway?" he asked in an exasperated tone. "Do I have to die for real before they know I'm not God?"

Reyna gasped.

"Do not even think such a thing, Lance," Arthur commanded, his voice firm and strong. "I almost lost you once. I shall not lose you again."

Ricky tossed off a disarming grin. "Besides, whose ass would I kick if you weren't around?"

Lance couldn't help but smile. "In your dreams, little man."

Ricky gave Lance another shove.

"You guys are too much alike, and you look *so* cute together," Reyna said, hands to her hips, eyes twinkling with amusement.

Lance went red in the face, and Ricky also turned crimson.

Reyna laughed delightedly. "Oh great. They even blush at the same time."

Lance threw her a look. "Careful, Lady Reyna, before I assign you KP duty."

Reyna tossed off that mocking laugh. "In *your* dreams, little man."

Arthur suggested Lance and Ricky work on the memorial for Jack and Mark. The mention of his friends instantly darkened Lance's mood, but he nodded and the boys left the Throne Room.

Reyna closed both double doors and turned back to Arthur and Jenny.

"They're so alike," Reyna said with amazement. "It's almost creepy, like two stars in perfect alignment. Maybe Ricky can help Lance get over losing Jack."

"Let us hope," Arthur agreed. "So, everything is arranged, then, Lady Reyna, for tomorrow?"

"I'll bring my speakers and we'll have music."

Jenny laughed hollowly. "Oh joy."

"Hey, I have some good music too," Reyna retorted with mock offense.

Jenny and Arthur merely smiled.

Reyna grinned as if to say, "You'll see."

Lance and Ricky talked with the lady who ran the Kabbalogy Institute about where they might find a display cabinet in the hotel. They explained their goal of putting Jack and Mark's swords and shields on display in the lobby so anyone entering would be able to see them straight away.

Director Killian led them down into the bowels of the hotel, to an enormous underground storage area, and they looked around at discarded furniture that had been stored there, some of it for decades. After searching in the dusty, cobwebby semi-darkness for thirty minutes, Ricky spotted something and called Lance over.

"How 'bout this?"

Lance stepped up beside him and gazed at a glass-enclosed ornately carved wooden display case with three shelves. The case looked to be seven or eight feet tall. Lance visualized it without the shelves, which he noted were removable. The swords and shields could be affixed to the back of the case with plaques beside them detailing the heroics of his friends.

"This'll work." Lance turned to the director. "Can we get this moved up to the lobby?"

She eyed him, as she always did, with uncertainty. Lance also noted that she kept her distance.

Would I be scared of me, too, he wondered, *if I was her?*

"Of course, Sir Lance. I'll have it cleaned and brought up at once."

Lance glanced at Ricky when the woman turned to lead them back to the elevator. Ricky shrugged and made a sour face behind her back, and they giggled like little kids.

As they awaited the delivery of the display case to the lobby, they returned to Lance's room to decide what to say about the two fallen knights. Having not known Mark at all, and barely knowing Jack, Ricky deferred to Lance for this task, saying he would look over whatever Lance wrote and give his opinion. So Ricky lay on Lance's king-sized bed while Lance sat at the ornate roll-top desk, pen in hand, struggling to sum up the lives of his two best friends in a few sentences.

There was so much he could say! But these needed to be short, almost like what you'd write on a gravestone. That reminded him of his need to tell Arthur what should be engraved on Mark and Jack's headstones, so the king could order them.

Maybe it should be the same — what's in the display case should also be on the gravestones.

Lance thought and thought, but even by bedtime he had not come up with the perfect words.

The next morning Lance awoke with a start. He'd been dreaming about Mark. And Jack. Once again they'd been heading up into the light without him.

And then, suddenly, it came to him! He knew exactly what to write for his fallen friends, and leaped from the bed to grab his pen.

He and Ricky ate a hurried breakfast and set about preparing the memorial before the other knights' arrival. As they worked, nailing hooks into the back of the cabinet, Ricky eyed Lance uncertainly as Lance lovingly cradled Jack's sword.

"Hey, Lance, can I ask you something?"

Lance looked up, his features riddled with sadness.

"Do you think you *were* in love with Jack?"

Lance glanced quickly around to see if anyone heard.

"It's okay," Ricky assured him quietly. "We're alone."

Lance gazed at his friend uncertainly. "I don't know. I don't know what love feels like."

Ricky nodded. That answer seemed to satisfy him. There was a moment of silence between them. Then he asked softly, "Do you think you might be gay?"

Lance trembled, and clutched the sword even more closely to his body. "I don't wanna be. It scares me." He paused a moment. "Do you think you might be?"

Ricky considered a moment. "I don' know, either. I never did nothing with girls, like I told you. Not even a kiss."

Lance thought a moment, considering everything Mark and Jack had told him about their lives. "Mark and Jack said they tried to be straight, but girls just didn't do it for them."

He paused again, and Ricky leaned in, hanging on every word.

"But you an' me, we got no experience with girls, so how do we know, right?"

Lance looked hopefully at Ricky, and the other boy nodded. "Adults keep saying it's a choice, right?" he went on excitedly. "That even though we fall for boys, if we really want to, we can make ourselves fall in love with girls, right?" Ricky nodded. He'd obviously heard the same things.

Lance leaned in conspiratorially. "So let's make it a goal to find girlfriends, Ricky, okay? To make ourselves fall in love with a girl. Whadda ya say?"

He knew his voice sounded desperate, and he *felt* desperate too.

Ricky smiled shyly. "Sounds like a plan."

They went back to work on the shrine.

The knights trickled into New Camelot throughout the day for the big gathering. On display, just inside the entryway, so it could not be missed, was the presentation case housing two swords and two shields. On paper, in rather fancy lettering – turned out that Ricky had another hidden talent he'd now put to use – were the names and dedications. Every knight who entered that day paused in reverent silence at the weapons, and Lance's written tributes to each boy.

Beside Mark's weapons Lance had posted: "In Loving Tribute to Sir Mark the Gentle, Knight of the Table Round. He was strong and decent, even when he didn't have to be."

Beside Jack's he had affixed a sign that read: "In Loving Tribute to Sir Jack the Self-Less, Knight of the Table Round. He gave his all, and when that wasn't enough, he gave his life."

The Throne Room could accommodate nearly one thousand people at a time, and most of Arthur's current Round Table members came to the mansion that day, some seeing it for the first time because of school and other commitments. They had to pass through the Lance Cultists waving signs or kneeling in prayer. Some of the signs begged Lance for a miracle — like a cure for some disease. Others proclaimed that 'The savior of the world resides within and we await his every appearance and his every word'.

In his room that morning, Lance looked desperately around for something to give Ricky. Because of the cultists outside and the constant media presence, Lance felt like a prisoner in New Camelot. Next week would mark his first official interview since coming back, but even that had to be done within the hotel.

"For security reasons," Arthur was told by Ryan and Gibson. The public was just too volatile and overwhelmed by Lance's resurrection to be trusted.

Thus, Lance was unable to shop for Ricky, and would have had a hard time anyway since the two were so joined at the hip these days that he wouldn't have been able to shop in private. So he searched through his meager belongings, and finally settled on another gold circlet Arthur had given him. This one was actually the one he was seen wearing in the enormous downtown mural. Without anything to wrap it in, he slipped it into a small leather pouch he'd also gotten from Arthur and tied the thin leather thong around it.

Around three that afternoon, Chris came to Lance's room, where he found Lance and Ricky hanging out on Lance's bed shooting the breeze.

"Arthur wants to see you guys before the gathering," Chris announced with obvious excitement.

He extended a hand to both of them and the older boys each took one. With Chris in the center, they made their way down the stairs from their second floor rooms, passed through the lobby, down a short hallway, and stopped at the closed double doors to the Throne Room.

The older boys exchanged a confused look at the closed doors. Chris opened them and darkness spilled into the lobby.

Lance and Ricky looked surprised.

"Did the gathering get cancelled or something?" Ricky asked uncertainly.

Lance shrugged. "Dad didn't say anything to me if it did."

Suddenly the glittering chandeliers sprang to life and hundreds of voices shouted, "Happy Birthday!"

The boys were visibly taken aback as they stood in the open doorway and gazed in at what looked like the entire membership of the Round Table.

Lance's eyes caught sight of an enormous banner strung up across the wall above the throne: "Happy 15th Birthday Lance and Ricky."

He flushed with embarrassed consternation, and turned to the equally embarrassed Ricky.

Simultaneously they said, "You told!"

Reyna, standing by the door to lead them in, laughed.

Then the boys blurted to one another in perfect synchronicity, "I'm gonna kick your ass for that!"

"Oh no, they're already thinking at the same time, too," Reyna chuckled.

The boys shared a laugh over their synergy before Reyna led them up to the front of the room where Arthur and Jenny stood before the seats of honor. There was an enormous cake and piles of presents on some long tables off to the side. The entire room erupted into applause and hooting and whooping and foot stomping as the boys passed up the center aisle toward the front, causing both Lance and Ricky to turn even more red.

As Reyna led them through the throng, the boys got slaps on the back and punches to the shoulder from the excited, whooping knights, all of whom were dressed in their usual tunics and pants.

Lance had chosen a scarlet tunic, in honor of Jack, and Ricky wore sky blue to honor Mark. Chris trailed behind as Reyna marched the birthday boys forward.

Arthur grinned as Reyna pushed them up onto the platform where the king and Jenny awaited. Jenny looked very much the queen in a long, almost sparkly white

MICHAEL J. BOWLER

gown that Reyna had helped her pick out. Arthur wore his most formal tunic and,
now cleansed of Lance's blood, the scarlet cloak he'd worn that fateful night. He even
wore his small crown, and Excalibur rested lazily against his side in its scabbard.

Lance was shell-shocked, and Ricky looked self-conscious.

Jenny leaned in to kiss Ricky on one cheek and then repeated the gesture with
Lance, beaming with joy and wishing each a happy birthday.

Lance then eyed Arthur uncertainly until the king reached out to pull him into
a hug. Releasing Lance and offering a smile filled with love, Arthur then embraced
Ricky, wishing both boys the happiest of birthdays.

Lance turned to look out at the throng. As the clapping and whooping continued,
he turned to Ricky, who looked mortified, and understood at once that Ricky, being
brand new to the crusade, didn't believe he should be part of this celebration at all.

He wanted to assure Ricky that he *was* part of the Round Table and more than
deserving, but his tongue stuck in his mouth. Emotions swelled within him as all his
previous birthdays flooded in at once, and he choked back the tears he feared would
come, especially as his gaze rested on the cake and the presents.

"Speech! From both!" Reyna called out as soon as the applause died away, which
brought back even more whoops and catcalls and foot stomping.

Lance looked at Ricky, tears burning his eyes, emotions threatening to drown
him. "I can't," he whispered desperately.

Ricky saw how troubled Lance appeared and his face fell with dismay. But he
took the microphone from an eager Reyna, who looked resplendent in her designer
tunic and tight-fitting leather pants.

Ricky gazed out nervously at all these kids he didn't even know, and who didn't
know him. "Uh, this uh, this party was supposed to be for Lance, not for me. He has
a big mouth, besides being a pushover when we spar."

There was laughter from the crowd, but Lance barely smiled, his head still
lowered.

"I'm new around here and most of you don't even know me," Ricky went on, his
soft voice cracking with nervousness. "I sure know I haven't done anything to deserve
so much attention from you all, but it's really cool and I, like, I really thank you for
making me feel I belong. And thank you, Lance, for having such a big mouth, and
a bigger heart."

He shoved the mic at Lance, who stood staring down at his brown leather boots.

When Lance looked up, tears dribbled from eyes. He couldn't hold them back.
Damn! He hated crying in front of others, especially hard guys like Esteban and
Jaime. He took the mic, sniffling, fighting back his emotions, barely able to look at

the suddenly silent crowd. Everyone waited in uncertain silence. The only sound was Lance sniffing into the microphone.

"I'm sorry," he finally managed to get out, his chest hitching. "It's not that I'm not, you know, thankful for all this..."

Reyna moved to his side and wrapped an arm around his shoulders. "It's okay, baby boy. Jack would want you to celebrate your birthday."

Lance shook his head, and used the hand holding the mic to wipe tears from his cheek. "It's not even that. It's just that...I... I never celebrated my birthday before."

There were gasps of surprise from the crowd. Ricky's mouth fell open. Even Reyna looked flummoxed.

"You mean," she said, the words tripping over her tongue in astonishment, "no one ever, like, I mean, you never had a party before?"

"I never even had a cake. Nothing." Tears dripped down his cheeks and Reyna stood stunned, her mouth open in shock. Then she engulfed him in a crushing hug.

Arthur placed a hand to his shoulder, and so did Jenny, Ricky, and Chris. Lance could feel the love emanating from every hand on him, but the moment was just too much for him. He shed his tears gratefully into Reyna's soothing shoulder.

Esteban shouted, "Long live Lance!" The throng turned it into a chant. "Long live Lance! Long live Lance! Long live Lance!"

Lance pulled his face from Reyna's shoulder and looked out over the shouting, stomping, cheering, whooping kids, and smiled. He glanced at Ricky and mouthed, "Thank you."

Ricky winked.

Reyna let go of Lance and announced, "We have cake to eat and they have presents to open. But first, we gotta dance."

There were some cheers and some groans from the crowd.

"And that means everyone," Reyna went on, her eyes twinkling with delight. "Arthur and Lady Jenny too. And of course, our birthday boys." She threw an arm around Ricky and Lance and pulled them in.

"Hell, no, Reyna," Lance announced firmly, still wiping away tears. "I'm not dancing. No way."

"Me, either," affirmed Ricky, shaking his head defiantly. "I can't dance."

Reyna tossed off that musical laugh that seemed to win over a room. "Everybody can dance to this."

She put on "The Cha Cha Slide" and some of the kids reacted with pleasure. Most knew this song from school dances. It was popular because the lyrics were the actual dance steps, so even if someone couldn't dance, at least they'd know what to do.

So the nearly one thousand knights lined themselves up in rows while Reyna dragged Arthur and Jenny, and Chris pulled the very reluctant Lance and Ricky out into the middle of the dance floor. They formed their own row and others melted in to fill it out.

The music began. The deep-voiced singer called out the words, and the directions. The crowd slipped quickly into the groove. It was simple, at first.

"Slide to the left, slide to the right,

Take it back now y'all..."

Everyone complied, and the directions continued, the music funky, the steps progressively more complicated with stomps and crouching and hand swiping. Lance and Ricky laughed at each other trying to keep up with the directions, stumbling, throwing a good-natured punch when one or the other missed a step.

Reyna was excellent – she obviously knew this dance well. Of course, she had Esteban in tow and laughed with delight at his attempts to mockingly show off his moves for her, but clearly this was something he'd never danced to in his life and he looked silly. Alongside Lance and Ricky, Chris, the youngest child there, laughingly stumbled his way through the number.

Arthur and Jenny tried to follow the directions, but they mis-stepped often and laughed like teenagers at their first high school dance.

The song was lengthy, the steps and moves funkier as it went on, and the room filled with laughter as everyone had fun. After the solemnness of the past two weeks, the laughter felt cathartic to Lance. When the song finally came to an end, everyone clapped and laughed some more. Lance shoved Ricky playfully, and was shoved right back.

Slightly out of breath, Reyna returned to the podium and announced, "Cake for all. And while everyone is eating, it's present time!"

Lance and Ricky exchanged a grin and a shrug, each trying to usher the other forward to where Reyna stood by the cake holding out a large cake-cutting knife.

Pushing and shoving their way, with more claps to the back, the boys stepped up and stood before the enormous cake. Three-tiered, it looked almost like a chocolate wedding cake, except it was decorated with little knights and horses and said "Happy 15th L & R!"

Cell phone cameras flew out as Reyna nudged Lance and Ricky into place just to the side of the cake. Reyna handed Lance the cutter, and then put Ricky's hand on it too.

Lance blushed. "We're not getting married, Reyna!"

Everyone laughed.

Reyna grinned. "Just cut the cake. We're all hungry."

Lance, with Ricky's help, cut through the bottom tier, to the accompaniment of cheers from the crowd.

The boys eyed Reyna to see if she was happy. "Now cut each other the first piece," she commanded, and Lance knew better than to argue.

He scowled, but cut a slice and handed it to Ricky on a plate. Ricky cut another slice, set it on a plate, and handed it to Lance. Eyeing one another suspiciously, they took small bites. Then, simultaneously, each shoved his piece into the other's face, dissolving into laughter as they did. Pictures were snapped of the two boys with chocolate frosting all over their faces and clinging to strands of their long hair.

Reyna shook her head. "Boys!" she announced through the mic, and laughed. Then she pushed them aside to begin cutting the cake for everyone else. Jenny moved in to help her, as did twelve-year-old Sylvia, Reyna's archery protégé. Others stepped forward too, and began distributing the cake as knights lined up to get a slice.

Ricky and Lance looked at each other's cake-smooshed face, grinning like two five-year-olds.

Lance reached up with one finger to scoop a bit of frosting from Ricky's cheek and put it on his tongue.

"Hmm. Tastes like someone who needs an ass-whupping."

Ricky swiped some off Lance's face and put it into his mouth. "This tastes like someone who already *got* his ass whupped."

They cracked up and handed each other towels to wipe off the chocolate.

After the cake had been consumed, the boys were placed at the long table and handed presents by Reyna and Chris. They got something from almost everyone. Some gifts were simple, some quite expensive. Lavern gave Lance an arrow into which he'd carved: "Sir Lance. Born November 6th. Long may he live."

Esteban stepped forward, gave Lance the little chin raise, and handed him a soft wrapped package. Lance ripped off the paper and gazed at an old, previously worn tank top undershirt. He looked up at Esteban quizzically.

"That's the shirt I wore when you kicked my ass, Lance," Esteban announced, loud enough for everyone to hear.

Lance's mouth dropped open.

Esteban appeared a bit embarrassed, especially with Reyna eyeing him expectantly. "You made me humble, Lance, and I been a better man 'cause 'a you. Happy birthday, *carnal*."

Speechless, Lance returned the look of respect he saw on Esteban's solemn face.

Ricky didn't get as many gifts because he was new and no one really knew him. But Reyna had made sure he got a lot of stuff. In fact, she offered her gifts to the boys last, handing each an identical sized package, wrapped in sports-themed wrapping paper.

Lance eyed her suspiciously. "It's not a bomb, is it?"

Laughing, she punched him on the shoulder. "Open them, funny man. At the same time." Up came her phone to grab a picture of their reactions.

Lance and Ricky watched each other unwrap the package, as though wanting to see the other's reaction more than his own. The paper came off, and both boys stared in open-mouthed amazement.

Reyna had given each of them a brand new iPad. Both stared in muted shock.

Reyna bounced up and down with excitement, clicking pictures and laughing gleefully.

"Oh, wow," Lance said finally, blowing out his breath in amazement. "I never got nothing like this in my life."

Ricky shook his head, cradling the box in his fingers. "Me, either."

Both boys looked up at her and said, "Thank you, Reyna," and gaped at one another for their simultaneous utterance, and then laughed.

Reyna engulfed them in a group hug. "What else is money for if you don't spend it on people you love, huh?"

Ricky, especially, was stunned. "You barely met me and you give me something like this." His face was locked into a state of shock.

Reyna grinned all the more broadly, lighting up her beautiful face. "If my baby boy loves you, then so do I."

That made both boys turn red again.

Finally, it was Arthur's turn to present his gifts. The king stepped up onto the platform in front of his throne and took the microphone from Jenny. He gazed out at his knights, at this vast army he'd assembled over the past eight months, at these young people who had come from so far from so little.

"Thursday was a day of deep mourning for us all, and yet a day of celebration, as well. For on that day, fifteen years in the past, my son came into this world, and the world has not been given a greater gift since. Nor have I. My love for this boy knows no bounds, nor my pride in him."

Lance reddened with embarrassment as Arthur spoke.

"And now I have been gifted with another son, Ricky," Arthur went on, smiling at Ricky as he spoke.

Ricky looked up at the king, startled.

"I have only known him a short time, and yet his devotion to me and, more importantly, to my beloved Lance, has endeared him to my heart and solidified his place amongst us as invaluable. So Ricky, to you I shall present my gift first. Kneel before me, squire."

Ricky climbed up the three small steps to the platform and stood before Arthur. The king motioned him to his knees, and Ricky complied.

Jenny stepped forward to hand Arthur a sword—the very sword Ricky had been using to spar with Lance all week—and placed it point down into a groove carved in the platform for that purpose. Ricky gazed at the sword, eyes wide with wonder, and then looked up at Arthur.

"Speak the oath, squire."

It took Ricky a moment to compose himself as the reality of what was happening slowly hit him. Then he recited the oath exactly as Lance had taught him. When he finished, Arthur raised Excalibur and gently touched it to each of Ricky's shoulders.

"I hereby dub thee Sir Ricky, Knight of the Table Round. May you for now and always guard Sir Lance and keep him from harm."

Ricky beamed with delight, his eyes welling with unexpected tears. He kissed the hilt of his sword before taking it in his hands and standing to face the crowd.

"I present Sir Ricky," Arthur boomed, and the crowd went wild with applause.

Ricky gazed out at the cheering knights, his sword held aloft, and looking happier than Lance had ever seen him.

Ricky looked over at him. The boys grinned, and then Arthur turned to Lance.

"My son, kneel before me."

Ricky stepped to one side, next to Jenny, who pulled him into a hug with a whispered, "Welcome."

Confused, Lance climbed the steps and, eyes never leaving those of his father, knelt before the king.

"As you are my son, Sir Lance, and liege lord in my stead," Arthur said as he removed the crown from his head and held it over the startled Lance's, "I hereby dub thee *Prince* Lance, my son and successor, who shall rule as king when my time is done." He placed the crown on Lance's head.

Lance held his breath, his heart thumping with wild abandon. He looked up at Arthur, who grinned down at him. Then with a wave of his hand, the king bade Lance to stand, which he did, on shaky legs.

Arthur called out to the crowd, "I present my son and heir, the Prince."

Lance saw Ricky grinning from ear to ear, and Reyna trying hard not to cry. The room exploded in applause. Reyna took the microphone from Arthur and when the crowd quieted spoke enthusiastically into it, "Now the birthday prince *has* to make a speech."

She shoved the mic at Lance, who felt like he'd been run over by a truck. Ricky moved to his side, still grinning, and bowed respectfully. Lance took the mic from Reyna and fought to gain control over his voice.

"I don't know what to say except... thank you. Thank you, everyone, for making this the best birthday I ever had. And Dad, I'll work hard to be the best son and the best prince and the best knight in the world."

Arthur smiled.

Lance gazed out at his fellow knights, his eyes afire with passion. "All of us here have a great task ahead. We know how amazing we all are, how important us kids are. We already showed them out there by what we done in our hoods. But we still have a long way to go, and it won't be easy. I'll do my best to be like my dad, our king, and lead the way in my words and deeds."

Seeing Lance choke up, Ricky leaned in to the microphone. "And if he doesn't, as his protector, I can kick his butt for you."

Laughter filled the room.

Lance chuckled, grateful for the save. "In your dreams, Sir Ricky." Both boys laughed, Lance handed the mic back to Reyna and she signaled the D.J., Sir Khom, to resume the music.

Lance stepped up to Arthur and threw his arms around him. Arthur hugged him back. No words were needed.

Then Lance, Ricky in tow, drifted over to the table filled with their now-open presents, and Lance suddenly remembered. "Oh wait, I almost forgot. I have something for you, fool."

Arthur heard that and cleared his throat, eyeing Lance with mock annoyance "Sorry, Dad, but he brings out the worst in me." Arthur grinned.

Lance reached beneath his tunic and pulled out the pouch. "Happy birthday, *Sir* Ricky."

Ricky looked uncertain, as though a snake might pop out. He opened the pouch and reached within. As he pulled out the shiny gold circlet, he gasped in surprise. Drawing it all the way out, he held it up to see it glimmer beneath the chandelier light.

"Oh Lance, I can't take this, man. This is like, your signature or something. It's the one in the..."

"Mural, I know," Lance said. "That's why I want you to have it. You're my protector. You're *my* First Knight."

Before Ricky could protest, Lance grabbed the circlet, removed the one Ricky was wearing, and placed the new one properly and securely around his head, restraining his cake-sticky hair.

Ricky looked unable to speak. Then he seemed to remember something. "Wait, I have something for you too." He slipped a small package, wrapped in newspaper, from his pocket and held it out to Lance. "It's not near as cool as what you gave me, but it's my favorite and I want you to have it."

Lance tore off the paper and glanced down in stunned surprise at a well-worn paperback book. "The Neverending Story?"

"Before you get mad, lemme explain. When I... when my parents took off for Mexico and left me behind, that book was all I had to keep me company on the streets. I was lost and had no hope out there, but then you came along and saved me. You were my Ivory Tower. I may be able to kick your butt in wrestling, but you saved me, Lance, and that's why I want you to have it."

Lance didn't know what to say, having not known Ricky thought of him so exaltedly.

"Thank you." He stepped close and they bumped fists. Then they gave each other the man-hug, which quickly turned into a tussle as the boys began trying to take each other down. Arthur and Reyna separated them, laughing with delight.

The party continued with more music and food and soft drinks and laughter. At no time did Ricky relinquish his sword or circlet, nor did Lance remove his crown or let go of *The Neverending Story*. For both boys, it was clearly the best birthday they'd ever had.

Agreeing to meet every Saturday afternoon as a full company to discuss and plan out their future moves, the knights departed as the party broke up. Jenny left for home, as did Reyna.

Lance cornered Sir Techie as the party wound down to ask about his phone.

Techie looked dismayed. "Sorry, Lance, I couldn't trace the number. Whoever the guy is, he doesn't wanna be traced."

Lance and Ricky frowned with concern as Techie explained that the call had been routed halfway around the world. He handed the phone back.

"I changed the number on it and texted everyone who's anyone in the Table your new one. That should take care of it."

Lance thanked him and went upstairs with Ricky. They paused at Lance's door, gazing at one another a long moment.

Both blurted, "Thanks," at the exact same time, and then cracked up.

"Man, that's a habit we gotta break," Ricky said, and Lance nodded. He gazed long and hard at Ricky.

"Jack was right about you."

"What did he say about me?"

"That you'd be a good friend."

They grinned and said goodnight, entering their respective rooms.

Lance stripped off his tunic and glanced at his reflection in the mirror. His chest and shoulders had filled out since the last time he'd looked. When was that? He couldn't even remember.

I'm fifteen, and I finally had my first birthday party! If only you could be here, Jacky, then it would've been perfect.

The phone in his pocket buzzed with a text. Lance frowned and pulled it out. Nine zeros faced him. A chill ran up his back, and he opened the message. 'Think you can ditch me that easily, Lance? No way. Your Jacky will always find you.'

Angry, Lance thumbed in: 'Who are r u?'

These words quickly materialized: 'You planning to cheat on old Jacky with your new bodyguard? That would so hurt my feelings. I want you all for myself. LOL 'Night, 'night, sweet prince.'

The phone went dark, and silent. Nothing more popped up. Frightened, Lance considered who could be behind such a cruel prank, and how did the person already know he was a prince?

He slipped out of his long leather pants, tossed them onto the floor of the closet, and pulled on some running shorts. Then he picked up *The Neverending Story* and crawled beneath the covers. He'd just begun to read when the door cracked open and Chris's head appeared.

"I'm scared, Lance. My room is so big and I feel all alone in there. Can I sleep with you?"

Lance smiled. His king-sized bed looked big enough for five or six. "You know it, little man. Just like old times."

Happiness washed over him as the small boy in the overly large nightshirt crawled under the covers beside him, just as it had always been. Chris no longer feared him, which was the best present Lance could have ever received.

Chris pointed to the book. "Will you read to me, Lance?"

Lance did.

CHAPTER FIVE
NOBODY'S TAKING ME AWAY FROM YOU

THE WEEK FOLLOWING THE BIG party marked Lance's first live interview, to be conducted within the Throne Room at New Camelot, and would feature Lance—and briefly, Merlin—one on one with Helen. The plan was to offer a live feed to every network and Internet site that wished to carry it, and do a sort-of call-in format because both the president and the Pope wished to talk with Lance and the people of the world simultaneously. That thought made Lance extremely nervous, and he spent his afternoons sparring with Ricky or having Ricky teach him wrestling moves to help quell his anxiety.

Just as Ricky had picked up swordplay quickly, Lance adapted rapidly to the sport of wrestling. At first, Ricky won every match, which only made Lance work harder. On Wednesday of that following week, Lance finally pinned Ricky by the shoulders, and whooped with triumph.

School also began that week. Two retired teachers volunteered their time, and three classrooms opened for business on that Monday morning. School ran from eight to noon, Monday through Friday, and knights flocked in from all over the city to attend. Most were ex-gang members who'd never had much use for school anyway. Jenny was pleased that they were now ready and willing to earn their high school diplomas within the less conventional setting New Camelot provided. Their afternoons continued to be spent organizing kids in their neighborhoods to work together on whatever improvements they deemed necessary.

Thursday finally rolled around, and a nervous Lance paced the lobby with Ricky at his side, awaiting the arrival of Helen and her film crew. When she did show up, Lance gaped at the lights and multiple cameras and cords and other equipment her crew hauled through the front lobby into the Throne Room. Arthur and Jenny chatted with Helen calmly as everything was set up, while Ricky kept trying to muss Lance's hair or wrinkle his shirt, and the boys laughingly shoved each other around.

Lance was dressed in a green tunic that Reyna insisted brought out his "beautiful eyes," his best leather pants and boots. His luxuriously thick hair was brushed and draped his shoulders and back, another of his gold circlets wound round his head to keep it off his face. Ricky thought Lance should wear the crown Arthur had given him, but Lance didn't want to seem like he was showing off or trying to be "all that."

Finally, Helen walked out of the hallway into the lobby where the boys were horsing around. She was dressed in a simple pale blue dress, and her make-up was more muted than usual. She cleared her throat.

Startled, the boys stopped tussling and looked her way, surprised and embarrassed to have an attractive woman see them acting like little kids.

Lance threw his hands to his shirt to smooth it out and then pulled the hair away from his face.

"Sorry, Lady Helen," he apologized. "We didn't hear you."

She grinned. "Not a problem. You guys look good together."

That made Lance burn with embarrassment, and Helen laughed. "We need you for a sound check, Lance," she said, and ushered him down the hall to the Throne Room.

Eyeing Ricky once more, Lance punched him the moment Helen's back was turned and then scurried away before Ricky could retaliate.

Arthur, Jenny, Ricky, Chris, Reyna, Esteban, Darnell and Justin sat in back of the Throne Room and watched the interview unfold live before them. It was broadcast on the large overhead flat screen, albeit with the volume muted, but the group could easily hear each question, and Lance's responses.

Helen introduced her guests, "Though they need no introduction," and then began with Merlin. She asked him how he was able to bring Lance back from the dead.

The older man shrugged and tried not to look uncomfortable. "My God-given power to manipulate nature, Lady Helen, has always been part and parcel of who I am. In Arthur's day I was called a 'wizard' and my powers 'magic'. In this era, I might be better termed a conduit, of sorts."

Helen's brows furrowed with confusion. "How do you mean?"

"Rather like the conduction of electricity, I can conduct the forces of nature and, to some extent, control them, even route them through my own body. Thus Sir Jack was able to use me to send his life force into Sir Lance. Some might call it deviltry or black magic, but I can assure you it is neither."

Helen tried for a conspiratorial smile. "Can you do any magic for us now?"

Merlin glowered. "I have just told you, madam, that it is not magic, and no I cannot do anything for some time, decades, most likely. Restoring Sir Lance has drained me, much like one of your rechargeable batteries. I can do nothing more."

Helen looked annoyed at having been chastised, but put on her professional face for the cameras and thanked the wizard. Then she turned her full attention to Lance.

She asked him to describe his experience of being "dead" and of coming back into the world.

Lance detailed his memories after saying goodbye to Arthur and drifting into unconsciousness.

"What do you think it all means?"

"I don't know," Lance answered honestly. "I believe Mark and Jack went on to heaven 'cause, what else could that light mean? It looked so amazing I wanted to go too. But, I guess God has other plans for me, so I need to do my best to make Jack's sacrifice count for something."

He also reiterated some of what he'd already said at the funerals, that he was neither messiah nor devil, but just a kid who'd been given an extraordinary second chance.

He exuded natural humility and charm, and Helen always managed to relax him, so it wasn't long before Lance settled comfortably into his chair and fielded her questions with ease.

When it came time for the president to join them live from The White House, that's when Lance started to sweat. He had no idea how anyone other than the Internet crowd felt about him and, after having dealt with Mayor Villagrana and his opposition to the crusade, he worried what the president might have to say.

Fortunately for him, or maybe due to the live worldwide feed, the president was very cordial and seemingly excited to be talking with him.

"You are, Sir Lance," he said with a serious expression, "for obvious reasons, the most famous person on earth, and I, for one, am pleased you're too young to run against whoever I support in the next election."

He smiled to assure everyone he was joking, but Lance's inner sense about people gave him the impression the man was not. But he laughed politely. "Yes, sir."

"As President, I'm proud to have Americans like you, Sir Lance, who put the needs of your community ahead of yourself. The First Lady and our kids would love to have you here to the White House for dinner. We could discuss your crusade and your future plans."

Him, in the White House? The idea almost made him laugh. "Thanks, Mr. President. That'd be cool."

After the President signed off, a live feed came in from the Vatican, and the Pope appeared on screen. He was an older Latino man wearing a white skullcap and white vestments.

The Pope spoke to Lance in Spanish, and someone on the network translated everything into English. Lance answered the Pope's questions, which were mainly about how he'd felt as he was about to cross over into the light, did he recall more details, and how he felt upon awaking.

Then the Pope spoke to the world with these words, "It is my firm belief, from all I have seen and heard, that the return of young Lance is a clear act of God, for reasons that remain known only to Him. Young Lance is a mystery, like so many others the faithful must struggle to comprehend. But he is not Jesus returned to earth. The Scriptures are clear that Jesus will not return as a boy. Likewise, Lance's return is not the handiwork of Satan. This boy has proven himself to be good and pure through his previous actions, and I ask all believers to accept him only for what he is – a gift from our Heavenly Father."

Lance felt great relief on hearing the Pope's words and, though he wasn't Catholic, he hoped the faithful all over the world would listen to this holy man and stop worshipping him. He thanked the pontiff in Spanish, and the Pope gave him a blessing before signing off.

The rest of the interview went well, and when the hour came to a close, Helen bade him goodnight and signed off.

Lance felt drained and nearly collapsed when the camera lights flicked off. Helen beamed at him from her chair and thanked him as Arthur and the others approached to congratulate both of them.

After that, life settled into a routine at New Camelot. Ryan and Gibson dropped by a few times to let Arthur know that the shooter had not been apprehended and, even though preliminary investigation suggested a hired assassin, they didn't want the king or Lance leaving New Camelot without police escort. Chief Murphy agreed with them and assigned both detectives to permanent duty as protectors of father and son. At this point, the men were on call anytime Arthur or Lance needed to go anywhere.

Lance complained about being a prisoner in his own house, but the detectives couldn't offer any alternative. With the gunman at large, and the two dead men in the limo under investigation, there might be more accomplices out there, as yet undetected. In addition, despite Lance's interview and the Pope's assurances that Lance was neither savior nor devil, people remained divided regarding his resurrection.

The week after the interview with Helen was Thanksgiving, and Arthur spent the day with his in-house knights, as well as others who chose to share the dinner with them. Lance and Ricky, as well as Chris and Lavern, basked in the glow of a real Thanksgiving feast with a real family.

Prior to eating, Arthur went around the table and asked each attendee to give thanks for something in their lives. Most gave thanks for Arthur, some for having a real roof over their heads, others for having a family.

Lance and Ricky both thanked God for the gift of each other, true friendship they hoped would last their entire lives. Merlin thanked God for heavy metal music and the opportunity to be of service in bringing Lance back into the world. Arthur gave thanks for the miraculous return of his son, whom he vowed never to take for granted again. He also thanked God for all of the amazing children he'd been blessed with, and for the gift of Jenny in his life, causing her to look slightly embarrassed.

Prior to Lance being shot, Arthur and his knights had taken down one hundred crack houses and/or meth labs in neighborhoods throughout Los Angeles. At Chief Murphy's insistence, Arthur agreed to allow the police to handle such matters from that night forward. His leadership team, from various neighborhoods throughout Los Angeles County, all agreed to use their influence over kids to try and locate every drug house, but not do anything more than report those locations anonymously to Sergeant Ryan. He was the only cop they trusted.

Murphy had set up a private, untraceable hotline for anonymous tips to be called in to Ryan for investigation. The knights had spent too much time and effort cleaning up their neighborhoods to allow criminals to take them over again. With the kids leading the way, the adults were happy to help keep the areas where they lived as clean and crime-free as possible. But everyone knew it would be an ongoing, daily battle requiring constant vigilance.

December brought with it a slew of TV chat shows for Lance and Arthur, always accompanied by Ricky, but Ricky never joined them in the interview chairs. Ryan and Gibson personally drove them to each and every venue, and only shows located within the Southern California area were considered at this time. Thus they appeared on Ellen and The Tonight Show. Other shows that wanted Lance, or anyone else from New Camelot, had to do a live feed from the hotel.

All of these hosts were cordial and excited to have Lance, in particular, on the air with them. Some, like Ellen, joked around by poking him a few times and proclaiming, "Nope, not a ghost" to uproarious laughter from her studio audience.

All asked him about his experience of dying, about his kidnapping, about Jack and his ultimate sacrifice. It never got easier to talk about Jack, Lance noted during those weeks. Every time Jack's name was mentioned, Lance choked up and almost couldn't respond. But he inevitably did, praising Jack with every compliment he could muster. It was Arthur's hope that by doing these kinds of shows, the public would be assured that Lance was indeed a normal boy and not one who could "walk on water," as one website had proclaimed him capable of doing.

December also brought some big news from Jaime, who'd been absent a lot because he had gotten a job through Homeboy Industries and attended school at Homeboy in the mornings. He joined the Saturday gatherings as often as he could, but in the second week of December he called Arthur to announce that Sonia, his girlfriend, had given birth to a seven pound, eight ounce son whom they'd named Arturo, after Arthur.

The king was thrilled, and expressed his pride in Jaime for working hard, as a man should, to care for his lady and his child. Jaime vowed to bring the family to New Camelot soon so everyone could check out his son.

Of course, Reyna was exhilarated at the prospect of organizing a baby shower and set her party planner brain to work on the idea immediately.

Sir Techie, with help from Lance and Ricky, had the New Camelot website up and flourishing, along with a Facebook page, and Twitter accounts for Arthur, Lance, Ricky, Jenny, Reyna, Esteban, Darnell, and Justin. Of course, Lance had his own fan page for people to follow.

The New Camelot page received over a million "likes" in just a few days. Lance's fan page managed fifty million in the same time period. "Sir Lance" fan clubs had sprung up all over the Internet, along with the cults, and it became clear that the superstar status of *The Boy Who Came Back* was here to stay.

Kids throughout California, and the whole world, were fascinated with the Round Table and wanted to learn more about it and how they could join. To that end, Arthur recorded "Chivalry Thoughts of the Day" videos that were posted daily on the website, short little lessons on how the Code of Chivalry applied to the world today.

Also, Arthur, Jenny, Lance, Ricky, Reyna, Lavern and Esteban created study guides for the website so newbies could learn about chivalry and the "war against children" the country seemed to be waging. There was also an on-line test, created by Jenny, that potential knights could undertake to show their knowledge of Round Table policies, the code of chivalry, and the oath they must swear in order to be knighted.

At Lance's suggestion, Arthur performed his first virtual knighting ceremony just before Christmas, live on the Internet. Hundreds of children and teens, most in California, but some from other states and countries, logged in at the same time and, en masse, recited the oath. Then Arthur pointed Excalibur at the camera and officially proclaimed them all knights of the Table Round.

The event would be but the first of a series of such ceremonies, as the increasing numbers of followers demanded. In addition, Lance and the other knights, including Chris, recorded short little videos about the lack of rights children had—they focused on California because of their ultimate goal for the following year's election cycle— and gave examples like the failure of the current school system and the excessively punitive nature of trying children in adult court.

They contrasted this lack of trust in the value of children with what they, under Arthur, had accomplished in Los Angeles over a period of months – the rejuvenation of neighborhoods, the reduction in gang affiliations, and the ferreting out of drug labs throughout the city. They encouraged kids statewide to get involved in their own communities and schools, to challenge the status quo that said anyone under the age of eighteen was worthless, to organize their own neighborhood rejuvenation programs, and to post their own videos or send in comments on what they had encountered and achieved.

The kids of California bought into this idea in a big way, and postings came in almost daily about this hurtful school policy or that anti-kid rule or this neighborhood cleanup. Some policies were as seemingly innocuous as certain gyms, notably YMCA's, which were geared toward the entire family unit, not allowing middle school kids, or even kids under sixteen, to use the weight room on the excuse that they were too young, even though these same kids played sports and worked out with weights at school. The real reason, it turned out, was these gyms promised potential adult members that there would be certain rooms where kids wouldn't be allowed so as to not "bother them."

There were anti-skateboarding ordinances and anti-loitering ordinances that applied only to kids. Apparently, adults could loiter, but not kids? The sheer number of these kinds of postings grew by the day. Lance and Ricky and Techie, the main three in charge of the Internet sites, often became overwhelmed by the volume and couldn't possibly read them all. Anything posted that was inappropriate, however, they took down, especially postings by the "Lance is the Anti-Christ" crowd, which did its best to make the crusade look like the work of Satan. "They're trying to take God-given rights away from parents" was a common refrain of such groups.

Still, in just over a month and a half, the crusade had vastly expanded, and the plan was to roll out in January the biggest component, the one that would likely consume all of their attention until the election next November.

Enrique and Luis, who with Lavern had spearheaded the amazing downtown mural of Lance, were noting how people had already starting selling shirts and posters with Lance's image on it. They felt that money should be coming into New Camelot, to support the crusade. They'd even worked on some preliminary designs for t-shirts, mocking and emulating a popular movie series at the same time.

In the Computer Lab one day, they proudly pulled up images they'd created of two shirts side by side. One had Lance's smiling face and the other Ricky's. One was emblazoned with the words, "Team Lance" and the other "Team Ricky."

Lance was mortified, and he saw Ricky was, too.

But everyone else laughed and thought it a great idea, especially when Enrique mentioned his marketing plan to have "Team Reyna," "Team Esteban," "Team Chris," and, of course, "Team Enrique" and "Team Luis" shirts, as well. They could make one for every knight, at least the most famous ones.

"We'll make a bundle!" Luis exclaimed as Lance looked on dubiously.

"Especially with your pretty-ass faces on the first two," Enrique said laughingly to Lance and Ricky.

The boys shook their heads in amazement, but Lance didn't say no. It was worth discussing with Jenny's uncle, Sam McMullen, who'd agreed to the job of attorney pro bono. Next time he dropped by, they'd bring up the idea of this side business.

During this period of transition, Lance received at least one text a week from the '00000000' untraceable phone number. All were the same – taunts, innuendo, comments about Jack. These messages creeped Lance out big time.

At first, he'd responded in order to get a clue who the sender might be. He even had Techie change his number again, but the mysterious stalker had the new one within days, despite Techie's attempt to keep it off the grid.

Then one day, Lance had a thought, one that terrified him. "Ricky," he said almost breathlessly. "I just realized…"

Ricky was lying on Lance's bed playing with his iPad, and sat up quickly. "What? Did you get another text from that scumbag?"

Lance shook his head. "I just thought about...what if it's him? You know, the boogeyman?"

Ricky's face turned thunderous. "You mean Dickwad?"

Lance nodded slowly, his heart already beginning to thump. "What if he's, like, watching us all the time?"

"How? We never go out."

"Yeah, but I just remembered he said something about you one time," Lance went on in a hushed whisper. "About you and...me, you know."

Ricky's face grew hot with anger. "Like I told you, Lance. He comes near you or me, I'll kill 'im!"

Lance saw Ricky was dead serious. He shook off his fear. Fear would undo him, if he let it, and they had too much to accomplish.

Ricky told Lance to simply delete each message as it came in and ignore the guy. So Lance did, and by Christmas the stalker seemed to have gotten the message that he would no longer rise to the bait, and the texts ceased. Still, in the back of Lance's mind always lurked the terrifying possibility that his personal boogeyman was still after him.

Ryan and Gibson kept Arthur and Lance apprised of any developments in the investigation into Mr. R. and Mr. L. Their real identities were now known and both men had been well respected within legitimate business circles. Much shock and outrage was expressed by private enterprise and government agencies regarding their secret double lives as a prominent drug cartel.

Because the overall extent of their operations had not yet been determined, and with the FBI heading up the investigation, Chief Murphy continued to insist on police presence for Arthur and Lance whenever they left New Camelot. It was his job, he maintained in a phone conversation with Arthur, to make certain the king and his kids remained safe.

The other huge fallout from that fateful night fell squarely on the shoulders of Mayor Villagrana. The cell phone of Mr. R. had been blown free of the limo wreckage and its memory remained intact. Thus, the authorities found the mayor's voicemail alerting Mr. R. to the fact Arthur had something planned for that evening. That significant find placed Villagrana front and center of a possible conspiracy to take down Arthur and destroy the Round Table. He was hit from all sides with calls to resign.

Head District Attorney Dooley, up for re-election the following year, went after the mayor with both barrels. Based upon the phone message, and evidence linking Villagrana to money laundering and drug trafficking, he charged the mayor with "conspiracy to commit murder," "conspiracy to traffic in illegal narcotics," "accepting illegal campaign contributions," and "money laundering."

When these charges were filed, the shell-shocked mayor was placed under arrest in front of City Hall and led away in handcuffs. After posting the million-dollar bail and vowing to fight the charges, Villagrana resigned from office and went into hiding to await trial.

The City Council stepped in and appointed one of the deputy mayors, Julian Soto, as interim mayor until new elections could be held the following year.

Jenny's uncle, and now Arthur's attorney, paid a special visit to New Camelot just before Christmas. A big, blustery Scotsman, Sam McMullen had always considered Jenny like a daughter to him and personally favored everything that Arthur had been doing to "shake up the system." Thus, when Jenny had asked for his help on the hotel deal, he'd eagerly agreed.

He and Jenny had been discussing the parentless kids Arthur had living with him, and what legal hurdles he might have to leap over in the future. They met in the library, which had become the almost exclusive purview of Merlin. The wizard preferred to remain out of the spotlight, for obvious reasons, and he loved reading the history of the world since he'd last walked upon it.

Arthur invited his old friend and mentor to remain with he and Jenny while Sam lowered himself into a soft easy chair, and popped open the briefcase on his lap.

"Once all the dust settles from Lance's death and rebirth, if it ever really does," the man boomed, his voice still tinged with a slight brogue, "especially with you fighting against the powers-that-be to gain real rights for kids in this state, it won't be long before the government will start moving against you any way it can."

Arthur and Jenny frowned, and even Merlin set down his book to listen more intently.

"They'll likely start with the underage children you have living here at New Camelot."

Arthur leaned forward. "How do you mean?"

"Any minor child living here must have written permission from their legal parent or guardian to do so."

Arthur nodded solemnly. "To the best of my knowledge, Samuel, only Lavern has a mother who may be found. Since my crusade began and the media prominently featured my knights, all but him have returned to their homes, with New Camelot used for training, schooling, or gatherings. Rarely do any have cause to stay overnight. Alas, Lance, Ricky and Christopher have no family save myself, and Jenny."

Sam explained that he must file paperwork with the courts for legal custody, and eventual adoption of these boys, to avoid having them taken away. "As for Lavern, the boy's mother must agree in writing to allow him to remain, or he'll be forcibly removed at some point."

Arthur's heart pounded with dread. To lose Lance and Chris? And Ricky? No. They were his sons and he would fight for them. "I shall cooperate in any way that I can."

Sam explained that he would start the process with the court. "There will have to be a due diligence to locate parents, but with all of the media attention you've already received, and with no parents having turned up to cash in, they likely won't be found. The U.S. won't search in Mexico for Ricky's family, so that's an easy one. This is what's called a pre-emptive strike, Arthur, getting all our ducks in a row before anyone sneaks up on us from behind."

Arthur texted Lance and requested that he and Ricky join him in the library. While waiting, Sam pulled out the necessary paperwork for Arthur to begin the adoption process.

Lance and Ricky, dressed in muscle shirts and workout shorts, appeared at the doorway. Arthur ushered them inside and asked them to sit.

Something about the way the adults looked at them disturbed Lance, and he exchanged a look with Ricky, who obviously felt the same bad vibe. Lance glanced at Merlin. The older man was wearing a Metallica shirt today, with the ever-present ear buds dangling out from under the collar of the shirt and down his front. He held a large hardbound book in his refined-looking hands and gazed at Lance soberly. As always, his face was unreadable.

Arthur explained as best he could what the attorney had told them. Lance's heart began pounding, and his face darkened as he listened. Ricky, too, looked suddenly small and afraid. When Arthur finished, the adults awaited a response.

"Nobody's taking me away from you," Lance insisted, his voice shaking with pent up fury. "You're my dad. I don't care about the law."

Arthur smiled. "And you, Sir Ricky? How do you feel about me adopting you?"

Lance exchanged a look with Ricky, the enormity of Arthur's words cutting through his anger. Brothers. They would be brothers for life, and Arthur would be their dad.

Ricky gazed wide-eyed at Arthur, seemingly overcome with emotion and looked for a moment like he might cry. "I think that would be the most amazing thing to ever happen to me," he whispered, and then cast Lance a little grin. "Besides kicking this guy's butt, I mean."

That earned a return grin from Lance.

"Good," Sam said. "At fifteen, you boys will have some say in the court, however limited it might be." His face clouded. "Chris, however, will not. How old is that boy?"

Suddenly Arthur and the boys exchanged a startled look, and Jenny drew a blank too.

"We don' know," Lance answered after a moment. "Hell, Dad, we don't even know his birthday." He saw Arthur frown at his language. "Sorry, but now I feel like a pig for not knowing."

"It is my job to know of these matters, Lance," Arthur reassured him, "and I shall find out. In fact, instruct Sir Techie to learn the date of birth for all of our knights and post them on a calendar so that we might have a monthly celebration to honor them."

Lance nodded.

Sam cleared his throat. "As I was saying, Chris might prove to be more of a problem, but again, if his parents haven't risen to cash in on his publicity by now, likely they're not out there to do it. We'll just have to see."

Lance turned his fiery gaze on Sam. "I'm not going back into that system, Mr. McMullen. This is my home and that man is my father." He pointed to Arthur. Then he threw an arm around Ricky. "And this is my brother." He glanced once at Arthur and Jenny, and then at Merlin. "If they try to take me away from my dad, I'll run. I will *never* go back to them. And you can tell whoever says different, and I apologize for this, Dad, to go screw themselves."

He turned amid a swirl of hair and strode from the room, slamming the door behind him. Ricky eyed Arthur apologetically before hurrying after Lance.

Arthur heard Merlin give a disgruntled "hummp" and turned to see him stuff the ear buds back into his ears and return to the open book in his lap.

Arthur fixed a long, hard look on Sam. "You heard my son, Samuel. Feel free to pass along his precise words to the powers that be."

Sam grinned. "With pleasure."

Christmas proved to be the best one Lance, Ricky, Chris, and Lavern could ever recall. There was a huge tree in the lobby that they had a blast decorating. There were presents and food and cider and lots of knights dropping in to visit and/or stay for dinner. As on Thanksgiving, the dining room was filled to capacity and everyone had a great time. The Centre Director and Arthur had agreed that come January, the hotel would once more open up to paying guests, and tours of New Camelot, which would mean audiences, of a sort, with Arthur and Lance in the Throne Room.

That Christmas, then, took on a special family significance with only the Knights of the Round Table in attendance. Jaime and Sonia arrived with little Arturo in tow, and everyone fawned over the adorable infant. Chris, in particular, loved to hold and rock the baby in his arms, and numerous pictures were snapped of the two children who looked so cute together.

Even Pastor Tom had dropped by that morning to conduct a service in the Throne Room, and he volunteered to do a service every Sunday at eight a.m. for whoever would like to attend.

For Lance and Ricky, who could never quite forget the possibility that the county might try to take them away from Arthur, the holiday was especially heartfelt and powerful because they felt the intense love of family surround them like a comforting blanket, and wanted nothing more for the new year than to have their family made permanent. It was a day filled with laughs, cheers, applause, fun, and love, one that none of the kids in attendance would ever forget.

New Years passed quietly, with Arthur and the boys watching the events in Times Square unfold on the big screen television. Jenny was there, too, and between them they tried to help the befuddled Arthur understand why people of this age made such a big deal about the New Year.

"I hate to say it, Dad," Lance offered, "but it's mostly just an excuse for people to party and get all wasted."

Ricky nodded, and Jenny explained to the uncomprehending Arthur what "wasted" meant.

"Alas, *that* behavior is no different from mine own era, I'm afraid."

Everyone laughed, but a thought ran through Lance's head for the rest of that night that he couldn't quite shake loose: would people ever change?

It was now the Saturday after New Years, and at their gathering that day the next phase of the crusade would be discussed. Lance and Ricky had worked with Reyna, Esteban, Justin, Lavern, and Chris to come up with ideas for the year, and everyone was anxious to move forward, especially with their big political campaign.

Lance woke that morning after a troubling dream, one in which he saw himself dragged away from New Camelot by the police as Ricky and Arthur stood in the open door helplessly watching. The dream actually woke him and he found his bare torso covered beneath a sheen of sweat. He shivered, reliving the dream images and feeling certain they related to Arthur's attempt at adopting him.

As a result, he was in a pensive mood during breakfast, and even Ricky couldn't joke him out of it. Afterwards, as Lance paced his room anxiously, Ricky tried to interest him in another "smack down on the wrestling mat." But Lance felt more restless than usual and wanted to get out. He almost never left the house anymore and hadn't been skating in months. Every time he did go out, it was with Arthur and Ryan. He needed some freedom.

"Let's go for a walk, Ricky," he blurted suddenly as he stopped pacing.

"A walk? Without Sergeant Ryan?"

"Yeah. I just need to get out for a few, you know?"

"We'll be swamped the minute we step out the door."

Lance paused. Both of them had received a lot of "regular" clothes for Christmas, and their birthdays, and there was a back gate at the far end of the gardens that led to a residential street behind New Camelot.

"We can disguise ourselves," Lance announced, as though the matter was settled, "and sneak out the back."

Ricky still looked uncertain. "What if we get recognized anyway?"

That brought a sly grin to Lance's face. "We run like hell."

Ricky laughed, and it was decided. Going through their drawers and closets, the boys selected jeans, rocker t-shirts, hoodie sweatshirts and beanies. They shoved all their hair up under the beanies and then flipped the hoodie up over that. Lance wore his skater shoes, and told Ricky to wear his.

Lance had made sure to get his soon-to-be brother good shoes and a new Flip skateboard for Christmas because he wanted to teach Ricky some cool skate moves. Of course, Ricky had gotten Lance a brand new Flip board, too, one designed by David Gonzalez, Lance's favorite skater. While Ricky was not as smooth on a board, he'd skated often enough as a youngster to be acceptable.

They snatched up their boards and peeked out the doorway into the hall. Lance figured if they could actually get away from the house for a while, they could do some skating in the neighborhoods behind the hotel. Since swords would've been a dead giveaway, the boys carried sheaths under their shirts housing dirks, just in case of trouble.

They snuck down the back stairs and out into the vastness of the hotel grounds and gardens, past the outdoor stage, and Lance was pretty sure no one had spotted them. Some of the cultists hung around in back, but since the media focused on their presence up front, and since being on television was a large part of their agenda, very few wandered too far behind the hotel. Thus, the boys surreptitiously slipped out the gate and then began walking casually along the sidewalk. Anyone who hadn't spotted them exiting the hotel grounds would simply see two skater boys ambling down the street, and wouldn't even take notice.

They talked a bit about the possibility of being taken away from Arthur, and Lance was adamant that would never happen.

"I'll die again before I go back in that system," he declared with quiet passion.

Ricky assured him he was too famous now for that to happen. "Hell, Lance, you ought 'a be able to get whatever you want now."

"Yeah, 'cept privacy."

Just as they passed beneath an enormous shade tree, a voice behind them caused both to whirl around.

"Well, well, well, if it isn't Jesus, Harry Potter and the Ivory Tower all rolled into one."

Lance reached under his hoodie for the knife as a very muscular boy stepped from behind the tree, but then paused when he recognized the speaker. It was the blond kid from Jack's funeral. Up close, Lance studied his hard, chiseled features and steely brown eyes that had a vaguely familiar look to them. But he couldn't recall anyone who'd ever had eyes so cold and empty and filled with scorn. Over six feet and body-builder wide, the boy would be handsome, Lance thought, if not for the mask of maliciousness dominating his face.

Ricky stepped protectively in front of Lance. "Whadda you want?"

"Just wanted to meet The Boy Who Came Back." His voice dripped with smarmy contempt. Even his bushy blond hair wafted dangerously in the cool morning breeze. Everything about this boy reeked threat.

"Yeah, well, we're busy," Ricky retorted.

"Worrying about the *law* taking you away from your beloved King Arthur?"

Ricky flashed anger. "That's none 'a your damn business!"

"Anything I want to know is my business."

Ricky took a dangerous step forward, gripping his skateboard with white-knuckled fury. "Get lost, scumbag!"

The boy laughed. "Or you'll do what, little girl?"

Lance stepped forward now. "It's okay, Ricky." He gazed long and hard at the boy's face. "You were at Jack's funeral. I saw you."

Those eyes... Lance felt drawn to them.

The boy tilted his head to one side, but didn't respond.

"Did you know Jack?"

The boy didn't answer.

Lance was unnerved by him, but determined not to show it. "What's your name?"

"Michael."

He didn't offer his hand, but Lance stuck out his. Michael didn't take it, just stared at Lance so intently that he became uncomfortable.

"Uh, yeah, well listen, Michael, we gotta get back. Big meeting today. See ya around."

He nodded to Ricky and they started back the way they'd come.

Michael stared after them.

Those eyes haunted Lance, and he impulsively turned back.

"You want to come? To the meeting?"

"Lance!" Ricky hissed.

Lance ignored him. "Check out the Round Table? Maybe you might want to join."

"I'm not much of a joiner." Michael shrugged his massive shoulders, and even that move was intimidating. "You want me to come?"

Lance didn't know why, but he answered immediately. "Yeah."

Michael closed the gap between them in a few steps. He was at least four inches taller. "Tell you what. I'll come to your meeting. Check out what you have going. But you have to party with me after."

Lance looked stunned. "Huh?"

"Party?" Michael grinned. "You know, booze, music, girls... *boys*." He said that last word with a knowing smirk.

Ricky stood fuming with rage.

Lance felt weak and indecisive. He knew Michael was mocking him. Was it just to get a rise out of him or for some other reason?

"What's the matter? Never partied, Lancey boy?"

Ricky leapt forward, right up into the bigger boy's face. "Don't call him that!"

Michael eyed Ricky with amused disdain. "You better tell your trained Chihuahua to back off, Lancey, or I'll have to crush him under my foot."

Ricky looked enraged, but Lance stepped between them and put a hand to his chest to keep him back.

He eyed Michael appraisingly. "Sorry. I don't party."

Lance grabbed Ricky and led him back toward New Camelot.

Michael's mocking laughter drifted over the morning air behind them. "What's wrong, Lancey boy? Afraid?"

Lance whirled in anger, his pride struck to the heart. "I'm not afraid of anything!"

"I'm smarter than any kid you got in your so-called crusade, Lancey," Michael tossed out like it was a fact everyone already knew. "You could use me."

Lance considered. Those eyes intrigued him. But no. The kid looked too unstable. "I think we can live without you."

They turned again to leave.

"There'll be girls at the party, Lancey," Michael tossed out tauntingly, and Lance stopped dead in his tracks, forcing Ricky to stop, as well.

"Hot girls," Michael went on, his voice smooth and velvety and reeking of temptation. "Only the hottest ones party with me."

Lance exchanged a look with Ricky, who shook his head vehemently. But Lance stood still, considering. Ricky's eyes pleaded with him to say no. But Lance turned back to Michael.

"Okay. Meeting starts at four. I'll leave your name at the gate."

Before he could change his mind, Lance gripped the furious Ricky and hurried him away down the sidewalk.

"You don't know my name, Lancey boy," he heard in that infuriatingly contemptuous tone.

Lance stopped, turned and did his best imitation of a smirk. "I'll just tell the guard up front to let in Michael the scumbag." Then he braced himself for the likely explosion to come. But whatever reaction he expected, he wasn't prepared for what Michael did next.

The boy's eyes flew open in stunned surprise, and then he threw his head back and laughed. A real laugh, Lance noted, not the smug, scornful type. And then Michael looked straight at Lance a moment, and for a split second his savage expression morphed into something almost... human. "That'll work."

Lance turned again to Ricky to push him forward. But then he remembered something and turned back.

Michael hadn't budged. He looked like a Greek statue.

"Michael, have you been texting me?"

Michael looked confused, and amused at the same time. "Why would I text you when I know how to find you?"

"Just wondering." Lance hurried Ricky away.

Once around the corner and out of sight, Ricky stopped and whirled on Lance. "What's wrong with you, Lance? That guy's a jerk! Why did you invite him?"

"Not sure." He really wasn't. It was a pure gut decision. "A feeling, like maybe he could be useful."

"Yeah, as a jerkbag to keep out the other jerkbags."

Lance smiled.

"And you said you'd party with him," Ricky went on soberly. "Arthur's not gonna like that."

"Which is why we're not telling him that part. I'll just say we're going to hang out with Michael and his friends."

"We?"

"You're my bodyguard, right? Where I go, you go."

"I don't like it, and I don't like him."

Lance stopped and put both hands on Ricky's shoulders, gazing deeply into those soft brown eyes. "Remember what we talked about, Ricky? About being gay?"

Ricky blushed, and nodded.

"There'll be girls there, Ricky," Lance went on quietly, but firmly. "You and me got no experience with girls, remember? This'll be our chance to meet some."

Ricky didn't look happy. "Okay, Lance. We'll go."

"Thanks, Ricky."

Ricky looked dubious as they headed back to New Camelot.

Arthur's Throne Room filled to bursting with eager youth, almost all of the Round Table being in attendance. The king had placed his leadership team in the front row, having added Lavern and Sylvia to the group. Though young, both were smart and could offer sage advice the older ones might not consider. These gatherings were semi-formal, so everyone wore their knightly garb – no street clothes were permitted.

Lance descended the stairs wearing his crown, with Ricky at his side, and greeted entering knights. After a few minutes, Michael strutted through the front door, wearing fancy Nike's, designer pants, and a stretch shirt even tighter than the one he'd had on earlier.

Ricky glowered as the boy sauntered up to them.

"So, any problem at the gate?" Lance asked casually.

Michael chuckled. "Nope. Said I was Michael the scumbag and the dude ushered me on through."

Lance smiled, recalling the guard's face when he'd left those instructions earlier in the day.

Surprisingly, Michael smiled back, again seeming almost human for a split second. Then he blew Ricky a kiss.

Before Ricky could fist up, Lance threw an arm around his shoulders and led him down the hall into the Throne Room, Michael striding in after them.

Since he was unfamiliar, everyone stared at Michael and murmured amongst themselves. Esteban scowled at the new boy's obvious haughtiness, and Reyna eyed the newcomer with disdain.

Lance stopped before Arthur's throne and released Ricky, who looked calmer now that he wasn't looking at Michael's smug, arrogant face. The two boys bowed to the king, and ascended the three steps to the platform. Jenny sat to Arthur's left. Lance's seat remained at Arthur's right, with one for Ricky on Lance's right.

Lance introduced Michael as a boy who might want to join the crusade.

Arthur welcomed Michael, indicating that he sit, and then the meeting commenced.

Arthur introduced Sam McMullen for those who hadn't yet met the loud, middle-aged attorney, as the official New Camelot lawyer, and indicated that he would pass legal judgment on their plans for moving the crusade forward.

Sir Techie updated everyone on the current status of the website and social networking sites. He mentioned Arthur's virtual knighting ceremony, but most everyone agreed that as the campaign for children's rights moved forward, Arthur would have to travel around the state to speak with kids in person, and conduct on-site knighting's.

Lance liked that idea because it would give a more personal touch to the spreading of their message. Besides, he'd never been out of L.A. and would love to travel.

"Alas," Arthur told his son, "if I am away from New Camelot, it will be you, the Prince, who must be in command."

Lance frowned at that, but nodded obediently. When given permission to address the assemblage, Lance stood and offered the idea he and Ricky had hatched. "It's a proposition that will go on the ballot for the November election," he said into the microphone, feeling Michael's cold stare on him the entire time and forcing himself to ignore it. "If the people pass our prop, fourteen-year-olds will have the right to vote."

Excited murmuring and chatter rippled throughout the room before Arthur raised Excalibur above his head to quell it.

"It is a very audacious plan," the king said. "As you all know, I believe in giving people a choice." Then he turned to the assemblage. "Opinions?"

"The grownups aren't going to just let us kids vote," Michael tossed out without raising his hand for permission to speak. "Too much power to give up. They'll stop you."

Sam agreed. "It will be an uphill battle, Arthur. We'll have to draft that proposition to allow fourteen-year-olds adult rights, get enough signatures to qualify it for the ballot, *and* we'll need to move fast if we're aiming for November."

Arthur was clearly out of his league, so Lance explained that since only adults could currently vote, it would be up to the crusade to convince them it was the right choice to make. "And, like Michael said, that probably won't be easy."

Again, Michael leaned forward and fixed those intense eyes on Lance. "First of all, you need to draft a proposition that clearly states your goal. What is your goal? Just kids voting?"

"No," Lance answered. "Kids can vote and drop out of school at fourteen, too, if they don't think school is meeting their needs. That's what we all talked about before, right?"

The leadership team, and many in the crowd, nodded their agreement.

Michael sneered. "That's all well and good, Sir Lancey, but even if you get it on the ballot, the people could just vote it down."

Arthur glowered at Michael for his rudeness, but said nothing.

Lance was offended by the nickname, but kept his cool. "You have a better idea, Michael?"

"Yeah. The prop can be written as an either-or situation. A yes vote means we kids are now adults at fourteen and have all the rights of eighteen-year-olds. A no vote would repeal all laws that currently make any kid under eighteen an adult for any purpose, be it criminal or even the crappy movie theaters make twelve year-olds pay adult rates."

"I think that's a great idea, Michael," Lance said quickly, aware that his dad wasn't liking Michael's tone. "We're fighting for adults to give us choices, so we need to let them make one too. That way they can't just vote us down and have nothing change."

Sam stroked his reddish gray beard with thick, cigar-like fingers. "The boys have a good point, Arthur. If we write it that way, the voters will have to make a real decision."

Arthur nodded, looked to Jenny and the others in leadership roles. Everyone nodded in agreement. "I agree. Be there more, Michael?"

Michael went on, suddenly sounding like a teacher. "Once you get the prop written, it has to be submitted to the state attorney general to get a ballot title. Then you have one hundred fifty days to collect at least 504,760 signatures. You really should get more – one hundred ten percent of what you need because they have to be verified and there are always phonies thrown in by people, especially if they want to screw you over. Then your initiative must qualify at least a hundred thirty one days before the election in which you want it included."

Lance sat in open-mouthed astonishment, especially because he and Ricky had only seen the bad side of Michael before.

Arthur looked awestruck. "Very impressive, Michael. How old are you?"

"Seventeen." Again, those cold, hard eyes went to Lance.

Sam leaned forward on his chair, obviously taken aback by the boy's knowledge. "How do you know all of this, young man?"

Michael shrugged. "I'm like Wikipedia, except I'm more accurate. What I want to know, I find out. They say I have a super high I.Q., but I think that's BS. I just have a perfect memory. I never forget anything."

"Perhaps you would like to assist us in drafting the proposition, Michael," Arthur asked, "since you appear very well informed on the procedure."

Sam jumped in with, "Of course, I'd check it over to make sure it's all legal and proper, once he does his draft."

Michael smirked. "No need, counselor. I never make mistakes."

Arthur eyed Michael cautiously. "Shall I take that as a yes, Michael, that you'd like to join our cause?"

"Sure. Till I get bored, anyway." He looked straight at Lance when he said it.

That penetrating look was not lost on Ricky, who scowled.

"Sir Lance," Arthur said, drawing Lance's attention away from Michael's eyes, "what was your idea regarding the procuring of signatures, and votes?"

Lance cleared his throat and forced himself to focus on his father. "Once we get kids from all over the state involved, which should be easy with Facebook and the website and all of your local visits, we get them all – or most, anyway – to commit to a few things."

He proceeded to lay out his plan for how the children of California could "force" their parents to sign the petitions. He glanced around at the rapt faces hanging on his every word. Even Michael lost the smirk and listened. When he stopped talking, Lance looked out at his peers for a reaction. The room was silent.

Reyna raised her sword and said, "I like it. It'll drive adults crazy. They'll sign for sure."

Michael tossed a sensuous look Reyna's way. "I agree with the hot lady. Good thinking there, Lancey."

Arthur looked irritated. "Michael, these meetings are conducted in a formal fashion. You must needs address my son as Sir Lance."

Michael bowed his head in mock deference. "My apologies, your highness."

It was decided that Michael would start coming to New Camelot daily, after school, to work with Lance and Ricky in drafting the proposition.

Esteban, Darnell, Justin, Lavern, and Sylvia would now take over the weapons training and sparring sessions, especially with new recruits. Reyna would assist both Arthur and Lance. Merlin would always be available for advice and wisdom.

The meeting finally adjourned after two hours. Since it was a Saturday, nothing else was scheduled that evening. Some of the kids wished to spar and train, so Esteban took them to the Training Centre. Others dispersed for home, or the Computer Lab to respond to incoming comments on the website.

Michael loitered up front near a scowling Ricky, leering at Lance.

Lance approached Arthur, who stood chatting with Jenny and Merlin. "Uh, Dad, Michael invited Ricky and me to hang out tonight. You know, without Sergeant Ryan. Is that okay?"

Caught off guard, Arthur exchanged a look with Jenny, but she just shrugged, indicating she knew nothing of this idea. Then he eyed Michael with caution. "What does 'hang out' mean, Michael?"

Michael spread his arms wide and grinned. "Chill with friends, spin some tunes, dance. I have my own car, so I can get them back, no problem."

Arthur gazed long and hard at the boy, sizing him up. Michael gazed right back, not the least bit intimidated by the bigger man. "Michael, kindly wait in the lobby while I speak with my son."

Michael tossed off that haughty look again before sauntering out of the room.

Reyna leapt up onto the platform and moved to Arthur quickly. "I don't like that guy, Arthur. Did you see his eyes? I felt like a serial killer was staring at me."

Arthur looked bewildered by the reference, but Lance jumped in before he could speak. "He's not that bad, Reyna."

Arthur caught Merlin's eye a moment, but the wizard's face remained noncommittal, and then turned back to Lance. "What exactly do you know about him?"

"Nothing, really." He knew he couldn't tell Arthur the real reason he wanted to go with Michael. He tried to meet his father's eyes, but couldn't.

Arthur turned to Ricky. "Sir Ricky, what is your impression of this Michael?"

Ricky wanted to share his true feelings about Michael, but knew Arthur would say no if he did. Lance flicked an imploring look his way, and Ricky sighed. "He's stuck-up, I guess, but so're a lot of kids these days."

Lance let out the breath he was holding.

Arthur studied Lance. "Son, it's been barely two months since... since I nearly lost you. I could not bear to lose you a second time. And you know we are under police protection."

"Dad, we're just gonna hang out. He's not gonna use me for target practice."

Reyna snorted, her arms thrown across her chest. "How do you know?"

Lance glared at her, but she didn't look away.

"Lance, have you perused the Internet very much of late?" Arthur asked.

Lance shook his head, not sure where this was going.

"Sir Techie brought to my attention certain websites that have emerged since..."

"Since I came back from the dead?" Lance tried not to glower. "Yeah, Dad, I've seen the hate groups out there. Hell, we got 'em parked out front. So?"

"Recall that some of these people believe your return is the work of Satan, and that you should still be dead. That you must *be* dead for Satan to be defeated."

Lance's mouth dropped open. Techie hadn't showed him those sites. "What the—? You mean they wanna kill me?"

"They do not quite go that far, son. But they do feel the world would be better off were you still dead."

Ricky stepped forward. "It sounds like they hope somebody takes Lance out, Arthur."

"Precisely my thoughts, Sir Ricky."

Lance gazed defiantly into his father's face. "I can take care of myself, and I have Ricky to protect me. I can't stay in this house all the time, Dad. I can't hide. Please. Let me go. We'll wear hoodies to hide our faces and we can sneak out the back, and I'll be home at whatever time you say."

Arthur looked at Reyna with raised brows. "Your thoughts, Lady Reyna?"

"Midnight. He needs to be back by midnight."

Arthur nodded in agreement. "Very well."

Lance gasped. "Midnight? Dad, I'm fifteen years old!"

Reyna eyed him coolly. "I don't think you should go at all. You tell Michael if anything happens to you, I'll cut his throat and laugh while he bleeds to death."

Arthur, Jenny, Lance and Ricky all stared aghast at Reyna. But Merlin smiled.

"What? He's my baby boy, and I'm sure as hell not gonna lose him again, either." She turned to Ricky. "You tell Michael what I said."

Ricky grinned. "You got it."

Arthur still looked dubious, but Jenny gripped his arm and squeezed gently.

"It's okay, Arthur," she said in that soothing voice Lance loved. "Lance is smart. He'll be fine."

"Be cautious, son. And you, as well, Sir Ricky. At the slightest hint of trouble, call me at once."

Lance still looked annoyed, but Ricky agreed. Then the two boys exited the room in silence.

Reyna watched them go before turning back to Arthur and Jenny. "I still don't like this, Arthur. Lance barely knows that guy."

"I know, Reyna. But Lance is growing up, and his return has created a restlessness within him heretofore unseen." He paused a moment, lost in thought. "The loss of Sir Jack, and the manner of his loss, has, I think, settled a guilt upon Lance's soul that will be difficult to erase. We must be patient with him."

"He's right, Reyna," Jenny agreed, taking the girl's hand in hers and squeezing. "I'm glad he has such a great sister."

That brought a smile to Reyna's face.

When Lance informed Michael that they could go with him, the boy mad dogged Ricky.

"I didn't invite girly boy here."

Ricky balled up his fists.

Lance stepped between them. "Where I go, he goes."

"Your bodyguard?"

"Something like that." Lance felt Ricky fuming behind him, and pressed back against him, hoping his physical touch would be calming.

Michael looked contemptuously at Ricky. "You'd be safer with a poodle. But whatever. I'll bring the car round back, to the tree where I found you this morning."

Then he was out the front door without another word. Ricky made a move to follow, his face contorted with rage, but Lance grabbed his arm.

"Remember, Ricky," he whispered, "we're not doing this for him. We're doing it to meet girls."

That seemed to mollify Ricky, who visibly calmed down. Then the two of them ran upstairs to grab their hoodies.

As they hurried through the expansive gardens to the back gate, Ricky asked Lance, "Do you think about Jack a lot?"

That stopped Lance in his tracks, and he turned to face Ricky. He sought his friend's eyes in the shadowy darkness. The night air was cool on his face and the scent of roses assailed his nostrils.

"Why do you ask?"

"Just wondering."

"Yeah, I do," he said back, almost reverently. "And I still have that weird feeling I told you about, that death wants me back."

Ricky eyed him in the dark. "You're not thinking it might be better if you were dead, are you?"

"No," Lance said, though he knew it sounded unconvincing. "But if I was, at least I'd have Jack." He resumed his walk toward the gate.

"Yeah, but who would I have?"

Lance stopped, frozen in place. Ricky waited, but Lance didn't turn around.

"C'mon, Ricky, Michael's waiting."

And then he strode to the gate while Ricky hurried to catch up.

Michael sat in a brand new, four-door silver beamer, his window down, arm poised on its lip, engine idling, music exploding from powerful speakers. Lance and Ricky gazed at the elegant car a moment and shook their heads.

"Lancey boy up front, bodyguard in back," Michael announced like a proclamation.

Ricky scowled, but Lance just nodded to the back. The street was quiet, even though it was a Saturday evening, and before anyone could spot them, Ricky slipped into the back seat and Lance eased into the front.

He felt soft, smooth leather beneath him and noted a fancy dashboard that looked straight out of a science fiction movie, all amber-colored lights and dials and gizmos. Obviously,

Michael came from money, Lance realized, which could explain the boy's haughty attitude.

As Michael gunned the engine and peeled off down the street, Lance eyed him in the darkness. "Don't call me Lancey boy, Michael."

Michael glanced over a moment. "Okay." Then his eyes returned to the road.

The quick agreement confused Lance. He studied Michael's profile in the dark. The boy was good-looking in a rugged kind of way, or could be if he didn't go out of his way to act so animalistic. He wore diamond stud earrings in his lobes and his blond hair was short at the sides, but tapered upward to sort of flop over at the top, giving him an innocent look that totally belied his attitude. Yes, Lance realized as he considered Arthur's words of caution, Michael was an unknown, and a potentially dangerous one at that.

Was meeting girls worth the risk?

He knew Ricky would say no. But then Richard's leering face rose from the bottom of his soul to fill his mind's eye, and he shivered.

Yes, it was worth the risk.

"Where we going?" he asked.

"My house first," Michael answered above the alternative rock blasting from his stereo system. He steered the car sharply into a turn, throwing both Lance and Ricky hard against the passenger side windows. "We'll kick it awhile and then hit the party straight off. Especially since your old man wants you back at midnight. Hell, my parents don't care if I ever come back. But of course, you're the goody-goody Sir Lance and wouldn't think of disobeying."

Michael whipped the car into another turn, almost throwing Lance into his lap. He grinned Lance's way as if to say, "Having fun yet?"

Lance ignored Michael's taunt, but it stung nonetheless. He wouldn't disobey Arthur. He couldn't, not after everything the man had done for him. He glanced back at Ricky, who looked very uncomfortable, and offered a slight smile.

Michael drove them into the ritzy Hollywood Hills area above New Camelot and Lance gaped out his window as mansion after mansion flew past their view. Most of these homes were bigger than New Camelot. One looked like an alien flying saucer perched atop an enormous concrete pole, but most were four and five-story family homes with light blazing from the windows, surrounded by high fences and locked front gates.

It was a daunting sight to see so much opulence causally dispersed amongst the rolling hills and curving roads, and Lance wondered if any of the owners ever considered how lucky they were to have such niceties. Or, like Reyna used to, did they take it all for granted?

As Michael pressed a button on his steering wheel, Lance's eyes were drawn straight ahead to enormous, wrought iron gates easily ten feet high that began to swing inward to admit them. The headlights from Michael's car illuminated a curved driveway surrounded by grass and trees on either side. Then Michael floored the accelerator and Lance hit the headrest hard when the beamer shot forward up the curved driveway.

In another couple of seconds, a gargantuan, five-story mansion loomed before his eyes as Michael whipped his car around and ground to a halt. Lance's astonished gaze travelled along the semi-circular front. Stairs led up to double front doors flanked by huge, dazzlingly lit bay windows. He looked up at the luminously lit upper floors, all with wide windows blazing with warmth. There were balconies and balustrades, ornate railings, copings and ivy growing up the sides on trellises, and it was just too much to take in all at once.

"You live here?" Lance heard himself ask, knowing it was a stupid question.

Michael snorted. "Hell, no. My parents live there. I have my own back house. That way we never have to see each other."

Something in his tone caught in Lance's mind for a split second, something that almost made Michael seem like a regular kid. But then it was gone as the boy wiggled his brows. "And I get more privacy."

He laughed at Lance's look of discomfort and exited the car with a flourish. Lance glanced back at Ricky, and even in the dim light saw the anger on his face.

"I know, he's a jerkbag," Lance whispered, and that got a smile out of him.

Both boys exited the beamer and followed Michael. They wended their way around the side of the mansion to a gate. Michael held up his cell phone and pressed in a code of some kind. There was a slight *click* and the gate popped open. After they stepped into the backyard, Michael didn't stop walking, so they followed. The gate closed quietly behind them.

There was a huge, L-shaped pool with the main part looking like something out of the Olympics, the smaller part of the L housing a waterfall hot tub that gurgled invitingly as the boys passed in wide-eyed wonder. Michael didn't give the fabulous pool so much as a glance.

The backyard beyond the pool looked like the jungles from *Jurassic Park*. There were trees and ferns and hedges and plants of all types, and flowers, and Lance gawked as he and Ricky wended their way along a path made of individual flat stones set into the grass.

Michael led them through the jungle to a smaller house, single-story, but still larger than anything either boy had ever lived in before New Camelot. Its white stucco walls gleamed in the moonlight and, like the main house, had a large bay window looking into what was likely the living room. The front door was built of solid wood, though Lance had no idea what kind. He did note the rather substantial deadbolt on the door and wondered why Michael would be so worried when it was obvious this entire estate would be hard to break into.

As Michael put a key into the bolt and turned, Lance asked, "So how come you live separate from your parents?"

Michael turned the key. The lock clicked. "We don't talk."

"Why not?"

Michael stared at Lance. "Fear."

That look sent a chill down Lance's back. "Why are you afraid of them?"

"They're afraid of me."

He pulled open the front door. Lance glanced at Ricky, who had that worried look plastered all over his face, and then stepped through the door.

There was a living room with modern black-leather sofas and chairs. In fact, the entire décor was based on the color black. Even the paintings on the wall were dark – macabre images of screaming faces or hellish landscapes. Michael didn't give them time to look around, but kept moving past an expansive, spotlessly clean kitchen that had the appearance of never being used, and down a hallway to the room at the very back.

Again, using his key, Michael unlocked another deadbolt that secured his room from the rest of the house. That, also, stuck in the back of Lance's mind. Why would Michael be so paranoid?

The bedroom was huge, with a king sized bed sporting a shimmery black cover, a large computer table housing two twenty- five inch monitors with an enormous black tower underneath, large dresser, a gigantic easy chair with built-in ottoman, what looked like a huge walk–in closet, and wide double doors leading out to the jungle-like garden.

Michael scooped up a remote from a shiny black night table and pressed a couple of buttons. The computer monitors sprang to life with psychedelic images and music began to play – techno, this time.

There were also floor-to-ceiling black-lacquered bookshelves filled with books, which amazed Lance, who stared at them in shock.

"What's the matter, Lancey, didn't take me for the reader type?"

Lance turned to find Michael standing by the bed. "No. And I told you to stop calling me that."

"To be precise, you told me not to call you Lancey *boy*, and I didn't."

Lance eyed him, but saw no mockery this time. That *was* what he'd said, wasn't it? And Michael *had* done what he'd asked. "Uh, yeah, well, 'Lance' works just fine."

Michael said nothing more, so Lance took that moment to peruse the book titles. Michael stepped closer and reached for a book on the third self, tossing it to him.

Lance glanced at the title quizzically. "Frankenstein?"

"You ever read it?"

Lance shook his head. "Seen some of the movies."

"The movies are crap," Michael declared, as though that settled the issue once and for all. "The book, however, is genius. Read it."

Lance looked surprised. "Uh, okay."

Michael tossed his car keys to Ricky. "Ricky boy, I left my jacket in the car. Go get it."

Ricky bristled. "I'm not your damned lapdog! Get it yourself." He raised his arm to throw the keys back, but Michael's piercing glare stopped him.

"Get a clue, little boy. We want some private time."

Ricky stood his ground, gripping those keys like he might a blunt instrument. "No way. It's my job to protect him."

Lance wasn't sure why, but he wasn't afraid of Michael. He sensed that Michael *wanted* everyone to fear him, but Lance's street-honed instincts assured him he was safe. And he was curious to know what Michael wanted to talk about alone.

"It's okay, Ricky. I got this. Go get the jacket, please."

Ricky looked at him with anger. And maybe hurt. Lance couldn't be sure.

"Lance!"

"Please?"

With a final glare at Michael, Ricky left the room and his footsteps could be heard echoing off the hardwood flooring of the hallway outside. Then a moment later the front door opened and slammed.

Without warning, Michael reached up and slipped off the tight shirt and tossed it onto the bed, causing Lance to gasp.

"Like what you see, Lancey?"

Lance looked away. "You just surprised me, that's all."

Michael laughed again—that infuriating laugh.

"I'm just nervous," Lance went on. "Thinking about the girls we're gonna meet."

"Right. The girls. Go ahead, take it off."

Lance gaped, his breathing accelerating. "What?"

"That parachute you're wearing, Lancey. You cannot go to one of my parties looking like one of the Three Musketeers. You'll wear something of mine."

Lance hesitated, but Michael's hard gaze never wavered. Nervously, Lance slipped off the hoodie and pulled his tunic up and over his head. He had nothing underneath, and he felt naked beneath Michael's penetrating stare.

Michael nodded approvingly. "Not bad, Lancey. I mean, *Lance*. You're built. No wonder Jack fell for you."

That startled Lance. "What are you talking about? How do you know anything about Jack?"

"It was broadcast live, your tearful goodbye, Jack pressing your hand to his heart. Young love. How very touching."

Lance felt his blood boil and he fought the urge to rush the bigger boy. "You're a jerkbag, Michael."

Michael chuckled. "True, but I'm honest. Are you?"

"Yes."

Michael moved closer, leaving only an arm's length between them. "Yeah? Then tell me—am I more buff than your Jacky boy?"

He flexed his chest and popped a bicep pose. He *was* bigger, but Lance would never give him the satisfaction of saying so.

"No."

"I thought you were honest."

Lance met Michael's gaze. "I am."

Before Lance could move, Michael threw both arms around him and planted lips firmly onto his. Lance pushed and fought, but Michael held him fast, his grip unwavering.

Finally, when Lance thought he'd suffocate for lack of air, Michael broke the kiss.

"What the hell are you doing, Michael?" he spat, wiping his lips with his hand.

Michael laughed.

"You're worse than a jerkbag, Michael!"

And then Lance saw Ricky watching in open-mouthed horror from the doorway, a leather jacket dropping from his hand to the floor.

"Oops, we made the bodyguard jealous."

Ricky flushed with fury.

Lance snatched up his shirt and hoodie from the floor. "C'mon, Ricky, we're out a here."

Michael sneered. "So the uber-honest Sir Lance is going to break his word after all?"

That stopped Lance at the door.

Ricky put a hand on Lance's arm, his voice potent and urgent. "This is different, Lance. You don't have to go through with this when he pulls crap like that!"

Lance looked pained, his heart still pounding. "I know. But I did promise."

"Lance—" Ricky protested helplessly.

Lance leaned in to Ricky's ear. "I still wanna meet some girls, Ricky. After that, I *need* to."

Ricky gazed at him in disgust. "Why's your shirt off?"

Lance blushed. "Oh, Michael wanted me to wear something else to the party."

"What, your birthday suit?" Ricky glowered furiously.

Michael, standing by the walk-in closet, chuckled. "Oooh, score onefor the bodyguard." He disappeared into the enormous closet.

Ricky whispered to Lance, "Lance, he kissed you, man! This guy's a freakin' stalker or something."

Before Lance could answer, Michael emerged wearing a very tight, sleeveless muscle shirt and carrying an even smaller one in his hand. He walked over to Lance and tossed the shirt at him.

Lance held it up in dismay. "No way, Michael. This thing looks too small for my little brother."

"Exactly." He snatched the shirt from Lance and slipped it over his head, glaring. "Arms." Lance reluctantly slipped his arms through and Michael pulled the shirt all the way down. Lance yanked his long hair out from under it and squirmed with discomfort. He felt like he was wearing a straitjacket.

Michael surveyed him a moment. "Perfect."

Lance started to remove it, but Michael's hand stopped him.

"Michael, it looks like I'm wearing nothing. This is embarrassing, man."

"And it shows every cut of your buff, rippling body, Lance. The girls'll love it." He paused. "And you did want to meet girls, right?"

Lance reddened, and caught Ricky's eye. "Will you wear one too?"

Ricky's eyebrows shot up, but before he could answer Michael sighed. "I hadn't planned on showing off the bodyguard, but if you insist."

He ducked back into the closet.

Ricky eyed Lance dubiously. "We better meet some really hot girls after all this," he said with a slight grin, and Lance grinned back.

Michael returned with another tight, sleeveless shirt. "Off with the tent, bodyguard."

Ricky looked embarrassed as he removed his hoodie and tunic. Lance's grin faltered as he noted how cut and defined Ricky looked, even more than when they'd first met.

Ricky grimaced as he slipped on the excessively tight shirt.

Lance gave Ricky the once over, as though seeing him for the first time. "Looking pretty hot there, Ricky, especially them guns. The girls'll faint when they see you."

Ricky grinned shyly. "You mean the ones who didn't already faint over you?"

Michael snorted. "You look like twins – twin girls."

"Not funny, Michael," Lance shot back, the brief moment of camaraderie with Ricky lost.

"You ladies ready to roll?"

Lance stood up to his full height and stared firmly at Michael. "Michael, you're the biggest jerkbag I ever met, and once I fulfill this promise, Ricky and me will never party with you again. If you wanna work on our prop, fine. But no more crap like this. Clear?"

Michael looked impressed, the smugness replaced with a sober nod of the head. "Crystal, Sir Lance. Let's go."

Michael scooped up his jacket and they followed him out to his car, making sure to bring their tunics and hoodies with them. Neither would be caught dead in these shirts at New Camelot. Lance also remembered to bring *Frankenstein*, slipping the paperback into his pocket as they left the house.

DARKNESS FALLS

CHAPTER SIX
YOU DON'T GOTTA PROVE NOTHING TO NO ONE

JENNY STAYED FOR DINNER AND then left for home. She asked Arthur to let her know when Lance returned. They kissed beneath the moonlight on the front steps of New Camelot and stood together in a companionable silence. Then they walked to her car and Arthur felt lonely as she pulled through the main gates and passed the sign-wielding crowds.

Seeing those crowds reminded him that Merlin must see the websites he'd instructed Sir Techie to keep hidden from Lance. He found his old mentor in the kitchen, eating ice cream directly from a tub.

"Arthur, this ice cream is but the most glorious of inventions," he exclaimed, licking the spoon clean, his face pulled into a look of ecstasy. "Would that we'd had it in your day – oh, the treaties we could have solidified."

His eyes twinkled, and Arthur laughed. It felt good to once more have his old friend available for advice and counsel. He finally coaxed the man to follow him, but only after Merlin had finished the last spoonful and dumped the empty half-gallon tub into the trash.

Sir Techie and a few other knights sat at computers, messaging, responding to comments, or just playing online games when the two men entered. Arthur asked Techie to pull up some of the nastier webpages. The wizard bent forward to scrutinize the content, commenting on the ingenuity of man to create such vast marvels and then to use them solely for the purpose of verbally abusing one another.

Some of the sites were hate-filled. Many of these included pictures of Jack holding Lance's hand to his heart from the night Lance died, and the comments accompanying these pictures were vicious. Jack was called everything from a faggot to a child rapist to a sick and twisted pervert who should rot in hell, and Lance was excoriated for associating with him. Some had begun attacking Lance as queer, too, because of the look on his face as Jack held his hand.

It broke Arthur's heart to see these stories, but he didn't know what he could do to prevent them.

"Arthur, we knew this could be the result of restoring Lance to life," Merlin finally said. "Human beings have not changed since you were a boy. Only their methods of expression have."

"I know, Merlin. I have seen ample evidence in just the months I have lived here. But this is Lance we are discussing, not some stranger. He is my son. How may I protect him from all of this?" He pointed at the computer screen.

Merlin placed a comforting hand on his shoulder, much like he'd done when Arthur was a boy. "You cannot, Arthur. I restored Lance to you so your noble and necessary crusade may yet succeed, because he is the key. But he must, as did you when you became boy-king of Britain, learn how to protect himself, how to wade through this emotionalism, how to rise above it and be the leader you require. You and I shall do our best to guide him. But the strength must come from within him."

Arthur offered Merlin a little smile through his well-trimmed beard. "Wise words, as always, my old friend."

"The road ahead will be rocky for Lance, and we adults must stay by his side no matter what. You most of all."

"Merlin, tell me true. Have you foreseen something of Lance's future that you choose not to share with me?"

Merlin looked thoughtful. "Just what I have said, Arthur. No matter what transpires, you must never give up on him."

Arthur nodded, his worries only intensified by the wizard's serious expression.

Michael drove them to another mansion and Lance gawked out the beamer's window at the fancy, super-expensive cars that filled the circular driveway. Every window in the sprawling two-story house blazed with light. Alternative music blasted from the open double front doors and silhouetted bodies slid into and out of the light.

Lance turned back to exchange a nervous look with Ricky as Michael eased his beamer to a stop behind a sleek new Jag and killed the engine. Lance and Ricky exited the car and stood a moment in awe. This house, though only two-stories, seemed to go on forever. Whereas Michael's was built more upward with its five floors, this one spread out for what seemed to Lance like miles and miles.

Michael turned and waggled a finger to follow. Lance felt naked and exposed in the super-tight muscle shirt, and saw the same discomfort on Ricky's face. They trailed Michael as he sauntered up the paving stone walk to the front door, giving the head nod to a few guys and girls loitering outside holding cups filled with liquid. These kids, Lance noted, acknowledged Michael, but made no attempt to engage or even greet him. That seemed odd, but he had no time to contemplate its reason because Michael strode right to the open doors and stepped inside. Nervously, Lance and Ricky stepped in after him.

Within a massive entry hall, teenagers milled about, some passing into an expansive living room on the left and others heading down another hall somewhere Lance could not see. Several flights of stairs leading to the upper floors were in evidence. The music, blasting from the living room, now switched to techno. Glancing in, Lance saw kids, cups in hand, dancing to the music. The smell of pot and cigarette smoke assailed his nostrils, and loud laughter hit them from all directions. Lance was agape with amazement, having never been in such an environment before.

A beautiful girl sidled up to Michael from out of the crowded living room and gave him a perfunctory hug. She was one of the prettiest girls Lance had ever seen. She sported bobbed blonde hair, several piercings in her ear lobes, a piercing through her nose, and lovely blue eyes that immediately brought Mark to mind.

Before Lance even had a chance to feel sad, the girl's eyes bulged with amazement. "Oh my God, Michael, you *did* bring him!"

Without awaiting a response from Michael, she giggled nervously. "I'm Bridget, Sir Lance. Oh, my God it's so dope to meet you! The Boy Who Came Back! I'm so stoked! I've gotta introduce you to everyone!"

Before Lance could speak, she grabbed his bare arm at the biceps and began dragging him toward the living room. Michael's hand shot out and gripped her forearm roughly. She turned with annoyance, but something in Michael's face must've scared her because she quickly looked more deferential.

"What, Michael?" she asked with a nervous sigh.

Michael leaned in to her ear and whispered something Lance couldn't hear. He glanced over at Ricky, but the nervous boy just shrugged.

Michael pulled back, but still gripped her arm, tightly, Lance noted with discomfort. Bridget scowled.

"Okay." She dropped her eyes from Michael's penetrating gaze, and he released her. Without another word, she dragged Lance out of the entry hall and into the crowd dancing in the living room.

Ricky stepped forward to follow, but Michael's hand to his chest stopped him. Ricky glared, his fists balling up. Michael didn't push, but merely blocked him from following. "He'll be fine with Bridget, bodyguard. Three's a crowd, remember? Follow me."

Ricky glanced at the swirling, writhing bodies pounding along to the techno beat, but caught no glimpse of Lance among the crowd. Reluctantly, he followed Michael down a hardwood floor hallway into a kitchen as large as the entire apartment he'd lived in with his parents.

All the cabinetry was white and clean and there was not one, but two gigantic refrigerators, a stove big enough for him to hide in, a large island in the middle with chairs around it, and dangling fixtures sending pools of light bouncing off the whiteness.

On the marbled top of the island sat a beer keg and a large punch bowl with fountaining streams of colored liquid pouring continuously into its base. Teens of varying ages lounged against the counters or loitered around the punch bowl, laughing, swigging from red plastic cups, even making out in between swigs. All were Caucasian, which made Ricky feel the odd man out with his brown skin. That and the fact that he'd never partied before made this whole world foreign to him. He thought of Lance in the other room and wondered what was happening. And he wanted nothing more than to get the hell out. This wasn't his scene and he knew it.

The kids not already drunk greeted Michael with guarded acknowledgement. Michael grabbed a cup away from one boy who was just about to press it beneath the streaming liquid of the fountain. The boy didn't object. In fact, he kept his eyes downcast and stepped out of Michael's path. Michael stuck the cup beneath a stream and filled it. Then he handed the cup to Ricky.

"Bottoms up, bodyguard."

Ricky took the cup and smelled it. He wrinkled his nose in disgust. Whatever this was, it was strong. "I can't get messed up, man. I gotta watch out for Lance."

"This is a party, Ricky boy, and the point of a party *is* to get messed up. I'll keep an eye on Lance, don't you worry. Now drink!"

The intensity of the command and that wild flash in Michael's eyes scared Ricky, and he didn't scare easily. Uncertainly, noting that Michael did not have a drink of his own, he raised the cup to his lips. He sipped, and the sour taste burned his tongue. He grimaced in disgust.

"It's not tea, Ricky boy," Michael said goadingly. "Chug it."

Feeling every eye on them, Ricky squirmed, feeling embarrassed by his ridiculously small shirt and Michael belittling him in front of so many peers. So he upended the alcohol into his mouth and down his throat. He gagged and choked, causing the kids around him to laugh. Michael joined in the laughter, and that seemed to encourage the kids. Ricky heard mutters of "pussy" and "lightweight" bandied about, and he flushed with humiliation.

Michael clapped Ricky on the back. "That's more like it, bodyguard. I'll make a man out of you, yet."

Just then, a lithe, shorthaired brunette in a sleeveless black shirt entered the kitchen. She had goth tattoos covering every inch of her slender arms and a piercing through her right eyebrow. She squealed with delight at seeing Michael.

"Oh, Michael, you finally made it." She grabbed him in a hug and squeezed the biceps with delight. Michael eyed her with disdain. Then she spotted Ricky grimacing beside Michael, the alcohol still burning his throat. "And who's this cutie?"

Michael chuckled. "Ricky, this is Carmen."

She giggled and leaned in to kiss Ricky full on the lips, startling him so much he nearly dropped his cup. She pulled away, laughing at his surprised expression. "Oooh, he tastes delicious." She looked seriously at Michael. "Is he..."

Michael shook his head. "Nope. He's all yours. Have fun, bodyguard."

And then Michael was gone, leaving Carmen to gaze hungrily at Ricky, who looked back at her uncertainly. Now what was he supposed to do?

When Bridget dragged Lance into the living room, she made a beeline for the stereo system—which looked more expensive than Michael's car—and turned off the music. The dancers stopped moving, heads turned, all conversation ceased. And all eyes widened in astonishment as they spotted Lance standing beside Bridget in his tight shirt, feeling exposed and naked and under a microscope he didn't want to be under.

His stomach churned with unease, and he hoped he wouldn't get sick. Hell, this was worse than speaking to all the people on the night he came back. These were his peers gaping at him, and this was a really hot girl beside him. Just the feel of her warm arm brushing against his sent tingles of nervous uncertainty through his body.

"Look who Michael brought, everyone," Bridget called out, but the stunned silence and gaping expressions revealed that Lance had clearly been recognized. "Let's welcome Sir Lance, The Boy Who Came Back!"

Lance turned red and became even more embarrassed by the silent, open-mouthed reaction of the crowd. It's like they were awed and scared at the same time. He felt like a true freak under their intense stares, and had just decided to bail when a girl raised her glass.

"Let's hear it for The Boy Who Came Back."

That broke the ice, eliciting a rousing cheer and swigging of drinks, and suddenly

Lance was mobbed by kids wanting to touch him, stroke his hair, squeeze his arms, ogle him, shake his hand and have their pictures taken with him. Girls rubbed their hands along his chest and abs, cooing at how buff he was.

He felt both mortified and exhilarated, and had no clue how to respond. These were teens like him, and they didn't fear him as he'd thought they might, but how was he supposed to act?

They threw a thousand questions at him, mostly what it felt like to be dead, what did God look like, could he walk on water or do any other miracles, that sort of thing. Lance tried to answer, but new questions kept cutting him off. Everyone wanted a picture with him and he did his best not to look uncomfortable when hot girls in skimpy clothes, and even boys, leaned against him so closely they made him squirm. He felt the beginnings of a freak out coming on, and desperately wanted to get out of there.

Finally, Bridget told them all to back off and let Lance party. She turned the music back on and the kids returned to their drinking, but always eyeing Lance as they did. Linking her arm in his, Bridget led him to a couch and grabbed a bottle of booze from another kid she passed. She pushed Lance onto the couch, and plopped down beside him, taking a swig from the bottle before offering it to Lance. He shook his head nervously, his heart hammering.

Bridget laughed, but not in any mocking way. Hers was a laugh of delight, as though seeing such innocence in a teen boy her age was refreshing. "This is a party, Sir Lance. It'll relax you. You're way too tense."

She forced the bottle into his hands and smiled as he timidly put it to his lips. She was right about tense. He felt more nervous and afraid than when he and Jack had been held prisoner by Mr. R. The music pounded in his head, and he couldn't quite get his thoughts straight.

"Don't worry – it won't kill you. You can't die anyway, remember?"

Lance frowned at her statement, not certain how much was jest and how much irrational belief, but her lovely smile was so infectious, so inviting, that he tipped the bottle and poured the sour-tasting alcohol down his throat. It burned, and tasted horrible, but Lance put on the best face he could for Bridget, fighting back the urge to spit it out. She grinned and took another swig herself.

"You're so much cuter in person, Sir Lance. Can I just call you Lance? The 'sir' part makes me feel like I'm talking to a teacher."

Lance nodded, the alcohol beginning to relax him, the panic starting to recede. He took the bottle and forced down another swallow before handing it back.

She swigged again, obviously having had a lot of experience with drinking.

"I've had a thing for you ever since you first started showing up on the Internet," she gushed. "You have the most beautiful hair I've ever seen." She reached out to lovingly stroke Lance's long, dark hair, pulling it toward her and running her fingers through it. "My hair is so lame, I have to keep it short. But yours is thick and *so* soft. And your face is drop-dead gorgeous."

Lance blushed, causing her to laugh. He liked her laugh. It was lyrical, and he relaxed a bit more.

"When Michael told me he was gonna get you to party with us, I almost wet my pants," Bridget went on excitedly, taking another swig from the bottle. "Normally, if somebody else said it, I'd think it was BS. But not Michael. If he wants something, he gets it."

Lance nodded, trying to focus on her words and not do or say something lame, while the alcohol went to work in his system. Feeling the need to do something, he took the bottle from her and swigged again, bigger this time.

Bridget eyed him with wide-eyed wonder. "You always this quiet, Lance? I saw you talk pretty good on TV, so I know you can."

"I'm just, you know, nervous. I never..."

"Partied before?" Her voice was light and inviting.

Lance shook his head.

"So tell me, how did it feel when you found out you didn't die after all? That must've been like, super weird."

Lance's face clouded, his thumping heart accelerating. He grabbed the bottle and took another long drink before answering. "It was. I almost crossed over to, well, wherever, and I actually wanted to go. But then I woke up and saw my Dad and Merlin, and felt really weird, and scared."

Bridget took his hand and gently squeezed, and Lance enjoyed the touch of her fingers entwined within his. "Why scared?"

Lance lowered his eyes. "Because right before I woke up, I saw Jack waving goodbye, and that's when I knew that *he* was dead instead of me."

He fell silent, fighting the urge to cry. The alcohol was loosening his emotional self-control very quickly. He felt warmth suffusing his body and knew it was the booze. But it felt relaxing, too, so he took another swig, gripping the mouth of the bottle like it was his only hold on life.

Bridget stroked his hand with hers. "That must've been so painful. I saw you guys say goodbye to each other – hell, I think the whole city did. Were you and Jack...?"

Fear gripped him, and his blood began to pound. "What?"

Bridget eyed him uncertainly, as though she didn't want to know the answer. "You know, like, boyfriends or something?"

Lance blanched "No! We weren't, but..."

Bridget smiled and seemed to understand. "But you loved him, didn't you?"

Lance nodded reluctantly, the alcohol unleashing the tension within. "Not like that," he quickly added. "He was like, well, my idol, my hero. I looked up to him, you know?"

"I get that. So, does that mean a girl like me has a chance?"

Lance frowned. "A chance?"

She smiled coyly and squeezed his hand again. "Yeah. A chance with you."

Lance blushed again, and nodded.

She laughed. "God, you're even hotter when you blush."

That drew smile to his face. Their eyes met, and then Lance quickly snagged another drink from the bottle.

As he lowered the bottle, Bridget leaned in and kissed him. When she pulled back, he smiled for her benefit, more than his. Had he felt anything during the kiss? He took another swig and fought the pending freak out.

Carmen had managed to pour enough alcohol into Ricky to relax him, and had finally dragged him upstairs into one of the numerous bedrooms. Sitting on the edge of a queen-sized bed with a floral covering, Carmen had wasted no time in getting Ricky's shirt up and over his head, tossing it onto the floor. He was mortified, but she was all over him and he had little time to think. Her hands groped his hard, wrestler muscles and her lips flew to his mouth before he could say a word. But when her hand moved lower, Ricky pushed her away and clambered off the bed. Blood pounding, he gaped at her in amazement.

She was very drunk – he knew that much. She'd polished off half that punch bowl downstairs and he didn't even know how she could still walk.

"What's wrong, pretty boy? Don't want me?"

"Hell no! I don't even know you."

Her eyes narrowed in anger. "You a Mexican faggot?"

Ricky felt his face burning, and the alcohol caused his temper to flare. "I gotta be gay 'cause I don't wanna do a stranger?"

She laughed mockingly, eyeing him with disdain.

"I'm outta here." Ricky grabbed his shirt off the floor and bolted from the room.

Moving past couples in the hallways and drifting by an open bedroom door with pot smoke wafting out into the hallway, Ricky slipped his shirt back on and checked his phone for the time. Eleven thirty. He needed to get Lance and they had to get home. He'd been drinking with Carmen for an hour, and he'd drunk far more than he should have. Hell, he was supposed to be guarding Lance and he had no idea where Lance was or what might have happened to him. Ricky made his way unsteadily down the stairs, gripping the bannister the entire way.

Michael watched as Bridget and Lance slow danced, she with her arms tight around him, his hands wrapped around her waist. Michael pushed the girl he was dancing with away and moved behind Bridget. He tapped her on the shoulder. When she turned her head, he eyed her a moment before she reluctantly released Lance, who could hardly stand up. Michael took her place, enfolding Lance in his arms and grinding against him.

Ricky stopped in the doorway and looked in, watching with horror as Michael kissed Lance, hard and with passion.

Furious, Ricky staggered through the dancers. His fists were balled at his sides, but he knew he was in no shape to take on the bigger and stronger Michael.

"Michael, we gotta go. We promised."

Michael looked annoyed at having been interrupted. Then he shoved Lance at Ricky, nearly toppling him. Ricky grabbed the dazed Lance and steadied them both.

"Better not let go, bodyguard," Michael taunted. "Little boy can't hold his liquor." He gave Ricky the once over and shook his head in disgust. "Looks like you're a lightweight, too. Let's go. I told his old man midnight and I keep my word."

Michael crossed the room to Bridget and said something Ricky couldn't hear. She raised a hand and waved goodbye. Then Michael grabbed the two boys, dragging and shoving them out the front door.

Arthur was up and pacing the lobby of New Camelot, holding his phone, anxiously awaiting Lance's return. He glanced again at the time on his phone. It was midnight. The phone beeped, and his heart leaped, but it was Reyna's picture that came up. He put the phone to his ear and heard her concerned voice asking the obvious.

"No, Reyna, he has not returned."

"Text me, Arthur, as soon as he does."

Arthur was so lost in thought he found himself nodding, despite the fact she wasn't there. "I shall alert you immediately. Thank you for your concern."

He ended the call just as Chris descended the stairs wearing pajama bottoms and a t-shirt that said, 'I Heart Sir Lance'.

"Arthur, is Lance back yet?" Chris asked, his small voice laced with unease.

"Nay, Sir Christopher. Soon, I hope."

"I can't sleep without Lance here."

Arthur tousled his shaggy blond hair. "Nor can I."

Just then, Ricky and Lance stumbled into the lobby from the back hallway, Ricky supporting Lance, who was very unsteady on his feet. Arthur groaned upon seeing them, for it was clear they were drunk. He'd been there himself as a boy, and remembered it all too vividly, and its repercussions.

"Sir Ricky, what happened?"

Ricky couldn't meet Arthur's gaze. "He drank too much, Arthur. I did, too."

Arthur gazed at the boy sadly, causing Ricky redden with shame.

"I didn't want to, Arthur, but everybody was drinking and this girl kept laughing at me and..." He trailed off. "I'm sorry, Arthur."

Lance had his eyes to the floor, embarrassed and guilt-ridden.

"Lance?"

Lance finally looked up, his face filled with humiliation. "I'm sorry, Dad. I just drank a little 'cause I was so nervous and then, well, I guess I had too much."

Without warning, he retched violently and threw up all over the floor at Arthur's feet. Vomit dribbling down his chin, he looked mortified as Chris leaped back in horror.

"Oh God, I'm so sorry. Dad, I'm so sorry."

Arthur's anger rose as he gazed upon this son whom he'd entrusted with the very survival of New Camelot. And he nearly lashed out with words he might have later regretted. But Merlin's advice returned to his mind: "You must never give up on him."

Arthur quelled his anger, but could not quite bring himself to look at Lance. "Sir Ricky, please take Lance upstairs and help him into bed. I shall clean this up. Sir Christopher, please assist Sir Ricky."

Chris stood stock-still, his eyes flicking from the vomit- splashed tile floor to Lance's pale, disoriented face, and nodded. He carefully stepped around the splash of sick and took one arm, while Ricky took the other, and they slowly guided Lance up the stairs.

Arthur watched them ascend, sadness and apprehension etched across his face. He pulled out his phone to text Reyna.

Ricky and Chris guided Lance haltingly, and with measured steps, up the stairs to his room and sat him on the edge of his bed.

"Hold him up, Chris, while I get something to clean his mouth."

Ricky staggered into the adjoining bathroom for a wet face cloth. He lurched back out, none too steady on his feet, and washed Lance's face. Lance looked at him sadly, and then at Chris, and began to cry, a keening sort of wail.

"What's the matter, Lance?" Chris asked, taking Lance's hand in his. "Are you sad?"

Lance stroked Chris's face and nodded, his emotions churning like a whirlpool. "I feel like crap—oh, sorry, Chris. Ricky, I dissed Jack. With Bridget. And then I let Michael kiss me... I hate myself! Why did Jack let me come back? Why?"

Ricky looked at Lance sadly. "You're drunk, Lance. I feel like sh—crap, too. I think it's the alcohol, man."

Lance shook his head dejectedly. "No, it isn't. It's me."

As Lance continued to cry, Ricky and Chris managed to remove the tunic and Chris eyed the skin-tight shirt underneath a moment in surprise before delicately tossing the vomit-stained tunic into a laundry hamper in the bathroom.

Ricky gently lifted Lance's arms and pulled off the shirt, slipped off Lance's boots and set them aside, and then laid him down on top of the bedcover.

"Grab a blanket from the closet, please, Chris."

Chris hurried to the closet and returned with a king-size blanket, which they used to cover Lance.

Ricky gazed down at him. "Well, uh, good night, Lance. I gotta crash, too. I'm sure we'll feel better in the morning." He tried for a smile, but failed.

Lance shot a hand out from beneath the blanket and grabbed Ricky's wrist. "Don't leave me alone, Ricky, please. I don't wanna be alone tonight. Stay with me."

Ricky blushed.

Chris stepped closer to the bed. "Can I stay, too, Lance?"

"'Course, Chris." Then to Ricky he implored, "I need you too. Please."

Ricky smiled. "Why not? This bed could hold fifty people." His smile did nothing to soften Lance's somber mood, however.

Chris went around to Lance's left side and crawled beneath the blanket. Ricky removed his shirts, pants and boots and set them aside. He flicked off the light on the nightstand and crawled in beside Lance on the boy's left, slipping beneath the blanket. He and Lance gazed a long moment into each other's eyes.

"Thanks, Ricky," Lance said tremulously, almost a whisper. "You're my best friend, just like Jack said you'd be. I'm sorry about tonight, man, I'm so sorry about everything…"

"Go to sleep, Lance. We'll feel better in the morning."

Lance continued to sniffle for a time, and then he knew no more.

When he woke, Lance clutched his head as a jackhammer began pounding away inside it.

Ricky pulled himself awake on the other side of the bed.

"I guess this is a hangover," Lance whispered, even the sound of his own voice sounding like a rock concert in his head.

"Yeah," Ricky acknowledged in a whisper, hands to his head. "I guess."

Lance leaned back against the headboard.

"You better today, Lance? You were super depressed last night."

Lance raised his head slowly, his bleary eyes round with guilt. "I didn't wanna dis Jacky, Ricky, really. It's just, I think, well, it seemed like maybe Bridget might want to be my girlfriend and I didn't want her to think…"

Ricky's eyes widened at that. "Really? Do you like her?"

"She's cool, Ricky. We mostly talked." He blushed. "We made out a little, too, but not much. I felt a freak out coming on, so she mostly held my hand."

Ricky frowned. "What about Michael kissing you? And grinding against you?"

Lance broke eye contact. "I don't wanna talk about that. I was drunk. Didn't know what I was doing."

Ricky nodded, but said nothing.

Lance looked up at him. "What about you? Anything happen?"

Ricky snorted in disgust. "Michael hooked me up with this chick, Carmen."

Lance looked startled. "Did you…"

"Hell, no! She dragged me upstairs and got mad when I told her no."

They fell silent a moment.

Then Ricky asked, "Are you gonna see her again? Bridget?"

"I want to. I need to see if I can fall in love with her, like we talked about." Then his face clouded. "But that probably means hanging with Michael too."

"There's something wrong with him, Lance. Can't you see it in his eyes?"

Lance considered that question, Michael's eyes haunting him with their mystery. "Yes, and no."

"What does that mean?"

Lance shrugged, because he didn't know what he meant. Not yet. It was just his gut instincts at work. There was more to Michael than the jerkbag he projected. Maybe working on the proposition together would help him understand the enigmatic boy.

"Lance, I don't want to do any more partying like that," Ricky affirmed, his face looking ashen from the hangover. "I hated every second of it."

"Me, too," Lance agreed, his head throbbing. "Besides, we have more important things to do. I'll just have to figure out some way to see Bridget without Michael knowing."

Ricky's face took on a look of sadness mixed with longing that Lance noted. "We'll find you a girlfriend, too."

Ricky nodded absently, but said nothing.

Chris barged into the room. "Lance, Arthur wants to see you and Ricky in the throne room as soon as you're ready."

Both boys winced in pain, and exchanged a guilty look.

Chris eyed Lance appraisingly. "Do you feel better today, Lance? You were so sad last night."

"I don't feel good, no, Chris, 'cause I did something stupid by going to that party, and then drinking too much. But I don't feel so sad, no. Did you stay with me last night?"

Chris nodded, and Lance pulled him into a hug. "It's so cool to have you as my brother."

Chris hugged him tightly and then turned to run back out into the hallway.

Lance eyed Ricky a moment. "Thanks, Ricky, for staying with me last night."

"No prob," he said with an off-hand grin. "'Cept you snore like an old cow."

Lance guffawed. "You made that up."

"Showers before we see Arthur? You pretty much reek, Lance."

Lance punched him in the shoulder. "Me? You smell like week-old underwear!" Ricky grabbed Lance and they wrestled for a few seconds before Lance called out, "Truce!" and they separated, his head pounding from the exertion.

"I'm gonna go get ready." Ricky slipped out the opposite side of the bed. "I'll come back so we can go down together."

Lance nodded, his head still throbbing.

Ricky went to his door, and then turned back. "Do you think Arthur'll be pissed?"

"Damn straight."

Ricky left the room.

Lance reached for his phone to check for messages. There was another text from '000000000'.

"Crap," he muttered. "All I need."

It read: 'Morning Lance. It's your boyfriend Jacky checking up on you. Better not be cheating on me with any other guys. Ha!'

Suddenly furious, Lance typed in a reply: 'Michael, I know it's u, so stop screwing around!'

Unlike before, an error message came up saying Lance's message could not be sent. He waited a moment to see if anything else appeared, and when nothing did he slammed the phone down on his bed and stalked into the bathroom.

It was nearly noon when Lance—Ricky by his side—entered the Throne Room to find Arthur quietly conferring with Jenny, Reyna and Esteban.

The conversation ceased the moment the two boys stepped through the double doors.

Arthur eyed them from across the vastness of the room. "Come in, son. You, as well, Sir Ricky."

As the boys hesitantly approached, Arthur turned back to Reyna and Esteban. "Lady Reyna, you and Sir Este please retire to the Computer Lab."

"Sure Arthur," Reyna agreed.

As she and Esteban walked past the two boys, he made a slashing motion across his throat, and her look would've killed a wild animal.

Lance knew he'd hear from both of them after he got it from Arthur. This was going to be a *long* day.

Arthur indicated that Lance and Ricky sit in the chairs directly in front of him. Jenny stood to Arthur's left, eyeing the boys with concern, obviously noting their bleary eyes and washed out appearance. Even the showers hadn't erased the visible effects of the hangover.

Arthur gazed down at them mutely, his eyes filled with what Lance interpreted as disappointment. He couldn't meet his father's eyes.

"I'm sorry, Dad," he offered, knowing it sounded hopeless and lame.

"Me, too," Ricky chimed in quietly, also with head bowed. "I was supposed to protect him."

"It wasn't Ricky's fault, Dad. I drank because I wanted to."

Arthur nodded. "And did you know there would be alcohol at this gathering before you left here?"

Lance nodded, eyes still downcast.

"So you lied to me?"

Those words ripped open Lance's heart and forced his eyes upward to meet the intense look directed at him. And he saw what he dreaded – disappointment.

"Not exactly," he blurted, the throbbing headache only getting worse as his blood pounded with shame. "But... yeah, I guess."

"Why?"

Lance gazed imploringly at Arthur, hoping his eyes revealed what his heart feared to say – "please don't hate me."

"Because we wanted to meet girls, Dad."

Arthur's eyebrows shot up in surprise, and he exchanged a quick look with Jenny.

Before they could respond, Lance plowed forward. "We're cooped up here 24/7, Dad, and we never get to be like regular boys and meet girls, maybe even find a girlfriend, you know? So when Michael said there'd be girls there, we wanted to go. I'm sorry."

"I am not entirely without experience in this arena, Lance," Arthur said, his tone one of deep understanding. "I was but sixteen when crowned High King of Britain and there was little I could do that was not watched or monitored or questioned."

"But you got Guinevere, right?" Lance blurted, hoping to make his father understand.

"Alas, Lance, in my day we had little choice in such matters. Guinevere was betrothed to me as part of a peace treaty. I barely knew her."

Lance's mouth dropped open. He'd forgotten that part of the story.

"I understand your need to feel like regular boys, but you are and never will be regular boys, my son." Arthur's look was grave and intense, causing Lance to squirm. "You shall always be, what is the expression this era uses, under the microscope, and your choices must be sound."

That irked Lance, though he knew his father was right. "It was just a party, Dad. I shouldn't have drank, I know that now."

"Why did you?"

Lance flushed with shame. "I was embarrassed, Dad. I mean everybody stared at me like I was a freak. Then this hot girl wanted to talk and I was nervous and I didn't know what to do, so I... the booze relaxed me, I guess."

"I see. And you, Ricky?"

Ricky looked as humiliated as Lance. "I never been to a party like that, either, and I was nervous, too, 'specially when this girl was all over me. I'm really sorry, Arthur. I'll never let it happen again."

"I'm sorry too, Dad," Lance chimed in, his throbbing head beginning to swim with roiling discomfort. "It won't happen next time."

"Next time?" That was Jenny, a shocked expression on her soft features.

Lance looked uncomfortable. "Well, uh, I do, I mean, well, I want to hang out with Bridget some more."

"And Michael, as well?" Arthur asked cautiously.

Lance frowned. "Not so much. But Bridget, Dad, she likes me. I think she wants to be my girlfriend."

"That's rather fast, Lance," Jenny put in, "even by teenage boy standards." She smiled to put him at ease.

Arthur frowned. "You only just met this girl, son. You know nothing of her true nature, or her motives. Did she become intoxicated, as well?"

"Yeah, but Dad it's only alcohol. It's not like we were doing any drugs. What could happen? Didn't you ever get drunk when you were my age?"

Arthur nodded sadly. "Alas, once, when I was sixteen and newly crowned. I had no experience with women. Morgause used her charms to intoxicate me with mead, and then took me to her bed. That one night begat Mordred and the beginning of the end of Camelot. Yes, Lance, I did get drunk at your age, and it cost me my kingdom."

Lance and Ricky exchanged a look, but Lance wasn't about to give up. Bridget might prove that how he felt about Jack was a fluke, and he couldn't let her go.

"Nothing bad like that's gonna happen, Dad and I don't even wanna do that stuff right now. But Bridget really likes me, I could tell. You should meet her."

Arthur considered a moment. Jenny offered a small smile to soothe him. "I should like to meet her. Invite her for a visit."

Lance grinned. "You mean that?"

"Of course. Anyone of interest to my son is of interest to me."

"I'd like to meet her, as well," Jenny said, with a smile of her own.

Arthur's face clouded over. "Now, as for Michael..."

Lance blurted quickly, "It wasn't Michael's fault I got drunk, Dad." Too quickly. "Don't blame him."

Ricky eyed Lance with surprise.

"Sir Ricky? Your appraisal of Michael?"

Ricky glanced at Lance tentatively. "I think he's a jerkbag, but I was nervous and drinking was something to do to fit in. Michael could still be useful, you know, to write our proposition and all."

"He *can* be a jerkbag, Dad," Lance put in impulsively, "I even told him that. But there's something about him..."

"That reminds you of Jack?"

Lance looked down at the floor.

"I have a bad feeling about Michael, Lance, something I cannot pinpoint. However, I will allow him access to our computer lab to write the proposition, provided you and Ricky watch him at all times. But you may not go out of New Camelot with him."

"Are we grounded?" Lance asked in surprise. Arthur looked puzzled. "Grounded?"

"He means, are you punishing us?" Ricky explained.

"Neither of you has ever given me any prior need for punishment. I shall hope last night to be an aberration that will not be repeated, though the repercussions of this one event could be long-lasting."

Lance couldn't believe his good luck. "We'll never do it again, Dad. I promise."

Arthur nodded, his face sad. For some reason, that sent a chill of fear rippling along Lance's back.

"Report to Reyna in the Computer Lab. Both of you."

Lance frowned. "Uh, does Reyna know about last night?"

Arthur nodded.

"Oh, crap, I thought you said we weren't being punished."

Arthur remained silent. Lance exchanged a nervous look with Ricky, then both boys bowed and left the Throne Room.

The Computer Lab was fairly busy for a Sunday. Those knights who arrived early for religious service, which Lance and Ricky had missed due to their hangover, often remained to add details or videos to the website. Enrique and Luis were working on their t- shirt business, checking orders and sales numbers.

Reyna sat beside Merlin, showing him how to navigate the Internet, while Esteban checked new website postings with Sir Techie. When Lance and Ricky entered, everyone paused to look their way, and all conversation ceased. Reyna smiled, but Lance could see it was forced.

"Welcome, brother. Come on in. I'm just showing Merlin how to find things with Google."

The boys exchanged a guarded look and then crossed the room to the computer station where Merlin and Reyna sat. Lance briefly noted Merlin's Led Zeppelin shirt, but mainly felt the power of every eye in the room tracking his movements. Something was up, and he didn't think he was gonna like whatever it was.

He tried to smile, but the pounding in his head wouldn't let it come out right. "Morning."

Reyna smirked, looking uncannily like a female version of Michael. "You don't look so good, little brother. Headache?"

Lance scowled, but knew better than to be a smart-ass with her.

Merlin turned to the boys, "This Internet is the most amazing of inventions, Lance. A marvel even I could not have foreseen."

Lance shrugged noncommittally. "Yeah, it's pretty cool." What were they were up to?

"For example," Merlin went on conversationally, "Reyna has demonstrated — not that I didn't already know — your culture's rather obsessive fascination for celebrities and their personal lives."

Merlin pointed to the screen. Lance and Ricky shifted positions so they could look over the wizard's shoulders. Within the Google search box was the name 'Celebrity Scandals'.

Lance noted the web pages devoted to famous actors and singers. The headlines were almost the same: 'Is he gay?' 'Celebs gone wild.' 'So and so has a new boyfriend or girlfriend.' 'This or that celebrity seen partying.'

Lance didn't understand why they were showing him this stuff. He didn't care about celebrities. "So?"

Reyna gazed at him solemnly. "These people are all famous, Lance, and famous people give up their privacy. They can't do anything without being photographed or reported on. Are you getting the picture here?"

"You mean me, don't you?"

"You were probably at least as famous as these people before you... died. But after you came back, Lance, you instantly became the most famous person in the world."

Merlin eyed him knowingly. "You are savior to some, devil to others. But you are unknown to no one on this earth."

"That's not my fault!"

Reyna tried for a sympathetic expression. "Nobody said it was. It's just a fact. What you did last night not only made *you* look bad, but the rest of us too. Lance, you can't do stupid things like regular kids. None of us can or we'll bring down Arthur and the whole crusade."

Lance looked abashed, and the headache constricted the blood supply to his brain, making it hard to focus. "I know that, Reyna, and I apologized to Dad already. I told him it wouldn't happen again."

Reyna and Merlin exchanged a look. Even Esteban and Sir Techie looked over.

A chill rippled through Lance. "What?"

"Merlin, Google 'Sir Lance'."

Merlin did so. The first page alone caused Lance, and Ricky, to gasp. Websites or blogs or threads appeared with such titles as:

'The Boy Who Came Back – good or evil?'

'The Boy Who Came Back can work miracles, witnesses say.'

'Sir Lance and Sir Jack: Lovers?'

'Sir Lance Parties Hearty.'

'Sir Lance's Girlfriend?'

'Sir Lance Gay?'

'Sir Lance Bisexual?'

'Sir Lance's New Boyfriend?'

Lance's jaw dropped open and felt the blood drain from his face. "What the hell..."

He reached out to take the mouse and clicked on the "Sir Lance and Sir Jack: Lovers" link. A page opened up showing pictures of him and Jack holding hands right before he died. Other pictures showed Jack pressing Lance's hand to his heart. Still others showed them in Hollywood, hugging in that little alcove, walking together, sitting on bus benches. There was even one of them sleeping huddled together against that building on Santa Monica Boulevard.

Lance scanned the story and found "witnesses" who said they'd seen them kissing, which Lance knew wasn't true because they never had, not until they were locked in R's bathroom. The two boys were now dubbed "Sir Lack," combining both of their names.

Feeling even sicker than he had upon awakening, Lance dropped into a chair, and a stunned Ricky leaned close to the monitor to get a better view.

Merlin exited that website and clicked on images and videos. The screen filled with shots of Lance from the previous night's party. Lance raising the bottle to his lips; Lance locking lips with Bridget, but photographed over her shoulder to make sure his face was clearly visible; Lance posing with girls and boys feeling his muscles, hands on his shirt or planting kisses on his cheeks. The worst were the pictures of Michael kissing him. As with Bridget, these were taken from behind Michael, so only Lance's face was visible. All that could be seen of Michael were his broad shoulders and scruffy blond hair.

Ricky opened a YouTube link to a video of Lance and Michael dancing and kissing. Comments beneath this were vicious:

'faggots!'

'Lance is disgusting .'

'I knew that boy was too good to be true.'

'I used to look up to Lance, but he's just a party boy. Boo!'

Dead silence filled the room.

Lance's head throbbed, and his heart pounded. "Oh my God...I had no idea, Reyna, I swear. I didn't know...I didn't think..."

Reyna looked soberly at him, not angry, but very serious. "No, you didn't. But in just one night, you managed to take over the media spotlight. Is Sir Lance gay? Who's that boy he's kissing? Who's that girl he's making out with? Is he a party animal? Did we misjudge Sir Lance? Is Sir Lance a hypocrite? Is—"

"Enough, Reyna!" Lance exclaimed, exacerbating the pounding in his head. "I get the point. I screwed up."

"I did, too, Reyna" Ricky threw in quickly, leaping to Lance's defense. "I should've been watching him better."

Reyna nodded, but said nothing.

Merlin placed a gentle hand on Lance's shoulder. "What's done is done, Lance. You cannot take back a mistake, merely refrain from repeating it."

Lance looked at the older man, and tears welled in his eyes. "This is all your fault! I *never* wanted to come back! I wanted *Jack* to live. This never would've happened if you just let me die like I was supposed to!"

"There's the rub, Lance. You *weren't* supposed to. I corrected a mistake."

"No. You made everything worse. I'm a screw-up, and I'm gonna ruin everything Dad and the rest have been doing. God, I'm so pathetic. Reyna, yell at me, please. I know you want to. I deserve it!"

Reyna eyed him with compassion. "No, baby boy, you don't. This is a set-back for us, yes, but it isn't terminal cancer. You made a mistake, that's all. I've made a few in my time." She tried for a smile.

"This is worse. Everybody in the world already thinks I'm a freak, Reyna. Either I walk on water or I'll send 'em to Hell with a bolt of lightning. Now I'm a drunk, a player, a queer boy, and a hypocrite too." He glared at Merlin. "You're wrong, Merlin. I should've stayed dead!"

He leaped up and bolted from the Computer Lab. Ricky glanced at Reyna and Merlin in embarrassment.

Reyna threw up her hands. "Well, don't just stand there, go after him."

Ricky pelted after Lance.

Reyna moved to Esteban. "You talk to him, Este, you know, one of those guy talks. Tell him the stuff you used to do. Tell him we're all behind him and we can get through this."

Esteban looked ill at the prospect. "C'mon, Reyna, you know I'm no good at that kind a thing."

Reyna leaned in and kissed him. "You don't need to be good at it, Este. Just be you."

He nodded and exited the room.

Reyna and Merlin exchanged a look of concern. "Did we make things worse?"

"I fear we may have, Reyna. But Lance had to know, and it had to come from us. Give him time, and support."

Lance made his way to the upper-most floor and then out onto the roof of the hotel. He strode to the very parapet and jumped up onto it, gazing down at the city eight stories below. Hair blowing in the cool afternoon breeze, he paced the narrow wall, clenching and unclenching his fists.

Ricky burst out onto the roof, breathless. "Lance!"

Lance stopped and looked down at Ricky, who stepped forward with caution.

"What you doing up there, man? Get the hell down 'fore you fall."

"I'm a skater, Ricky. I don't fall." Lance turned away, hair in his face. "'Less I want to."

"Lance, please," Ricky implored quietly. "You're scaring me, and I hate being scared."

Lance kept his eyes fixed out over the city.

"So you'd just kill yourself, after everything Jack did to save your sorry ass?"

Lance spun his head around. "Don't you talk about Jack!"

Ricky looked stung by Lance's anger, but didn't lash out. "I know he thought you were better than he was."

Lance stared down at his best friend, someone who, in just a few months, had become invaluable to him, and regretted his harsh tone. "He was wrong. He was a thousand times better. But he *was* right when he said we're kids, and kids screw up. I'm a screw up, Ricky, don't you get that? Dad was wrong to make me First Knight."

"Lance, we both screwed up, me even more 'cause I was supposed to be watching out for you."

"You're not The Boy Who Came Back, Ricky. I'm the one everybody expects to be perfect. But I'm just a kid, man. Just a screwed up kid who doesn't even know if he likes girls or boys. Why am I even still here?"

Ricky moved closer, but not too fast. "Remember the book I gave you for your birthday?"

"Yeah. So?"

Another step. "When I was on the streets, Lance, and saw you on the Net doing all the amazing things you were doing, like when you gave that speech about how us kids were gonna make the world better, I bought it all, man."

He gazed up at Lance, squinting his eyes against the glare of the sun. "I didn't meet you by accident. I heard on the streets you was looking for Mark, so I made sure to be out there that night. When we met, everything I hoped about you turned out to be true. You *were* the Ivory Tower. You gave me hope. That's who you are. That's why you're here. That's why you came back, 'cause us kids need you. You're epic, man."

Lance smiled, in spite of himself. "That's the most I ever heard you say at one time. Maybe you ought to give the speeches, not me."

"Hell no!" They laughed. "But I'll stand by you, like I promised. And we'll get through this. And I'll still kick your ass in wrestling."

Lance smiled. "You and what army?"

Ricky held out his hand. Shyly, Lance took it and jumped down off the ledge. They looked at each other a moment, and then a cleared throat caused both to pull their hands apart quickly.

Esteban stood in the doorway. "Sir Ricky, lemme talk to Lance a minute."

Ricky nodded, and reentered the building.

Lance gazed soberly at Esteban, who approached slowly, as though uncertain what to say.

"You gonna chew me out, too?"

Esteban shook his head. "Hell, no, Lance, not after all the crap I pulled at your age."

"Like what?"

Esteban actually looked embarrassed, something Lance had never seen, and shuffled his feet. "Robberies, drive-bys, drug deals, drunk-ass parties, drugs, hangovers, sex with any female that let me."

Lance's eyes widened. "Really?"

"Really. And I ain't proud a none of that, Lance. Back then I was... hell, I had sex with an eighteen-year-old when I's thirteen. Used to think I was all big and bad. Truth was, I was too scared *not* to do those things 'cause of the homies. It's that peer pressure thing, I guess."

"What's it like, Este, with a girl?"

Esteban looked surprised. "You sound like you done it with guys before. I, well, I thought you were a virgin, Lance."

Lance shook his head sadly, the childhood memories potent. "Not since I's six years old, Este."

Esteban's stoic face crumpled into shock, and Lance filled in the horrified ex-gang member on his past.

The bigger boy listened, his posture stiffening with each sickening detail. "No wonder your head's screwed up."

Lance scowled. "Thanks."

Esteban looked apologetic. "Sorry, man, didn't mean it like that. Look, Lance, yeah I had sex at your age, but it sure as hell didn't make me a man. What made me a man was, well, to be honest, Arthur and this crusade. And Reyna." He paused a moment, and sighed. "You know, I wish *I* was still a virgin."

That stunned Lance. "You do?"

Esteban nodded. "Cause whenever Reyna and I, well, you know, that'll be how it's supposed to be, making love, not hooking up."

Lance's eyebrows shot up. "You mean you and Reyna haven't...?"

"No more hookups for me, Lance. I want the real deal. And I think I found it."

Lance nodded, cocking his head slightly, seeing Esteban in a brand new light. "What's it feel like, Este, being in love?"

Esteban smiled and it lit up his face like sunshine. "It's amazing. It's hard to explain. She makes me smile just when I think of her, and you know me – I hate smiling. And I, well, I think about her all the time, and hardly never think about me no more. And I'm gonna tell you something else, Lance, but if you ever tell Reyna I'll kick your ass, even if you are a better fighter than me."

"Not a word."

"I'm gonna marry that girl someday, if she'll have me."

Lance's jaw dropped open. "Really?"

"Really. Look, Lance, none of us care if you're into girls or guys, okay? We follow you 'cause you're the most badass kid we've ever known, down for a fight when you got to, but right up there caring about everybody when you need to. None of us ever seen nobody like you. You don't gotta prove nothing to no one."

"What about to myself?"

"You wanna prove something to yourself by gettin' drunk and banging some chick and hoping that'll change how you felt about Jack?"

Lance flicked his eyes up to the other boy's face, stunned. "You knew?"

"I got eyes, man. So do the rest a the guys."

"But nobody said nothing."

"That's what I been trying to tell you, Lance. Nobody said nothing 'cause it don' matter, man, and it never will. And you know something else?"

Lance leaned in, wanting to know everything.

"Jack an' me, not so different, man. Gangsters and gay boys're more alike than we wanna admit."

"How?"

"Both paranoid, always watching our backs, always worrying about what others think of us, holdin' our breath just waiting for the next time we get jumped or disrespected. So yeah, Jack an' me, not so different, 'cept I could get out, and he couldn't. I got tired, Lance, tired of trying to prove myself to people who didn't matter, 'cause none a them gave a crap about me."

Lance knew his mouth must have been hanging open. He'd never thought about big, bad Esteban, in that way.

"And you wanna know what else I think?"

Lance nodded.

"Find yourself someone like that badass Ricky boy who'd fight a whole army to protect you. Whether you know it or not, man, he's already making you better. That's what you need, like what I got with Reyna. And it don' matter to us if you pick male or female." He gazed solemnly a moment into Lance's shocked face. "Don't screw yourself over 'cause you're afraid of stuff like that. You're too important. We need you, *carnal*, just the way you are."

Then he strode to the door and reentered the building without another word.

Lance stood there dumbfounded, but also encouraged.

When he went back downstairs, he found Arthur and Jenny conversing with Helen in the Throne Room. When he eyed Helen quizzically, Arthur stepped forward.

"Lance, Lady Helen has informed us that there are a large number of media out front seeking answers to the images of you from last night."

Lance's face fell in shock. "Already?"

"Word travels fast on the Internet, Lance." She gazed at him sympathetically.

"Lady Helen feels it best that you answer their questions before more rumors begin to spread."

Lance silently cursed his stupidity. And his head was killing him. What he really wanted to do was go up to his room and turn off all the lights and sleep. "Dad, do I have to? I'm still—I still have a headache and..."

"I'll be out there with you, Lance," Helen offered reassuringly, "to try and steer the questioning away from the usual tabloid stuff they like to ask."

"This will not easily vanish, son."

Lance glanced at Jenny, and saw how much she hurt for him, and then looked abashed at Arthur.

"Did Merlin and Reyna show you those pictures?" Arthur nodded silently.

"I'm so humiliated, Dad. I really let you down. Big time."

Arthur strode forward to embrace him. "No, son, you have not let me down. You slipped and fell. Is it not my job as your father to help you rise again to your feet?"

Lance looked up, and Arthur gave him an encouraging smile.

"I love you, Dad," Lance gushed.

"I love you, as well, son. Shall we?"

He indicated Helen waiting by the large double doors. Lance sighed. With Helen in the lead, they met Reyna, Este, Ricky, and Merlin in the lobby by the front door. Apparently they'd all been alerted to the media onslaught.

Helen offered Lance a smile of encouragement and pulled the doors open. They strode out onto the front stoop and down the short cobbled pathway to the main gate.

Reporters shouted questions and cameras began rolling, but the locked gates kept everyone at bay. Helen and her cameraman were the only ones who'd been admitted to the grounds. Lance and the others approached the fence through which a barrage of questions was being flung at him.

Helen held up a hand for quiet. Gradually, everyone settled down.

"Arthur has given Sir Lance permission to answer some questions. Arthur, would you like to make a statement first?"

"Thank you, Lady Helen. I granted my son permission to go out last night with his friend, though I did not know they would be at such an event, or that such events be so commonplace amongst the youth of today. Having said that, I stand by my son. He—I believe the current terminology is—*messed up* last night, and he has apologized. He is not a hypocrite as some have said on the Internet, nor is he a *bad kid* as others have said. He proved to me very early in our crusade to be a boy of many gifts, but he is still a boy and far from perfect. I remain exceedingly proud to be the man he calls 'Dad'."

Lance looked gratefully toward Arthur, who grinned at him and nodded.

Helen stepped forward with her microphone, her cameraman training the whirring camera on Lance's agitated face. "Sir Lance, would you like to say something before we open it up to questions?"

Lance winced under the bright January sun. "Uh, yeah. Like my Dad said, I messed up, big time. I never been to a party before. I never even drank before 'cause a my skating and all. And not being twenty-one, of course. I guess I don't handle alcohol so good and I lost control. I'm sorry if I let anybody down. It won't happen again."

He finished, and hands instantly flew up. Lance pointed to one. The man asked, "Who was that girl you were kissing, Sir Lance? Is she your girlfriend?"

Lance blushed. "No. I just met her."

Lance pointed to another reporter, a guy who looked disturbingly like Richard. Same shade of yellowish blond hair. A chill rippled down his back. It wasn't Richard, but all the same... Fighting to suppress the rising memories, he attempted to focus on the man's question.

Yellow Hair gazed through the fence looking far too smug for Lance's taste. "What can you tell us about the boy you were making out with, Sir Lance?"

Lance blanched. "Nothing. I was drunk."

Yellow Hair leered slightly. "Are you gay, Sir Lance?"

Lance paled, and his heart hammered with fury. "The hell?"

Alarmed, Arthur stepped forward. "Lance..."

Lance whipped his head around to his father. "No, Dad, he got no right to ask me that!" He turned back to Yellow Hair. "What the hell is wrong with you, asking a kid something like that? You some kind a pervert, is that it?"

Helen's face dissolved into panic and she quickly stepped between Lance and his view of Yellow Hair. "Lance, calm down..."

Now another reporter chimed in with, "We're just asking about what we saw in those pictures, Sir Lance."

Lance stepped around Helen and saw Yellow Hair smirking again. It made his blood boil. "This is why we kids are fighting for our rights, so scumbags like you can't harass us about personal crap like that and get away with it. You want some gay guy, man, go find one your own age. Screw this, I'm outta here!"

He whirled around and stalked back into the house. The pack of reporters went rabid, tossing questions at Arthur and Reyna and even Ricky. Helen leaned in to Arthur as reporters continued to hurl more questions at him. Arthur nodded and waved everyone back into the house, leaving the shouted questions unanswered.

They found Lance in the Throne Room, pacing angrily. Arthur said quietly to Helen, "Helen, give us a moment."

Helen stepped out into the hallway.

Arthur placed himself squarely in front of Lance and put both hands on his shoulders.

Lance shrugged him off.

"Lance. Be calm."

Lance's face bordered on livid and it scared Arthur. He'd never seen his son this way before.

"How can I be calm with people like that?"

"Alas, son, I do believe you gave them precisely what they wanted."

"What?"

"An angry, petulant youth whom they can easily paint a bad boy, a troubled boy, a boy losing control."

Lance forced calm back into his voice. "Maybe that's what I am, Dad. A boy losing control."

"No, son, you are merely a boy. As brilliant as you can be, as insightful, as good a teacher and mentor as you have proven yourself, you are first and foremost a boy. And I vividly recall being a boy. T'was not easy in my time, but in this era it seems to be a miracle of God to survive boyhood unscathed."

"I'm sorry, Dad. I know I keep saying that."

"No need for apologies, Lance, but you do understand that we must repair this damage, for you and the crusade."

"But how?"

"Lady Helen would like to conduct an interview here, in this room, wherein you calmly and without rancor share your feelings on what transpired last night and why. Can you do that, son?"

Lance considered a moment. "Yeah. Lady Helen still likes me."

Arthur's eyes twinkled. "Correction – Lady Helen still *loves* you."

Lance smiled, his heartbeat calming, the pounding in his head subsiding. Arthur waved him over to his usual chair beside the throne and went to usher Helen and her cameraman into the room. He asked the others to wait in the lobby so as not to distract Lance.

Helen eyed Arthur awkwardly. "Arthur, do you mind if I sit in your... throne?"

Arthur smiled and waved her over. Helen sat within the massive wooden throne, eliciting a smile from Lance. He already felt more relaxed just in her presence.

Helen smiled back. "Okay, Lance, I'll ask you some questions and you know I won't get overly personal or anything, but we have to address your outburst outside since everyone will see that on air very soon. Okay?"

Lance nodded.

Then Helen's face lit up and she grabbed her cell phone from her purse. "Hold up, Charlie," she told the cameraman, who was prepared to start rolling. She punched in a number. "Dave, Helen. I'm here with Sir Lance and King Arthur at New Camelot. I've got an exclusive interview about those embarrassing pictures. Lance didn't do so well with the rabid dogs out front and I thought maybe we could go live with this? Yeah, I know it's midafternoon on a Sunday, but this *is* The Boy Who Came Back and it *is* breaking news. Okay. I'll give Charlie the phone. Let him know when to roll."

She handed Charlie the phone.

Lance suddenly felt nervous. "This'll be live?"

Helen looked at him soberly. "It's best, Lance, before those scenes of you losing control make it on air. We can outmaneuver them with the real you."

Lance reluctantly nodded, still edgy.

Helen waited for her cue from Charlie. He gave her the thumbs up, tossed an encouraging grin at Lance, and shut off the phone. The camera light came on and he pointed.

"This is Helen Schaeffer for Channel 7 with a breaking news story. I am seated with the boy who came back, inside the Throne Room of New Camelot. Sir Lance attempted to answer some questions of my fellow journalists out front, but became flustered and angry at the intrusiveness of their inquiries. He's agreed to speak with me one on one to discuss the firestorm of controversy over some pictures and videos that have surfaced, many just last night. Sir Lance, how do you feel today?"

Lance grimaced. "Not so good, Lady Helen. I was drinking last night and I never done that before. I guess this is the hangover part." He looked shamefaced.

"I think most of us can relate, Sir Lance." She smiled warmly and that put him somewhat at ease. "So, let's start with last night. Can you tell us just what happened and perhaps enlighten us on some of those images we've seen, images that many feel have tarnished your reputation?"

Lance cleared his throat. "I, uh, well, I went with this friend of mine. Well, he's not a friend, really, 'cause I haven't known him very long, but I promised to hang out with him if he came to one of our meetings. I didn't really know what we was gonna do except go to some party."

"You had Sir Ricky with you, is that correct?"

"Sir Ricky is my backup, like my bodyguard in case anybody tries to mess with me. Mi—my friend had us wear these really tight shirts 'cause he said we'd look better. Even though I didn't want to, I did 'cause I never been to a party like that before and didn't know what to do." He blushed at that. "Anyway, everybody was like, all over me, and I was nervous. I didn't even know what to say or do. This one girl, she, like, took me aside and helped me get calm."

"Was that where the alcohol came in?"

Lance nodded. "It wasn't her fault. *I* did the drinking. Ricky, too. We were just so nervous and out of place and everybody kept looking at me. Anyway, I... well, I got drunk and, well, the girl and me made out a little and then one of the boys kissed me and danced with me and... Oh God, Lady Helen, this is embarrassing. I never drank before and I got so drunk I didn't even know what I was doing. And that's scary. I saw those pictures today and freaked. I didn't even know anybody was takin' 'em. I'm really sorry, and it won't happen again."

"How has your dad reacted?"

Lance smiled. "He's been amazing, like he always is. He loves me and stands by me. Oh, and I apologize to the guys I yelled at out front. My head's still kind a pounding and I just lost it for a minute."

"That's understandable, Sir Lance, especially given the blunt nature of their questions. Since much of what's been on the Internet these past few weeks revolves around you and the late Sir Jack, may I ask you about him?"

Lance stiffened, but nodded warily.

"You and Sir Jack were close?"

"He was my best friend, absolutely amazing."

"Were you and Sir Jack...that is, did you have feelings for him other than friendship?"

Lance froze, considering how best to answer that. "If you're asking did I love him, damn straight I loved him. He was the greatest man I'll ever know except for my Dad. But if you're asking were we boyfriends, the answer is no."

"Some photos show you two holding hands..."

Lance sighed. "Why is this country so nutty about boys holding hands or boys being gay?" He looked at Helen soberly. "Lady Helen, hold my hand, please."

He stretched out his hand and, caught off guard, she clasped it.

"Does this mean you and me are dating, Lady Helen?"

She almost blushed, but kept her aplomb. "Of course not."

"Exactly. Holding someone's hand is, like, the most basic human contact there is and, I don't know about you, Lady Helen, but sometimes I just need that from someone. So did Jack. Especially after we... lost Mark."

He pulled his hand back and she smiled.

"Good answer, Sir Lance. Anything else you'd like to add?"

"Yeah. I know some of you, well maybe a whole lot of you, out there, are disappointed in me. But not as disappointed as I am in myself. I know I'm The Boy Who Came Back— and thank you *so* much, Lady Helen, for that nickname."

He smiled to let her know he was teasing, and then turned back to the camera.

"I don't walk on water, and I can't do miracles. I don't know why God let me come back—and yes, it was God, not the Devil—but Jack gave his life for mine and I don't plan on lettin' him down again."

He let out a sigh. "I'm just a kid, everybody, just a fifteen-year-old kid who needs to figure out who he is and what his place is in this crazy world. I messed up, I know that, and I'll do my best not to mess up again. But if I do, stick with me. Please. I need you much more than you need me."

Helen smiled and faced the camera. "This is Helen Schaeffer live with Sir Lance at New Camelot."

The camera light went off and Helen gazed at Lance in wonder. "That bit with the hand holding was brilliant, Lance." She smiled. "We'll rerun this later, of course, and provide it to all the national and cable outlets. Hopefully, it will help polish up your image."

"Thanks, Lady Helen. You're the best, even though you did give me that annoying title."

Helen laughed.

CHAPTER SEVEN
I DON'T CARE WHAT PEOPLE SAY

IN THE SCHOOL ROOM THE following day, Lance and Ricky still felt the aftereffects of their drinking binge, but fought to pay attention to Jenny's teaching so they could assist the younger children.

After a quick lunch, they wanted to spar and wrestle in the Training Centre before Michael arrived to work on the proposition. Due to his behavior at the party, the idea of working together with Michael made Lance skittish, and he needed to burn off some of that nervous energy. After changing into their tank tops and workout shorts, the boys paid a quick visit to the Computer Lab. Lance needed to check on how his interview with Helen had gone over with the public.

As always, Sir Techie sat glued to his seat, fingers flying over the keys, gaze pinned to the flickering flat screen before him. As Lance navigated his way between the tables, he wondered, as he often did, if Techie even ate, since all his time at New Camelot each day seemed to be in front of his computer.

"Hey, Sir Techie."

"Sir Lance," Techie replied without looking away from the screen. "How goes the battle?"

"With geometry, not so good," Lance offered with a chuckle. "How goes the battle for my image?"

Sir Techie stopped what he was doing and rapidly Googled "Sir Lance." YouTube links instantly appeared of Lance ranting against the reporters outside, and others of his chat with Helen. Links popped up to almost every major newspaper headlining something about him, either yelling at the reporters or apologizing to Helen or commenting on his "bad boy behaviors," as they were now officially dubbed.

Lance felt heartened to see encouraging comments beneath the video links like 'You go, Lance. Stick it to those jerks!' or 'You're too cute to be a bad kid, Sir Lance.'

Of course there were some that were negative or just plain weird, like 'The Boy Who Came Back is really a space alien - that's why he can't handle liquor.' Nasty ones read along these lines: 'Pretty boy faggot!' or 'Shut up, Lance. We got all the proof we need in these pix' or 'Since you like boys, post up that girl's phone number for us real men.'

Then one comment caught Lance's eye, and he leaned in for a better look. It read, 'I don't care what people say, Sir Lance, you're my hero. All us kids mess up – I saw my brother do worse than you. I got cancer, Lance, and don't know if I'll even grow up, but if I do I want to be just like you. Hang in there! Your friend, John.'

Lance's heart pulled tightly in his chest. Cancer? "Did you see that last one, Ricky?"

Ricky nodded. "See, Lance, it's like I told you. Hope, man."

Lance smiled, saddened by the boy's message, but feeling a little better because of it.

"Could be worse, Sir Lance," Techie said, interrupting his thoughts. "I think your apology helped, but pix of you are still the most downloaded by a long shot."

Lance frowned. "I probably shouldn't ask, but can you tell which ones are the most popular?"

Sir Techie's fingers swept deftly over the keyboard and he brought up the website with the data he sought. "Looks like your most popular pic is the one of Jack holding your hand to his heart."

Seeing that image again made Lance's heart lurch.

Techie opened the next image. "Next would be...oh. The one where the dude is kissing you."

Lance groaned. "I don't wanna see any more. Thanks, Sir Techie."

He walked quickly from the lab. Ricky had to jog to keep up.

Lance and Ricky entered the workout arena. Some knights were already sparring or practicing at the indoor archery range. They spotted Esteban sparring with Chris and gave both the chin nod. Then they entered the armory just off the training area. No one was in there as they gathered up their weapons.

Ricky watched as Lance picked up his sword and shield, and sighed. "Lance, what're we gonna do about Michael?"

For some reason, that irked Lance. "Whadda you mean? We're gonna help him with the prop, just like Dad said."

Ricky shook his head. "That's not what I mean and you know it." He suddenly looked guilt stricken. "I lied to Arthur for you, Lance, and that man has done everything for me."

Lance glared, the hangover and his guilt clouding his better judgment.

"There's something wrong with Michael and you know it," Ricky went on in a whisper. "Hell, man, he kissed you twice, once in front of everyone."

Terror filled Lance as images of that video he'd seen of him and Michael flashed through his mind.

"What is it with you and Michael?" Ricky asked hesitantly. "Are you crushing on him?"

Lance instantly threw up his defensive walls. "Hell, no! I refuse to be gay, Ricky. I'm a real boy."

Ricky bristled. "And I'm not?"

"You said you weren't sure."

Ricky's face dropped in shock. "So did you!"

"Well, now I'm sure."

"Just because you kissed a girl?"

Lance didn't respond.

"If you're such a *real* boy, how come you kissed Michael, huh?" Ricky grabbed his sword and shield and exited the armory.

Fuming, Lance dropped his weapons and rushed out to tackle Ricky, knocking him to the mat and sending his sword and shield flying.

Chris and Esteban instantly stopped sparring.

"Lance, stop!" Chris shouted, but the boys heard nothing.

Ricky rolled immediately upon being struck, partially dislodging Lance and causing the latter's fist to strike the workout mat instead of his face. All of his wrestling skills clicking into gear, Ricky rolled out from under the enraged Lance and jumped on him before the other boy could recover, pinning him to the mat with his body weight, holding his hands down as best he could while Lance struggled like a trapped animal beneath him.

Esteban charged over and pulled Ricky off. Then Chris leaped into the fray and grabbed Lance as he rose to his feet. Lance was so angry that he threw Chris off and the boy fell hard to the mat. Chris gaped in horror at Lance, who suddenly realized what he'd done.

"What the hell's goin' on, Lance?" Esteban shouted, still holding the squirming Ricky in his iron grip. "And you, Sir Ricky, you're supposed to protect him, not beat him up!"

Ricky and Lance glared at one another, but Ricky ceased fighting and Esteban released him. The two boys panted and mad dogged one another.

Ricky looked livid. "Don't ever tell me I'm not a real boy. Ever!" He extended a hand to Chris. "C'mon, Chris, I'll spar with you."

Still shocked by Lance's behavior, Chris took Ricky's hand and got to his feet.

Lance was guilt-stricken. What had gotten into him? "Chris, I'm sorry, I'm really sorry."

Chris looked at Lance as though he'd never seen him before, and followed Ricky back into the armory.

Esteban gazed long and hard at Lance. "I'll work out with you, Lance. Looks like you need to cool down."

Lance waited for Ricky and Chris to exit the armory and move to another side of the Centre before he entered to retrieve his own armaments.

Neither Lance nor Ricky even looked at each other as they passed.

A little before three o'clock, Lance anxiously paced the lobby awaiting Michael's arrival. Over and over his mind replayed the fight with Ricky. What had gotten into him? They hadn't spoken to each other for hours, the longest non-communication between them since Ricky's arrival. And Lance felt the absence bitterly. Part of it, he knew was the residual hangover, part the nasty messages he'd seen posted up about him, but most of it was Michael. Or was it? Maybe it was Esteban's words on the roof yesterday, words that kept coming back to haunt him. Words about Jack, and Ricky. And him.

No. He pushed aside those thoughts. He was gonna make this thing with Bridget work. He had to. He could never become... He shuddered at the very idea.

Suddenly, he stopped up short, realizing Ricky was standing on the bottom stair gazing at him. He hadn't even heard him approach. They made eye contact, and Lance saw lingering hurt in Ricky's gentle brown eyes. And that nearly broke his heart.

Unable to stand the silence between them another second, he said quietly, "I'm sorry, man, for saying you weren't, you know, a real boy. You were real enough to kick my ass pretty fast." He smiled hesitantly.

Ricky broke into a grin, flashing the smile that always made Lance feel he was the only person on earth. "Damn straight."

They laughed and clasped hands, once more inseparable.

Then the doorbell chimed. Arthur and Jenny appeared from the hall leading to the Throne Room, apparently awaiting Michael's entrance. Lance hesitated, wondering for a moment how Michael might be dressed.

Arthur eyed him. "Lance, the door?"

Lance shrugged off his nervousness and pulled it open.

Michael stood on the stoop, dressed in another of those shirts that almost looked painted onto his skin. "Lance."

Ricky strode to Lance's side.

"And the always charming Sir Bodyguard." Michael's eyes narrowed. "May I enter, Sir Bodyguard?"

Ricky glared, but stepped to one side. Michael pressed his way past, and then Arthur and Jenny were there.

"Welcome back, Michael," Arthur said in greeting. He nodded to Jenny. She stepped forward with an extra-large tunic in black, which seemed to be Michael's favorite color.

Jenny looked slightly uncomfortable as she held out the shirt. "You may wear this while here at New Camelot, Michael."

Michael smiled as he took the tunic and eyed it like he would a dishrag.

Arthur studied the boy. "It's protocol."

Michael shrugged. "Ah, well, when in Rome..." And he stripped off his tight shirt.

Arthur looked quizzically at Jenny and she said, "It's just an expression."

Michael handed Lance his shirt and made certain to flex as much as possible as he pulled the tunic over his head. He turned to Arthur and Jenny, spreading his arms wide. "Better?"

"Most certainly," Arthur said with a nod. "If I may have a word, Michael?" He indicated the direction of the Throne Room. Michael rolled his eyes before strutting past Arthur and Jenny down the hall and into the room. Arthur turned to Jenny. "Jenny, would you escort Lance to the Computer Lab, please?"

Lance didn't like the sound of that. "I thought you wanted me in charge of Michael."

Arthur gazed firmly at him. "Sir Ricky shall escort Michael. Please go on ahead and log in to the website Samuel has authorized us to use."

Lance nodded dutifully and followed Jenny out of the lobby.

Arthur looked Ricky right in the eye. "Watch Michael like a hawk, Sir Ricky. I do not trust him."

Ricky agreed, pleased that Arthur didn't like the jerkbag, either.

Arthur entered the Throne Room and closed the double doors. When he turned, he found Michael seated in Lance's chair. Knowing the boy was testing him, Arthur remained nonplussed as he strode casually forward.

"That chair is, and always shall be, for Lance alone, Michael."

Michael rose slowly, challenging the king with his stare, as though daring the man to get physical. Arthur merely stared at him until Michael smiled.

"You don't like me, do you, King Arthur?"

"I do not know you, Michael, but your attitude, tone, and posture speak of one who is arrogant and strong-willed."

"You got that right."

"I am appreciative of your desire to assist us, Michael. Your knowledge can be a great asset to our cause. However, should I ever feel you to be a threat to my son or anyone else within these walls, you shall have me to answer to."

Michael bristled, puffing out his chest. "Is that a threat?"

Arthur just smiled. "Nay. Merely a promise."

Michael looked him straight in the eye. "I like a man who lets me know where he stands. Anything else?"

"No. Sir Ricky will escort you to the computer lab."

Michael rolled his eyes, but wisely said nothing. As he crossed the room to the double doors, he turned back. "You worried I'll hurt the famous Sir Lance?"

"You have already hurt him, Michael, with your party," Arthur responded, his gaze pinned fiercely to the boy's face. "Tread cautiously, young man."

Michael exited the room.

In the lobby, Ricky stiffened as Michael strode haughtily up to him. "Well, Sir Bodyguard, I do believe his highness wants you to escort me. I might steal the tapestries or something."

"You're a jerkbag, Michael."

"Yes, Lance already covered that. A rather quaint term, but I like it. And your point?"

Ricky made direct eye contact, not about to be intimidated by the larger and stronger boy. "I've seen how you look at him."

Michael tilted his head in wonder. "I'm not in the mood for riddles." He started down the hall.

Ricky rushed on ahead and stopped Michael with a hand to the chest. "You hurt him, Michael, you even *try* to hurt him, and I'll kill you."

Michael pulled a face of surprise, and then laughed disdainfully as Ricky lowered his hand. "You got a couple of brass ones, bodyguard, I'll give you that." Then his brow furrowed, and his face darkened. "But you ever touch me again and it'll be the last thing you do on this earth."

Ricky stood his ground, but the savage look in Michael's eyes chilled him to the core. He turned and led Michael down the hall.

Lance sat before a computer terminal. His phone beeped. He pulled it out and found a text: 'Hey Lance. Bridget. Michael gave me your number.'

Lance smiled, but also tensed because now he knew for sure Michael had been sending those 000000000 texts. He typed: 'Hey urself. How r u?'

The answer appeared. 'Good. Sorry about the party. Didn't pay attention to all the camera phones. Damn technology. Lol'

Lance thumbed in: 'No worries. When can I see you again?'

'When Michael says so."

Lance frowned and typed: 'What's Michael gotta do w/it?'

This message appeared: 'Michael calls the shots, Lance. Oh, my mom's calling. Later'.

The screen went blank. Lance frowned. What did that mean, Michael calls the shots?

As though on cue, Michael entered the lab with Ricky. The look on Ricky's face told Lance they'd had some kind of altercation, but he'd find out about that later. Michael was his usual smug self as he plopped into a chair beside Lance, and Ricky glowered as he headed over to Sir Techie's station.

Michael grinned. "Ready to rock and roll, Lance?"

Lance said, "I wanna see Bridget again, but she said you call the shots. What's that mean?"

"Just what it says. I'm the alpha. I call the shots for my posse."

Lance wanted to argue, but then thought of how he called the shots, essentially, for the Round Table, and decided not to get into a war of twisted words with Michael.

"Okay, so when can I see her again?"

"You already kicked it up pretty badly with last weekend's party. Best to wait."

"I didn't mean at a party. I wanna invite her over here."

Michael shrugged. "We can arrange that. Long as I'm here, too."

"Why, Michael? Are you jealous?"

"Of course not, Lance. Bridget and I are old news."

Lance froze. "Uh, how long did you guys date?"

Michael scoffed. "I don't *date*, Lance. I see something I want and I take it." Michael's hand settled on Lance's leg, close to his crotch.

Lance's breath stopped, and his heart leapt into his throat. It suddenly wasn't Michael touching him... it was Richard! Touching and whispering how good he could make little Lance feel. And then his bedroom – darkness around him. Only the nightlight illuminating his humiliation. And the pain. The searing, burning pain. And the sock in his mouth to stifle his cries. And Richard's cooing voice, "You like that, don't you, my little fagboy..."

Ricky returned and saw everything. "Get your hand off him!"

Michael complied without question. His eyes narrowed as he watched the erratically breathing Lance.

Ricky put both hands on Lance's face. He forced Lance to meet his gaze. "Lance, it's me, Ricky, man. Snap out of it. You're okay. I got you."

Lance's eyes seemed to gaze at something horrifying before finally focusing on Ricky and actually seeing him. "Ricky? Where am I?"

"Computer lab, man." Ricky removed his hands from Lance's face. "You had a flashback. You're okay."

Lance gulped and nodded, reassured by Ricky's voice, his thudding heart beginning to ease. "Thanks, man. I'm good now."

Then he turned and saw Michael scrutinizing him. The smugness was gone. The arrogance was gone. Michael's expression was unreadable.

The blond boy eyed him a moment longer. "You okay to work, Lance?"

"Yeah. I'm good. Let's do this."

Michael nodded.

For the rest of the afternoon, they worked on the proposition. The three boys focused on the content of the prop and Michael translated that into legalese that would pass muster with the state. Lance was astonished by Michael's knowledge of the law and his writing skills. The arrogance vanished completely as the intellectually gifted Michael dove headfirst into the project, and the boys actually enjoyed themselves, even laughing at their temptations to slip cheeky little asides into the prop to see if anyone would catch them.

Before they knew the time, it was almost six and they found themselves alone in the Lab. Everyone else had gone to dinner. The Kabbalogy Center maintained its own kitchen staff and operated the dining rooms as restaurants for visiting celebrities. Random drop-ins were no longer allowed and reservations were a must.

Arthur and his residents preferred to eat in the smaller, less ostentatious dining room for breakfast and lunch, but dinner was always served in the Renaissance

Restaurant, and the food was excellent. Hotel guests were once more in residence, most of them rich and privileged folk who wanted to be seen with the famous King Arthur or the even more famous Boy Who Came Back.

As they saved their work and stood to stretch, Lance felt good about how far they'd gotten. He stared hard at Michael, giving him a look of deep admiration. "You're pretty amazing, Michael, knowing all that stuff."

Ricky eyed Lance, and scowled. "Yeah," he agreed, trying to keep the sour note out of his voice.

Instead of crowing like Lance expected, Michael just nodded, looking at him with an expression Lance couldn't quite fathom.

"Uh, you wanna stay for dinner?" Lance asked before he could stop himself. "They got some really good cooks here."

"Sure. Why not."

Lance smiled, wondering again what it was he saw in Michael's eyes that made him think there was more to this boy than the arrogant jerk he played so well. He led the way, Michael followed, and Ricky brought up the rear.

Lance led Michael up to his room. Ricky followed them and silently opened the connecting door to his own so he could wash up for dinner.

Michael watched him go. "Cozy, that connecting door. You and bodyguard can have all sorts of fun without anyone knowing."

Lance reddened, but said nothing as Michael spotted *Frankenstein* and *The Neverending Story* on Lance's nightstand. "You read Frankenstein yet?"

"Started it."

"Let me know when you finish. Interested in your take." That surprised Lance, but he remained silent. Michael picked up *The Neverending Story*. "This book kicks ass too. You reading both?"

"Yeah, Chris likes Neverending Story, so I read him some every night."

Michael nodded approvingly, all trace of arrogance gone from his face. Then he eyed the king-sized bed and the smarmy look returned. "Now *that's* a bed, Lance. You could have a veritable orgy on that bed."

Embarrassed, Lance pointed to the bathroom. "Bathroom's in there, Michael. You go first."

Michael turned to him with an inviting grin. "We could wash each other, if you want."

Lance scowled. "No, Michael."

Michael shrugged and stepped past Lance to enter the bathroom.

Lance sighed. Then he stepped into Ricky's room and stopped short when he saw Ricky shirtless at his bathroom sink, washing his hands. Involuntarily, his eyes did a quick once over of Ricky's torso and toned six pack.

Ricky looked over, disconcerted. "Lance, you startled me, man."

Lance shook his head to clear his thoughts. "Sorry, Ricky. Michael's back to his old self, making me uncomfortable and stuff, so I came in here. Figured I could wash up with you."

Ricky smiled. "I guess the straight-up Michael is like Dr. Jekyll from those movies, huh? Only shows up once in a while."

Lance laughed. "You got that right. Can I?"

Ricky moved to one side of the sink so Lance could stick his hands beneath the faucet. They playfully jostled each other under the water, like two little boys trying to one-up the other. Both laughed and began splashing each other, until a cleared throat drew their attention to the door.

Michael stood there. "You guys are just too cute together. And Ricky boy's looking semi-buff. Not bad, bodyguard."

Ricky scowled. "Get out of my room, Michael. I didn't invite you."

"Oh yes, us bloodsuckers need an invitation, don't we?" He chuckled and returned to Lance's room.

"Can I change into one of your tunics?" Lance asked, a trifle hesitantly. "I mean, we're about the same size and I don't wanna take my shirt off in front of Michael."

"I get that. The perverted Mr. Hyde is back in full."

Their eyes held a long moment, and then Ricky hurried from the bathroom.

Lance removed his shirt and gazed at himself in the mirror. He and Ricky had strikingly similar builds, though Lance sported a bit more muscle since he'd been training with heavy weapons for longer. Ricky's return with a blood red tunic caught Lance off-guard, especially with Ricky's eyes fixed on his upper body.

"Lookin' pretty buff there, Lance," Ricky said, hesitantly handing over the shirt.

"Uh, thanks. I was thinking the same thing about you." He pulled the shirt over his head. "You think girls'll think we're built?"

Ricky grinned. "Damn straight."

Lance laughed. "You copying me now?"

"Lance, the whole world's copying you."

Lance punched Ricky on the shoulder. "Hopefully not copying what we were doing the other night."

Ricky agreed.

They re-entered Lance's room and found Michael lounging on the bed watching them.

"You can get off my bed now, Michael."

Lance extended his arm toward the door. Michael smiled before sliding off the bed and making his way into the hall. Ricky looked like he wanted to say something snarky, but Lance just grabbed his hand a moment and squeezed.

"Basic human contact."

Ricky nodded, squeezing Lance's hand and releasing it. They stepped out into the hall and led Michael down to the dining room.

Since New Camelot was also a fancy hotel, the dining rooms were set up in high style. Lance always felt like he was aboard Titanic or something every time he entered the Renaissance Restaurant. Tonight, it was almost full, with Arthur, Lavern, Techie and Chris sitting with hotel guests and chatting amiably, as well as holdovers like Reyna and Esteban, who would return home after dinner. They sat at a table with Darnell and Justin. Hotel guests filled in the other tables, and all eyes followed Lance as he led Ricky and Michael to Reyna's table.

"Hey, room for more?" he asked, uncertain as to their response. Esteban cast Michael a dirty look, and Reyna's expression would've melted cast iron.

"Of course, brother," Reyna answered icily, her glare boring into Michael. "Why not sit Michael next to me and you guys sit wherever."

Her tone indicated something was up, and even Esteban looked oddly at her. Lance pointed out the empty seat next to Reyna, and Michael sauntered over to sit down like he owned the place. Lance and Ricky sat across from them, in between Justin and Darnell, who nodded their hellos.

"So what epicurean delights would you recommend, *Lady* Reyna?" Michael asked.

Reyna turned to Michael with a forced smile. "In your case, Michael, may I suggest something with pig in it? How about pork chops?"

"The other white meat?"

"Everything here is quite tasty, Michael."

Michael eyed Lance. "I can see that."

Lance stared right back, struggling to comprehend this enigmatic kid who could be so brilliant one minute and disgusting the next.

Reyna placed a hand on Michael's thigh and leaned in close. "May I offer a word of advice?"

Michael glanced down at her hand on his leg. "Absolutely, Lady Reyna."

Reyna's smile broadened, her voice soft, but etched with steel. "You hurt my brother, I'll rip your balls off, shove them down your throat, and laugh while you choke to death."

Then she grabbed Michael by the balls, hard, and squeezed. He jumped and nearly cried out, his face screwed up with excruciating pain.

"Clear?"

Michael winced, his eyes tearing up. "Crystal," he croaked, and she released him, patting the angry Esteban lovingly on the leg and grinning at Lance.

Both Lance and Ricky had to refrain from busting up as Michael readjusted himself and forced composure back into his face.

"Let's order, shall we?" Reyna announced to the table at large.

To his credit, Michael said nothing more for the remainder of the meal, and everyone else settled into their usual relaxed, jovial personalities. Lance and Ricky jostled one another and even tasted some of each other's food, which had become a nightly ritual. Esteban and Reyna exchanged a knowing smile, as though they saw something no one else did. Michael eyed the behavior with a sour grimace.

The next few weeks passed without further drama from Michael. Sure, he was still smug and arrogant when Reyna wasn't around, but she'd taken it upon herself to be working on the website when Michael, Lance and Ricky worked on the prop. If she saw or heard Michael do anything rude, she'd casually walk past him and do a snip-snip motion with her fingers, smiling genteelly all the time. Michael always smiled right back, but he got the message, loud and clear.

Lance began texting Bridget with such regularity that he ignored Ricky more than he intended to. It was mostly at night, after dinner. Lance would lounge on his bed with his iPad and converse with her for an hour, sometimes two, either by Facebook messaging or Skype. He learned more about her likes and dislikes and the more he learned, the more he wanted to see her again. He vowed to get a date out of Michael that Bridget would be allowed to visit.

Lance also received more texts from the 00000000 number, mocking and teasing him and making inappropriate remarks. Michael denied all responsibility when confronted, but Lance was certain it was his way of getting around Reyna.

Sam dropped by to alert Arthur that a court hearing had been set up for the following month. He still believed that Lance and Ricky, at fifteen, wouldn't have much trouble with the court about remaining with Arthur until the adoption went through. But Chris's age could be a problem. DCFS might want to take him away to a foster home while awaiting the finalization of the adoption.

Lavern's mother had agreed to sign a legal document allowing him to stay with Arthur, as long as Lavern sent her money every month. Lavern wished more than anything that Arthur could adopt him, too, but his mother refused to allow that.

Bridget was finally able to visit New Camelot at the end of January. She bubbled with excitement when she met Arthur and Jenny, and they chatted amiably in the lobby. Esteban, Darnell and Justin all gave Lance the chin nod of approval, but Reyna acted very cool towards her.

Lance reached out to shyly take her hand for the tour of New Camelot. Reyna, Ricky, and Michael followed them, none looking happy at Lance's exuberant chattering about everything they encountered and his obvious excitement at being with her. Lance and Bridget talked and laughed as though the others weren't even present.

Utilizing the old female excuse of needing the ladies room to freshen up, Reyna took Bridget up to the bathroom she used whenever she stayed overnight, and shared some of her toiletries. Bridget gushed over how beautiful the hotel was and how nice everyone was and how Lance looked even more beautiful here than he had at the party.

Reyna pinned the other girl with her intense gaze. "What is it you want with Lance, Bridget?"

Bridget turned her face from the elegant vanity mirror. "What do you mean?"

Reyna folded her arms across her chest. "I know your type. Party girls who like picking up boys and playing with them awhile before moving on to the next one."

Bridget bristled with indignation. "You calling me a hoe?"

"Don't know that, but you're an opportunist."

"How am I that?"

"How old are you, sixteen, seventeen?"

"Sixteen."

"And you've been around with boys, I can tell." Before Bridget could respond, Reyna held up a hand. "Would you really be interested in Lance if he wasn't The Boy Who Came Back?"

Bridget shrugged. "Why not? He's hot. He's sweet. He's—"

Reyna cut her off. "He's the greatest trophy in the world. Who wouldn't want to brag that she screwed the famous Sir Lance, The Boy Who Came Back? Make you pretty popular, wouldn't it?"

Bridget looked offended. "It's not like that, Reyna. I'm attracted to Lance. I mean, who wouldn't be? But I'd never push him to do anything he didn't want to do."

Reyna looked dubious, but said nothing.

"He and I have been talking a lot the past few weeks, and he's not like any boy I've ever met. He's sweet and sensitive and really cares about other people, but he's still all boy, you know? I don't know how to explain it. He's just different, but in an amazing way. And he sure loves you."

That caught Reyna off-guard. "He talked about me?"

Bridget laughed. "He told me what you did to Michael."

Reyna's eyebrows shot up and the girls shared a conspiratorial chuckle.

"He adores you, Reyna, and loves having you for a big sister." Her face and tone grew serious. "Trust me, the last thing I want to do is hurt Lance."

Something in her tone convinced Reyna that her intentions were honorable. "I'm sorry for being so hard on you. But that boy is the most important person in my life other than Este, and I almost lost him. That's not gonna happen again if I can help it." Her eyes narrowed. "Hurt him, break his heart, and I'll rip yours right out of your chest."

Bridget blanched, but then Reyna offered a smile.

"But somehow I don't think you wanna hurt him. Still, my warning stands."

Now Bridget relaxed. "I'm happy he has you looking out for him. And Ricky is sweet, too."

Reyna nodded, her thoughts drifting to Ricky, hoping that sweet boy wouldn't be thrown under the bus with all of this drama.

"Ricky is, in his own way, as amazing as Lance, and those two fit together perfectly, like pieces of a puzzle."

Something in Reyna's tone caused Bridget to frown, but she didn't reply.

Then Reyna brightened. "We better get back or Lance'll think I drowned you in the toilet."

Bridget stayed for dinner and everyone had a good time, chattering and laughing. By the end of the evening, Bridget felt at home with Arthur and Jenny and all the knights. Even Reyna remained warm and congenial after their little showdown.

Michael and Ricky didn't say much during dinner, and as he watched Lance play around with Bridget, laugh and giggle and even sample each other's food, Ricky felt the odd man out for the first time since joining the crusade.

After dinner, Lance excitedly asked Arthur if Bridget could stay over-night since they had so many rooms, and tomorrow being Saturday she could hang out and attend the weekly gathering. Jenny instantly suggested that it was not a good idea, and Arthur agreed. Both adults clearly saw Lance's infatuation with the girl and did not seek to give him opportunities for more scandalizing behaviors.

Lance kissed her goodbye at the door. Arthur glanced at Jenny, who raised her eyebrows. Reyna looked casually at Esteban, who grinned, but Ricky flushed red with discomfort, and Michael's face was unreadable. Then, with a wave, Bridget was down the steps and gone.

Early February brought perhaps the biggest surprise visitor to New Camelot yet: former mayor Villagrana. He'd been in hiding from the media since his arraignment, while awaiting a preliminary hearing to determine if the case would go to trial. No one had seen nor heard from him since the beginning of the year.

Arthur was stunned to see the man on his doorstep. "Mr. Mayor."

Villagrana struck Arthur as looking humble, vulnerable even. The haughtiness was gone, the ego deflated. He wore a simple gray suit and ordinary tie. "I imagine you never expected to see me here, Arthur."

"True enough. Come in."

The mayor stepped over the threshold as though entering sacred ground, and Arthur ushered him down the short hallway to the Throne Room.

Villagrana took a vague interest in the surroundings. "You've greatly improved this place, Arthur, and your presence elevates it more to the standards of the old L.A. it sprang from."

The king nodded, and pointed to a chair.

"I prefer to stand."

"To what do I owe the honor of this visit?"

Villagrana scoffed, his usual smug facial expression now replaced with one of genuine regret. "Honor? More like a mea culpa, Arthur. I came because I know you've seen and heard everything on the news about my relationship with that man. I wanted to tell you in person that I had no idea he would try to kill you. He promised to stop your crusade, which I thought meant defuse it, marginalize you, discredit you somehow."

"In other words, the usual political dirty tricks, as I've heard them called."

"I'm not going to lie to you, Arthur, and my attorney would kill me for saying this, but I knew R. wasn't on the up and up. He never said how he made his money, but I knew he wasn't legit. I looked the other way because..."

When the man said nothing more, Arthur filled the vacuum. "Because you sought power?"

Villagrana nodded.

"In my experience, Mr. Mayor, men who eagerly seek power generally make the poorest of leaders."

"Arthur, what happened to Lance... I never expected... I never thought R. would hurt any of your kids, especially Lance. I hope you believe me on that score."

Arthur gazed deeply into the man's eyes. "I believe you. Is that why you're here, to apologize to my son?"

"Partly." Then Villagrana's face took on a look of awe. "And just to see him up close, you know, the miracle."

That response surprised Arthur, for he'd seen no previous indicator that this man had any spiritual leanings whatsoever. "I shall send him here to you."

Arthur called Lance and Ricky out of Jenny's classroom and informed them of the mayor's visit. Lance was surprised, but curious, and agreed to see the man. Ricky, of course, followed close on his heels. After everything that had gone down involving the mayor, Ricky refused to leave Lance alone with the man, and Arthur agreed.

When Lance entered the throne room, Ricky at his side, the mayor gazed at the boys in wonder.

"What?" Lance asked, checking his shirt to make sure he hadn't spilled something on it.

Villagrana shrugged. "You two look so alike, is all. How unusual." Then he collected himself and cast Lance a serious look. "Lance, may I speak with you alone?"

Ricky stepped in front of Lance protectively. "You were in with the guy who tried to kill Lance. I seen it on the news. I'm not letting him out a my sight, Mister Mayor."

The former mayor appeared stung by Ricky's assertion. "I would never hurt you, Lance."

Lance looked the man in the eye, and saw his soul. "It's okay, Ricky. I'll be all right. Do you mind waiting in the hall?"

"Are you sure, Lance?"

"Yeah. Thanks, man."

Reluctantly, Ricky left the Throne Room and closed the doors behind him.

The mayor gazed at Lance in wonder, as though seeing something beyond belief. "I watched you die, Lance, and you likely won't believe this, but my heart broke at that moment. I was never against *you*, just Arthur, and only because..."

"He made you look bad?"

"Because he did my job better than I did."

Lance nodded. That answer made sense to him. "Why did you want to see me?"

"I was raised Catholic, Lance, and heard all about miracles and saints and Our Lady of Guadalupe from my grandmother, but I haven't believed in any of that for decades."

He looked into Lance's eyes and scanned his face, as though convincing himself this moment was real. "You, Lance, you are a living miracle, and I saw it with my own eyes. You *were* dead, and yet here you stand. I don't know why, but if God saw fit to return you to us He must've had a damned good reason. I just want you to know I never intended, nor suspected, that any harm would come to you from R."

Lance scowled upon hearing the name of the man responsible for Jack's death. "How well did you know him?"

"Not well. He supplied the money for my campaign, and I did him favors, gave him zoning variances and the like. I never knew him at all."

"I did, from the streets."

The mayor's eyebrows shot up in surprise.

"He tried to get me to work for him, sell drugs and stuff. I told him no, and I guess no one ever did that before. I was on his hit list before I even met my dad. So I don't think you set me up. He already had it in for me."

Villagrana released an excited breath, and smiled, the most real facial expression Lance had ever seen on the man. "Thank you, Lance, for telling me that, but I still should've warned Arthur about R. If you had... well, stayed dead, I'd have had to live with that the rest of my life."

"Jack is still dead."

Villagrana looked stricken. "I know, and for that I'm truly sorry."

Lance studied him a moment. "Why are you here, Mr. Mayor? I might only be a kid, but I know you didn't just come here to tell me this stuff."

"You may be a kid, Lance, but you're smarter than most adults." He smiled slightly, and Lance nodded at the compliment. "I don't know what's going to happen to me, and I don't worry about it, because watching you come back like you did, well, now I know God is out there and I need to get my act together if I'm ever going to get the chance to meet Him. I know it's a lot to ask, given all I've done to hurt you, but would you be willing to pray over me?"

That caught Lance off guard. "What?"

"A prayer, Lance, for a repentant man."

Lance stared open-mouthed at the mayor, and saw the man was dead serious. "Why me?"

Villagrana knelt before him. "Because you're the one God sent back to us."

Lance shivered, suddenly feeling those creeping fingers of death grasping again at the fringes of his soul. "I don't much know how to pray."

"It's no matter. Just rest your hands on my head and I'll believe God might give me a second chance." Without awaiting Lance's response, he humbly bent his head forward and clasped his hands prayerfully at his chest.

Unsure, Lance hesitantly reached out and placed both hands on the bowed head of the mayor, who clasped his hands even more tightly at the touch. As was so often the case when push came to shove, Lance suddenly knew what to say.

"Father God, watch over this man who seems to want to make right all the wrongs he has done. If you can, Father God, forgive him for those wrongs, especially what he did against me, 'cause, well, I think he's sorry for it. Amen."

Lance removed his hands and Villagrana tilted his head up, looking genuinely touched. "Thank you, Lance. I shall try my best to be a better man. God knows I couldn't get much worse."

Then he stood and exited the Throne Room without another word. Ricky entered as the mayor hurried past him and down the hall toward the front door.

"So, what did he want?"

Lance looked at Ricky with astonishment. "A prayer."

Ricky tilted his head and Lance shrugged. Then he slipped out his phone and checked the time. Noon. He grinned.

"School's out, little Ricky, time for me to kick your sorry ass on the wrestling mat, and then with the sword."

Ricky grinned right back and punched Lance in the abs. "You and what army?"

Laughing, the two boys exited the Throne Room, shoving and jostling each other. They found Arthur descending the stairs.

"Did the mayor leave?"

Lance nodded. "And you know, Dad, he's different now, not as big a jerk as before."

Arthur smiled. "A miracle, isn't it?"

Lance grinned. "Yeah."

Lance, Michael and Ricky were nearly finished with their revised draft of the prop when Michael pointed out that if it passed, AMBLO would be very happy.

Lance eyed him with confusion. "What's AMBLO?"

"It's an acronym for American Man Boy Love Organization. They want to lower the age of consent so grown men can have legal sex with boys. This prop gives them that permission, at least if they find some hot fourteen-year-old they like."

Lance blanched with horror, Richard's face instantly assailing his consciousness. "Is that true, Michael, or are you just making that up?"

Michael looked oddly sincere, an expression Lance seldom saw on him. "On my honor. They'd like the age to be ten, but they'll settle for fourteen, I'm sure."

Ricky exchanged a look of dread with Lance. "We can't let that happen, Lance. But he's right. If fourteen years old is an adult, than any adult can have sex with any fourteen-year-old, girls too."

Michael snorted with disgust. "This is what's known as 'the law of unintended consequences'. Happens with lots of laws. Unless we put in some kind of clause forbidding anyone eighteen and older from having sex with fourteen-year-olds, it will be legal. And I'm not sure such a clause would pass legal muster. AMBLO could challenge it in court."

Lance looked white with fear, and Ricky equally dismayed. "Crap, Ricky, we never thought of that. Only thirteen and down would be safe from perverts like that."

Michael's voice turned cold. "No kid is safe."

Lance and Ricky eyed one another uncertainly, but when the older boy said nothing more, they quickly got to work limiting the rights fourteen-year-olds could have under their proposition.

They decided that this age group could only vote on statewide issues and offices, not federal; they could not give consent to have sex with adults eighteen or older; they could not drop out of school to join the military—because this was a state prop and would not apply to the Federal Government—unless the military specifically offered them a Job; they could drop out of school if school was not meeting their needs, but only if they obtained a job of at least thirty hours per week; they could only drive a car if they were tall enough to see clearly and reach the floor pedals. There were a few other minor restrictions, as well, but for the most part, if the voters passed this prop, fourteen-year-olds would finally have real rights and real power in California, including the power to sit on criminal juries and render verdicts. And if the people chose to vote 'no', all laws making kids under the age of eighteen adults for any reason became null and void as of January first, and no new such laws could be proposed.

They sent the finished draft to Sam for proofing, and he reported back to Arthur that the prop was flawlessly written, with not a single mistake, all clauses articulately explained and completely legal. Astonished at Michael's legal and writing acumen, he went ahead and filed it with the state Attorney General to get it approved for signature gathering.

Lance suggested posting the full text on the website and Facebook pages so people all over the state could read and "Like" it. He wanted to credit Michael with the writing, but Michael almost angrily forbade it. His name was to appear *nowhere* on the document or the Internet. He insisted Lance and Ricky take full credit—it was their ideas he wrote up, anyway.

"Not all of 'em," Lance insisted, but Michael remained adamant: if his name appeared anywhere, there would be hell to pay.

Lance agreed, as did Sam, though the attorney couldn't understand why Michael wouldn't want to take credit for such an outstanding piece of legislation.

"Better written than most by men my age, Michael," he told the boy admiringly. But Michael declined, and now Lance began to seriously wonder what Michael was hiding.

The days passed quickly, with the website and Facebook pages generating tons of attention, with school and training and getting the main points of the prop out to the public. Arthur called a press conference before anything was posted on line, and appeared with Lance, Ricky, Reyna, Esteban, Darnell, Lavern, Justin, Enrique, Luis, and Chris in front of New Camelot to officially announce the proposition. The kids excitedly told reporters when and where the prop would be posted for viewing and threw out a few of its main points.

That yellow haired guy was back, and asked Lance if any more parties were in the offing. Lance kept his cool and announced that his partying days were over.

"What about the girlfriend?"

"I'm working on that."

Everyone laughed.

CHAPTER EIGHT
WE WON'T GET CAUGHT

THE DAYS FOLLOWING THE ANNOUNCEMENT were a whirlwind of activity for everyone at New Camelot. Michael decided, despite finishing the prop, to continue showing up most days after school because he wanted to train with the sword, always asserting that he could beat Lance and Ricky combined, but never quite gaining the advantage over either. His size and strength ensured he never got knocked down, and seldom tired, but he only ever managed to fight either boy to a draw, and that seemed to annoy him.

Lance juggled school, physical training, and recording video spots for YouTube and the website encouraging kids all over the state to join their cause and support their fight for equal rights.

Kids throughout the state, and the whole country, for that matter, became part of the New Camelot family by way of the website and Facebook pages. They loved the live chats Lance held every few days for an hour after school. Many promised to learn the Code of Chivalry and join the Round Table. The crusade for children's rights was taking flight, and Arthur realized he would soon have to start traveling the state, meeting with kids and their parents, pitching the proposition, and knighting those youth who had prepared themselves. An old school bus had been donated to New Camelot for Arthur's travel needs, and plans began to be formulated.

In the wake of the prop announcement, celebrities and politicians inundated Reyna and Jenny with requests to drop in and chat with Arthur and Lance. After a few of these, Lance quickly discerned that many of the rich and famous merely wanted a photo-op to further their own public image, rather than out of any support for the crusade.

After discussing the problem with Ricky, Lance alerted Arthur not to meet with anyone who brought a photographer with him or her unless the celebrity signed an agreement that any proceeds from the photo would go to some charity. If anyone actually brought along a news camera or reporter—as some of the politicians did— the boys made the person in question promise, on camera, to support their crusade before allowing the cameraperson to record anything else.

Arthur had eyed Lance and Ricky with wonder when they'd offered this idea. "Very insightful. In this way they cannot later deny their allegiance to our cause."

The boys grinned with pride.

The Department of Children and Family Services came to New Camelot in early February to inspect the premises prior to issuing a report for the court regarding Arthur's bid to assume permanent custody of the boys. The social worker, youngish woman wearing a crisp business suit, introduced herself as Ms. Hanson.

Arthur greeted her warmly and introduced the three boys. She acknowledged them and asked to inspect the entire hotel. Arthur and his boys gave her a tour of the schoolrooms, the bedrooms, the kitchen and dining areas, as well as the Computer Lab and Training Centre. She said very little during the inspection, jotting copious notes while viewing the Training Centre, taking particular note of the armory.

Hanson interviewed each of the boys individually, and then interviewed Arthur alone. Sam had acquired birth certificates on all three boys and had made certain Arthur had a TB test during January to be ready for the hearing. All appropriate legal paperwork had been completed, and the due diligence to locate parents had been ongoing since December.

The initial court hearing took place the second week of February. Sam had informed Arthur and the boys that the purpose of this first appearance was to convince the judge to grant Arthur custody of the boys until the adoption could be finalized.

Arthur dressed in a modern light gray suit, picked out for him by Jenny. He squirmed beneath the tie and tight collar, and Jenny kept nudging him to stop. The boys were likewise dressed in new suits and, despite sharing Arthur's discomfort regarding their ties, looked "Very handsome," according to Jenny, who took great delight in adjusting Lance's hair or Ricky's tie or Chris's collar.

Sam met them all in the corridor outside the courtroom and reminded them, "Let me do the talking."

Reyna, Esteban and many other knights chose to show up in support and sat in the gallery. Sam led Arthur and the boys to a table in front and slightly to the right of the judge's bench. The boys eyed the Great Seal of the State of California, the massive judge's bench, the court reporter and bailiff with trepidation.

Sam gave a head nod to DCFS representative Ms. Hanson and her attorney, seated at the other table.

The bailiff instructed everyone to "Rise for the Honorable Judge Harold Baker."

Everyone stood as a portly, middle-aged man with thinning brownish hair and wearing a black robe entered from a door behind the bench and climbed up into his seat, looking out at the participants and spectators alike. The bailiff told everyone to sit.

Lance turned once to catch Reyna's eye, and she blew him a kiss. He smiled, feeling a surge of strength.

"Welcome King Arthur, and welcome boys," Judge Baker began jovially. "As everyone knows, this hearing will determine whether or not you boys may remain in Arthur's custody pending completion of adoption proceedings. Now this is Family Court and you boys will have an opportunity to speak. But it is customary to begin with DCFS. Ms. Kelly, as the attorney representing Department of Children and Family Services, you may present their report and recommendations."

Kelly stood. "Thank you, your Honor. DCFS has conducted its usual investigation into the suitability of Mr. Pendragon as an adoptive parent, including, but not limited to, examination of the living environment and schooling situation."

"And your findings?"

"Despite Mr. Pendragon's fame and obvious contributions to some of the poorer neighborhoods within the city, we have serious reservations about these boys remaining in his care."

Lance almost leaped to his feet, but Sam's meaty hand on his arm stopped him. He opened his mouth to speak, but Sam shook his head and gently lowered him back into his chair.

"Such as?" asked the judge. "It was my understanding today's hearing was a mere formality."

"The living conditions within New Camelot, as the former Kabbalogy Center has now been renamed, are, of course, quite adequate. Each child has his own room and access to privacy when bathing and dressing. However, it is still a celebrity 'hang out,' of sorts, and many of those people are not the best influence. While the home schooling set-up passes muster with the state, we always prefer to see children in regular school to obtain a proper education. Also, there are several workout areas within the hotel containing dangerous weapons, and even younger boys, such as Chris, are allowed access to those weapons. They wear protective clothing and are supposed to be supervised at all times, however, children have been known to break rules from time to time."

She paused a moment. "We fear Chris may gain unsupervised access to these weapons and hurt himself. In addition, Mr. Pendragon's own past is, shall we say, murky. We have no birth certificate, no paperwork of any kind. He purports to be the same King Arthur who lived centuries ago – a preposterous claim at best. To DCFS, he is a blank slate, and that is always a red flag. Now I know the older boys, Lance Sepulveda and Ricky Delgado, may choose to stay with Mr. Pendragon. The younger boy, however, under California law, has no such right. Based on some of the recent scandals involving young Mr. Sepulveda and Mr. Delgado, we do not feel they are a proper influence over young Christopher. If we grant Mr. Pendragon custody over all, the two older could very easily be a negative influence on the youngster. Therefore, we motion the court to remove either the two older boys or Christopher Wallis from New Camelot until a final determination can be made on permanency. Thank you, your Honor."

She resumed her seat.

Lance could hardly contain himself during her recitation, and several times had to be restrained by Sam's large hand on his shoulder. Hearing the recommendation, Chris began to cry, throwing his arms around Arthur as though fearful the bailiff would drag him away.

The judge waved to the court clerk. She scurried over to Arthur's table with a box of tissue for Chris. Arthur thanked her and Chris snatched a handful of tissue, weeping into it.

"Mr. McMullen," announced the judge, "you may now state your case before the court."

Sam stood, dressed flamboyantly in a royal blue suit with a really loud power tie. "Your honor, with all due respect to Ms. Kelly and DCFS, my client has been in the public eye with these children for nearly a year and has already proven a better parent than those who brought them into this world. As to my esteemed colleague's specious allegation that the younger boy is in danger of acquiring unsecured weapons, there are no firearms on the premises, and all knives and swords are secured within a locked room when not in use. The only people who have a key to the armory are Arthur, Jenny, and Lance."

Kelly jotted something down on her legal pad.

"Mr. Pendragon is an international figure at this point in time, Your Honor, and nothing he does goes unnoticed by the press. DCFS doesn't need to watch these kids because the whole world is doing so. As to the so-called 'celebrity hangout' status of the hotel, yes, it has been that in recent years. However, any celebrities who wish to meet with Lance or Ricky, or any of Arthur's knights, must be given prior approval before entering the premises. There are no 'drop-ins' allowed. Sir Lance has made it quite clear that neither he nor any of his fellow knights are to be used for 'photo-ops' to better anyone's visibility. In addition, if said people do want to take pictures with him or the others, Lance has insisted they pledge a public contribution to the charity of their choice. A very astute and well-groomed young man, if I may say so, Your Honor, and clearly a testament to the parenting prowess of Mr. Pendragon. There is no evidence for Ms. Kelly or DCFS to conclude that any of these boys, including young Christopher, would be any safer or better cared for within our overburdened foster care system."

Kelly stood up quickly, reminding the fuming Lance of a Jack- in-the-Box. "If I may make a point, your Honor?"

"Yes, Ms. Kelly?"

"As I've previously mentioned, we already know of the disturbing behaviors these two older boys have been involved in. We've all seen the pictures and videos. Now I'm to understand that the so-called boy who came back has a key to the armory? A minor, and a party boy? I maintain that these older boys pose an inherent risk to the younger one."

The judge peered over his wire-rim glasses at Sam. "Mr. McMullen?"

"Your Honor, whatever Ms. Kelly may try to claim, Lance has proven to be a paragon of responsibility, especially when caring for, and setting a proper example for, his younger sibling, and yes, they already consider themselves brothers. Admittedly, Lance had that one fall from grace. But then, he is a teenager, and I suspect Ms. Kelly had her own less-than-responsible moments as a teen, just as we all did. If it please the court, Your Honor, Sirs Lance and Ricky would like to address you."

"Absolutely. I wouldn't think of denying their right to speak. Who shall go first?"

As Sam resumed his seat, Lance indicated Ricky, who stood nervously. Chris peered out from behind Arthur's sleeve, sniffling, but watching his older brother with keen eyes.

"Your Honor, I been with Arthur the least of all us guys here, but him and Lady Jenny and Lance and Chris have been more family to me in a few months than mine ever was. My dad hated my hair, he hated my wrestling, he hated that I liked reading. I think he just hated me. I wasn't what he wanted in a son. When he found out I really admired some boy he called me a faggot and beat me."

Ricky paused to compose himself.

The judge frowned deeply. "Ricky, are you telling this court your father beat you for being gay?"

"No, Your Honor, because he *thought* I was gay. And then when they decided to move back to Mexico because they couldn't make enough money here, he kept telling my mom that he wouldn't be seen with this *maricón* of a son in his home country. The other men would laugh." He lowered his eyes in shame.

The judge looked confused. "For the court reporter, Ricky, what is *maricón* in English?"

"Faggot."

"Thank you, Ricky. I know this is difficult. Please continue."

Ricky exhaled a deep breath. "Anyway, they just up and left one day, moved back to Mexico without me. I stayed with friends for a while, but finally ended up homeless on the streets. I didn't want to get locked up in juvy, so I never went to the cops."

"How did you survive on the streets?"

Ricky lowered his gaze. "It wouldn't be right to say, Your Honor, in front of Chris."

Judge Baker turned to Kelly. "Is this boy's history in your report, Ms. Kelly?"

She shook her head. "No. He never told us this part."

The judge turned back to Ricky. "Ricky, I always want the full picture before I make a ruling. I'd like you, both attorneys and the court reporter to adjourn to my chambers and we will continue there."

Nervously, Ricky glanced at Arthur and Sam. Sam nodded. Then Ricky looked at Lance, who grinned and mock punched him. Ricky grinned back.

They exited the courtroom and the others waited. Chris raised his hand to Sam.

Sam smiled with amusement. "You're not in school, Chris. What is it?"

"Are they gonna take me away?" Tears were once more brimming.

Sam placed a hand on his shoulder. "They want to. But we're fighters, Chris. They won't win."

"Can I talk to the judge?" Chris's light blue eyes were blurs of hope.

"Normally children your age don't have the right to speak at these hearings. But Judge Baker is a fair man. Why not ask him, eh?"

He winked and Chris nodded.

Lance fidgeted, and wrestled a bit with Chris to calm him down. Ten minutes elapsed before the door to the judge's chambers opened and everyone re-entered the court. Ricky slipped back into his seat beside Lance, looking as though he might cry, and Lance surreptitiously slipped his hand between their chairs and took Ricky's in his, gently squeezing, but keeping his eyes on the judge. Ricky returned the squeeze.

"Back on record in the adoption proceeding for Mr. Arthur Pendragon and three minor children," the judge announced upon resuming his seat. "Sir Ricky, based upon the horrific life forced upon you by your parents, and your stated wish to remain with Arthur Pendragon, I hereby grant your request."

Ricky's face melted into almost tearful relief and he turned to Lance. The boys grinned at one another, and squeezed their hands together more firmly.

The judge now fixed his gaze on Lance, and smiled encouragingly. "Sir Lance, you would like to speak?"

Lance released Ricky's hand and stood, stepping around the table and standing just in front of it. He sucked in a deep breath, and exhaled.

"Thank you, Your Honor." He turned and pointed to Arthur. "That man is my father. And those are my brothers." Then he turned and pointed at Kelly and Hanson. "Nothing these ladies or anyone else says will ever change that. I know Ricky and me messed up going to that party. People all over the world think I'm perfect or I'm gonna do miracles or something 'cause I came back. But Your Honor, I'm just a kid who got sold to a stranger for drugs. You wanna know what these people—" He pointed at the DCFS table "—done for me in their system, then we gotta go in back 'cause I don't want Chris hearing it. Ricky knows, and my Dad, but no one else. Just know this, Your Honor. I'll *never* go back to them. You try to take me away from my Dad and I'll run. I'll run so far you'll never find me."

The judge looked troubled. "Don't be afraid, Lance, I don't want to separate you from your father. Let's go back into chambers and you can share your story."

The court reporter again gathered up her stenotype machine and stepped through the door behind the bench, then the judge signaled Lance and the two attorneys to follow.

Ricky looked nervous, and Arthur placed a hand on his shoulder. Chris took Ricky's hand and held it tight.

After another fifteen minutes, during which the gallery was awash with indistinct murmurings and whispers, the door opened and everyone resumed their places. Lance looked pale, his eyes red with pain, as he slid back into his seat between Ricky and Chris. The little boy instantly grabbed one hand, and Ricky took the other one. The three boys faced the judge straight on, awaiting his decision.

"Back on the record in the matter of the Arthur Pendragon adoption proceeding," the judge intoned again. But then his face softened, and his tone became more compassionate. "In light of Lance's testimony, do you still feel he should return to the custody of DCFS?"

Kelly glanced at Hanson. She actually looked shattered. "No, Your Honor."

"Very well. Sir Lance, you are hereby to remain in the custody of the man you call dad until the adoption becomes final. Congratulations, son."

Lance almost burst into tears and turned to hug Arthur. But then he let go and turned back to the judge fearfully. "What about Chris?"

The judge's grin faltered. "Alas, Lance, he is another matter."

Chris impulsively leapt from his chair and stepped forward, raising his hand in front of the judge's bench.

Amused, Baker said, "Yes, Christopher?"

"Permission to speak, sir," Chris said, his voice strong, but quavering a little.

Kelly stood at once. "I object, Your Honor. This child is too young to know what he wants."

"Is he?" Baker looked down at Chris. "How old are you, Chris?"

"Seven years, three months and fourteen days, Your Honor," Chris replied with wide-eyed innocence.

The brought a smile to the judge's face. "Indeed? You must be good at math."

"Yes, sir, I am. Ask me a math problem."

The judge considered a moment. "How about twelve times twelve?"

Chris pulled a face. "That's for little kids, Your Honor. It's too easy. One-hundred-forty-four. Ask me something hard."

The judge chuckled. "All right. How about twenty times three hundred forty? If it's too hard, let me know."

Chris's face scrunched up in thought. "Six thousand eight hundred," he announced proudly.

The judge looked astonished and turned to the clerk. "Is that correct?"

The clerk used the calculator on his phone and punched in the problem. He looked up and grinned, giving Chris a thumbs-up. "Yes, Your Honor."

The judge beamed. "Very impressive, Chris."

"Your Honor," Chris went on excitedly, "I'm learning more with Lady Jenny and the other teachers than I ever did at school. And my mama left me in an alley 'cause she didn't wanna feed me no more. Arthur is my Dad, and Lance and Ricky are my brothers. You can't let these people take me away, sir. We need each other. Don't take me away! Please!"

He broke down into another spate of tears. Lance leapt up and hurried to him, engulfing him in a hug, and allowed Chris to cry into his shoulder.

Lance looked up at the judge. "See, Your Honor? We're a family. Don't let them do this. Don't let what happened to me happen to Chris. Please."

The judge sighed. "Well, I've never been known for taking the conventional approach to anything so, having gone on record as approving that Lance and Ricky remain with Arthur, I hereby order that Christopher Wallis also remain at New Camelot with Mr. Pendragon pending finalization of the adoption." Then he beamed brightly. "Congratulations, boys. You're a family."

The boys whooped and hollered, hugging and high fiving each other. Lance and Ricky hugged, taking each other's hand for a moment, squeezing and grinning foolishly.

"This is highly irregular, Your Honor," Kelly stated flatly, "and I hereby lodge a formal objection to your decision."

"Duly noted in the record, Ms. Kelly. This court is adjourned."

The sound of his gavel was the sweetest sound the three boys ever heard.

Of course, the formalization of them as a family was just the excuse Reyna needed to throw another party. All the knights attended and there was food and dancing and lots of laughs and hugs and "congratulations" thrown around. And, naturally, Reyna made everyone dance to the "Cha Cha Slide." Esteban shocked Lance by actually being good at it this time, and when he spotted Lance gaping like a grouper, he winked. That's when Lance knew – Esteban had been practicing since the birthday party so he could impress Reyna.

Yep, Este's in love all right.

It was a fun night for all, especially with Chris and Ricky inundating Arthur with 'Dad this' and Dad that' so they could get used to it. Arthur laughed, joked and danced the night away with Jenny in his arms, and a grand time was had by all.

The California State Attorney General approved the ballot initiative by the end of February and informed Sam that formal signature gathering could begin, reminding him that all signatures had to be collected by June to qualify the initiative for the November ballot.

This was exciting news for everyone at New Camelot. Even Michael was proud of his efforts, though his diffident attitude wouldn't allow him to offer much more than a "Course it passed muster – I wrote it" kind of remark. He had not attended the party, nor any weekly gatherings since his "job" concluded.

Techie immediately put signature-gathering forms on line and tweeted links so people all over the state could download the forms and begin the collection process. All signers had to be registered voters and residents of California.

Thus, the race to qualify their proposition, now officially named "Proposition 51—The Child Voter Act," began in earnest.

Despite their success with the state attorney general, and Michael's pivotal role in it, nobody but Lance could endure much of the boy's attitude, especially since he showed up at least three times per week to work out in the Training Centre. Though he wouldn't say it aloud except to Jenny, Arthur was glad Michael had ceased attending their Saturday gatherings.

Lance still didn't understand why he tolerated Michael, especially given how much trouble he'd gotten into because of him. He not only didn't hate Michael, but actually believed there was more to him than just the swagger. After all, Michael had stopped calling him 'Lancey,' had stopped making inappropriate comments (at least in person, if not via texts), and had taken the prop-writing process seriously – all because Lance had asked him to. In his mind, especially given the overall purpose of their crusade in regards to giving kids second chances, all of that indicated Michael wasn't a lost cause. Lance truly believed there was some good in him, and he determined to find it.

March would mark a major turning point in the crusade, for Arthur dropped a huge bombshell during their final gathering of February: he would take Llamrei and a group of knights and leave New Camelot for most of March, and probably April, as needed, to travel the state in support of the campaign.

His announcement, already known to Jenny and Merlin, stunned the assemblage, and Arthur had to quell their excited mutterings with a raising of Excalibur.

Lance and Ricky gazed at one another in shock. Though the need for travel had been discussed, they'd had no idea a decision had been made.

Lance stood as the crowd of knights settled back down. "Who will be in charge here with you gone, Dad?"

Arthur lowered Excalibur. "Why, that would be you, son, the Prince."

Lance was stunned. He'd known this day would come, but now that it had, he was terrified.

Arthur addressed the crowd. "Sir Lance will be assisted by his brothers, Sir Ricky and Sir Christopher, and I shall leave Lady Jenny, who will live here in my absence, and Merlin, as advisors."

The assembled knights were abuzz with excitement.

"My son shall also have the redoubtable input of the ever capable Lady Reyna."

There was some applause as Reyna's own face registered shock and amazement. She glanced at Esteban, and he squeezed her hand lovingly.

"The following knights shall accompany me," Arthur went on. "Sir Esteban, Sir Lavern, Sir Darnell, Sir Enrique, Sir Khom, Sir Duc, and Sir Luis."

Lavern whooped loudly with delight and then covered his mouth in embarrassment. "Sorry, Arthur," he muttered sheepishly.

The king merely smiled at the boy's gaffe.

Esteban's thick eyebrows flew up in surprise, but Reyna's expression clouded and she gripped his hand even harder, almost afraid to let him go.

Lance stood still, all his old insecurities rushing back in on him. Command? Him? What if he made the wrong decisions? What if somebody got hurt? What would he do? He eyed Ricky and mouthed, "I'm gonna need you more than ever."

Ricky smiled back encouragingly.

Arthur continued to lay out his plans for the campaign, and instructions for those who remained at New Camelot in his absence. Lance and Ricky would need to travel south to Orange County and San Diego to campaign, while Arthur and his crew would cover middle and northern California, finishing up in San Francisco.

Responsibilities were laid out for all, with the two camps remaining in contact via Skype. Sam had already begun making arrangements, with Jenny's help, for Arthur and his kids to stay at various motels along the way. Llamrei would have her horse trailer and only in big cities would they need to find a suitable place to stable her. Most of central California was farmland and ranches, so the mare should feel right at home.

The following weekend would be Arthur's last at New Camelot, and they would all gather again on Sunday, rather than the customary Saturday, for last minute assignments. The knights in charge of neighborhood watch and clean-up duties would continue those activities in his absence, while always encouraging adults along the way to sign their petitions.

Since New Camelot existed as a non-profit organization, and with money flowing in from all over the world, Arthur's trip was fully funded. The donated bus would be used for transport throughout the state.

Esteban, at Reyna's urging, had just gotten his driver's permit, so he was eligible to drive, if needed. But Sam had hired a driver for the bus, to which Llamrei's trailer would be hitched.

Lavern put up his hand and asked what color the bus was, and Arthur said, "Yellow." When Lavern pulled a face, Arthur asked what was wrong.

"That be an old school bus, Arthur," the boy announced with a snort of disgust. "Part of what we be against is schools." Then his young face lit up. "I know! We can bring paint along and kids we meet can paint over the ugly yellow with whatever they want and even sign their names on it."

Arthur grinned, and Lance smiled at the idea, as well.

"Brilliant, Sir Lavern," the king said in praise, and the twelve-year-old beamed with pride.

The meeting concluded with the promise that all other details would be finalized next week.

Lance sat stunned when it was over, but so many knights came up and assured him he'd be an awesome king that he finally began to relax. A bit. He wouldn't completely fall apart with terror, he knew, until he was alone in the shower and the overriding panic would rip through him like a bullet.

Michael, who knew nothing of Arthur's plans, stopped by that Tuesday and invited Lance to another party on Friday night. He casually mentioned it while stowing their gear in the armory after a sparring session.

"I think it's been long enough, Lance. Your rep seems to have cleaned up enough, thanks to all those fireside chats you've been having online."

Lance shook his head, and explained what was going to happen the following Monday. "My dad won't let me go with you to any more parties, Michael. And I promised him I wouldn't, anyway. Especially now, when he's gonna put me in charge. I can't screw that up."

"So break your promise. He'll never know. Sneak out and meet me. And ditch the bodyguard while you're at it."

Ricky entered just then. "Ditch me where?"

Michael snorted. "Ah, busted."

Ricky turned to Lance. "What's up, Lance?"

"Michael wants me to come to another party with him."

Michael raised his eyebrows. "Your wanna-be squeeze Bridget will be in attendance, I might add."

Lance looked over at that, but Ricky caught his eye. "No way, Lance. You promised Dad. You're gonna be king next week, remember?"

"I can't, Michael. Ricky's right. If I screw this up, I could ruin everything."

Michael eyed Ricky. "As I was pointing out to Lance before *you* entered the conversation, promises to parents are meant to be broken."

"I can't, Michael," Lance repeated. "My dad never breaks his promises to me."

Michael shrugged his shoulders. "Suit yourself. I guess Bridget'll have to make out with some other guy."

For some reason, that thought scared Lance even more than getting in trouble. Bridget was his only hope, right?

"Okay, Michael, we'll go," he blurted before he could change his mind. "On one condition."

Ricky opened his mouth, but Lance placed a hand on his arm.

Michael's eyebrows shot up in surprise. "And what would that be?"

"No pictures," Lance insisted. "You gotta make sure no one takes my picture, or Ricky's."

Michael stood there, eyeing him with amused disdain.

Lance stood firm. "Otherwise, no deal."

"I can arrange that. I'll text you Friday night at eleven-thirty. Be ready. Oh, and wear the tight shirt again."

Then Michael left the armory to return home.

Ricky whirled on Lance. "Why did you do that? You promised Dad! You promised everyone on TV, man!"

Lance did not raise his eyes from the floor, because he didn't want to see the truth in Ricky's eyes. "I know. But I wanna see Bridget and this is the only way I can."

Ricky folded his arms across his chest in anger. "Dad'll let her visit any time. You know that." He eyed Lance suspiciously. "You sure it's not Michael you really wanna hang out with, somewhere Reyna won't catch you?"

"Don't go there, Ricky."

Ricky shook his head in disgust, looking like he wanted to punch a wall. "If we get caught, Lance, there goes our reputation again. Especially yours. You'll be a liar now, not just a party boy. We might really ruin everything this time, for real, man, for the whole crusade!"

"We won't get caught. Besides, this'll be the last party I can go to before I have to be in charge. And you might meet a nice girl this time."

Ricky looked very dubious.

"We just gotta not drink and make sure about the no picture rule," Lance added firmly.

"How we gonna make sure of that?"

"If anyone tries, we threaten to lock 'em in a room with Michael for a week." He offered a weak smile.

Ricky didn't return the smile. "How do you know it wasn't Michael who set you up the first time?"

Lance met his gaze with narrowed eyes. "Whadda you mean?"

"Those pictures," Ricky said. "He's such a control freak he had to know they'd be taking your picture."

Lance considered. It would be like Michael to try to ruin his reputation, just to see him grovel to get it back.

"I don' know." He honestly didn't. "But I don't think so."

Ricky scowled. "Why?"

"I just see something in his eyes, something that isn't all bad."

"You and people's eyes. You're like a soul-whisperer or something." Ricky paused. "Ever think you see in them what you wanna see, and don't see in them what you don't want to?"

Lance scrunched up his face in amusement. "If I ever figure out what you just said, maybe I can give you a smart-ass answer."

That was all they needed to break the tension, and Ricky grinned.

"What?" Lance said.

"I was thinking maybe now's a good time for another smack down. You know, before you become king and can throw me in the dungeon."

Lance scoffed. "*You* smacking *me* down?"

"Damn straight."

"Bring it on."

With that, they headed out of the armory and took to the wrestling mat for another hour-long workout. The exertion left them sweaty, but calmed their nerves and anxieties about Friday night.

The remainder of the week was a headlong rush to prepare everything for Arthur's journey. The knights who were to accompany him had to get permission slips signed by their mothers, and that wasn't a problem. The bigger issue was how to school them while they traveled. Sir Techie suggested that Jenny's lessons be Skyped live and the knights could watch on a couple of laptop computers Arthur had been given. The boys would take along their textbooks and the completed work would be mailed back to Jenny at New Camelot. It seemed an equitable solution and very "21st century," Arthur stated with a smile.

Lance and Ricky met with Arthur throughout the week to discuss the running of New Camelot. Lance wanted to announce at their Sunday gathering that in Arthur's absence, and with him filling in as prince and acting king, he would have Ricky as his First Knight. Arthur heartily agreed.

The boys grew increasingly restless as Friday approached, and each moment at Arthur's side weighed heavily on their consciences. Lance was tempted more than once to text Michael and cancel their plans. But then he thought of Bridget. How beautiful she looked. How much she liked him. And then thoughts of Michael's potent kisses rushed in and his resolve hardened. He couldn't turn into... Just the thought made him shiver with terror. He *had* to make this Bridget thing work.

Dinner that Friday was a nerve-wracking affair, with everyone excited about Arthur's journey and the campaign ahead. Lance and Ricky barely said two words, picking nervously at their food. Reyna frowned suspiciously, and even Chris wanted to know if they were sick.

Pretending to be tired after a particularly strenuous workout session that afternoon, the boys excused themselves before dessert and hurried up to Lance's room to hide until Michael contacted them.

Later that night, after making sure to tuck in Chris, who comfortably slept in his own bed now that he knew he had a real family, and having said goodnight to Arthur, Lance and Ricky met back in Lance's room. Lance had decided, and Ricky had whole- heartedly agreed, that they would *not* wear the shirts Michael had given them. He didn't care if Michael got mad or not. Instead, they slipped on band t-shirts and hoodies.

Lance glanced at Ricky and frowned, suddenly feeling an overwhelming surge of guilt.

"What's wrong, man?"

"I feel like dog crap for lying to Dad. He's leaving me in charge, Ricky, 'cause he thinks I'm responsible."

"This was your idea, you know. We don't have to go."

"I know. But I really wanna see Bridget."

Ricky eyed him uncertainly. "You like her, don't you?"

"Yeah, I think so. But I can't know unless I spend more time with her."

His phone buzzed with a text. It was Michael, waiting in his car out behind the hotel.

The boys exchanged another hesitant look before heading quietly out of the room.

Once in Michael's car, the older boy gave Lance the once over, obviously noting that his orders regarding the tight shirt had been ignored. But rather than get mad, as

Lance had expected, he nodded approvingly. As before, Lance sat in front and Ricky in back.

"Where are we going?" Lance asked cautiously.

Michael spun the wheel sharply into a turn, sending both boys flying. "My place. Parents are gone and I got both houses to myself."

"Bridget will be there, right?" Lance asked suspiciously, rubbing his shoulder where it had slammed into the passenger side window.

"She'll be there. I might even let you take her back to my private room for a while."

Lance shivered. Him, alone with Bridget where anything could happen? That's the last thing he wanted right now.

Brushing that thought aside, he asked, "Michael, you didn't set me up the last time, did you?"

"How so?"

Michael made another sharp turn with Lance almost spilling into his lap. The car sped upward, taking curves at a breakneck pace, rapidly ascending into the Hollywood Hills.

"All those pictures?" Lance explained, his voice suspicious. "Especially the ones of you and me?"

Michael grunted angrily. "Hell no! I never let anyone take my picture. I find out who took those, I'm gonna kick his ass!"

His burst of vitriol shocked Lance. They rode the rest of the way in silence.

As they neared Michael's house, Lance said, "Tell them not to take any pictures of me, remember?"

"How about bodyguard? He fair game?"

Ricky leaned forward angrily.

Lance put up a hand before Ricky could speak. "No. Not Ricky, either."

Michael chuckled. "Okay, I'll make it so."

The party was already in full swing as Michael led them into the main house, easily larger and more luxurious than the one which had hosted their first party. Nine-foot ceilings with fancy copings around the edges, chandeliers, hardwood floors, all-wood furniture, chairs and sofas soft enough to sleep on. Lance knew that if he attended a hundred of these parties, he'd never fit in with this lifestyle, or be truly wanted except by virtue of his fame.

As soon as they entered the crowded living room, with music blaring, kids dancing and drinking, Michael strode over and stopped the DJ with a wave of his hand. Everyone ceased their talking or dancing and turned to look.

Michael stood proudly, his painted-on shirt making him look even more muscular and dangerous than usual beneath the soft interior lighting.

"As you can see, I've got The Boy Who Came Back and his little-ass bodyguard back with us tonight."

Murmurs of excitement went through the crowd. Bridget stepped into the living room, her face alight with joy.

Michael's eyes narrowed, his wolfish expression not to be challenged. "Pictures are strictly off-limits. I find out anyone took pix of either of them and you know what'll happen. Party on, dudes."

He waved a hand at the DJ and the pounding alternative rock song resumed.

Bridget excitedly elbowed her way through the crowd, drink in hand, and latched onto Lance's arm like it was the most important thing in the world.

"You're finally here!" She leaned in for a kiss, catching Lance off guard with its intensity.

Squirming, Ricky glanced down at the floor.

Bridget pulled back, her face flushed with pleasure.

Lance blushed. "Wow."

Bridget laughed with delight. "C'mon, Lance, I want you to meet some friends of mine."

She glanced uncertainly at Michael as though for permission, and he nodded. She pulled Lance away through the dancing crowd of teens.

Michael eyed the confused look on Ricky's face. "Knock yourself out, bodyguard. Wander, find yourself a girl... or boy... to play with."

He moved off to mix with a group hanging out by the wet bar.

Ricky headed back toward the foyer. It made him too uncomfortable to be there with Lance and Bridget, especially when he knew they'd be kissing. Was it jealousy? Did he envy the fact that Lance had found a girl who was totally into him?

With these confused thoughts coursing through him, Ricky spotted a girl sitting by herself on the stairs leading to the second floor. He stopped up short to look at her. She was cute, though not model-type beautiful like Bridget, with longish brown hair, long lashes, and dimples that made her look especially appealing. She sat, elbows on her thighs, with her chin resting on her hands. She looked lonely, and did not appear to be having a good time. Sensing a kinship, Ricky stopped in front of her.

"Hi." He knew it was lame, and his heart pounded with terror.

She looked up quickly. "Hi," she said, obviously startled.

Ricky fought to keep his nervous voice steady. "Uh, you okay? You look kind a lost."

She smiled shyly. "I am. Not the party type. I came with Bridget. You know her, right?"

Ricky looked surprised. "Yeah, but how did you know that?"

She shrugged and offered a little smile that Ricky found appealing. "Everybody knows you, Sir Ricky. You're like Lance's other half."

She laughed, and Ricky joined in.

"Actually, I think you're cuter than Lance." Her hand flew to her mouth in embarrassment. "Oh God, I can't believe I said that. Please don't tell him."

Ricky grinned. "I'm cuter than Lance? Wow. Thanks. What's your name?"

"Ariel."

"That's awesome. From The Little Mermaid, right?"

She laughed. "Yeah, my mom loved that movie."

"Cool." He gazed down at her a moment, realizing he liked her already. She seemed natural and real. "You know, I'm not much for partying, either. Wanna go sit somewhere and talk?"

She smiled shyly again. "That'd be great."

He reached out and took her by the hand and they moved off deeper into the house.

In the crowded, noisy living room, Lance sat nervously beside Bridget in a loveseat off in one corner, uncertain and scared. He'd wanted so much to be with her, and now that he was, he didn't know what to do, or even what he wanted to do.

"Relax, Lance," she cooed with an inviting smile. She rubbed his hand gently in an attempt to calm his nerves.

Lance felt almost sick to his stomach. When she rubbed him, even like that, it unnerved him. He pulled his hand away. "I don't know why, but I'm always super nervous around you."

She reached for a bottle of vodka resting on the table beside the loveseat and offered it to him.

He shook his head. "I promised Ricky I wouldn't drink tonight."

She shrugged, and giggled. "Okay, but I'm nervous, too." She took a big swig from the bottle and then fixed those lovely blue eyes on him. "I like you, Lance, a whole lot. Do you like me, too?"

He nodded nervously.

"It's hot. Why not take off the hoodie?"

Lance nodded nervously, and slipped the hoodie up and over his head, laying it on the loveseat beside him.

She ran a hand slowly along his torso. "I like this band."

Lance nodded. He'd not even paid attention to which band shirt he was wearing. Her hand slid down to his leg and rested there a moment, and Lance froze. He started flashing, the gesture too much like... He felt the freak-out coming on and snatched the bottle from her, downing an enormous swig of the bitter-tasting alcohol. It burned his throat, but warmed his insides.

"Better?" she asked gently, removing her hand from his lap and taking the bottle.

He nodded, fighting to stave off the panic.

"It relaxes me, too," she said with a sly grin.

"Yeah." He grabbed the bottle back and upended it, needing the alcohol's power to keep his nerve, to keep the freak out at bay.

Bridget eyed him curiously as he lowered the bottle and wiped the dribble from his chin. "You sure don't seem nervous on TV, Lance. I loved the way you told off those reporters who wanted to know if you were gay."

"They were scum." He grabbed the bottle and took another gulp. "Bridget, do you... I mean, do you think I'm gay?"

"You don't kiss like you are. Why would I think that?"

He looked down. "Because of, you know, that stuff with Michael the last time."

She waved that off dismissively. "That's just Michael, Lance. Don't sweat it."

Lance took another swig, finally feeling the effects of the vodka. "He told me... that you and him, well, that you... dated."

Now it was her turn to grab for the bottle. "Yeah. He can be addicting, almost like this stuff. And he's hotter than hot, that's for sure."

Lance stiffened, feeling a rush of insecurity overwhelm him.

"But it's like he's the light and dark sides of the Force all at the same time," Bridget went on, her tone tinged with fear. "Be careful, Lance. I don't want anything to happen to you."

"What could happen?"

Bridget looked around to make sure no one was listening, and then leaned in close. "Once, at a party, someone took a picture of Michael and me dancing, and Michael went ballistic. He beat the hell out of that kid and would of killed him if a bunch of us hadn't pulled him off."

Lance shivered, and swigged again, feeling more loose and relaxed now. "Wow. I've never seen him like that."

Bridget's face clouded with anxiety. "Promise me you won't piss him off."

"I'll try."

"Feeling better now?"

Lance nodded, and took her hand in his.

She grinned. "Basic human contact, right?"

Lance laughed.

"Do you want to kiss me now?"

Lance nodded again, and did just that.

In the den, where the loud music from down the hall didn't pound so loudly into their ears, Ricky and Ariel sat on a fancy divan and talked. They talked about their interests, their families, and the crusade, and Ricky gushed about how Arthur was adopting him and how he was so happy to finally have a family that loved him.

They enjoyed each other's company, without drinking, until Ricky realized that over an hour had passed without him checking on Lance. He asked her if he could call or text her, because he'd like to see her again, and they exchanged numbers. He told her he'd likely be right back after making sure Lance was okay, but if he didn't, that meant there was a problem and he'd be in touch.

Ricky made his way back toward the living room and spotted Michael standing at the doorway gazing raptly into the room. As he approached, Michael leaned against the door.

"You become a man yet, Ricky boy? I heard you turned down Carmen last time."

Ricky's temper rose, but he didn't take the obvious bait. "Like I wanna do it with a stranger?"

"Keep telling yourself that, bodyguard. Maybe you'll eventually believe it."

Ricky followed Michael's gaze, and spotted Bridget and Lance kissing on the love seat. Ricky lowered his eyes in shame, and disappointment.

Michael started into the room. "Time to break those two up."

Ricky put out a hand to stop him. Michael turned and cast a vicious look his way.

Ricky didn't drop his hand. "Why, Michael? Why break them up?"

Michael stared at him, but didn't answer.

"Michael, I know how you feel about Lance. But you can't do that to him."

"Whatever are you talking about?" Michael looked mildly curious.

Ricky struggled to control his thumping heart. "You know..."

"You think I want to...?" Michael trailed off, but his meaning was clear.

Ricky gulped and nodded.

Michael squinted at him, and then, before Ricky had time to react, Michael grabbed him by the upper arm and dragged him away from the living room. "You and me are gonna chat, bodyguard."

Ricky struggled, but allowed himself to be led down a long hallway, away from the party and, to his relief, away from Lance.

In the living room, Lance pulled away from Bridget, knowing he was drunk, feeling an intense wave of despair wash over him.

"What's wrong, Lance?"

Lance didn't know, but something didn't feel right. *He* didn't feel right. "I don't know, but I feel really down all of a sudden."

She took his hand and held it. "Probably just the alcohol." She smiled. "You like kissing me, don't you?"

He nodded. Did he? He pulled her in close, resting her head against his chest. He didn't want her to see his face, because he wasn't sure what emotion she might find.

What's wrong with me?

Ricky ended up in a small bedroom, likely a guest room because the decorations looked like they belonged in a furniture ad.

Michael shoved him inside and closed the door, cutting off the music wafting down the hall.

Ricky stood his ground, ready to fight if Michael wanted to settle their enmity once and for all.

But Michael didn't come at him, or make any threatening moves. He studied Ricky, like for once not knowing what to say.

"What, Michael?"

"I wanna know why you're so worried about Lance's virtue, especially when it comes to me."

Ricky didn't respond. He promised never to tell anyone.

Michael ambled around the room, looking thoughtful. "I know where *you're* coming from in all this. It's written all over your face every time you're with him."

Ricky lowered his gaze, and that's when Michael pounced. He leaped behind Ricky and wrapped those thick arms around his neck, cutting off his air supply.

"Now, bodyguard, you're gonna tell me about Lance, because I know there's something he keeps hidden from the world."

He released his grip a little, but not enough for Ricky to get loose. He struggled, helpless beneath Michael's thick, powerful arms.

"I can't tell you, Michael. It's private!"

Michael increased the pressure. "Oh, you'll tell me, Ricky boy."

The grip relaxed a smidgen.

"I promised..." Ricky croaked, beginning to see stars.

"You promised Arthur no more parties too, and yet here you are. Cough it up, bodyguard."

The grip tightened again, and Ricky feared for his life. "I can't breathe, Michael!"

Michael's hands relaxed slightly, and then Ricky heard Michael gasp.

"Wait a minute..." Michael said quietly, his breath tickling Ricky's earlobe. "It has something to do with that provision we put in the prop, doesn't it, the one about men and boys."

Ricky fought to get free, but the grip intensified and white dots swam before his eyes. In his conscious effort to breathe, he could almost hear the gears shifting in Michael's brain as he put the pieces together.

And then Michael's body stiffened, and he let go. "Oh, hell!"

Ricky collapsed to his knees, choking and gagging for air, his throat burning with pain. He glared upward at Michael, and saw on his face that he'd figured it out.

"How old?"

Ricky shook his head, not comprehending.

The brown eyes flared. "How old was Lance?"

"Six," Ricky croaked, feeling weak and shameful all at once. He'd betrayed Lance. How much more worthless could he become?

Michael stared past Ricky toward the closed bedroom door, his eyes wild with anger, lower lip quivering as if fighting off an impending explosion.

Ricky rose shakily to his feet, still rubbing his throat, eyeing the silent, steaming Michael with uncertainty.

Michael strode to the door and flung it open, disappearing into the hallway beyond.

Fear engulfed Ricky as he stumbled out after him.

Making his shaky way down hall, he almost collided with Carmen, who was heading toward the living room carrying a bottle of what looked like vodka.

Carmen sneered, eyeing Ricky with utter contempt. "Well, if it isn't the boy who couldn't get it up."

Ricky flared with anger. "Carmen, I didn't *want* to get it up with you, okay? There's a difference. Now move, I gotta find Lance."

She smirked, obviously very drunk. "Maybe you can get it up for him, huh?"

He tried to push past her, but she grabbed his arm.

"What?"

She held out the bottle. "Give this to him, will ya? Save me the walk."

He looked at the bottle, her tottering form and smudged makeup. "Why would I give him that?"

He started past when her words stopped him. "Because some guy paid me a Ben Franklin to give it to him."

Ricky whirled around. "Some guy did what?"

"Paid me a hundred to give Sir Lance this bottle." Her words slurred slightly.

Ricky took the bottle and examined it. It looked full, but it had been opened already. He sniffed it. Smelled like vodka. "Where is this guy?"

She threw her thumb back over her shoulder. "Kitchen, I think."

Ricky glanced toward the living room, but couldn't see in, and then pushed Carmen toward the kitchen. "Show me, Carmen."

With a shrug, she led him down an expansive hallway, past a library and the den where he'd been chatting with Ariel. He glanced in as he passed, but Ariel was gone. They rounded a corner and entered a kitchen the size of a restaurant. It was packed with kids eating and drinking, laughing and talking. Ricky didn't care about any of that.

"Which one?" he asked, his voice anxious, his blood pounding with fear.

She looked around, but shrugged again. "He's gone."

"What did he look like?"

"I don' know. Mexican, maybe, bald head. Maybe nineteen or twenty. Seemed like a real man, not like you."

Ricky turned rigid a moment, not from her insult, but from the description. Other than him and Lance, there wasn't a brown face at this party. Something was wrong. *Very* wrong. Gripping the bottle tightly, Ricky sprinted from the kitchen.

When he entered the living room, he was shocked to see Bridget sitting by herself on the love seat, looking sad and forlorn. He pushed through the dancers to drop down beside her.

"Where's Lance?" he asked loudly, to be heard above the throbbing techno blasting from speakers built into the walls.

Bridget looked up, tears welling in her eyes. "Lance started crying and I couldn't stop him."

"Where is he?"

Her eyes widened with fear. "Michael took him."

"What!" A chill enveloped him. "Where did he take him?"

"To the back house."

He stood to leave, but she grabbed his hand and pulled him back. "Ricky, I really like Lance, you know. I think I'm falling for him. He's just so, I don't know, so different." She was clearly drunk, but not so far gone as Carmen.

Ricky nodded. "I know."

She looked at him in a way she never had before, and something about that gaze made Ricky squirm. Like she knew something he didn't. "What?"

"Nothing. Michael doesn't want me or anyone else to have Lance," she said as loudly as possible without drawing attention to them.

Ricky's heart pounded. "I know that, too."

"Please don't let Michael hurt him." Her damp blue eyes were imploring and desperate.

"Over my dead body," Ricky asserted and pulled away to leave again.

Bridget again grabbed his hand. "Be careful, Ricky. You're a sweet boy, and Michael's... dangerous."

"Don't worry, Bridget." And then he was through the room and out into the hall.

Lance was sprawled out atop Michael's bed, and Michael stood staring down at him with an unreadable expression.

Lance felt pathetic, and his thoughts would not clear. Confusion almost drowned him and he struggled against another wave of tears. What was wrong with him?

"Michael, I feel like crap, man." His voice sounded weak and desperate.

"You're just drunk again, Lance," Michael said soberly, without emotion. "It'll wear off. Lie there and sleep. I'll come back for you."

Lance called out, "Don't leave, Michael!" He struggled to prop himself up on one elbow. "Stay with me, please, Michael. I'm scared. I don't know why, but I'm scared to be alone."

"Man, Lance, you can't hold your liquor."

Lance shook his head, the softness of the bed beneath his back already pulling him down toward sleep. "It's not that, Michael. I'm just afraid of myself. Please stay."

Michael hesitantly lay down on the bed beside him.

Lance grabbed him around the neck and rested his head on his chest.

"It's okay, Lance," Michael said with a quiet sigh. "I'll stay with you."

"You're not all bad like everyone says," Lance said softly.

"Yeah, I am."

"What's wrong with me, Michael?"

"You're drunk, Lance. That's all."

"Not what I meant," Lance mumbled, struggling to merge his feelings into some semblance of coherence. "Sometimes… sometimes I think I love Bridget, you know, and sometimes I think I love you. But mostly… mostly I feel like I'm falling in love with…"

He said nothing more.

"Who?" Michael whispered.

But Lance was already asleep.

"Never mind. I know what you were going to say. Don't worry. You'll forget everything by morning."

Ricky burst into the bedroom, still clutching the vodka, but Michael's stern look silenced his mouth. Panting from his frantic run, he stopped and stared at Lance holding onto Michael.

"He's sleeping," Michael whispered. "And he wanted me to stay with him."

"He wanted *you*?"

Michael didn't look smug. "Yeah. Let him sleep it off, Ricky."

"I'm not leaving him alone with you, Michael."

"Didn't expect you would. Bed's big enough for you, too, or you can take the chair. Your choice."

Ricky eyed the two of them, and his heart caught in his throat. "I'll take the chair."

He circled the bed and sat down in the plush chair off to one side, propping his feet up on the large ottoman and sliding the vodka bottle down beside him.

His wary eyes never left Michael. "I won't let you hurt him, Michael."

Michael eyed him, but said nothing.

Ricky watched until Michael drifted off to sleep before his own exhaustion overpowered him and sent him into a dreamless slumber.

No one awoke when the door to Michael's bedroom crept open ever so quietly. Someone slipped inside, and several snaps of a camera later, exited as quietly as they had entered.

The click of the front door woke Michael. His head flew up, eyes scanning the room. Carefully, he extricated himself from Lance and climbed off the bed. He padded out to the living room and saw the front door closed. He opened it and heard music wafting over from the main house, but there was no one anywhere by the pool or in the back yard.

Returning to the bedroom, he woke Ricky.

"C'mon, bodyguard, time to get you and Lance home before your dad finds out. I'll be in the car."

He left and Ricky shook sleep from his eyes. He eyed Lance, still knocked out on the bed, and felt sadness well up within him. Rising to his feet, he climbed on to the bed and crawled over to Lance, gently jostling him awake.

"Michael?" Lance said, still groggy with sleep.

"No, it's Ricky."

Lance looked up at Ricky's downcast face. "You been with me all night?"

Ricky nodded, tried for a smile. "'Course."

"Where's Michael?"

"In the car. We gotta get home, Lance, 'fore Dad finds out we're gone."

Ricky sat Lance on the edge of the bed while he retrieved the vodka bottle from beside the chair. He held out his hand to Lance.

Uncertainly, Lance took it. His eyes met Ricky's.

"What?" Ricky asked.

Lance looked confused. "I don't know. Something I was telling Michael before I fell asleep. But now I can't remember."

"You drank too much, Lance. Probably wasn't important anyway."

Lance looked uncertain. "But I think it was."

Ricky shrugged and helped Lance to his feet, threw one arm over his shoulder, then slowly and carefully led him out to Michael's waiting car.

CHAPTER NINE

IF HE ISN'T, THERE IS NO ONE ELSE WHO IS

THE NEXT MORNING, RICKY WOKE Lance with some orange juice and coffee, rousting him out of bed. Lance's hangover raged more acutely than the previous one. Just the sound of the coffee mug striking his bedside table sent slivers of pain arcing through his head.

"You gotta pull yourself together before Dad suspects something."

"I know." He sat back against his headboard, feeling drained and exhausted, not even noticing that he had been undressed and put to bed by someone. He could barely remember anything about last night, and just thinking made his head throb. He sipped some juice and then some coffee, grimacing at the bitter taste.

Ricky was clothed in workout shorts and a tank top. He sat carefully on the bed and gazed sternly at Lance.

"What?" Lance asked.

"You promised you wouldn't drink." Ricky looked disappointed.

"I know. I'm sorry, Ricky, I just..."

"Just what?"

"I don't know. I just can't seem to be with Bridget and not drink. I get so nervous."

Ricky looked at him solemnly. "She's falling for you, Lance."

Lance's eyes widened in surprise. "Why do you say that?"

"She told me."

Lance set down the coffee mug on his table. "Wow. That means I have a girlfriend?"

Ricky nodded, his expression unreadable. "Looks like."

Lance eyed him, trying to discern the meaning behind that expression. "What about you? Meet anyone last night?"

"Um, yeah, I did." He told Lance about his conversation with Ariel.

"You think she wants to be your girlfriend?"

"Maybe. She did say I was cuter than you."

"Then she must need glasses." Lance laughed, and pain shot through his head. Ricky punched him in the chest, causing him to wince. "Oh, sorry. Forgot."

Lance smiled, despite the pain, despite the breaking of his promise. He didn't remember enough about last night to recall why he'd become so sad, but today he felt good. "We have girlfriends, Ricky. That means we're real boys."

Ricky's face clouded.

"What?"

"I know you don't like me talking about Jack."

"No, it's okay. I just feel sad when I do. And guilty. What about him?"

Ricky eyed Lance cautiously. "Would you call Jack a real boy?"

Lance bristled, sending a surge of blood pounding into his skull. "Damn straight! The baddest and realest I ever knew!"

"But Jack only liked boys, right?"

Lance's eyes narrowed with anger. "So? What's wrong with that?"

"Nothing," Ricky added quickly. "But if Jack could only fall in love with boys, and he was a real boy, if it turns out that, well, that maybe you and me can only fall in love with another boy, then how come we're not real, too?"

Lance opened his mouth to respond, but nothing came out.

Because Ricky was right.

A bit later, while Lance was in the shower, Ricky closed the connecting door to their rooms, pulled out his cell and dialed Sergeant Ryan.

"Sergeant Ryan?" Ricky asked when the call was answered. "It's Ricky Delgado. When you and Sergeant Gibson come over today to check out everything, I need to talk with you, but I don't want Dad or Lance to know." He paused and listened to something on the other end. "Because I think someone tried to kill Lance last night. Thanks, Sergeant. See you later."

He ended the call and eyed his closet, where the bottle of vodka sat in the darkest corner. Was he just being paranoid? Better to be safe than sorry.

Lance and Ricky went downstairs together for breakfast, Lance's head pounding unmercifully. But he knew he had to put on a good show, so no one would know he was hung over. They were later than most of the kids, but being a Saturday with no school, almost no one showed too early, so they had the dining room to themselves. The boys ate cereal and horsed around a little, joking about their girlfriends and how they could double date.

"If Michael will let us, that is," Ricky added with a scowl, thinking back on what Michael had done and said in that guest room, and how he'd betrayed Lance by telling Michael the secret. He felt like the lowest form of scum there was, even worse than when his father called him *maricón.*

Lance frowned. "I'm sure he will."

Ricky looked unconvinced. "You're surer than me."

They were almost finished eating when Reyna entered the dining room. She looked furious.

"What's wrong, Reyna?"

She glared at Lance and jerked her finger toward herself. "With me, little brother. You too, Ricky."

The boys exchanged a look. Somehow, they'd been caught!

But how?

She led them to the Computer Lab. Lance eyed Ricky with trepidation. The Computer Lab could *not* be good.

When they entered, a number of the computers were occupied. All activity stopped and everyone stared coldly at Lance and Ricky. The boys looked at one another – they knew it must be bad, maybe worse than before. But no one had taken pictures – Michael had insisted, and Michael ruled those kids. Didn't he?

Reyna went to stand beside Sir Techie and waved the boys over. Esteban rose from his computer and stood next to Reyna, arm around her, sliding his hand up and down her arm in a calming gesture.

When Lance and Ricky approached, Reyna pointed to the computer screen. There was a video playing of Lance kissing Bridget, over her shoulder like the previous ones. The bottle of vodka was plainly visible in Lance's hand.

"Oh, God!" Lance whispered, stealing a glance with Ricky, who looked almost as dismayed.

"It gets worse," Reyna said, and went back to the images page and clicked on one, enlarging it. Michael and Lance lay together on Michael's bed, Lance's head resting on Michael's chest.

"Oh, no!" Lance was in shock. The room was dark, so Michael's face was obscured, but Lance's hair was plainly visible. Suddenly, he felt knuckles rap his head. Pain shot through his temples and stabbed its way from front to back.

"That hurt, Reyna!"

"It wouldn't have if you didn't have a hangover."

Lance lowered his gaze to the floor.

"You promised, Lance. You promised me, Este, your Dad. You *promised!*"

Lance lifted his head, the pain ramping up his anger. "Okay, Reyna, I screwed up again, don't rub it in! I thought there was no pictures last night. Michael told everyone to back off or else."

Reyna threw her hands to her hips and tilted her head back with a sneer. "Obviously they didn't listen. Arthur's going out next week to campaign for our prop and you pull this crap? What were you thinking?"

"I wasn't thinking, okay, Reyna. I wanted to see Bridget and didn't think anything bad would happen."

Reyna then turned on Ricky. "And where were you while Lance was getting plastered?"

Ricky flushed with embarrassment. "I was talking to a girl."

Reyna was more pissed off than Lance had ever seen her.

"Well, *brother*, now you're bisexual again, with more people leaning toward gay. Happy? Look at the comments on you and Michael." She leaned in to the computer screen and read aloud, "'Was this pic before or after sex?' 'Which one is the girl?' 'Lance is the girl – look at the hair'. You wanna hear more?"

"No!" Lance's head was splitting open. "You have no right to attack me, Reyna. I'm your boss, remember?"

Reyna stepped back, her expression so explosive even Esteban gave her a wide berth.

For a moment, Lance feared Reyna would haul off and hit him. But instead she offered the nastiest smile he ever saw.

"You're right, *little* brother. When Arthur leaves, I take orders from you. But I sure as hell won't let you or anyone else destroy everything we've worked for because you're a little boy trying to prove he's a man by acting like a little boy! So yeah, you're my boss. But... you *ever* give me attitude like that again and I'll slap you down so hard you'll never get up!" She stormed out of the lab like a retreating tornado.

Esteban turned. "Reyna, wait..." But she was already gone.

He looked at Lance, but not with anger. "Remember what I tole you, Lance. You don't gotta prove nothin'." He hurried after Reyna.

Lance felt humiliated and guilty, especially now that he had to apologize to

Arthur, which was going to be the worst thing yet. Would Arthur trust him at all after this?

He glanced around the lab, at the looks of betrayal directed at him from everyone. He *had* betrayed them, he'd made them look bad in the eyes of the world, and felt such extreme shame he couldn't meet any of their angry eyes.

Sir Techie pointed out a comment beneath the picture of Lance. "Hey, you still have at least one supporter, Lance."

Lance leaned in and looked. The comment read, 'You're still my hero, Sir Lance.' It was signed, 'John.'

Lance scrunched up his face. "That name sounds familiar."

"C'mon, Lance," Ricky said with a sigh. "Let's go find Dad and get this over with."

Arms around each other's shoulders, they ambled from the Computer Lab, Lance feeling like he was on his way to a firing squad.

They found Arthur, Jenny, and Merlin in the Throne Room, staring at Jenny's laptop. Lance already knew what they were looking at. As he and Ricky approached, Lance expected some kind of explosion. But Arthur sat calmly on his throne, the computer on his lap, Jenny standing to one side and Merlin to the other. All three looked at the boys, not with anger, but with something resembling regret.

"Dad," Lance began, but Arthur raised a hand to silence him.

"I know, son, you're sorry. Just as you were the last time."

Guilt swamped Lance.

"I have already been fielding phone calls this morning from members of the press," Arthur went on. "Would I care to comment on my son's girlfriend? Or speculate upon the identity of his boyfriend? Or was I concerned that he might be having unprotected—"

"I get the point, Dad!" Lance said before he could stop himself. Then he looked mortified. "I didn't mean to sound like that, I'm sorry. It's the hangover."

"Yes, the hangover. Another promise broken."

Lance practically wilted beneath his father's disillusioned gaze.

"Lance, I am to leave in two days to travel the state and make our case that youth of your age should be given adult responsibilities. What am I to say to them when they mention these behaviors of yours?"

Lance looked up at Arthur sadly, but defiantly. "Tell them the truth, Dad. I'm not The Boy Who Came Back. I'm just the boy who keeps messing up." He lowered his head. "Put Ricky in charge."

"What?" Arthur looked shocked.

Lance met his father's gaze, tears burning his eyes. "Put Ricky in charge while you're gone. He's your son, too, and he's more responsible than me. He's not sad or emo all the time. He's not trying to be what he thinks a real boy should be. He's just... better than me."

"Lance..." Ricky sounded more shocked than Arthur.

Arthur exchanged a look with Jenny and Merlin.

"Why are you so unhappy, Lance?" Jenny asked softly. "Don't you know how much we all love you?"

Lance began to cry, softly and despairingly, fighting for control, but losing. "I don't know, Lady Jenny. Ever since I came back, it's been all wrong. Nothing seems to work for me. Nothing except Ricky. He's the one keeping me together, Dad. He should be in charge." He paused and expelled a breath. "I just keep wondering..."

Merlin spoke this time. "What is it you keep wondering, Lance?"

Lance looked at him. "I keep wondering how much better everyone would be if you never brought me back."

Arthur stood and handed the laptop to Jenny. He placed his hands on Lance's shoulders. "No one would be better, Lance, of that I can assure you, me least of all. I love you and I would have died, slowly and despairingly, had Merlin not returned you to me."

Lance looked confused. "But how can you still love me when I keep embarrassing you like this?"

"You don't embarrass me, son, but it pains me to see you embarrass yourself. You are too good for that."

"Dad, it's my fault too," Ricky put in, stepping closer to Lance. "I was supposed to make sure he didn't drink."

"Nay, Ricky, you were supposed to make sure he didn't go in the first place."

Ricky bowed his head in shame.

"I love you both, with all my heart. But can I trust you? Can you be men of your word or not?"

Neither boy responded.

Arthur turned to Merlin and Jenny. "I must give this matter much thought before tomorrow's gathering. It may have to be that Lance shall be in but nominal command of New Camelot in my absence. You Jenny, and you Merlin, may have to be the ones who are really in charge, with all decisions passing through one of you first."

Both adults nodded.

Lance and Ricky exchanged a devastated look between them.

Arthur looked solemn. "Alas, Lance and Ricky, based upon your actions, that may have to be my decision. I'm sorry."

Lance looked shell-shocked. "I understand, father."

Ricky nodded.

"May we be excused?" Lance asked. It was barely a whisper.

"Yes, you may."

Lance grabbed Ricky and practically bolted from the Throne Room. Arthur turned back to Jenny. She stepped forward and hugged him tightly. Merlin looked thoughtfully after the retreating boys.

Lance told Ricky he needed to be alone for a while, so Ricky watched him ascend the stairs. The doorbell rang, and Ricky went to open it. Ryan and Gibson stood outside with Justin. Justin and Ricky did the handclasp, fist bump handshake, and Ricky shook hands with both men. Arthur, Jenny and Merlin entered the lobby and crossed the tiled floor to greet the men.

"Thank you for coming, sergeants," Arthur said by way of welcome.

"Just making sure New Camelot will be secure in your absence, Arthur," Gibson said.

As Gibson and Justin accompanied Arthur and the others in the direction of the Throne Room, Ryan asked to say hello to Lance. When Ricky explained that he was upstairs, Ryan excused himself and followed him up.

When they got to his room, Ricky hurriedly shut the door and made sure Lance wasn't next door before hurrying to his closet and pulling out the bottle.

Ryan eyed it quizzically. He took the bottle and frowned. "Vodka?"

Ricky looked ashamed. "Lance and me was at a party last night."

Ryan lowered the bottle. "Yes, I know. Everyone knows."

Ricky burned with embarrassment.

"You said you think someone tried to kill Lance. How?"

Ricky pointed to the bottle. "I think it might be poisoned."

Ryan flinched. He pulled off the top and sniffed. "Smells like vodka." He replaced the top. "Tell me everything."

Ricky recounted everything that happened regarding Carmen and the bottle. When he finished, Ryan's frown had deepened.

"It is suspicious behavior. You're sure this Carmen was telling the truth when she claimed not to know the man who gave her this?"

"Carmen's the type who knows *every* guy she wants to." He turned red again and looked down at his skating shoes.

Ryan frowned, making the deep creases on his face. "Are you saying she knows *you* like that?"

Ricky looked up, mortified. "Hell, no! She tried, but I'm not like that. Anyway, I believe her."

Ryan frowned again. "Her description only fits about a million residents of L.A. County."

"Maybe I'm just being crazy, Sergeant, you know, over-worried about Lance."

"No, Ricky, you were right to call me. I got a friend at the lab, owes me a favor. I'm gonna have him do a rush toxicology on this and I'll let you know." He paused. "We need to tell Arthur."

"No!" Ricky blurted. "Please, not yet. It might just be me being nutty and I don't wanna worry him about me and Lance any more than he already is."

Ryan looked dubious. "I don' know, son…"

"Please, Sergeant, if it turns out to be poisoned, then we'll tell him. Okay?"

"By then, he'll be on the road."

"I know."

Ryan took a long moment. "Okay. But we're stepping up security here even more than we'd planned. Anytime you and Lance go out, especially if you're speaking to a crowd, I want the schedule in advance. Gib is telling your Dad right now – there's a lot of people out there who want you to fail. And they'll do anything to make that happen. Promise me something, Ricky."

Ricky's stomach clenched with worry. "What?"

"No more sneaking out to parties, for you or Lance. No more going out, period, without full security – your knights and my men. I need you to promise me that."

"I promise, Sergeant." Then he paused. "But I can't speak for Lance."

"Understood," Ryan said firmly. "I'll talk to him. Where is he?"

"The roof."

Ryan's eyebrows shot up.

"It's where he always goes to think."

Ryan nodded.

Lance sat on the parapet, legs dangling over the city, lost in thought. He didn't even notice Ricky's approach. He looked up, startled, and then smiled wanly. Ricky sat beside him and they looked shyly at one another.

"You need to be more alert, Lance," Ricky said, trying for a light tone. "If I was a bad guy, I could've pushed your dumb ass off the roof."

"Why would somebody wanna do that?"

Ricky turned serious. "Cause I think somebody tried to kill you last night."

Lance's mouth dropped open in shock.

Ricky explained what happened and how he didn't want their Dad to know until Sergeant Ryan tested the vodka.

"You called Ryan?"

"Hell, yeah. He's here now. Wants to talk to you."

He nodded back toward the door to the roof. Ryan stood there, shifting on his heels, hands in the pockets of a light brown jacket that was probably ten years out of style.

Lance turned back to Ricky, and Ricky grabbed his hand a moment. "This is serious, Lance. Dad's not the only one who'd die if something happened to you."

Ricky squeezed his hand and then retreated past Ryan to the door, leaving a stunned Lance staring after him.

Ryan gingerly approached. "Morning, Lance. Mind if I sit?"

"No, go ahead."

Ryan sat cautiously beside him, keeping his eyes off the eight-story drop in front of him. "Sorry. Heights aren't my favorite."

"How you been, Sergeant?"

"Doing pretty well, Lance. Thanks for asking."

Lance smiled, but didn't respond.

"You're having a rough time of it these days, aren't you, son?"

"You know, huh?"

"Everyone knows, Lance," Ryan said, confirming Lance's worst fears. "You can't sneeze that it isn't front page news."

"I'm sorry, Sergeant," Lance said, really meaning it. "I let you down too."

Ryan hesitantly placed a hand on Lance's shoulder. "No, you haven't. I was a party boy at your age, Lance, believe it or not."

"You?"

Ryan nodded, pulling his hand back and twiddling with the hem of his jacket. "And a drinker. Started when I was twelve, maybe. My parents put up with hell, Lance, let me tell you. Looking back, I'm not sure why I did that stuff. Wanted to fit in, I guess, didn't want to always be the *good* boy who never did anything wrong. Been sober now for twenty-five years, but it cost me a lot."

"You mean you turned into a drunk? Oh, my bad, I mean a, what do they call it, alcoholic?"

"Yep. Addicted by the time I was sixteen. Been fighting that demon ever since."

"Don't worry, Sergeant. I'm not gonna become a drunk."

"That's what I said."

Lance looked into Ryan's eyes and saw the truth.

"I can't say I know what you're going through, Lance, because I don't. You're the most famous person on earth, and that's a heavy coat to wear. I don't know why you came back, son. Don't know about God and all that. I just know you *did* come back. And I intend to make sure you *stay* back. There's a lot of people out there who want to stop you and your Dad. I'm gonna go down now and talk with him. I want you there, too. Okay?"

"Thanks, Sergeant Ryan."

They stood and moved to the door. As Lance held it open, Ryan looked seriously into his eyes. "You've stumbled, Lance, but don't let yourself fall. It's not only the kids you've given hope to." Then he was through the door and starting down the corridor.

Stunned, Lance hurried after him.

They stopped on the way down from the roof and grabbed Ricky before joining Arthur, Jenny, Merlin, Gibson and Justin in the Throne Room.

Gibson, looking larger than life in his slick suit, power tie, and thick mustache, greeted Lance warmly. "Long time, no see, Lance." They shook hands. "You look good."

Lance offered a shrug. "Yeah, for a dumb-ass party boy with a hangover, I guess."

He did not look his father's way, but Gibson smiled reassuringly. "Did some dumb-ass stuff myself, Lance, and not always as a kid." He glanced over at Justin, who grinned with understanding.

The detective turned back to Lance, all humor gone from his face. "I've been telling Arthur and the others about all the groups lining up to stop you, from the teacher's union to the prison guards to the D.A.'s – well, practically every union in the state."

"But why?" Lance asked, confused. "Wouldn't teachers want kids to have more rights? And if we all become adults, that could mean even more of us in prison, so those guys should be stoked. I don't get it."

"It's about power, Lance," Arthur chimed in. "No one, adults most of all, willingly cede power to others. If you could vote, you could help make laws and take absolute power away from them."

Lance still looked confused.

"See, Lance, this is how it is," Justin explained, looking excited to be in on important knowledge. "Let's take school, man. If them school unions knew we could quit any time we want and go to work, if they gonna keep their jobs, they gotta make school somethin' we wanna come to every day. That takes hard work."

"Exactly," Gibson affirmed with a prideful nod toward his son. "And trade unions don't want more competition for jobs because that might lower their pay scale, especially if a youngster can do the job better, or at least faster."

"And the district attorneys sure as hell don't want you kids sitting on juries," Ryan put in solemnly. "They like the uninformed types. You kids are too streetwise."

Gibson turned back to Arthur. "As I was saying, Arthur, you need a head of security here, especially with you traveling."

"I agree, Sergeant. A wise precaution."

Lance piped up immediately. "I nominate Justin, Dad."

Gibson turned in surprise toward Lance. "Justin?"

"Why not? He's, like, the biggest guy we got 'sides Este, and, well, he's had the best teacher, hasn't he?"

Justin stood straighter, his six foot two-inch height and muscular chest making him seem larger than life, nodding his thanks to Lance.

Ryan slapped Gibson on the back. "Got you there, didn't he, partner?" He winked at Lance, who grinned.

Arthur nodded approvingly at Lance. "I agree with my son. I cannot think of anyone more suitable, with your permission, of course."

Justin practically burst out of his already tight tunic with pride, obviously pleased by Arthur and Lance's support. He looked at his father, his eyes saying all that needed to be said.

Gibson grinned. "Agreed."

Justin high-fived Lance.

Then Ryan glanced at Lance, and Lance knew he wanted to tell Arthur about the possible attempt on his life, but Lance frantically shook his head.

"We can't do anything about protesters outside unless they try to enter the grounds," Gibson explained. "We'll step up patrols in this area, and any time Lance or any of your kids are out in public, especially if it's a rally for your prop, we'll provide police protection. The new mayor is determined not to have any more of your children shot or injured." He involuntarily glanced at Lance.

"I am most appreciative, Sergeant," Arthur said with a bow of respect.

"We need to check how this place screens visitors before they enter," Ryan said. "Your tech guy will have to run names through us and we can check them in our database."

"Is that really necessary, Sergeant?" Jenny asked, her face clouded with worry. "You really think someone might come in here to harm us?"

Lance and Ricky looked at each other, but Ryan retained his composure. "It's a contingency measure, Lady Jenny. Just covering the bases." He tried for a smile, but it just made his craggy face look lopsided.

Gibson pointed to Justin. "With your permission, Arthur, I'd like your new head of security to show me around." He grinned and Justin grinned back. "I can make better recommendations when I have the full lay of the land."

"Of course," Arthur replied with a bow. "Sir Justin, please take your father and Sergeant Ryan any place they'd like to see."

"Yes, Arthur," the boy affirmed with a return bow. "Follow me, Dad."

The two men followed Justin out of the Throne Room.

Arthur gave Lance a long, appraising look. "A very astute suggestion, Lance, Justin as head of security."

Lance looked down at the lush carpet a moment, and then back up. "See, I'm not always a failure."

He turned to leave, and Ricky almost had to run to catch up.

"Lance."

Lance turned back.

The king looked hurt. "Is that what you believe I think of you?"

Lance shook his head. "No, Dad, I know you don't. It's what *I* think of me."

He turned to leave again, and Ricky moved to follow.

"Boys," Arthur called out again. They turned as Arthur approached. When he stood before them, he looked first at Ricky, and then at Lance.

"Lance, you may try my patience at times, as I did that of Merlin when I was your age." He cast a quick glance back at the older man, who nodded vigorously. "But you will never truly disappoint me, son. Never."

Lance almost teared up. "Thanks, Dad." Then he hurried from the room.

Ricky looked at Arthur silently.

"Nor will you disappoint me, my son. Watch over him, Ricky. Keep him safe."

"I will, Dad. You can count on me."

Then Ricky hurried from the room to catch up with Lance.

Merlin smiled knowingly. "They make quite a team, do they not?"

"They do, indeed." Then Arthur grinned. "Was I such a great source of exasperation to you, Merlin, back in our time?"

"You could age me ten years in a day, Arthur."

Jenny laughed, and Arthur joined her.

Ricky caught up with Lance as he was ascending the stairs. Lance swiped away a few tears. "How did we get so lucky, Ricky?"

"Whadda ya mean?"

"To have a dad like him."

Ricky threw his arm around Lance's shoulders. "Maybe 'cause we're both kick ass boys who wanna be just like him."

"Yeah, maybe." Then Lance frowned. "I need to call Michael about, you know, last night."

Ricky flushed.

"You were there, weren't you?"

"Course. I wouldn't leave you alone with him."

Lance felt confused. "I was way out of it, I know, but did I say anything to him or you?"

"You were asleep when I got there."

Lance frowned. "I think I was telling him something important, something about me and… but then I fell asleep and now I can't remember."

"You said that last night, but if you don't remember, oh well, huh?"

"Yeah, I guess."

"You want me there when you talk to him?"

"I know it's just on the phone, but yeah. First, I gotta find Reyna and apologize."

Ricky grimaced. "I'll sit that one out. You come back with a big ole handprint on your face, I'll know it didn't go so good."

Lance chuckled.

He found Reyna and Esteban in the Training Centre practicing with the bow and arrow. Of course, Reyna was the expert, but Esteban had become a very accomplished bowman. Arthur wanted his skills improved before they set out on their tour, so Reyna had been coaching him all week.

Lance entered warily. They both turned to look, but Reyna instantly went back to her shooting, ignoring Lance completely.

Esteban approached and they bumped fists.

"How mad is she?" Lance asked. "One to ten?"

Esteban pulled a face. "About a fifteen."

Lance winced. He had a feeling this might make his hangover even worse.

"Go for it, Lance. You can work your magic on anyone."

He patted him on one shoulder and moved off to advise some of the other boys practicing with swords and shields.

Lance walked cautiously forward, almost afraid she would turn and shoot at him. "Reyna?" It was almost a whisper.

She fired her arrow. It struck dead center of the target. She whipped her head around, long hair flying over her shoulder. "Yes, sire? You have new orders for me?" Her tone reeked of sarcasm, and anger.

Lance lowered his eyes to the floor. "I'm sorry, Reyna, for acting like a jerkbag. You're the most kick-ass sister a guy could ever have and I'd never think I was better than you. I'm not. And I need you." He almost choked on his words, his voice barely a whisper. "I need your advice. I need you to help me make better choices. But mostly, I need you to never stop loving me." He looked up, straight into her wide eyes. "You think maybe you can still do that, even after all I done?"

Reyna stepped closer, hesitant and thoughtful. Then she softened, and that lovely smile lit up her face like sunlight. She engulfed him in such a tight hug, he thought he'd suffocate. "I'll never stop loving you, baby boy, even when you are a jerk."

She let him go and they laughed.

"I'm just having a hard time, Reyna. I don't know why."

"It's tough to have the whole world on your shoulders, Lance. Never forget you have a big family here to help."

"Thanks, sis."

He turned to leave.

"Where's Ricky?" she called after him.

Lance turned back. "Upstairs in my room."

She smiled, as though knowing something Lance did not. "Don't forget what I told you before, Lance, the day of Jack's funeral."

Lance looked startled a moment. "I haven't. Este told me the same thing."

She nodded, and he left the room.

Esteban looked over and gave her a big grin. She puckered and blew an air kiss his way. He reached up to catch it, and they both laughed.

Lance found Ricky in his room reading *Frankenstein*.

He looked up when Lance entered. "You still reading this?"

"I'm almost finished. It's really sad."

"Can I read it when you're done?"

"Sure."

Ricky set the book down. "Ready?"

"No, but I gotta call anyway." He pulled out his phone and called Michael, putting the phone on speaker mode.

A sullen voice answered. "Yeah?"

"It's me. Lance."

"Like I don't see your number on my screen?"

Lance frowned. "Sorry."

"Hello, Ricky boy. I know you're there, too."

Ricky sighed. "Michael."

"You calling about the picture, Lance?"

"Yeah. How do you think they got it?"

"I woke up 'cause I heard the front door close. Someone snuck in and snapped it. He's gonna regret that, Lance, let me tell you." His voice sounded almost demonic.

Lance and Ricky looked at each other in surprise.

"It's okay, Michael," Lance said. "You couldn't even see your face. Only your friends'll know. I'm the only one getting slammed for it. But don't worry – I won't tell anyone who you are."

"I know you won't. But nobody takes my picture without permission. Nobody. When I find out who it was, I'm gonna pound him so badly he'll never take another picture again!"

Lance shivered. "It's not that big a deal, Michael."

"It is to me."

"You, uh, you coming for the gathering tomorrow, Michael? Dad's leaving on Monday for his tour, remember?"

There was a long pause. Then, "You want me to come?" Ricky shook his head no, and Lance hesitated.

"I already know bodyguard doesn't want me," Michael's voice eerily echoed Ricky's head shake. "Do you?"

Lance paused, met Ricky's eye, and then said, "Yes, Michael. I want you to come."

Ricky cursed silently and left to enter his own room.

There was a pause on the line. "What time?"

"One o'clock."

"See ya then."

With a quick blink the call ended, and Lance looked up at the open door connecting his room to Ricky's. He slipped the phone back into his pocket, climbed off the bed and entered. Ricky stood at his vanity looking at a photo in his hand.

Lance approached. It was a photo of the two of them, arms over each other's shoulders, standing on the roof of the hotel attempting to punch each other and laughing like fools. It was taken a few months back, shortly after they moved in.

Lance smiled when he saw it. "That's my favorite picture of us. Shows me kicking your ass, like always."

Ricky set down the photo and turned to Lance, not playing their usual one-up game. "You know Michael isn't right in the head, don't you, Lance?"

"That's not true. He's just..."

"A jerkbag?"

"Well, yeah. But there's more to him than that."

Ricky crossed to his bed, plopping down dejectedly. "That's what you keep saying, Lance, but you're the only one who can see it. All I see is Michael Myers."

Lance sat beside him. "He's not *that* bad."

"Did you hear his voice? Just 'cause somebody took a picture? He sounded psycho. I don't trust him, Lance, especially after—"

Lance's eyes narrowed suspiciously. "After what?"

Ricky didn't answer, but Lance saw something in his eyes. "You think he was behind that bottle of vodka, don't you?"

Ricky flinched. He'd actually been thinking about his own disturbing encounter with Michael, and what the unstable boy might do with Lance's secret, but now that Lance mentioned the vodka, that possibility sounded all too plausible.

"Yeah. He's like, obsessed with you. And it's like he doesn't want anyone else to have you."

"If that's true, why try to kill me? Why not kill Bridget instead?"

"Maybe he just figures if he can't have you, he'll make sure nobody else can, either."

"Don't sweat it, Ricky. Michael would never hurt me."

Ricky looked at him soberly. "You're gonna risk your life on a hunch?"

"Yeah."

Ricky turned away a moment in dismay. "Okay, smart guy, then we'd better get you more wrestling practice, 'cause if a small guy like me can kick your ass, you're no match for a psycho buff boy like Michael."

Lance grinned. "You're on, little man." Then another throb of pain assailed his head, and he paused. "Well, maybe you're on in a few hours. Think I'll just chill and read Frankenstein."

"Okay. I'll warm up with Chris. When you're ready for an ass-whupping, come on down."

Lance laughed and returned to his room.

The next day was to be Arthur's last at New Camelot for two months. Ricky and Lance rose early and got Chris up, dressed and washed, and then all three attended the worship service with Pastor Tom. Arthur was already present, head bowed in prayer, and Lavern entered just after them.

Sometimes, other knights arrived for the eight o'clock service, but since today's gathering was scheduled for one p.m., most elected to arrive later. The service was brief, and the boys prayed for the success of their respective missions, and for the safety of Arthur and the others who would be traveling.

After Pastor Tom bid Arthur a fond farewell and left, the king retreated upstairs to make certain Jenny's room would be ready for her to move into, while the boys headed off to the kitchen for breakfast. They grabbed some cereal, milk, and bowls and headed out to the dining room. Per the orders of Ryan and Gibson, the hotel could not admit any paying guests while Arthur was away unless they had been vetted by a police background check. Thus, the entire hotel, for the moment, belonged to this handful of boys.

Lavern downed his cereal with gusto, more enthusiastic than usual, no doubt due to the journey he was about to embark on. "I never even been out of L.A. before," he gushed to the others, as they sat and shoveled cereal into their mouths.

Lance still felt residual dullness in his head from yesterday's hangover, so he ate slowly and didn't raise his voice too much.

"It's gonna be so cool, Lance," Lavern continued over a mouthful of Lucky Charms. "Arthur wants me to demonstrate my archery skills for kids who come to our rallies, and Sir Rique and Sir Luis and me'r gonna paint some murals too."

Lance smiled. Lavern was almost thirteen. The birthdays of all the knights had by now been put into a Google calendar, so each could be celebrated, at least on a monthly basis. Lance knew Lavern would celebrate his on the road, and made a mental note to remind Arthur on that day.

"I'm happy for you, Lavern." Then he frowned. "But be careful too. Sergeant Ryan says there's a lot of protestors against us."

"Your dad'll keep me safe."

Lance smiled.

Then Lavern's young face clouded over. "I wish he could adopt me too, but my mother won't let him."

Ricky placed a hand on the younger boy's shoulder. "You're still our brother, Lavern. Never forget that."

"Never," echoed Lance, and Lavern beamed brightly.

Chris leaned over and grabbed him in a hug. "Thanks for the drawing lessons, brother."

Lavern hugged him back. "No sweat, little man." It seemed everyone had adopted Lance's nickname for Chris, and hardly anyone ever called him Chris anymore.

Lavern leaped to his feet. "I gotta pack the rest 'a my stuff. See you later, brothers." He pelted through the double doors into the kitchen to wash his dishes.

As Lance and Ricky sent Chris in after him with his empty bowl, Ricky asked, "You sorry you're not going with Dad, too?"

"Kind of. But at least I still got you here."

"You mean someone to beat you down?"

Lance chuckled. "No, someone to be my tackling dummy in the workout room."

"In your dreams."

The boys finished their cereal and headed into the kitchen to clean up.

Michael arrived just before one, much to the chagrin of Reyna and Esteban. But Lance welcomed him. Ricky acknowledged him with the basic head nod, his mind flashing back to images of the boy's strong arms wrapped around his throat, cutting off his breathing and making him feel closer to death than he'd ever been before. And what about Lance's secret? So far, Michael had kept the knowledge to himself, at least so far as Ricky knew. Would he use it to blackmail Lance down the line, or maybe turn Lance against *him* for breaking his promise? The various possibilities terrified Ricky because, despite Lance's opinion to the contrary, he believed Michael was capable of anything.

Knights had been pouring in all morning, and the Throne Room filled to overflowing by the time the meeting was called to order.

Up front with Arthur sat Lance in his usual chair, Ricky beside him, and Chris beside Ricky. On Arthur's other side were Jenny, Merlin, and Reyna.

Arthur raised Excalibur to call the gathering to order.

"My noble knights and ladies. As you all know, tomorrow I embark upon the first leg of my journey to win the hearts and minds of the people in Northern California. We have millions of supporters throughout the state amongst the youth, but we must win over their parents, as well, since it is they who will vote on our proposition. This journey is but the first phase of our campaign. Reyna will coordinate with Merlin and Lady Jenny all public appearances within Southern California, so that you who remain may drum up support for our cause. In my absence, command of New Camelot and the final arbiter over all of you shall be my son and heir, Sir Lance. Sir Ricky shall act as his First Knight. Approval of any action, however small, which may in any way reflect upon New Camelot or our crusade, must go through them. They will have as advisers Lady Jenny, Merlin and Lady Reyna. Does this be clearly understood?"

Lance's mouth dropped open in shock.

There were head nods and murmuring from the assembled knights, some sounding disgruntled. One boy said a little too loudly, "Just 'cause he's Arthur's son. If I pulled that crap, I'd be kicked out."

Lance heard the comment, and embarrassment washed over him.

The dissenter was a skinny, scruffy-haired Caucasian boy named Charley, who was scowling at the boy beside him.

"Sir Charley, you wish to speak?"

Charley looked mortified at having been caught. "No, sire."

Arthur gazed at him from atop the stage. "Step forward, Sir Charley."

Reluctantly, Charley disengaged himself from his row, worked his way up the center aisle and stood before the king. "I apologize, Arthur. No disrespect intended."

"None taken, Sir Charley. But, did I understand you to say that if you had behaved foolishly, in the manner of so many teenaged boys, that I would kick you out of the Round Table?"

"Well, yeah. I mean, I'm not your son or nothing, so I figured..."

"Sir Charley, what is the reason we launched this campaign in the first place?"

Charley considered a moment. "Cause adults in this state don't wanna give us kids a second chance, or sometimes even a first one? Cause they just wanna throw us away if we screw up?"

"Crudely, but succinctly put, Sir Charley. So why would I, who am fighting against such behaviors, engage in them myself?"

Charley's mouth dropped open. "I didn't think of it that way, Arthur. I just thought..."

"You thought I was favoring my son over others."

"Yeah."

"Thank you, Sir Charley. You may retake your seat."

Embarrassed, Charley slunk back to his seat and Arthur looked out over the throng. "My knights and ladies, the entire purpose of our crusade is to remind the adults of this state that youth such as yourselves are going to *screw up*, as Sir Charley so eloquently put it, and that it be our job as adults to give you as many chances as you need to get it right. My son has been running through a dark place since returning to us in so painful a fashion, and he has made mistakes. Embarrassing mistakes. But he is still my son. I love him, and I forgive him, and I will never give up on him. That is the message, ladies and gentlemen, the message we must impart to every adult in this state. Can you all do this?"

They shouted their vociferous assent.

Arthur turned to Lance, who still had his mouth open in surprise. He'd been sure Arthur would castigate him in front of everyone. "My son, would you like to address the company?"

Surprised, Lance hesitated. Ricky elbowed him and grinned supportively. Lance looked out at the first row and spotted Michael grinning at him. Not smirking as usual, but grinning, as though with admiration. Lance stood and Arthur resumed his seat.

Lance cleared his throat as he scanned all the faces, some of which clearly showed their disappointment in him. "I take this moment to apologize to you all for my behavior, and any embarrassment it might've caused you. I guess I picked the wrong time to become a stupid, selfish teenager."

There were a few laughs at that.

"I won't let you down again. With Dad—that is, King Arthur— gone, I'll do my best to be a leader like I used to be, one you can all respect and follow. I got Sir Ricky ready to kick my butt if I don't."

More laughter.

"And I told Lady Reyna that if I step out of line again, she can slap my face in front of everyone."

The company laughed again.

"And she'll do it, too. Besides, I also have Lady Jenny and Merlin on my team, so I'll be okay. We're ready for this. We're gonna go out there on this campaign, and we're gonna kick butt. Right?"

The kids cheered and whooped and hollered.

"I didn't hear you!" Lance called out with a hand to his ear. The knights roared thunderously, and Lance grinned.

Michael threw him a thumbs-up sign, which made Ricky frown.

Lance resumed his seat and Arthur concluded the meeting with a prayer for their success.

When the knights scattered to the Training Centre or Computer Lab or weight room, or any of the other places they liked to hang out, Lance and Ricky stayed behind. Michael hovered near the door, obviously waiting for Lance to finish with Arthur.

Lance gazed awkwardly at his father. "I thought you were gonna, ya know, tell 'em I wasn't fit to command, like you said yesterday."

Arthur tilted his head quizzically. "I said you weren't fit to command, son, or you did?"

"I did." He studied his father's face. "You still believe in me, right?"

"I would not leave you in charge, Lance, if I did not."

Lance felt such an overwhelming rush of gratitude that it almost made him weak. "I'm gonna earn back your trust, Dad. You'll see."

Arthur smiled.

Lance understood that *he* was the only one who could win back Arthur's trust, not with his words, but with his actions.

Then the king cast an uncertain eye toward Michael hovering by the door, and leaned in to Lance and Ricky. "I require a solemn oath from you both. Can you give it?"

"Sure," Lance agreed at once, and Ricky nodded his assent.

"You must promise me to go nowhere with Michael in my absence. He may come here. Bridget may visit, as well."

"What about Ariel?" Ricky asked hurriedly.

Arthur's eyebrows shot up curiously.

"She's a girl I like," Ricky explained from beneath a slight blush.

"Of course, Ricky, she may visit, as well. But you may not accompany Michael or the girls to any venues beyond the public speaking engagements Reyna will set up. Do I have your word, boys? Your solemn word as knights of the Round Table? Your word as my sons?"

"You have mine, Dad," Lance affirmed.

"And mine," Ricky asserted.

Arthur visibly relaxed. "Thank you. Now, if you would not mind awaiting Michael in the lobby a moment. I must speak with him."

The boys headed toward the door. As they passed Michael, Lance said, "My Dad wants to talk to you. We'll wait in the lobby."

Michael sauntered up to the front of the room and looked disdainful. "Yeah, Arthur?"

Arthur knew the ladies and Merlin were watching intently, but he ignored them. "I give you permission to visit New Camelot in my absence, and to accompany Lance and the others on their speaking engagements, if you so desire. However, neither of my sons is to accompany you to any parties or venues that are not part of our crusade. Do I make myself clear, Michael?"

"Crystal, sire. Anything else?"

"I don't trust you, Michael, but Lance does, and he wishes your presence near to him. However, if anything should happen to my son, if you in any way harm him, I shall hunt you down and, boy or no, I shall kill you."

Jenny gasped, but Reyna nodded approvingly.

Michael glared up at Arthur, anger replacing smugness. "I'm not afraid of you." He turned to leave.

"Michael," Arthur said, and when the boy turned he found the point of Excalibur at his throat. Another half inch and he would've been dead. "You should be. Mark my words."

Michael made no sudden moves until Arthur pulled back the sword. He met Arthur's fierce gaze with an unreadable expression. Then he offered a half bow before turning to exit the Throne Room.

Jenny hurried up to him in shock. "Arthur, I can't believe you threatened him. He's a boy."

Arthur gazed at her soberly. "Aye, but a dangerous boy. Reyna thinks as I do, do you not, Reyna?"

"Hell, yeah."

"Watch him, Reyna, whenever he is on the premises, and whenever he is near to Lance."

"I will, Arthur. Trust me on that."

"And have Sir Techie seek out information on his background. We know nothing of him."

"I'll get on that. Don't worry, Arthur. He won't hurt Lance, or Ricky. He'll have to go through me, first." Reyna grinned, and Arthur patted her on the shoulder.

"That's my girl."

She smiled and left to find Esteban so they could pack up the weapons Arthur would need for his trip.

Jenny turned to Merlin. "Merlin, what's your opinion of Michael? Do you think he's dangerous?"

Merlin looked thoughtful. "He is an enigma to me, as well, Lady Jenny. I think, in this case, Arthur made the right call."

Jenny shook her head in disgust. "Men. You always go to violence first."

Arthur looked at her. "Not first, but always if it is required."

She sighed. "I've got to organize my room and prepare lessons for the week." She leaned in and they kissed before she exited the Throne Room, leaving Arthur and Merlin together.

"Well, old friend, tell me true – do you believe Lance is up to the task I have set before him?"

Merlin shrugged, one ear bud in and the other out, as always. "As I explained when I brought him back, Arthur, if he isn't, there is no one else who is. Let us hope and pray."

"And what of Ricky? Was he in your vision?"

Now Merlin frowned with confusion. "No, which somewhat confounds me. He could make or break Lance, and yet he remains invisible to me."

Both men fell silent, contemplating what the future might hold, for them and for all of New Camelot.

EQUALITY UNDER THE LAW

CHAPTER TEN

ALL THEY WANNA DO IS THROW US AWAY

As Monday morning dawned and Arthur bade everyone goodbye before boarding the bus with his entourage and setting out, Lance and Ricky, though titular rulers of New Camelot in his stead, alas were forced to succumb to California law and attend school as usual. It felt both odd and comforting to be sitting with Lady Jenny as regular boys on the one hand, and strange to know that at any moment either or both could be called away on crusade business.

First, however, Lance called Helen and told her they'd scheduled a press conference for Tuesday to answer questions about the prop, and the new unflattering images of him. He'd expected her to express her personal disappointment in his behavior, especially after giving him that live one-on-one interview last time, but she was enthusiastic and professional, as always. As he hung up, Lance wondered why more people in the media couldn't be as understanding as her.

Calls had been coming in all weekend regarding Lance's behavior, with requests for interviews from numerous magazines, not to mention the mainstream news outlets. Helen did ask Lance when they spoke if he could handle another barrage of questions, given his outburst the previous time. He said he could, because this press conference would focus on the prop and he would only answer a few questions about his bad behavior.

Lance was called away during morning break to take a phone call from the new mayor, inviting him and Ricky to his office to discuss Arthur's requests for public speaking permits, and the opportunity to use City Hall as one of them. Mayor Soto sounded cordial and eager to meet "the most famous boy in the world," which made Lance cringe a little.

They agreed on Tuesday at two o'clock in his office, right after the press conference, which the mayor agreed could be held in front of City Hall. That way any interested elected officials could easily attend. Several council members and Chief Murphy would also be present at the office meeting. Hanging up, Lance felt he'd handled himself in a very professional manner. When he turned to leave the front office, he found Ricky grinning at him from the doorway.

"So, Lance, when you gonna run for mayor?"

"How about never!" They shared a laugh and high fived. "You're coming with me tomorrow, so don't think you got a day off."

"Of course I gotta come. Who's gonna watch over your dumb ass if I don't?"

Lance eyed the other boy warmly. "Is that what you do?"

"Damn straight."

Lance grinned.

Later that afternoon, while knights were in the Training Centre or doing their homework, Lance and Ricky met with Reyna and Techie in the Computer Lab to plan out the speaking events. Techie had put up on their website and Facebook page a link so organizations could request Lance and his knights to come and speak to their members. Reyna's job would be to sift through them and select the ones she felt would maximize their visibility in promoting the prop and their mission.

Unfortunately, with the latest inflammatory pictures of Lance making the Internet rounds, some organizations had already rescinded their previous requests, especially church groups. Lance understood it was his fault, and so did everyone else, but he was grateful his fellow knights didn't rub it in.

Sifting through the existing requests, they settled on a fairly large number, one or two per day for the next two months. It would be a daunting schedule, especially since the kids could only go on the road after noon on school days. Weekends were different, and would be utilized as often as possible.

Sir Techie then showed Lance a specific request he'd received from the Make-A-Wish Foundation. A young boy had requested to spend a day at New Camelot with Lance.

"What's the Make-a-Wish Foundation?" Lance asked.

"It's a group that grants last wishes to dying kids," Techie answered matter-of-factly.

Lance was stunned. "What do you mean?"

Reyna shrugged. "You know, kids with cancer and stuff."

"Oh, wow," Ricky whispered.

"This boy," Techie went on, "wrote to the organization that his hero is Sir Lance of the Round Table and his wish is to spend a day with Sir Lance at New Camelot and experience what it's like to be a knight for a day."

Lance was almost speechless, glancing at Ricky and then at Reyna.

Reyna smiled. "See, brother, you're still a hero."

Lance nodded, something stirring in his memory. A post he remembered from a kid with cancer...

"What'll I tell them, Lance?" Sir Techie asked when Lance remained silent.

"Oh, sorry. Of course, tell them it's okay," Lance replied, still stunned at the thought of a young child dying from cancer.

Reyna nodded. "But have Justin run this link through his dad to make sure it really *is* Make-A- Wish contacting us."

"Good thinking, Reyna," Ricky acknowledged, tossing her a smile. "Gotta keep my boy safe."

Lance was lost in thought, amazed that a kid would want to spend some of his last precious hours with him. With great fame came great responsibility, he realized.

After working out their appearance schedule for the next two months, Lance and Ricky headed off to the Training Centre. Before sparring, both texted their girls and invited them to come over whenever they wanted, and also to attend any of the rallies they had planned.

Both Bridget and Ariel expressed nervousness about coming to New Camelot without Michael's permission, but the boys assured them it was okay. They would pick days Michael would not be there.

After this, the boys wrestled for a time. Each won and lost several matches. Then they worked out with swords, and finally bows and arrows. Chris joined them for sword and shooting practice, and the boys had a tiring, thorough workout.

Michael did not show or call or text.

After showering, Lance lay on his bed, head up against the headboard, reading *Frankenstein*. He'd thrown on some shorts, but no shirt, and was engrossed in the story when Ricky wandered in from his room, wearing shorts and drying his hair with a towel.

"Hey Lance, can I borrow your hairdryer, man? Mine crapped out on me."

Lance looked up from his book. "Uh, sure. Under my sink."

"Almost finished with Frankenstein?" Ricky asked, approaching the bed.

"Yeah," Lance answered, his voice wistful.

His tone prompted Ricky to climb onto the bed and sit beside him. "Is it scary at all?"

"No, mostly sad, like I told you before."

"Isn't it about a monster, like in the movies?"

"Yeah, but he didn't start out that way. People made him into a monster."

"What does that mean?"

"I'm almost done and then you can read it. See for yourself."

Ricky nodded, and they fell silent a moment.

"Wonder why Michael wanted you to read that," Ricky finally said.

"Dunno," Lance replied thoughtfully. "Maybe he can relate to it somehow."

"Well, he is kind of a monster."

"I was thinking more of Victor, the creator. He's an arrogant genius."

"Yeah, that's Michael, too. Genius *and* monster."

Lance eyed him carefully, searching his face and uncertain eyes for insight into his mood, but found nothing to "soul-whisper," as Ricky called his unique talent. Deciding to change the subject, he said, "Wow, your hair is catching up to mine."

Ricky smiled and they held eye contact a long moment before Ricky threw his towel at Lance and started to climb off the bed. But Lance tackled him and they rolled around on the huge bed, each trying to gain an advantage over the other, laughing like two kids without a care in the world.

Finally, Lance landed on top of Ricky, straddling him and pinning his hands to the bed, their faces suddenly close together. Their laughter ceased, and awkwardness overwhelmed them.

They looked uncertainly at one another before Ricky, panting slightly, said, "Okay, Lance, you win this round. You can get off me now."

Lance hesitated, as though in a daze.

"Lance?" Ricky whispered, almost desperately. "Please get off me."

Lance suddenly awoke from whatever realm he'd dropped into and rolled off Ricky. "Sorry."

"No prob. I'll be on top next time." Realizing what he just said, Ricky's face flamed red.

Then they laughed.

Lance threw the towel back at him. "Time to dry your hair, fool."

Ricky leapt off the bed, heading into Lance's bathroom. Lance found his eyes following Ricky, trying to figure out what had just happened, and why he so often felt awkward around him these days. Deciding he didn't want to think about it, he picked up *Frankenstein* and resumed reading.

A few minutes later, there was a knock at his door. "Come in,"

Jenny entered.

Lance immediately pulled a pillow up over his naked torso, and Ricky stuck his head out of the bathroom, also looking embarrassed.

"Lady Jenny," they both said simultaneously, and Jenny couldn't help but laugh.

"It's okay, Lance and Ricky," she chided good-naturedly at their discomfort. "I have seen a few boys with their shirts off in my time."

Both boys relaxed, Lance dropping the pillow back beside him before getting off the bed. "Sorry, Lady Jenny. You just surprised me."

"I understand." She indicated the book. "Is that one I assigned you?"

"Michael gave it to me." He showed her the cover.

She nodded approvingly. "Michael has good taste. A very thought-provoking story."

"Yeah, it is."

Jenny eyed him, also noting Ricky staring at the two of them from the bathroom door, hairdryer in hand. "I just wanted to see how you're doing, Lance, if you're ready for the press conference tomorrow."

Lance shifted uncomfortably. "I guess. I know the prop stuff real good, but I know they're all gonna attack me about those pictures." He cast a look Ricky's way.

"Don't let them, Lance," Jenny said. "Say what you want to say about what happened, take a few questions about it, and then close that door for good. Stick to the prop after that and don't… well, let them upset you."

Lance grinned. "You mean, don't yell at 'em like I did before."

She laughed, and so did Ricky. "Yeah, that's what I mean. I just spoke with your dad and he said to tell you he loves you both and he'll be watching tomorrow before they have their first rally in Fresno."

"Cool. When can I talk to him?"

"He's your dad, honey. You can call any time you want."

"Awesome. I'll check in after dinner."

Jenny handed him a piece of paper. "Something your dad said yesterday made me think of this quote. I think it's from a book or maybe the movie of the book. I can't recall exactly. But it reminded me of you and I wrote it down as best as I could remember. Maybe it'll help." She smiled reassuringly. "Don't forget, I'll be with you tomorrow. Anybody who takes an unfair shot at my boy will be down for the count." She smiled and made a swinging motion with her fist.

Lance's eyes widened. "You'd cuss 'em out?"

"Better me than you."

Lance frowned. "I want Dad to be proud of me, Lady Jenny, like he used to be."

She placed both hands on his cheeks so they could make eye contact. "He's never stopped being proud of you, Lance." Then her gaze included Ricky. "Both of you. See you at dinner."

Lance grinned and she exited. Ricky returned to the bathroom to finish his hair while Lance sat on his bed to read what Jenny had given him. He nearly gasped aloud. It fit him so perfectly, he could've written it himself. In fact, it fit his whole life, even the part he still kept hidden from Arthur, the part that scared him most of all. How had Jenny come up with something so perfect?

Ricky came out of the bathroom and sat beside him. "What'd she give you?"

Lance scooted over and they both read the typed words.

"Wow," Ricky whispered. "That's me."

"Me too. More than you know."

Ricky looked at him seriously. "Anything you wanna tell me?"

"Naw. But I'm gonna use this tomorrow."

Ricky nodded and went back to his room to dress for dinner.

Lance felt nervous during school lessons, and couldn't focus. His mind was on the press conference. He'd spoken with Arthur the night before and the king assured him that he would do just fine. As long as he didn't allow anyone to goad him into losing his temper, he would come out the winner. Arthur's words helped him a little then, but now his stomach was churning with anxiety. Jenny excused her classes early so she could get Lance and Ricky ready for the press conference and subsequent meeting with Mayor Soto. The boys dressed in their finest tunics, Lance's green contrasting with Ricky's red, and freshly pressed pants. Both had matching circlets around their brows to restrain their hair and wore their standard knee-high boots. Ryan and Gibson arrived to provide police escort to City Hall.

The boys queried Ryan about the vodka, but he shook his head. "Might hear something today," he added, and led them out to the car.

There was a huge phalanx of reporters and news cameras in front of City Hall, as well as an enormous crowd hoping for a glimpse of The Boy Who Came Back. Hundreds of cops held back the multitude and blocked off the area around the stage, once again set up along the Temple Street entrance. As Ryan and Gibson escorted Jenny and the boys through the crowd, people reached out to touch Lance, as though just a touch would somehow bless them. He did his best to smile and nod and say thanks when people called out support for him. He heard "queer" and "pervert" shouted a few times, but chose to ignore those. When they reached the stage and climbed the several steps to the podium, Helen was right there waiting for them. She smiled as they approached.

"You ready, Lance?"

Her smile calmed him a bit. "Yeah."

"I'll let everyone know you're going to make a statement and then open up the floor to questions."

Lance nodded, catching Ricky's eye as he did. Ricky flashed a look that somehow made him feel special and unique. How Ricky did that, he didn't know. But it relaxed him and that's what mattered.

Jenny also smiled Lance's way and he tossed her a grin.

Helen stepped to the podium and spoke into the microphone. "As you all know, Sir Lance is here to make a statement on the most recent photos and videos that surfaced over this past weekend. Then he will entertain a few questions. However, the main purpose of this press conference is to discuss Proposition 51, The Child Voter Act. I'll turn it over to Sir Lance."

There was substantial applause from the crowd, but not from everyone, Lance noted, as he moved to the microphone and looked out over the massive throng.

"Good afternoon, everyone," he began, anxiety sweeping over him as the hundreds of faces stared at him with expectation. "As Lady Helen said, I'm going to explain as best I can about the embarrassing stuff I did over the weekend, but mostly I'm here to talk about our prop and answer your questions."

Hands immediately shot up and questions began to be shouted.

Lance raised his hand to silence them. "Please, no questions until I've said what I have to say."

He paused, glanced at Ricky standing just to his right. Ricky gave him that look again, and Lance relaxed. "I'm going to start by reading something Lady Jenny gave me. It kind of sums up my life, especially where I'm at right now."

He pulled the paper from his pocket and began to read, "For every child, there comes a time of running through a dark place, and there's no word for a child's fear, and no one to hear it if there was a word, and no one to understand it even if they heard."

He stopped and lowered the paper, looking solemnly out at the expectant faces. "That's been me all my life, until my Dad found me and took me in and showed me what real love was. I had a lot of fears growing up, and I'm still running through that dark place, 'specially since I came back. I don' know, maybe it's 'cause of Sir Jack, or maybe it's just 'cause I still don't know who I am, or why God brought me back. Everyone expects so much from me, and that's scary. I wanna be a regular kid, too, but I can't."

He paused a moment, sweeping his eyes over their expectant faces. They were listening. "I snuck out with Ricky last Friday night 'cause I wanted to see the girl in that video. And no, don't ask her name 'cause I won't tell you. I'm glad you can't see her face clearly because I don't want her being messed with. Is she my girlfriend? I think I'd like her to be, you know? But my life isn't normal, so things like having a girlfriend are harder for me than for other kids. When I'm with her I get super nervous and I drink, and I can't drink. When I drink, that dark place gets darker, and I get more scared and really sad. My whole life comes flooding back in, and I think of Mark and Jack and whether or not my Dad will be disappointed in me."

He paused again to take a breath, emotions roiling through him, those butterflies in his stomach dancing like crazy.

"Anyway, yeah, I was obviously kissing the girl – the alcohol brings that out too. But that video didn't show me start to cry, or my friend grabbing me and taking me to his bedroom so I wouldn't embarrass myself in front of everyone. He put me on his bed and was gonna let me sleep there, but I begged him to stay. I was lonely and sad and didn't wanna be alone. So he lay there with me till I fell asleep. I guess he did too, 'cause somebody took that picture."

He paused and looked out over the crowd.

"I didn't do anything with him, or with her. I'm not ready for that yet. But I can tell you that was my last party, and my last bottle of booze. It's illegal anyway for us kids, and I need to set a better example. And there's no way I'm gonna become a drunk and disappoint my father, or anybody else out there who looks up to me. I'm not perfect, but I'm not bad, either. I may be the Boy Who Came Back, but I'm still just a boy, and I have a lot to learn. Adults used to be willing to give kids a hand when we fell, a second or third chance to get something right when we screwed it up."

Again, he stopped and gazed at them intently. Some were nodding their heads, others just staring.

"But not anymore. You can't wait to pounce on me every time I do something stupid or show bad judgment. You seem to like watching kids fall. You're all like, what's the word, voyeurs? I'm not some reality TV show and neither is any other kid out here who screws up. I always thought adults were s'posed to help us kids when we messed up, but I was wrong. You just wanna laugh or mock or throw us in jail or kick us out of school. That's pretty much why we launched this campaign, and it's the whole purpose of our prop. Since you adults won't look out for us kids any more, us kids gotta look out for each other."

When he finished, the crowd applauded, much louder and with more support than before. Hands shot up instantly from the reporters.

He scowled when he saw the yellow-haired guy up near the front, and pointed to someone else.

"Sir Lance, why was your head resting on his chest?"

"I, uh, don't know, really. I was pretty drunk and fell asleep right away."

The same reporter continued, "It's a very romantic picture, Sir Lance, you have to admit, your head resting on his chest."

Lance felt his face grow hot. "There you go again with the voyeur stuff. Look, I was unhappy and lonely and he was there. He was being a friend. Why is it so horrible for boys to comfort each other?"

Another hand shot up, and Lance pointed.

"You're a role model for kids all over the world, Sir Lance," the male reporter said. "We appreciate you explaining the drinking and vowing to stop that behavior. But the provocative nature of these pictures leads kids everywhere to think you're sexually active, possibly with both girls and boys. How do you feel about that image you've cultivated?"

Lance's jaw dropped open, and Ricky put a hand on his arm to keep him from exploding.

But Lance was too stunned to explode. "If the people of California vote no on our prop, it'll be illegal for you to ask a kid that question. It should be now, but obviously it isn't. I already told you, I'm not doing anything with either that girl or that boy, or anyone else. Now we're done with the party questions. It's the prop from here on out."

Helen, right in front, put up her hand and Lance pointed to her. "Can you tell us, Sir Lance, in so many words, the purpose of your proposition?"

"I already just told you part of it, Lady Helen. It's because adults don't want to parent us kids or mentor us or help us when we fall or give us second chances. All they wanna do is throw us away. If I'm adult enough when I get in trouble out in the streets, then I sure as hell am adult enough to vote for these kinds of laws and to sit on juries when you put us on trial. At least with our prop, kids'll have a jury of their peers who actually know what's up out here, and we'll be more fair than the adults who got no clue what it's like being a kid today."

Another reporter raised her hand. Lance pointed. "Why do you want fourteen-year-olds to be able to quit school if they can find a job?"

"Because the schools and the people in Sacramento running them don't care about us or what we might wanna do in life," he answered firmly. "Just from all our clean-ups last year, I learned a lot of job skills, career skills to make a good living, more useful stuff than I ever learned in high school. All we hear is college, college, college, whether we want it or not. Why college? Is it for us? No, it's for the money. More money to the state and more to the student loan program. I've done my homework. What's wrong with trade school? Why can't high schools start teaching us those skills, too? If we kids have a choice to stay or leave school, the teachers and administrators are actually gonna have to work hard to keep our business. That means they have to offer us more than the same one-size-fits-all classes that might not be what we want to do with our lives. I've heard the teacher's union is against us on this. Wonder why. Next question."

More hands flew up excitedly. Lance pointed to a female reporter with big hair.

"What about the other unions, Sir Lance? Pretty much all have come out against you. As have most of our elected officials."

Lance offered a little smile. "I think everyone is afraid of the competition. We proved last summer that we can be pretty effective plumbers and carpenters and electricians, and work harder than a lot of the real ones, and we learn fast. If we become legal adults, we can make our own decisions about apprenticing ourselves out to whoever might take us, and they don't have to pay us minimum, either. We can take less, if we want, in exchange for learning the trade. Isn't more competition always a good thing?"

He looked outward, heartened to see some heads nodding in the crowd. Quite a few, actually.

"As for why the D.A.'s don't like us, that's a 'duh'. They wanna put as many of us in prison as they can, and the prison guards love that 'cause then they got kids in there for life. But the D.A.'s sure as hell don't want us sitting on juries because we know how life goes down out here and we're not gonna convict every kid, or every adult, just because the guy's charged with a crime. And you said the elected officials are against us? They don't want more voters who can fire them when they don't do their job. Big surprise there. Next question."

Yellow Hair put up his hand. Reluctantly, Lance pointed to him. "What about your stipulation that even though fourteen-year-olds will be adults in some ways, they cannot consent to have sex with anyone over the age of eighteen?"

Ricky came and stood beside Lance.

Lance shivered, but fought down the shakes. "That's in there because adults having sex with kids is wrong. It's perverted. It's evil."

There were gasps from some in the crowd.

"Do you have personal experience in that area, Sir Lance? Is that why it's in there?" Yellow Hair awaited his response.

Lance hesitated.

"Well, Sir Lance?"

Lance took a deep breath, turned to a worried Jenny, and then to Ricky. He had that look in his eyes, that special look. Lance gave him a shy little smile of thanks, and then gazed out at the crowd.

He froze.

Like Freddy Krueger rising from the depths of his deepest, darkest nightmares, there he was, standing at the very back of the crowd, leering up at him.

Richard!

The boogeyman.

The demon of his dreams.

Lance sucked in a terrified breath.

"What's wrong?" Ricky whispered, leaning in closer.

"It's him!" Lance whispered back, barely breathing, his heart suddenly pounding.

"Who?"

"Richard."

Ricky's eyes scanned the crowd.

Lance saw Richard duck behind some other people and could no longer tell where he was.

"Where?" Ricky asked.

"Out there, in the back."

Ricky leaned in. "I'm gonna tell Sergeant Ryan."

Lance grabbed Ricky's hand. "No. Don't leave me."

"I won't."

Lance released his hand.

The reporters and the crowd were murmuring, obviously wondering what was going on up there.

Lance saw Yellow Hair smugly awaiting an answer to his question. He regained control over his shaking, leaned back in to the microphone, looked straight at the man and said, "Yes, I have personal experience in that area."

There were gasps from the crowd.

"When I was six years old."

The crowd exploded with stunned surprise, and cameras flashed like mad.

Lance composed himself as best he could while they settled back down.

"This city put me in a foster home with a pervert who raped me and did sex stuff with me and threatened me and scared the crap out of me for three years till I finally ran away. You asked why I been acting out. Now you know one of the biggest reasons. So yeah, that part of the prop is real personal."

Yellow Hair wasn't deterred. "But you weren't fourteen. What about the age of consent being fourteen?"

Ricky stepped boldly forward. "I got raped last year, when I *was* fourteen, by older men who used me for sex. I was homeless and didn't have no one or nothing. We're not gonna let sleazy groups like AMBLO have their way with us. Hell no!"

Hands rose and questions flew at Lance. He held up a hand for quiet.

"I've said all I'm gonna say about my childhood. You can't understand it 'cause it wasn't you. Like I said before, there's no word for a child's fear, and no one to hear it if there was a word, and no one to understand it even if they heard. It's something I've been running from ever since, and I'm not sure I can ever stop. Now, are there more questions about the prop?"

Helen raised her hand again.

"Yes, Lady Helen?"

"Given all the opposition to you and your proposition from so many unions and other groups, how will you get the signatures required to qualify your measure for the November ballot?"

Lance smiled. "Children can be very persuasive, Lady Helen. Wait and see."

He glanced at his phone. It was nearly two p.m. "Thank you all for coming out here. I have an appointment with the mayor and don't want to be late. We have some knights circulating with petitions, if any of you wish to sign and support us. Members of the press will be emailed our schedule of campaign stops for the entire month, just in case you want to come out and heckle me, or maybe even support me. Have a great day."

Lance turned to Ricky and their eyes locked a moment. "Thanks for backing me up, Ricky."

"I always got your back," Ricky said as they did the fist-bump.

Jenny engulfed him in a tight hug. "I'm so proud of you, Lance. You were amazing."

He pulled away and met her eyes. "You think Dad's proud?"

"I know he is." She held up her phone. Arthur's face floated in the center of the screen, grinning with pride.

"There have been many an occasion, Lance, for which I have felt immense pride in thee, but none more so than today," he said. "You handled that masterfully."

Lance could scarcely breathe for a moment. "Thanks, Dad. I'm trying to be like you."

"With what you just did, son, and what you revealed to the world of your suffering, you are far and away a greater man than me. I do not believe I would've been courageous enough to do what you did. I love you, Lance."

Lance almost burst into tears. "Love you, too, Dad."

"And where is my other son?"

Ricky stuck his face in front of the phone. "Hi, Dad."

"I say to you what I said to Lance. Your courage to reveal your pain for the good of our cause humbles me. You, too, make me proud, and I love you, Ricky. Never doubt that."

Ricky grinned. "Thanks, Dad."

Jenny put her face to the phone. "We've got to go, Arthur. They have an appointment with the mayor."

Arthur smiled. "Thank you, milady."

"Good luck up there," she said back and then the call ended. She turned to the boys. "Ready? The mayor awaits."

When Ryan and Gibson led Jenny and the boys through the expansive City Hall lobby to the elevators, Lance shivered, flashing back to that night last October when he'd awakened within the City Council Chambers and found his beloved Jack dead. Ricky slipped his arm behind Lance's back to squeeze his hand in quiet support. Lance offered a tight smile of thanks.

Neither boy had ever been inside the mayor's office, and thought it ostentatious with its massive oaken desk, plush, expensive-looking chairs, flat-screen television on one wall, high-end artwork adorning the others. There were four people present, but Lance only recognized the police chief.

Mayor Soto, a short, stocky man with a crew cut and big ears, greeted Lance warmly with a hearty, "Well, if it isn't the young Mr. Lincoln."

"Excuse me?" Lance said uncertainly.

The mayor extended a hand. "Julian Soto, at your service, Sir Lance. This is Police Chief Murphy, Council President Sanders and Vice President Gale."

Lance, Ricky, and Jenny shook hands with all of them.

"It's an honor to finally meet you, Sir Lance," Gale said, eying him appraisingly. She was African-American with big hair, red lipstick, and round cheeks. "I never got the opportunity after you… well, came back."

Lance nodded, and then turned to the mayor. "Why'd you call me young Mr. Lincoln?"

"The way you handled those reporters, that crowd, it was brilliant, Lance. You have the gift, young man, just like our sixteenth president."

"Gift?" Lance echoed.

"How to charm a crowd," the mayor affirmed. "How to mollify the belligerent without seeming uppity yourself. You're a natural, son. I can see why Arthur put you in charge. How's he doing up north, by the way?"

"Okay, I guess. The first campaign stop is this afternoon. You'll see it on the news, I'm sure."

"I'm sure I will. You know, I'll be officially running for mayor this fall, so if your proposition passes, you don't plan to challenge me for the job in the next election, I hope?"

"Hell, no!" Lance exclaimed, and everyone laughed.

They all took seats, with Jenny sitting off to the side to let the boys do the talking.

"If I may begin, Mr. Mayor?" Chief Murphy asked, and the mayor nodded his agreement. "Sir Lance, I was very disturbed to hear about your abuse as a child. Did you ever report this man to the authorities?"

Lance looked embarrassed and shook his head. "I was too scared of him."

"The statute of limitations may have run out by now, Lance., but I'd like the man's name. There are probably other victims. If he's still out there I want him arrested and brought to justice."

Justice? Lance thought. What did that mean? How could he get his innocence back, his childhood? He shivered and looked at Murphy. "He's still out there. I saw him in the crowd."

Everyone reacted with shock.

"Why didn't you tell me then?" Ryan blurted, leaning forward in his chair.

"Cause he took off right when I saw him," Lance whispered, heart thumping.

Ricky put a hand on his arm and gave Lance that look again. It helped.

"Give us his name, Lance, and we'll find him," Murphy assured him. "He won't get to you again."

"It'll be over my dead body," Ricky affirmed.

"Mine too," Ryan added, and Lance felt some measure of security.

"His name is Richard Thornton," Lance finally said, after a pause.

"Sergeant Gibson, get on it."

"Yes, Chief," and Gibson stepped out of the office.

The mayor sat back and looked at Lance appraisingly. "You're a brave kid, Lance. Unlike my predecessor, I admire that, and what you're trying to do."

Lance frowned. "What's gonna happen to him, Mayor Villagrana?"

Murphy spoke up. "He's in serious trouble, Lance. At the very least, he's an accessory to murder." Then he looked embarrassed when Lance's eyebrows shot up. "Sorry, son, I mean attempted murder."

"I don't think he knew what R was gonna do, and I don't think he ever wanted to hurt me."

"What makes you think that, Sir Lance?" Sanders asked.

"Something R said, when he had us prisoner in his limo. Called the mayor a useful idiot, or something like that."

Sanders and Murphy exchanged a look, but it was Soto who spoke up. "His attorney would probably want to hear that, Sir Lance. I have to confess that Villagrana was vain and weak, but he was something of a friend and I'd like to think he wouldn't stoop so low as to sanction the murder of a child, or anyone else, for that matter. Can I let his attorney know what you said?"

Lance shrugged. "Sure."

Ms. Gale looked rather astonished. "He almost got you killed, Lance. He *did* get you killed, actually."

"He came to see me a while back to ask for forgiveness, Ms. Gale. I could tell from his eyes, he didn't know what R was planning."

She studied him a moment, but said nothing more.

"So, Sir Lance," the mayor began, "we know Arthur left you and Sir Ricky in charge of New Camelot while he is traveling, and my office is at your disposal. You'll have all the police security you need, at all of your venues. Permits will be processed according to your itinerary and any protestors who appear the least bit violent will be arrested immediately. There'll be no more dead kids on my watch."

Lance blanched, and looked down, embarrassed.

The mayor's face fell. "Sorry, Sir Lance, I didn't mean to suggest you weren't alive. It's just, well, I was watching like the rest of the city when you... died, and then came back. I'm still processing that reality."

"As are we all," Sanders echoed. He was older and Lance had been told he'd been on the council for nearly twenty years. "To bear witness to such an event, well, it's shaken us all, Lance, let me tell you. No one present that night will ever be the same."

"Me, either, Mr. Sanders. But Jack's still dead, you know."

A hush fell over the room as though everyone suddenly remembered a boy *had* died that night.

Soto cleared his throat awkwardly. "You're right, Lance, and we can never forget his sacrifice."

Lance shifted uncomfortably in his chair, but his chest felt tight and he couldn't respond.

They conversation switched to the campaign and what could be done to minimize potential security risks. As the meeting progressed, Ryan got a message on his phone. He checked it, and his face registered shock.

"Problem, Sergeant?" Murphy asked.

Ryan looked up at the chief, and then over at Lance. "Toxicology on that vodka, Lance. It was filled with arsenic."

Everyone looked at Ryan curiously as both Lance and Ricky paled with dread.

"What are we talking about here, Sergeant?" Soto asked.

"Somebody tried to poison Lance at that party the other night," Ricky put in, still shaken by the reality.

Between him and Ryan, they filled the group in on what had transpired. Ryan confirmed the arsenic was probably taken from rat poison, and there was more than enough in that bottle to have killed Lance.

"Hell." The mayor looked shaken. "Now we really have to step it up. Murphy, I want Ryan and Gibson assigned 24/7 to Lance. They'll live at New Camelot as needed, they'll go wherever he goes, and security at every campaign stop is hereby doubled."

"You got it, Mr. Mayor," Murphy replied, clearly disturbed by the news.

"You okay, Lance?" Ricky asked, placing one hand on his shoulder.

Lance looked at him, his heart filled with so many emotions he could hardly speak. "You saved my life, Ricky."

"That's my job, right?"

"What would I do without you?"

"You'd have to find someone else to kick your ass in the training center, that's what."

Lance grinned.

Jenny pulled a petition from her purse and held it up.

"Any of you care to support our cause?" Lance asked everyone with a smile. "I mean, you all did say you're on my side, didn't you?"

That caught them off-guard. The mayor and council members exchanged uncertain looks, but Chief Murphy reached for it.

"Hell, why not? Without you kids helping, we'd never have busted half the drug houses we have. Gimme."

Then the mayor took it. "You're a slick one, Mr. Lincoln."

Everyone laughed, but they all signed.

Finally, Soto told Ryan and Gibson, who'd returned from making his calls, to take the boys and Jenny home and secure the premises. Gibson told them he'd put Thornton's name into the database and they would soon have everything that was in the system. The meeting ended and the group returned without incident to New Camelot.

Arthur's campaign stop in Central California took place on the Fresno City Hall steps. The monstrous glass and metallic building looked like a flying three-quarter pyramid from the future had planted itself right in the heart of the city. Its roof tapered up into twin triangles and the front surrounding the double doors was made of enormous mirrored glass panels. Sloping steps rose from the street level up to meet in the center at the front entrance, and it was right before those front doors that Arthur and his knights stood with the mayor and other local dignitaries.

The massive crowd of spectators gathered on the grass one floor below them, so Arthur had a clear view of everyone. Men, women, and especially children of all ages cheered when the mayor introduced him.

Speaking into the microphone provided for his use, Arthur looked down at the crowd below. The mayor seemed pleased to have the king and his group, but there were some boos when he was introduced.

He outlined the purpose of their initiative, much as Lance had done, and then opened the floor up to random questions from the crowd. After a spate of inquiries deftly answered by Arthur and his knights, Lavern and Esteban demonstrated their archery prowess. Enrique threw apples high into the clear blue sky and either or both archers would spear them in mid-air, much to the delight of the youth in the crowd.

But then, a middle-aged guy with thinning hair and wearing overalls stepped forward to the front of the crowd and glowered up at the king.

"Why don't you go home to Los Angeles," he called up, his voice sounding like a belch. "We don't want you here!"

Arthur and Esteban exchanged a look. The boy flashed anger, but Arthur smiled reassuringly.

"And your name, sir?" the king asked politely.

"My name doesn't matter," the guy called out. "But I got your number, for sure. You and those kids 'a yours wanna push us union guys out and undo good laws, laws to keep dangerous punks like that one—" he pointed straight at Esteban "—off the streets so our good kids'll be safe. You're nothing but a rabble rouser, Mr. so-called king and you're not gonna get any support here in God's country."

Esteban bristled and inched closer to Arthur during the man's tirade, but Arthur calmly glanced at him and Esteban settled down. They'd been expecting opposition, after all.

"You call this 'God's country', sir," Arthur began, "and yet you do not seem to act in a God-like fashion. It has always been my understanding that the Creator does not approve of condemnation or the throwing of stones at others."

"Don't try to twist my words, mister," the man shot back. "I'm just calling a spade a spade." He glared up at Esteban again. "You, there, boy, the gangbanger. You even legal here?"

Arthur nodded to Esteban, who stepped forward, clearly fighting back the urge to put an arrow between the man's eyes. "Yes, sir, I was born here. I'm as American as you."

"Like hell you are! I never been a criminal in my life, my kids neither. I bet you've done more 'n enough to send your ass to prison for life. Am I right?"

"This is a nice area around here, sir. Clean. Don't see no graffiti, probably not much crime. Am I right?"

"Damn right, 'cause we keep punks like you out a Fresno, or throw 'em in prison where they belong."

The female mayor behind Arthur shifted with obvious discomfort.

Esteban nodded. "It sounds like a good place to grow up. But see, my hood was a hellhole. Everything there was bad. Don't kids gotta be taught how to act good 'fore they can? You can talk trash about me all you want from your nice little town up here, but bring your kids to my hood and stay a month or two. Learn what you're talk'n 'bout 'fore you start throwing them stones."

He gazed out over the faces. The adults might have been surly, but the kids in the crowd were mesmerized.

"I never had no real choices," he went on, "not till this man came along and showed me how to be good, how to be a man, how to make a difference for other people. All we're campaigning for is fairness, sir. You say kids like me are adults when we get in trouble. Fine. Then we're also adults when it comes to voting for laws and props and sitting on juries. You can't have it both ways no more, mister. If I'm an adult one minute, then I'm an adult the next. Only thing guys like you are worried about is us kids voting for laws that might put your ass in jail for being a bigot. Sir."

He gave a respectful bow to the enraged man, and the kids in the crowd let loose with a resounding roar of approval. Even the mayor applauded. The man looked outraged, especially when Esteban offered him a kindly smile. Many of the adults looked upset, and glowered at their own children, who ignored the looks and kept on clapping.

CHAPTER ELEVEN
YOU ARE EFFECTIVELY KING

L ANCE RECEIVED A HERO'S WELCOME upon returning to New Camelot. Everyone applauded how skillfully he'd handled the crowd, and many hugged him or viewed him in a new light, especially Chris, who eyed his brother sympathetically, big blue eyes filled with sadness.

Lance went to the small boy and squatted down before him. "I never wanted you to know what happened to me when I was your age, Chris. I'm sorry you had to find out like that."

Chris gave him a toothy grin. "It's okay. I love you, Lance." He threw his arms around Lance and held on tight.

Lance cradled him a moment. "I love you too, little man, so much!"

Lance released Chris as Michael sauntered across the lobby toward him.

Surprised, Lance looked at Reyna and Justin with raised eyebrows.

"Techie needed help with the petition drive and Michael showed him what to do," she said with obvious distaste.

Lance turned to face Michael, while Ricky tensed up beside him.

"Pretty gutsy move, Lance, telling everyone what that maggot did to do," Michael said, without his customary smirk.

"Yeah, well, it just seemed the right time. I'm tired of hiding."

"Why didn't you kill the son-of-a-bitch before you ran away?"

Lance was appalled, especially when it became obvious Michael wasn't joking.

"Why would I do that?" Lance finally asked when he found his voice.

"Justice." Michael turned and left the house without another word.

"I told you he's a monster, Lance," Ricky whispered, shaken by Michael's coldness. "He really *is* psycho."

But Lance was lost in thought. "I wonder." He caught Reyna's eye as she shook her head in disgust, taking Chris by the hand and exiting the lobby. Justin cast Lance an uncertain look before following them.

Lance's mind remained fixed on Michael and his ideas of justice. Lance had done nothing to stop Richard all those years ago. Even Chief Murphy had suggested there were probably more victims. How many other boys had the man raped? Was that his fault?

Deep within a thoughtful silence, Lance followed Ricky upstairs so they could get cleaned up for dinner.

While dressing, Ricky considered the events of the day. Since Lance had told the world his secret, hopefully he'd never have to find out what happened between him and Michael that night of the party.

If Michael didn't say anything today, Ricky thought to himself, *maybe he never will.*

After dinner ended, Jenny, Merlin, Ryan and Gibson called Lance and Ricky into the Throne Room and insisted Lance inform Arthur about the attempt on his life.

"No," Lance said instantly. "He'll just turn around and come back."

"That's his decision, honey," Jenny said. "But he has to know."

"We agreed, Lance," said Ryan, "that if the vodka turned out to be poisoned, we'd call your dad."

Lance *had* agreed to that deal. "Okay, but let me do the talking."

Ricky nudged him. "Try out the young Mr. Lincoln thing on Dad. I wanna see that."

That made Lance smile.

Arthur was Skyped through the flat screen mounted to the wall because it had a built in camera. The king sat in a motel room with Esteban and Lavern. He beamed when he saw Jenny.

"My night is now perfect," he said. "Is everything well?"

Jenny nodded. "How did it go for you today?"

Arthur patted Esteban on the shoulder. "Sir Este won the day for us."

"Congratulations. Um, Lance has something to tell you."

That made Arthur sit up and take notice, especially when Ryan and Gibson entered his camera view behind Lance and Ricky.

"Uh, Dad, I don't wanna worry you, and we got it under control, trust me."

"What is it, son?"

"Well, someone tried to, well… kill me."

"What?" Arthur leaped off the bed and almost dropped his phone.

Lance, Ricky, and the two detectives filled him in on what had happened, causing Arthur's face to crease with worry lines at each additional detail.

"I'll be back there straight away."

Lance leaped toward the screen, his face filling Arthur's phone.

"No, Dad, please, it's okay. The campaign—"

"Is not as important as you, son," Arthur affirmed, cutting him off. "I made that mistake once before. Never again."

"But Dad," Lance insisted, "listen a minute, please."

Arthur paused and sighed, reseating himself. "I'm listening, son."

"Ricky saved me, Dad," Lance said with a glance toward Ricky. "Just like he was supposed to. And now I got Sergeant Ryan and Sergeant Gibson and Justin and the whole LAPD. The mayor is on my side, the Police Chief. I'm not going anywhere without armed guards, Dad, and definitely not to any more parties. There's nothing more you could do by being here, and we need you more up there right now. I got everything covered down here, just like you wanted me to."

Arthur considered. "Sergeants Ryan and Gibson, your assessment?"

"Lance is right, Arthur," Gibson said. "We're covering all the bases. Nothing you could really do here except worry, and you could do that up there. As one father to another, I share your fear, but I promise you Lance will be safe. And he's handling everything better than I could. You should've seen him with the mayor."

Ricky laughed. "Yeah, the mayor called him young Mr. Lincoln 'cause of the way he handled the crowd. We'll be okay, Dad, trust me. I'm even gonna sleep with Lance to make sure he's never alone."

Lance chimed in with a playful shove at Ricky. "He even offered to shower with me, Dad, but I said hell no!"

"He's so lying!" Ricky put in, shoving Lance right back.

"Am not," Lance added, giving another shove.

"Dad, this fool's gonna be bald by the time you get back 'cause I'm gonna cut off all his hair while he's sleeping," Ricky threatened.

"Ricky, you know how I feel about that word," Arthur said.

"I know, Dad, but if he's playing the fool, isn't it the right word?"

"Point taken," Arthur said.

"Dad!" Lance called out to the screen in mock annoyance.

Arthur sighed. "Well, it heartens me to see you two be not terribly worried about all this."

Lance shrugged. "They already killed me once, Dad. What else can they do?"

"Kill your ass again?" Ricky put in, and they busted up.

Arthur reluctantly agreed to continue his end of the campaign, but ordered that any new information, no matter how trivial, be relayed immediately.

The boys, and the adults, all promised and the call ended.

Merlin eyed Lance with a twinkle in his eye. "Very clever."

"And very thoughtful," Jenny added.

"Did I miss something?" Gibson asked.

Jenny nodded her head toward the boys. "Their little performance, Sergeant, put their dad at ease, which was their intent."

Now Gibson looked impressed. "Pretty slick, boys."

"What performance?" Lance asked, feigning offense. "This fool really did wanna shower with me."

"And this fool's gonna have a fat lip in a minute," Ricky threw in, and then they laughed and high fived.

Suddenly, all of them were less worried about the future than they'd been a few minutes prior.

Later that night, Lance sat up in bed wearing only his workout shorts, reading *Frankenstein*. Ricky came in through the connecting door dragging some bedding.

Lance lowered the book. "What're you doing with that stuff?"

"Figured I'd sleep in the chair. Gotta keep an eye on your ass, remember?"

"Fool," Lance said, "this bed is big enough for six people. You don't need the chair, man."

Ricky hesitated. "I just thought, you know, it might be weird."

"What's weird about sleeping in the same big-ass bed?"

"I guess," Ricky said and dragged his bedding back into his room.

When he re-entered, Lance realized Ricky, too, wore no shirt. He quickly turned away to set down his book on the night table while Ricky crawled under the covers on the opposite side of the bed.

"You don't snore, do you, Lance?"

"How should I know?"

"If you do, I'm gonna pound you."

"Oh yeah, you and the army of which country again?"

"The country called Lanceisaweakassfool."

Lance threw a pillow at him.

Both boys scooted down under the covers and turned off the lights. There was a moment of silence before Ricky asked, "Hey, Lance?"

"Hey, what?"

"Did you mean it downstairs, when we were talking to Dad?"

"Mean what?"

"You made it sound like, well, you wouldn't care if you died again."

There was a long moment of silence.

Then Lance's voice came through the dark, soft and almost chilling. "Dying wasn't all that bad, Ricky. Pretty easy, actually."

And then nothing more.

It took Ricky a long time to fall asleep after that, and when he finally did, he dreamed of losing Lance over and over and over again, until he finally lost himself, too, and only darkness remained.

The rest of that week was more of the same. Lance, Ricky, and some of the other knights appeared at Boys and Girls Clubs, at YMCA's, and other venues, to speak on their prop and have adults sign the petition. They also recorded YouTube videos to run on Facebook and their website explaining the prop and why it was necessary, and alerted people how to get petitions or where knights would be stationed within the L.A. area for people to sign.

Lance and Bridget texted and Skyped, as did Ariel and Ricky. Bridget said she wasn't able to attend his public appearances because her parents wanted her focusing on school. Lance agreed it was best for her to stay away so she wouldn't be under the media microscope and lose her privacy.

Lance received another mocking text from the all-zeros number and ignored it. He figured it was Michael in one of his moods. Michael began making it a routine to drop by each evening to check out the status of the prop and the signature gathering.

They sparred almost daily in the Training Centre where Michael insisted on changing his shirt in front of Lance. He obviously wanted Lance to notice, but Lance always forced his eyes away so as not to encourage the older boy.

Michael announced on Wednesday that there would be another kick-ass party Friday night, but both Lance and Ricky flat out told him no. Michael shrugged and told them he wouldn't come by that night, but would see them at the Saturday gathering.

Seeing an opportunity, Lance and Ricky quickly invited Bridget and Ariel to dinner at New Camelot Friday night, and they readily agreed. When the girls arrived, the boys made it a point to hold their hands, especially while giving Ariel the tour, since this was her first visit to New Camelot. But during dinner, where Lance and Ricky sat in their usual spots beside each other, Reyna noted that they almost ignored the girls, focusing on each other like they did every other night, goofing and bagging and passing little asides back and forth.

The girls, excited to be there, didn't seem to notice as they chatted with their tablemates. Later, when it was time for them to leave, both boys kissed their girls goodbye in the lobby, while Reyna and Jenny looked on. They exchanged a look between them, but said nothing to either boy.

Arthur's troupe fared better after Fresno, and received warm greetings in Modesto and other cities and towns. The local kids were thrilled, and Arthur knighted some along the way in very visible, televised ceremonies. The new knights were given ceremonial replica swords Arthur had purchased over the Internet, and all were invited for supervised training, using the real weapons, should they ever choose to visit New Camelot at any time in the future.

The collection of signatures was progressing, but not as fast as Lance would like. However, it had barely been one week, and Lance decided to give it a month, at least. Then, if adults were not cooperating, the next phase – dubbed Operation Silent Treatment - would be initiated throughout the state.

After the Saturday gathering, Michael—who said nothing about the previous night's party—wanted to work out with the boys, which was their usual custom.

However, when they got to the training room, Michael said, "How 'bout we wrestle today, Lance? Me against you."

Lance was about to respond when Ricky stepped forward. "Why you wanna wrestle him, Michael? Cause you outweigh him by forty pounds?"

"Just wanna see what The Boy Who Came Back can do."

"I'll take you on, Michael," Ricky challenged. "I'm the wrestler here, not him."

"Ricky, really, it's okay. I can—"

"I got this, Lance," Ricky insisted, and Lance eyed him, realizing that Ricky's animosity toward Michael was the main reason, and it might get him seriously hurt.

Michael shrugged. "Works for me. Bring it on, bodyguard."

Lance stepped back as Ricky and Michael stripped off their tunics, tossed them to the side, and then circled each other around the mat. Michael's muscularity and size were intimidating. Ricky was ripped and solid, but smaller and clearly outmatched in strength. Having technique and experience on his side, Ricky was able to put a few moves on Michael right away that would've easily taken down an opponent in his weight class.

But Michael's prodigious strength dislodged Ricky every time, throwing him hard to the mat. After this happened several times, and Ricky lurched unsteadily to his feet, Lance could tell Ricky was weakening and that Michael was purposely slamming him harder than necessary. Michael's torso was slick with sweat, his breathing heavy, but Ricky positively dripped, gasping for air as they circled each other like alley cats.

Lance wanted to step in and stop the match. He had the authority. But would Ricky forgive him for the embarrassment?

The boys continued circling and Ricky dove in to grab Michael's legs for a take down. But Michael elbowed Ricky to the chest and sent him sprawling. Then Ricky kicked out with both legs, scissored Michael's waist and spun him down to the mat, hard.

Michael rose to his feet, furious. He reached down and grabbed Ricky with his powerful arms, wrapping them like an anaconda around his chest and squeezing the air out of him. Ricky gasped and gagged for air.

Lance jumped to his feet as Michael shifted his grip and lifted the struggling Ricky above his head, and, eyes wild, prepared to slam him down, a move that could easily break his back.

"Michael!" Lance shouted, leaping forward to stand before him. "Enough. You win. Now put him down, gently."

Michael glared at Lance, with Ricky squirming and struggling futilely above his head, and Lance feared he'd throw the boy right at him, injuring them both.

"Michael. I said let him down."

That uncontrollable look gradually slipped from Michael's eyes, and he lowered the struggling Ricky into Lance's arms. Lance lowered Ricky to his feet, and held the furious boy back.

"You bastard, Michael!" Ricky spat, struggling to squirm out of Lance's tight embrace.

Michael smoothed back his mussed mop of blond hair. "Better tell bodyguard to watch his mouth, Lance. Or else."

Ricky was about to say something more, but Lance grabbed his hand and squeezed.

Michael eyed the hand holding and grinned. "I'll see you boys on Monday."

And just like that he snatched up his tunic and made his way to the door.

Lance held Ricky's hand firmly as Michael stopped at the door and turned back. "You ever finish reading Frankenstein, Lance?"

That caught Lance off-guard with its randomness. He nodded.

Michael raised his chin slightly. "So who made the creature into a monster – the creature himself or Victor?"

"Victor."

Michael smiled. Then he turned and was gone.

Lance let go of Ricky.

"Why do you trust him, Lance? Hell, he almost killed me. *He's* the freakin' monster, not the one in that book!"

"I'm sorry for what he did, Ricky. He is like a monster. But he stopped when I told him to. Would a real monster do that?"

"I don't ever want you alone with him to find out. I swear, if he hurts you, Lance, I'll kill his ass!"

Ricky limped out of the Training Centre, leaving Lance to ponder what had just happened.

The following week passed much like the previous. School in the mornings, public appearances each afternoon. Lance also went on a couple more talk shows via Live Feed from the Throne Room.

He and Bridget continued their online relationship, as did Ricky and Ariel. Michael showed up every afternoon, but made no mention of Saturday's confrontation.

Then, on Thursday, Michael did something else that threw Lance for a loop. When Ricky was off helping Chris with something, he gave Lance a key to his private back house.

"I don't need this, Michael," Lance told him, confused, trying to hand it back.

"You never know. It's someplace you can go to get away from the cameras and paparazzi. You could even be alone with someone, if you wanted." He wiggled his eyebrows.

Lance's face grew hot.

Michael shoved Lance's hand with the key back at him. "Any time you want, it's cool. I don't have to be home." Then he patted Lance on the shoulder and turned to leave. But he turned back to Lance. "Do *not* tell bodyguard. Clear?"

Lance nodded, still confused.

Michael left without another word.

On Friday, Michael didn't come by, but it was too late to invite the girls over. So the boys just chatted with them via Facebook messaging on their iPads. After having said goodnight to Bridget, she suddenly messaged him back and attached a video. 'Watch this and call me'.

Lance clicked on the video. It was a news story off YouTube, dated that day, about a high school football player in Los Angeles who'd been badly beaten the night before. But what was most strange was that the assailant had broken all of his fingers, and both hands too. Stomped on them, it looked like. The boy never saw his assailant's face – he got jumped from behind.

When Lance saw the boy's picture, he gasped. It was a kid from that party at Michael's house. He remembered because he'd joked to Michael that the kid looked more buff than him and had a cool letterman jacket.

He hurriedly Skyped Bridget. "Did you watch it?"

"Yeah. Wasn't that guy at Michael's party?"

Bridget nodded. "And I think Michael beat him up."

Lance's blood ran cold. "What do you mean?"

"His cell phone was smashed, stomped on, just like his hands."

"So?"

"So," Bridget went on, "I think maybe he's the one who took that picture of you and Michael. He's always been jealous of Michael, anyway."

"Oh, hell," Lance whispered.

"Lance, I'm scared," Bridget whispered.

"It's okay, Bridget," Lance assured her. "Michael wouldn't hurt you."

"It's not me I'm worried about, Lance, it's you."

"Me?"

"I think maybe, well, I think… I'm falling in love with you, Lance."

Lance was stunned, and speechless.

Bridget looked down shyly. "It's okay, Lance, you don't have to say anything."

"No, it's uh, it's not that, it's just, well, I'm surprised, that's all."

"Why?"

"I don' know."

"You're not like any boy I know, and you're so amazing that I, well, I just think I love you."

Lance expelled a breath. "Wow. I guess I never thought…"

"Thought what?"

"It could happen to me."

She almost laughed. "You're like, only the hottest, most popular boy in the whole world, Lance."

He smiled shyly. "I'm not exactly sure what it feels like, Bridget, but I think maybe I love you, too."

She beamed, making her face even more beautiful. Then she frowned. "Michael's obsessed with you, Lance. You know that, right?"

"I think you're exaggerating."

"No, I'm not. I went out with him, remember? He's got this *thing* for you and I don't even know what it is. Please be careful, Lance. Never be alone with him. Promise me."

Lance thought of the key in his pocket, and Ricky's very same admonition. "I promise."

She smiled shyly again. "Okay. Good night, Sir Lance of the Table Round. Love you."

"Love you back."

And then she was gone, and Lance sat back to contemplate the conversation. Had Michael beaten up that boy? He *had* threatened to mess up whoever took the picture, after all.

But then Lance smiled. On the other hand, he now had a real girlfriend who *actually* loved him.

"Gotta tell Ricky," he said aloud and went to share the news.

Michael sat back from his dual computer screens, replaying Bridget's words, "Never be alone with him," and then froze the image and stared at Lance's face. He lounged back in his desk chair, his face contemplative, his expression unreadable.

Ricky tried to act excited for Lance when he heard about the confession from Bridget. Like Lance, he talked with Ariel virtually every night by text or Skype, and he liked her a lot, but somehow Lance's news that Bridget was in love with him and that he might be in love with her bothered Ricky, made him feel jealous and selfish at the same time. Still, for Lance's sake, he took the news as a great development.

The weeks slid by, and Arthur's travels likewise settled into a daily routine. There were no more attempts on Lance's life, or any plots that the police had detected against him or New Camelot. Unfortunately, they were also unable to locate the whereabouts of Richard Thornton. It appeared he'd changed his name after DCFS began to suspect he was up to no good. The paper trail ended on the Thornton name four years prior. Lance didn't spot him at any other speaking sites save that first one, but the police had his old photo from his years as a foster parent and were on the lookout for him at every venue.

Justin and Techie confirmed that the Make-A-Wish request was legit, and Lance approved the visit by ten-year-old John, a victim of bone cancer who wasn't expected to survive the year. That revelation saddened Lance, and he almost dreaded the visit, scheduled for Saturday.

Promptly at nine o'clock Saturday morning, the visitors from Make-A-Wish arrived on the New Camelot doorstep. Justin, tall and imposing in his dark brown tunic, sword at his waist, checked their I.D.'s, as Gibson had taught him, to ensure they were the right people. There was a representative from Make-A-Wish named Barbara. Mom's name was Karen Aragon. She and John were Filipino.

Ten-year-old John entered in a small wheelchair that could he maneuvered with ease. Mom explained that the cancer was in his legs and he'd finally stopped walking a couple of months ago. He had longish black hair, dropping past his shoulders, which Mom explained was a tribute to his idol, Sir Lance. When she said his name, however, she scowled slightly.

Lance, Ricky, and Jenny greeted them in the lobby. The boys were decked out in their knightly tunics, pants and boots, and Jenny wore a formal white gown in honor of their visit.

Mrs. Aragon took to Jenny right away, but remained barely cordial to Lance and Ricky, who seemed surprised and confused by her attitude toward them.

But John gaped awestruck at the enormous, gorgeously appointed lobby with its tapestries and ornate staircase leading to the upper floors.

Lance grinned broadly at John, who looked small and frail, but whose eyes were alive and filled with wonder.

"Hey, John nice to meet you, man." He shook hands with the excited boy.

"Me, too," Ricky offered, also shaking his hand.

"This is so cool!" John gushed. "I never thought I'd get the chance to be a knight, even for one day. Thanks for having me, Sir Lance."

Lance smiled warmly. "Since you and me are buds, John, just call me Lance. And this goofball is just Ricky. Got it?"

John nodded, still in awe of them.

Ricky turned to Lance with a bow. "Shall we give John the grand tour, Sir Lance?"

Lance tried for a serious expression, with a hint of British accent. "I do believe that would be in order, Sir Goofball."

Both boys cracked up, and John joined them. All three high-fived and Lance led the way. As was customary, they showed the group the memorial to Jack and Mark, now with permanent plaques set within the glass-enclosed case and Lance's words engraved upon them.

John was especially solemn, Lance noted, perhaps thinking of his own impending death. After this, they toured the Throne Room, where Lance suggested that John sit in Arthur's throne for a picture.

"No," Mrs. Aragon insisted. She and Barbara hovered protectively in the background, just to make sure John was safe.

John's face fell. "Oh, mom, they can help me."

She shook her head. "No way. You're too fragile."

John looked at the two boys imploringly, but Lance didn't see any way of convincing mom to change her mind.

Then he got an idea.

"I know," he said, to John. "Ricky and me'll put you and your wheelchair right in front of dad's throne, and then him and me will squat down right in front of your chair when the picture's taken. That way, if the camera angle's right, it'll look like you're on the throne." Then he turned to John's mom. "That work for you, Mrs. Aragon?"

She looked at both Barbara and Jenny, and both ladies nodded assent.

"Okay," she said to Lance, "But be careful lifting his chair onto the platform."

Lance chuckled. "No prob. Ricky and me been working out and getting stronger." Then he threw a "look" at Ricky. "Well, *I* have, anyway."

Ricky grinned. "I'm gonna tell you true, John, this boy thinks he can beat me at wrestling, but he's so wrong, it's not even funny."

"Maybe we'll give John a demo match later. Would you like that, John?"

"Oh, yeah. I wanna see everything you guys do here, so I can feel like I'm part of the Round Table, too."

Lance and Ricky exchanged a serious look, as John wheeled himself to the platform. The boys easily lifted the chair up onto it, Lance noting that John and his chair weren't very heavy. They arranged the wheelchair directly in front of Arthur's throne. Lance had Ricky squat down in front and then stepped over to where Mrs. Aragon and the others waited. She had her camera out, ready to take the picture.

Lance held out his hand. "May I?"

Almost reluctantly, she handed it over. Lance hunkered down and framed the shot to do what he'd envisioned in his mind. Then he explained to Mrs. Aragon that she needed to take the picture from this exact position and it would work. She agreed, and he rushed back up front, squatting down beside Ricky, the two clasping hands across John's knees, blocking them from the shot. Mom took several pictures and Lance checked them before they showed them to John. The boy was stoked. It *did* look like he sat on the throne with the two boys at his feet.

"Man, that looks awesome," he gushed. "Thanks, Lance!"

Lance grinned, and the three boys did the fist-bump before the tour resumed.

With the elevator, they were able to take John up to every floor and he was thrilled to see their rooms. He liked the Computer Lab and they spent some time checking out the website and looking at people's comments.

While they were there, John asked Lance, "Did you see my comments a while back?"

At first, Lance looked at him quizzically. "What comments?"

"Back when all those stupid pictures of you kept showing up," John explained.

Lance burned red with embarrassment. "Oh, yeah, those pictures."

"I was the one defending you, Lance, 'cause I knew you were a good kid."

"How'd you know that, John?"

"Cause you been my hero since you first started your crusade. Man, ask my mom, I got every video and every picture of you on my computer, and every news story too. Even the bad ones." He laughed.

Lance laughed, too, noting Jenny and the other ladies chatting in a corner, not too close to overhear, but still close enough to make Lance nervous.

"You know, John, I did some really stupid things. They don't make me any kind of hero."

John just waved it off. "You were running through a dark place, Lance. So am I. But for all the other stuff you've done, man, you are a hero. I wish I could live long enough to be as cool as you."

Lance's breath hitched in his chest, and Ricky choked back a shocked gasp.

John noticed their reactions. "It's okay, guys. I know my future. That's why today is so perfect." He grinned. "Can we go to the Training Center? Think I could wield a sword? I know the whole code and the oath and everything."

Lance looked dubious. "We can show you how to fight with the sword and use a bow, but… think your mom'll let you?"

John winked. "I have my ways."

Once within the Centre, John met Chris and other knights who were practicing, and was in instant awe. Chris gushed over him and wanted to suit him up right there, wheelchair and all.

Mrs. Aragon emphatically said no, but John told her he wanted to speak with her in private. She wheeled him just outside the door, and they were gone a few minutes. When they came back, his mom looked ashen, but John was grinning. He wheeled himself up to the waiting boys and vigorously nodded his head.

"How'd you convince her?" Ricky asked.

John leaned in and they all gathered in close. "I told her that today was *my* wish, not hers, and I was going to do what I wanted. Period. It's called a cancer perk."

Lance blanched in horror.

John smiled slightly. "Having cancer has to have some perks, doesn't it?"

"You're amazing, John," Lance said and they went to the armory to find some chain mail and protective gear to put on John's small, frail body. They found a sword that Chris was sure John could handle, and placed a helm on his head.

Mrs. Aragon and Barbara shot lots of pictures and video as the boys took turns controlling the wheelchair while one of them taught John how to parry and thrust. He seemed a natural, or had been practicing a lot at home, because he quickly got the hang of it.

Lance and Ricky gushed over his skills, and Chris even said, "You learned this stuff a lot faster than me," and fist bumped the boy. John was so excited he couldn't contain himself.

By the time they got to the archery, Reyna had arrived and she gave her usual dazzling demonstration, bested only by Lance who once again, as he had back in the beginning, pierced her shaft with his own. John clapped excitedly. Reyna and Lance then told the story of the first time they met, and John thought it was hysterical.

They fitted him out with an archer's glove and found the lightest bow they had. Reyna chatted with Mrs. Aragon while Lance and Ricky showed John how to take aim and shoot at the target. Chris and Sylvia practiced their shooting at the same time. After a wobbly start, John got the hang of it and almost got two bulls-eyes. He radiated excitement.

By this time, it was noon, so everyone went to the dining room for lunch. Lance and Ricky kept John enthralled with tales of their experiences, and Lance told the boy about things that happened before Ricky joined up. Lance grew quiet and sad as he mentioned Jack, and their escape from Mr. R.

John reached out and took Lance's hand.

Lance gazed at him in surprise.

"Basic human contact, right?" John said, and Lance had to smile.

"Wow, you do watch everything I do, don't you?"

"I know you're sad about Jack. I can see it in your eyes. But Jack did the right thing. And you have Ricky, now." He paused as Lance and Ricky exchanged a look. "I know what Jack looks like, Lance, so if see him on the other side, I'll tell him what's up for you."

Lance felt an almost overpowering desire to hug the child. How could this stranger hit so close to his heart like that? "Thanks, John."

John prattled on about the code of chivalry, amazing the boys with his expertise on its rules and bylaws. He even recited the oath of knighthood verbatim and everyone applauded.

Lance, however, got an idea. He excused himself to use the bathroom, but instead ran upstairs to his room and grabbed his cell phone. He called Arthur.

"Hey, Dad, you got a minute?"

Arthur smiled on the Skype connection. "Always for my son, as many minutes as you need. All is well at New Camelot?"

Lance assured him it was, and briefly filled him in on what they'd been doing all morning with John. "Dad, when you're gone, I'm Liege Lord in your stead, right? Like it says in the code?"

"You are effectively king."

"That means I can knight someone?"

"Yes, son, you can knight someone and it shall be no different than had I had done so."

Lance's heart beat with excitement. "Cool. Today, at the gathering, I'm gonna knight John into the Table."

Arthur broke into a grin. "I should like to watch my son in action. Please Skype us the ceremony."

"You got it."

As Lance was about to end the call, Arthur said, "Oh, and Lance."

"Yeah, Dad?"

"I'm proud of you, son."

Lance flushed with pride. "Thanks." Then the call ended. He was giddy with excitement as he hurried back to the table before anyone would wonder at his absence.

After lunch, Jenny showed everyone the schoolrooms, which gave Lance a second to tell Reyna and Ricky about his plans for the afternoon. He instructed Reyna to send out a blanket text to get as many knights to the gathering as possible. They were all supposed to be there, anyway, because next week would begin Operation Silent Treatment, but Lance wanted to make sure the room was filled for John. Reyna excitedly went off to take care of it.

Ricky looked at Lance very seriously. "This is a way cool thing you're doing, Lance."

"Yeah?"

"Hell, yeah. Wish I'd thought of it first."

The boys grinned and resumed the tour. They encountered Merlin in the library sitting in his usual chair reading, and Lance introduced them. He stood to greet the newcomers, and John's pale, thin face lit up with wonder.

"Awesome!" he gushed. "You gave us back Lance. Thank you so much for that!"

Merlin bowed. Mrs. Aragon frowned with distaste at his Iron Maiden shirt, but said nothing.

"You're quite welcome, Master John," Merlin said, drawing a smile from the boy.

"Was that a miracle, Merlin?"

Merlin looked down at the boy, and then squatted so they could be at eye level. "That's difficult to say, young John. My ability to manipulate nature was innate – I was born with it. Presumably it was God who gave me this gift. I personally believe that Lance, himself, is something of a miracle, and thus, I suppose, you could say my bringing him back was miraculous."

John soaked up every word, and then frowned sadly. "Is it true you have no more power?"

"Alas, John, no more miracles for me. Lance was my last for a very long time."

John looked sad a moment, and Lance surmised he'd had some hope Merlin could cure him. His heart tightened in his chest, and he reached instinctively for Ricky's hand, squeezing it lightly.

"You made the right choice, then, Merlin," John said with emphasis. "We need Lance, don't we?"

Merlin stood. "Indeed, we do."

Lance felt impending tears and had to fight them off. John turned to eye Lance and Ricky, observed them holding hands, and didn't look surprised. They noticed him looking and released their hold on each other.

"Lance, is it true, what people say on the Internet?"

"Is what true?"

"That since you came back you can do stuff, like walk on water or... cure diseases?" He flushed when he said that last, as though he had no right to ask.

His mother choked back a sob, and Jenny took her hand for comfort.

Lance was speechless. How could he tell this little boy, this dying little boy, that he couldn't do any of those things without hurting him more than he already hurt? Ricky looked at him intently, awaiting his answer. And as Lance looked into Ricky's soft brown eyes, he saw the answer.

"Tell ya what," he told John seriously, "Have Ricky take you outside by the pool and I'll show you what I can do. Just gotta run to my room for a sec."

Mrs. Aragon sucked in a startled breath, and Ricky almost gasped. "Lance, what—"

Lance shushed him with a look. "I'll be right out." Then he dashed out of the library.

Looking confused, Ricky wheeled John out to the backyard patio and over to the enormous pool. The adults followed behind, Mrs. Aragon casting harried looks Jenny's way.

Jenny leaned in and whispered, "Don't worry, Karen. Lance would never do anything to hurt your son."

She looked dubious, but remained silent. After a few minutes, Lance re-appeared, still dressed the same, and approached the edge of the pool. He turned to John, not with a grin, but with a serious expression.

"People say I can do miracles, don't they?"

John nodded.

"And one of those miracles is to walk on water, right?"

John nodded again.

"Well, then, I'm gonna show you how I walk on water, okay?"

John clapped excitedly, casting looks toward his mom and Ricky.

Ricky tossed a "what are you doing?" look at him, but Lance ignored it.

Lance slipped out of his boots, pulled off his socks, stripped off his shirt, and then his leather pants. He wore swim trunks underneath.

"This, John, is how The Boy Who Came Back walks on water."

Turning slowly and dramatically, Lance lifted one foot and allowed it to touch the surface of the water. He stepped all the way in, and promptly sank like a stone to the bottom.

John gasped in surprise as Lance's head broke the surface and he swam over to the side, flashing his most comforting smile. "So, whadda ya think? Pretty cool trick, huh?"

John broke into a grin. "It was awesome!"

Ricky laughed too, reaching down to grasp Lance's hand and pull him from the pool. Their eyes met a moment, and Ricky's gaze lowered to the water droplets cascading down Lance's chest before returning to his face.

Hair plastered to his shoulders and back, Lance squatted and clasped John's hands. "Never have I wanted so much to be able to do a miracle as right now, John." He blinked back tears. "I'm sorry."

John squeezed Lance's hand. "This is a miracle, Lance. This whole day with you. Don't sweat it, man. I'm good."

Filled with sadness, Lance stood. "Well, now I need to dry off and get dressed for our gathering. We've got some important business to cover, John. You're gonna love it." Then he winked. "Ricky, why not take John back to the training area and let him work out some more while I get ready."

John nodded vigorously. "You read my mind, Lance."

Lance gathered up his clothes before sprinting back into the house.

He showered, blow dried his hair, and wore the small crown Arthur had given him. He dressed in his fanciest green tunic and beige leather pants, and even went to Arthur's closet down the hall for one of the king's regal cloaks, which he wrapped around his shoulders. He slung his leather sword belt around his waist, and checked himself in the mirror. This was to be his first knighting ceremony, and he wanted to look right.

Satisfied, he started down the stairs just as Ricky was ascending. Ricky stopped and gaped. "Wow. You look freakin' hot, Lance!" he blurted, before catching himself in shock. "Sorry, I meant, like, amazing, man, you know, like a real king."

Lance grinned. "King for a day."

They high-fived.

"Did you leave his sword out?"

"Chris has it."

"Cool," Lance said, his eyes noting Ricky's sweat-drenched shirt, revealing the outline of his pecs beneath. Then he pulled his eyes away. "Better hurry or you'll miss my first knighting."

"Hell, no!" Ricky blurted and bolted up the stairs to get cleaned up.

Lance sought out Chris, who also marveled at his appearance, and got John's sword from him.

When Reyna saw Lance, she gawked. "You look beautiful, brother!"

He laughed. "Please don't call me beautiful in front of everyone, Reyna. I am a boy, after all."

Hands to her hips, she feigned annoyance. "Yes, you are, Lance. A beautiful boy." And then she hugged him. "Of all the amazing things you've done for people, this is the best."

She kissed him on the cheek and went to prepare the Throne Room, taking the sword to place it into position before everyone arrived. Techie would Skype Arthur so he could be part of the proceedings, as well.

Lance found John and his mom in the kitchen. John was having an afternoon snack after his second workout of the day.

"Wow!" blurted John, his mouth full of food.

"I second that wow, son," Mrs. Aragon said, eyeing Lance as though seeing him in a new light, at least a different one from when she'd arrived in the morning.

"Do you always dress that fancy for gatherings, Lance?" John asked.

"No, but today we have something special going on. You're going to witness one of our number being knighted."

John dropped his fork in shock. "No way!"

"Yes, way. This boy has been preparing for a long time and he's very deserving. And, my father, King Arthur, will also be with us through Skype, so you'll get to meet him, too."

The boy's eyes were as wide as saucers. "Did you hear that, mom?"

She smiled. "Yes, I did. Pretty cool, John."

"It's super cool!" he exclaimed, and ate some more of his dessert.

Mrs. Aragon eyed Lance again, but he merely smiled and bowed. "We'll call you when everyone gets here."

The others began streaming in, and within thirty minutes the Throne Room was packed. Chris brought John, Mrs. Aragon, and Barbara to the front row, removing one of the chairs so John's wheelchair would fit.

Once they were in place, Chris sat beside the boy. A sword stuck out of the platform in front of Arthur's throne, and John looked around at everything in wide-eyed wonder.

As was the custom, Reyna entered from a hallway behind the throne and stood before her seat. Then Jenny emerged and stood before hers. Both ladies were decked out in their finest gowns and glittery shoes. They even wore shimmery tiaras in their hair that gave them a fairy tale quality. Next came Ricky, looking nearly as regal as

Lance, with his hair washed and brushed, Lance's circlet round his brow, royal blue tunic and brushed leather pants and boots, sword at his waist.

When Lance emerged, crown on his head, thick, shimmering dark hair streaming down his back, sword at his belt, Arthur's cloak dragging behind him, there were gasps of surprise and wonder. He bowed to the assembled, and they bowed back.

"Welcome, knights of the Round Table," he began, his arms outstretched to the crowd. "We have important business to cover today, matters crucial to the crusade. But first I want to introduce our guests."

He proceeded to introduce John, his mother, and Barbara, explaining their presence at New Camelot. The crowd applauded them politely.

"Now, because of the importance of this meeting, my father, your king, wishes to take part." He motioned to Techie, who switched on the big screen. Arthur's bearded face appeared, with Esteban and Lavern beside him.

"Welcome, Knights of the Table," Arthur began. "As you well know, next week begins Operation Silent Treatment and we shall need all of thy cooperation."

"Yes, sire!" the massive crowd shouted in unison.

Arthur smiled. "Lance?"

Lance grinned at his dad and then turned back to the crowd. "Before we cover the details of that campaign, we have a special event planned, one that I'm really excited about. As Liege Lord while my father is away, it's my job to perform all kingly functions, including the initiation of new knights into the Table."

There was excited chattering and murmuring.

Lance waited until it died down.

"There is someone here who has amazing strength, and who has, in one day, showed us what true courage really is." He dropped his gaze to John. "John come before me to be knighted."

John's jaw dropped open in astonishment, and his mother gasped. There was surprised murmuring from the crowd. John pointed a finger at himself, and Lance nodded, waving him forward.

Almost in shock, John began to wheel his chair toward the platform. His mom stepped in to help, but he turned and looked at her imploringly. With obvious reluctance, she stepped back to her seat. John stopped, uncertain how to get up the stairs. Lance waved his hand toward the side, where a makeshift ramp had been put in place. John grinned and wheeled himself over and up the ramp with obvious effort.

Ricky was about to step forward to help, but Lance's hand on his arm stayed his motion.

John struggled up the ramp without assistance and Lance saw the look of accomplishment on his face.

John rolled up and Lance indicated that he place himself right in front of the sword sticking up from the groove. John's eyes widened as he obviously recognized it as the very sword he'd been practicing with all day.

Lance pulled his sword from its sheath.

On the flat screen, the traveling knights crowded in with Arthur to get a better view of the proceedings.

Recalling his own knighting, Lance gazed down at John with a big grin on his face. He couldn't help himself – he was too excited.

John looked shyly up at him.

"Now, because we swear the oath before God," Lance announced to the assemblage, "you all know that the squire normally kneels. But—"

John cut him off. "I can do that."

Terrified, his mother started forward, but Lance's upraised hand stopped her. He nodded toward John and then watched, heart in his throat, as the little boy slowly, painfully eased himself forward in his chair. He used the handle of his upright sword to stabilize himself as he gradually sank down onto his knees, grimacing in pain, his brow beaded with sweat. He tilted his head proudly up to Lance, grinning with triumph.

"Speak the oath, Squire."

John took a deep breath and bowed his head. "I thank thee, Heavenly Father, for permitting unto me the use of this sword to repress the wicked and defend the downtrodden. You, who in your wisdom created the order of chivalry, and who planted goodness within my heart, hereby charge thy humble servant before thee to never strike anyone unjustly, but to use this sword only to protect. Grant me, Lord, the strength to be for now and all time, a warrior, not for might, but for right."

Looking up, John almost seemed ethereal in the overhead chandelier light and Lance eyed him with wonder.

Did I have that same look on my face, he thought, before raising his sword and touching the tip, first to John's left shoulder, and then his right.

"I hereby dub thee Sir John the Bold, Knight of the Table Round."

John trembled with exhilaration and looked ready to cry from happiness. He leaned in and kissed the hilt of his sword. Then Lance's breath caught in his throat as John gripped the hilt so tightly his knuckles turned white, and began pushing himself slowly and painfully to his feet.

There was a gasp from Reyna, and a horrified Mrs. Aragon started forward, but Lance raised a hand and shook his head. She stopped, reluctantly, and stared with a mix of horror and amazement as John slowly, inexorably, agonizingly forced himself to a standing position on legs that were thin, wobbly, and weak.

Ricky stayed close to Lance, in case the boy fell, but John gained his feet unaided. He stood, unsteady for a moment, brow furrowed with torment. Then he astonished everyone even more. He pulled the sword from its groove and raised his arms above his head, held the gleaming blade aloft, then slowly turned inch by inch to face the stunned assemblage, his sword raised on high, his face one enormous grin of elation.

"I present to you, Sir John the Bold!" Lance announced to the crowd, and the entire room burst into thunderous applause. Mrs. Aragon began sobbing, and Barbara had to prop her up.

John gazed around him at all these young knights clapping and whooping for him. Then, he turned back to face Lance, tears of joy on his face.

Lance and Ricky helped ease John back into his chair, then Ricky handed him the sheath.

John slipped the new symbol of his rank into its soft leather cover and looked up at Lance with awe.

"Thank you so much for that!" The exertion had clearly sapped his strength, but his blurred eyes shone with gratitude and love.

Lance offered him a radiant smile, and placed a hand gently on his trembling shoulder. Then he nodded to Ricky, who wheeled John back down the ramp and over to his mother, who tearfully embraced him.

Lance glanced up at Arthur on the screen, and his dad beamed with pride. Esteban and Lavern both gave him a thumbs-up. Finally, once all the clapping died down, Lance continued with the meeting.

Later, after everything was arranged and everyone knew his or her assignments, the gathering disbanded. There were refreshments to celebrate John's knighthood, and lots of kids swarmed around to congratulate him and wish him well. And then, all too quickly, it was time for John and his mother to leave. His day at New Camelot had come to a close.

Sheathed sword across his lap, John looked exhausted, but overjoyed beyond measure. "This was the best day of my life, Lance. Thank you so much. And you too, Ricky."

And then he hugged them both at the same time, pulling all three of them together in a group hug that he seemed reluctant to have come to an end. When it did, Lance knelt down and slipped a piece of paper into John's pocket.

"That's my personal cell number, John. You call me any time you want. Day or night. It doesn't matter. You're one of us, now. You're our brother."

John looked on the verge of tears again. "Thank you, Lance. My real brother died, but now I'm not alone anymore."

Lance was shocked, but fought to mask it. "No, John, you're not alone." He smiled, and John returned it.

As Barbara wheeled John out to their car, Mrs. Aragon hung back. Jenny and Reyna were there, having said their goodbyes, and she thanked all of them. But then she looked shamefaced.

"I almost didn't let him come today, Lance." She shook her head as though to say, "how could I have been so selfish?"

"Why not?"

"Because of all your bad boy antics, the both of you." She included Ricky in her gaze.

"Oh," they said simultaneously.

"Uh, what changed your mind?" Lance asked awkwardly.

"John. He reminded me that even good boys mess up sometimes, like his own brother."

"He said his brother was dead..." Lance said, uncertain if he should.

She nodded sadly. "Car crash. Coming home one night from a party. Drunk. He was sixteen, and he was a good boy, Lance, like you're both good boys. He just did something really stupid."

"I'm sorry," Lance murmured.

"I almost humiliated John today. But you stopped me. When he struggled to stand?"

Lance nodded.

"How did you know how badly he needed that moment?"

"'Cause there's just some things us boys gotta do for ourselves, Mrs. Aragon. It's what makes us boys."

Her eyes pooled with tears. "My son was right about you, Lance. Today was a miracle, and you *are* a gift from God."

She kissed him on the cheek, and then kissed Ricky too. "I know you have Lady Jenny, but if either of you ever need an extra mom at any time, even just for a hug, call me."

Stunned, and fearful he would start crying, Lance nodded. Ricky threw his arm over Lance's shoulders and pulled him in close. Mrs. Aragon said goodnight to the ladies and left the house. Reyna and Jenny stepped forward to hug the boys, and the four of them stood that way for a long time, processing all the emotions swirling through them. This day had been one none of them would ever forget.

CHAPTER TWELVE
YOU'RE THE BEST FRIEND I EVER HAD

THE NEXT DAY, MICHAEL SHOWED up – on a Sunday – and even attended services with Pastor Tom. Lance was surprised to see him, but Michael simply shrugged as if that was explanation enough. Ricky and Reyna's mutual disapproval showed, but Michael ignored them. After Pastor Tom departed and Reyna went off to oversee the appearance schedule for the week, Ricky took up his protective spot beside Lance and eyed Michael suspiciously.

Lance tried to straddle the gulf between them. "Why are you here today, Michael?"

"Just wanted to see the response you get to the silent treatment plan. Good job, by the way, Lance, knighting that sick kid yesterday. He'll die happy now."

"You scumbag!" Ricky spat.

"Hey, just keeping it real. You wanna come at me, bodyguard? Finish what we started?"

Ricky started forward, but Lance got between them. "Stop it, now!"

He stood tall and commanding. Much to his surprise, both boys backed down.

"How'd you know I did that yesterday?" Lance asked Michael. "I made sure it wasn't on the news."

Michael grinned and folded his huge arms across his chest. "I snuck in, saw the whole thing."

"I didn't see you."

"Me, either," Ricky echoed, suspiciously. "Didn't want to be seen."

Something about that answer bothered Lance. He wasn't quite sure what it was, but his mind was still on yesterday—and today—so he let it drop.

Tension filled the air as the three boys made their way to the Computer Lab. Every knight who was available showed up that day to take turns at all the computers.

Techie, Reyna, Lance and Ricky had written a "Message" to all of their youthful followers in the state, now in the millions. This status update was to be sent out today via Facebook, Twitter, and their website.

"Operation Silent Treatment," which kids statewide already knew about, was set to begin on Friday of that week. The knights would be at the computers all day to handle responses and field questions or comments. Lance and Ricky and Reyna would be roving the room, checking those comments and advising what the most appropriate reply might be to each.

New Camelot's Status Update read as follows:

"Attention Children and Teens of California – The Camelot Crusade for Equal Rights is about you and it's for you. As you know, we are gathering signatures to get our proposition on the ballot for the November election. We need your help – all of you. We need six hundred thousand signatures before the middle of May, and only you can make sure we get them. You think you have no power over your parents and other adults? Think again. Beginning this week we start Operation Silent Treatment. The rules are simple: You stop talking to every adult in your life until they sign one of our petitions. You may verbally speak with each other, but only when no adults are present. This means you do not speak to parents, teachers, ministers, priests, store clerks – EVERY adult. As needed, you may text your parents or write a note or response to a question. Think of it as having a cell phone with no voice plan. Go to school, but do not enter the buildings. Sit out on the football field or in some large common area in complete silence for the entire day. Do not interact with each other except by text, and do not speak to anyone. Sounds boring, yes, but if you want to be treated as equals in this state, you must fight for it. In the event you are herded into classrooms, same rules apply, except there you may not text one another until passing periods. Just do your work in silence and go home. We will win this fight, if all of you cooperate. This is a non-violent protest so we do not want anyone fighting with any adult. Sadly, you will be the bad guy in any such altercation, not the adult who started the fight. This is one of the many inequities we must change in California. LIKE this status if you plan to participate, or post a YES on our website or Tweet an "I WILL BE SILENT" to us. We begin next Friday, with however many of you jump on board. Send us comments, reactions, opinions. Keep us updated on the progress in your town or city. Know that we here at New Camelot are always on your side."

Techie turned to Lance. "You wanna change anything 'fore I post it and tweet a link to it?"

Lance looked to Reyna and Ricky. "Whadda you guys think?"

Reyna shrugged. "Looks good to me."

"It's a start," Ricky added. "We gotta follow up with re-postings like every hour, right, Techie?"

"Good idea. Make sure everybody sees it no matter when they log on."

Lance smiled at Ricky. "Good idea."

Ricky grinned.

Michael moved off to an empty computer, planting himself in front of it. The others ignored him. Lance nodded to Techie, and he hit "Post."

Lance smiled nervously. "Now we sit back and watch the haters attack."

Reyna grinned and took her place at the computer beside Techie. Lance wandered over to where Michael sat intently watching something on the monitor. Ricky trailed after. Lance stopped and looked over Michael's shoulder. The blood drained from his face. Michael was watching the video of him and Lance dancing and kissing from that first party he went to.

"Why are you watching that, Michael?" Lance whispered, and Ricky cursed under his breath.

"I miss those good ole days."

Humiliated, Lance reached over and closed that website. "I don't."

Then he turned to walk away, but remembered something and turned back.

"By the way, did you ever find out who took that picture of us?"

Michael's expression gave away nothing. "I took care of it."

His voice was so chilling, so matter of fact, that Lance knew immediately it *was* Michael who'd beaten that boy so badly. He turned to walk away, but Michael reached out to grab his hand, causing Ricky to leap forward.

Lance held up his free hand to stop Ricky, all the while looking firmly at Michael. "Let go of my hand, Michael."

Michael looked him straight in the eye. "Remember what I told you, Lance. Any time." Then he let go and pulled up the New Camelot Facebook page, ignoring the boys completely.

Lance led a fuming Ricky away.

"What did he mean by that, Lance?"

"Nothing. Let's get online and watch the 'Likes' come in." He patted Ricky on the back and they moved to computers as far from Michael as possible.

Having observed the exchange, Reyna turned to Techie beside her. "Techie, can you do a background check on Michael? I promised Arthur we'd find out everything we could about him."

"Sure. What's his last name?"

She frowned. "I don't know. But I'm gonna find out."

She casually wandered over to Michael's computer and sat beside him, much to his surprise.

"Looking for a little action while the boyfriend's away, Lady Reyna?"

Her glare was the only answer he needed. "Can't blame a guy for trying." He returned his eyes to the screen.

The "Likes" were starting to pile up already.

"So, Michael," Reyna said, "how does it feel to have the prop you wrote become so popular with kids everywhere? We're even getting likes from other states."

"It's whatever."

It was obvious he felt proud of himself.

"Tell me something, Michael."

He turned to face her.

"You've been with us now for a few months and I don't even know your last name." She put up a hand quickly. "Not that I need to, by the way. You may be hot, but you're an arrogant jerkbag, as Ricky likes to say, and I'd never date you in a million years."

He chuckled at her nasty tone.

"But how does it feel to have created, or mostly created, the most important part of our crusade and then not get to take credit for it? For a guy as narcissistic as you, that must be hard."

"Sitting here with you, that's not the only thing that's hard."

She hauled off and slapped him.

He only grinned the more. "Getting to you, eh, Lady Reyna?"

Feigning indignation and fury, Reyna leapt to her feet in a huff. "So much for my being friendly."

She turned with a swish of hair to walk away, and heard from behind, "It's Maitland."

Reyna smiled to herself, but then turned her head and put on a furious mask.

"In case you want to look me up," Michael finished with a sly grin.

"As if." She whipped her head back around, smile returning, and headed for Techie's station.

Lance and Ricky, having observed the exchanged, looked mystified.

Ricky leaned in. "Whadda ya think all that was about?"

Lance shrugged. "Michael being Michael."

"You ever wonder if he gets tired of having dog crap for a personality?"

That drew a laugh from Lance and they high fived.

For the next few hours, the room filled with chattering as everyone reacted to the comments and postings about their plan. "Likes" came in by the second, which filled Lance with hope. But the threats came too. Threats to destroy New Camelot, to send The Boy Who Came Back straight to Hell where he came from, to rid the world of punks like Lance who wanted to take rights away from parents.

Lance had expected this because haters were so prominent online these days, but Justin noted every single one, copied the sender's email or Facebook address, and instantly sent the data to his dad's computer at police headquarters, where these people would be checked out and possibly charged with making "terrorist threats."

When Lance raised his eyebrows at that, Justin said, "That's the legal term, Lance. My dad taught me."

There were no speaking events scheduled for that Monday, purposely to build suspense for Tuesday's press conference, and to allow the proposed Operation Silent Treatment to build plenty of buzz. Other than morning school, the rest of the day was free, so Lance texted an invite to Bridget and Ariel to visit after school. He wanted to hear the reaction from her classmates, and it would give him and Ricky some time with the girls. Lance assured her that Michael had had a run-in with Reyna the previous day and wouldn't show.

Happily, she agreed and said Ariel would be excited, too.

Jenny and her classes, as well as the other two teachers and their classes, discussed the possible ramifications of the silent treatment if enough kids bought in and followed through, and how every knight needed to be extra careful when venturing outside the gates of New Camelot because there would be many angry adults out there.

The mayor called to speak with Lance. He, Ricky, Jenny and Merlin went into the Throne Room so they could use Skype and see each other. The mayor expressed concern over this silent treatment idea.

"But isn't it just civil disobedience, Mr. Mayor, like Thoreau did?" Lance said. "Lady Jenny taught us about him and we're not telling the kids to do anything violent, either."

Jenny gave Lance a smile of satisfaction that he referenced her teaching.

The mayor nodded. "And I thank you for that, Lance, but simply because the kids are not behaving in a violent fashion, this upheaval of the civic order could easily spiral into violence."

"How?"

"Adults might become frustrated with their uncooperative kids and take it out on them physically," the mayor responded soberly.

Lance blanched. "But that's a crime, isn't it? At least it's supposed to be. We told everyone to report that if it happens."

Now the mayor shifted uncomfortably. "At the risk of dredging up bad memories, Lance, you didn't report your own abuse because you were afraid."

Lance paled.

"What makes you think these other kids will be any braver? I'm sorry to bring this up, but I don't want to see kids getting hurt."

Ricky put a hand of comfort on Lance's shoulder.

"I don't, either, Mr. Mayor," Lance assured Soto. "But we need this prop passed if kids are gonna be treated fairly. The kids who participate know their own parents better'n you or I do. They'll do what works for them."

"You know I'm going to face a firestorm of criticism from the school boards and PTA groups throughout the city, don't you? For supporting your prop?"

"Yes, sir, and I'm sorry for that." Then he offered his most endearing smile. "But you can kick it here with us any time you want, just to get out of the fire."

The mayor grinned. "I might just take you up on that offer. If things really go south, do you have a permanent room for me?"

Lance laughed. "You know it."

The mayor hung up and Jenny eyed Lance appraisingly, as though seeing him in a new light.

Lance felt uncomfortable. "What?"

"I was just thinking the mayor was right about you."

Lance scrunched his brows. "About what?"

"You are the young Mr. Lincoln."

Ricky slapped him on the back. "That's my boy." He bowed. "Mr. President."

Lance punched him and they cracked up.

Bridget and Ariel showed up around three-thirty and the boys let Jenny know they'd be upstairs in their rooms listening to music.

"Leave your doors open," she instructed, and Lance knew she wasn't joking.

"Okay, mom."

That made Jenny grin as the four teens headed upstairs.

Since both had iPads and speakers given to them as birthday gifts, they played their own music, or music off the girls' phones. At first, they all hung out in Lance's room, but then Ariel and Ricky drifted into his and left Lance and Bridget alone.

290

They kissed a little, but Lance felt restless, wishing desperately for some alcohol to calm his nerves.

He pulled away from her and clambered off the bed, causing her to frown.

"Better check on Ricky and Ariel." He laughed nervously, and she offered an expression he couldn't read.

"You two guys are like, separated at birth or something," she said, envy creeping into her voice.

"We're like soul mates."

Her eyebrows shot up in surprise.

Lance suddenly realized what he'd said and flushed deep red. "I meant soul brothers, without the black part."

She gazed at him long and hard, but he had a tough time meeting her eyes.

"I love you, Lance," she whispered, almost pleadingly, as though she were holding on to him by the thinnest of threads.

"Love you, too." He shifted awkwardly, gave that breathy little nervous laugh, and stepped through Ricky's door. He found Ricky and Ariel lying on his bed, listening to a sad song on Ariel's phone.

"What's up, guys?" Lance said, announcing his presence.

They looked up, slightly startled. It was obvious both had been lost within the lyrics.

"Just chilling," Ricky announced. "Ariel's got some sad-ass beats on her phone."

Ariel smiled shyly. "I'm kind of a melancholy person, you know?"

Lance nodded as Bridget appeared behind him.

"Not having too much fun in here, I hope," she said, with a laugh.

Ariel blushed.

A knock at the main door startled all of them. Jenny stood there. "Everything okay?"

Ricky and Lance looked at each other, and then at Jenny. "Yes, Mom," both said, giggling like little boys.

Jenny cracked a grin. "Just thought I'd let you know Michael is here, down in the Computer Lab."

Everyone exchanged a look, the girls one of fear.

"What did you tell him?" Lance asked.

Jenny shrugged. "I told him you were in your rooms chilling. I don't think he believed me."

"Why not?" Ricky asked.

"Because he asked didn't I mean you boys were up here studying biology with a couple of girls." She sighed. "You know how I feel about him, Lance. Your father, too. If he's in the house, I want you watching him at all times."

"I'll be right down."

Jenny left, and Bridget panicked, scurrying to gather up her purse and phone. "We should go Lance, before he sees us."

Lance and Ricky exchanged a look, and both shook their heads. "Hell, no." Lance said firmly. "You're guests in our house and if Michael doesn't like it he can—"

"He can what?" came a cold, hard voice from the hallway as Michael sauntered in, cool and collected. "How's the bio lesson coming along, boys and girls?"

Ricky sat up, furious. "Get your ass out of my room, Michael. Now!"

Michael looked bored. "Or what, bodyguard? What's a little bitch like you gonna do to me?"

Ricky jumped off the bed to the floor. Lance bounded in front and blocked him, while Ariel tried to grab one of Ricky's flailing hands.

"Stop it, Ricky!" Lance shouted.

"No, Ricky," Ariel cried out, getting hold of his hand.

Ricky yanked his hand viciously away from her. "Let me go! That bitch is mine!"

Lance grabbed Ricky's head and forced their eyes to meet. "No, Ricky," he said calmly, but forcefully. "That bitch is *mine*."

He released Ricky, who looked stunned by his response, and turned to Michael. "In the hall, Michael. Now."

Michael turned to step into the hall and Lance followed, slamming the door behind him.

Bridget turned to Ricky. "You okay?"

He nodded, and turned to Ariel. "I'm sorry, Ariel, for pushing you away. I just wanna kill that guy sometimes."

Bridget nodded. "Don't we all."

Ricky took Ariel's hand, looking flushed and embarrassed. "About what he called me..."

"It doesn't mean anything, Ricky," she offered, squeezing his hand.

Bridget stared pensively at the door. "Whadda you suppose is going on out there?"

"Let's find out." Ricky strode to the door and grasped the knob firmly. He eased it open and peeked through the crack.

Lance and Michael were down the hall near the top of the staircase, and Lance was clearly angry. However, he was speaking so quietly Ricky couldn't hear him. Then Lance took Michael's hand and put something into it, something Ricky couldn't quite discern. Michael shoved it right back at Lance, forced open the smaller boy's hand and stuck in in there.

"You *will* need it one day, Lance. Mark my words," Michael said, loud enough for Ricky to hear.

Lance hesitated, and then put whatever it was into his pocket. "Get out, Michael. You ever talk to Ricky like that again and he won't have to kill you, because I will."

He stood his ground, fists clenched, glaring at the bigger boy. Ricky feared Michael might grab Lance and toss him head first down the stairs. But he just smiled and strolled past Lance down the stairs. As Lance started to look in his direction, Ricky quickly pulled the door shut, feeling an unexpected warmth overcome him at Lance's declaration on his behalf.

"Well?" Bridget asked anxiously.

"Lance kicked his ass out. Told him not to come back."

Ariel smiled with relief, but Bridget looked afraid. "It's not over, Ricky. It's never over with Michael."

The door opened and Lance appeared. "Coast is clear," he announced. "I sent him home." He approached Ricky. "You okay?"

Ricky nodded. He didn't want Lance to know he was spying, but he really wanted to know what Michael had insisted he keep.

Bridget looked at Ariel, who was still shaking, and then at the two boys who suddenly seemed more interested in each other than in them. "I think it's time for us to go, Ariel," she announced.

"You don't have to," Lance insisted, but it was a weak insistence.

Ricky could plainly see that Lance didn't want the girls to stay.

"Yeah, we do," Bridget insisted. "I told Ariel's mom I'd have her home for dinner."

Lance nodded, looking relieved. The girls gathered up their stuff and the boys walked them down the stairs and out to Bridget's car. They waved goodbye as Bridget drove to the gate, where the security guard waved her through.

Neither boy noticed Michael standing across the street with the cultists, eyes narrowed, face expressionless as he watched Bridget's car drive off down the street.

Arthur and his company had held a rally in Stockton, and were staying the night before moving on to Sacramento. Lavern sat watching TV while some of the others tightened their bows or sharpened their swords. Arthur had knighted a large group of children this day, but the response to Lance's Silent Treatment proposal was mixed. The kids were enthusiastic; their parents were understandably not, and Arthur had overheard some telling their children there "would be hell to pay" if they tried to participate.

The kids, now newly minted knights, nodded their heads in agreement, but then turned when parents weren't looking to salute Arthur with their plastic swords.

Arthur sat with Esteban in a couple of hotel chairs, the two relaxing after a long afternoon of campaign stops. Esteban caught Arthur unawares when he suddenly asked, "Arthur, are you in love with Lady Jenny?"

Arthur eyed him a moment before smiling. "Yes, lad, I am."

"Have you said it to her yet, you know, those words?" His face was dead serious.

Arthur shifted uncomfortably. "Well, not in precisely those words, but I feel quite certain Jenny knows my heart."

"I never told Reyna *those* words."

"Is that how you feel about her?"

Esteban grinned. "To quote your son, 'damn straight.'"

Arthur smiled. "He does say that often, doesn't he?"

"You remember what he said at Jack's funeral, about somethin' Jack told him once?"

"Refresh my memory, Sir Este."

"He said, 'it's the things we don't say to each other that make the biggest difference.'"

Arthur nodded. "I do recall it."

Esteban looked him in the eye. "What if, like, something happened to me, or to Reyna, and I never said those words to her..."

Now Arthur understood his meaning. "Thy wisdom, Sir Este, never ceases to amaze me. We shall call our ladies this night and tell them what is in our hearts."

That surprised Esteban. "You mean right now?"

"No time like the present. Call Lady Jenny, if you will, and ask her to find Reyna and go to the throne room. We shall Skype them there."

Esteban grinned. "You got it."

When Jenny got Esteban's call, she was surprised. She hadn't expected to talk with Arthur again until tomorrow, after Lance's press conference about Operation Silent Treatment. She sent a text to Reyna, who was still hovering around the Computer Lab, and asked her to meet in the Throne Room.

When Reyna arrived, her eyes wide with questions, Jenny opened the Skype connection to Arthur. The king's face filled the screen, instantly joined by Esteban beside him.

Reyna beamed upon seeing him, and he grinned right back.

"Is everything all right, Arthur?" Jenny asked, concerned by the king's obvious nervousness.

"Of course, Jenny. All is well. It's merely that, well, Sir Este and I have been talking and, well, we were recalling Lance's admonition that what we do not say to one another makes all the difference in life."

He paused, and the two ladies exchanged a curious, amused glance. Neither had ever seen Arthur so strapped for words.

The king cleared his throat. "What I'm trying to say, Jenny, is that, while I know the crusade requires my presence here in this far-away place, my heart is bereft without you. I have been reluctant to say these words due to the uncertainty of my time here in this era, but they have been on my mind and in my heart for months, and I must needs share them."

He paused a moment to take a breath. "I love you, Lady Jenny, with all of my being. I have not loved any woman as I love you, and my heart feels empty without you by my side."

Jenny's hand went to her mouth in startled shock at his words, and she nearly burst into tears. Reyna wrapped an arm around her excitedly.

Now Esteban took center stage on the monitor. "I can't speak all tight and kingly like Arthur, and I said these words before to girls, 'cept they was just words to get what I wanted. Now I really know what they mean, 'cause I love you, Lady Reyna, with all my heart and soul. Man, I'm so in love with you, I can't believe it myself. Me, the badass gangster turned knight is scared out of his mind right now 'cause I'm afraid maybe you don't feel the same."

He stopped then, his poignant eyes urgent and wide with uncertainty.

Reyna's breath caught in her throat, but she didn't betray her feelings as Jenny had. Too many years of winding her emotions into a tight coil prevented that.

Esteban looked almost ill as he awaited her response.

"Well, do you?" he prompted, blushing with embarrassment.

She smiled in that haughty way she'd perfected. "It's about time you said it, Este. You expect a girl to wait forever?"

He still looked worried. "But, do you, you know, love me too?"

"Of course I do!"

He broke into a huge grin of relief and Arthur reappeared beside him.

"I know you to be a very independent woman, Jenny," Arthur said. "You need not express feelings you may not have. But I felt compelled to tell you—"

"I love you, Arthur!" Jenny blurted. "Of course I love you." She chuckled wryly. "I think I fell in love with you that first night in Eucalyptus Park when I saw you go flying off Lance's skateboard. Oh, Arthur, I don't care how much time you have here. I want to spend every minute of it with you."

Arthur looked relieved. "And so you shall, once our tour of duty has ended."

Jenny placed her hand on her heart. "My heart will count the days."

Arthur copied her motion. "And mine, as well."

The call ended and Reyna stared a moment at the blank screen. Then she screamed—shrieked actually—and grabbed Jenny in a tight hug. "He loves me, Jenny, he loves me!"

Jenny hugged her back. "Of course he does, Reyna. How could he not?"

Reyna screamed at the top of her lungs. "He loves me!" Then she looked quickly at Jenny. "Don't tell him I did that, please."

"It'll be our secret."

The double doors burst open and Lance and Ricky rushed into the room, swords at the ready.

"What's going on?" Lance asked anxiously. "We heard screaming."

Reyna ran to him, scooped him up, sword and all, and planted a huge kiss on his cheek. "He loves me, Lance. Este loves me!"

She put down the startled Lance and then did the same to Ricky, nearly crushing him.

Lance shrugged. "I knew that, Reyna, a long-ass time ago."

She threw her hands to her hips and glared at him. "And you didn't tell me?"

"Hey, us guys gotta keep some stuff to ourselves."

She waggled her finger at him and then practically waltzed from the room.

Lance turned to eye Jenny, noting her own radiant expression. He smiled broadly. "Dad finally got up the *cajones* to say he loves you?"

She blanched at his choice of words, but nodded excitedly, fighting back the tears.

"It's about time!" Ricky said, and the boys high-fived. Then they took turns hugging her.

Lance stepped back. "Does this mean we can start calling you *Mom* for real?"

He grinned, and she laughed delightedly. "I guess it does. Son." Then to Ricky, "Other son."

They all hugged again and the boys left her alone to go on up to their rooms.

Jenny gazed in wonder at the throne, feeling euphoria and fear simultaneously. Just how much time *did* Arthur have here, anyway?

Later on, after pulling on their usual sleeping shorts, Lance and Ricky sat on Lance's bed.

"Do you think you're in love with Ariel?" Lance asked out of the blue.

"I don't know. I told her I might be. I'm not sure. You think you're in love with Bridget?"

"I told her I was," Lance answered. "But I wonder if it's 'cause I wanna be, more than I really am."

Ricky thought on that a moment. "How does it compare to your feelings for Jack?"

"I don't know," Lance admitted after a pause. "Jack and me went through so much, especially when I thought we were both gonna die, you know?"

Ricky nodded, hanging on every word.

"I never knew what it felt like to be in love. Still don't, I guess."

"Me, either."

"I don't think what I got going with Bridget is like Dad and Mom, or even Este and Reyna. Este told me he thinks of Reyna, like, 24/7. I'm not always thinking about Bridget."

"I don't always think about Ariel, either."

Lance sighed. "Maybe we just want girlfriends so bad, Ricky, that we're fooling ourselves. And them."

"Maybe," Ricky agreed, not quite able to look Lance in the eye.

Lance slipped under the covers on his side of the bed.

Ricky did the same on his.

They extinguished the lights, and silence filled the dark room.

"You know, Ricky," Lance whispered, "what I accidentally said to Bridget today?"

"No, what?"

"She said you and me were separated at birth, and I told her we were like soul mates. I meant to say soul brothers, but mates came out instead. Crazy, huh?"

"Yeah, crazy."

"Ricky?"

"Yeah?"

"You're the best friend I ever had."

"And you're mine."

"'Night."

"'Night."

The following day, Lance felt anxious about the press conference, even more so than his first one about the proposition. The Facebook page and website had gotten millions of "Likes" and "Yes's" from kids all over the state, the country, even, and he knew he'd face some hard questions. He and Ricky didn't discuss the girls any more, but sent them both "good morning" texts before school began.

The press conference was held once again in front of City Hall at three-thirty, and this time the mayor and City Council sat up on the dais with Lance, Ricky, and Jenny.

"Thank you all for coming out here today," Lance began cordially, waving to Helen in front. "I suspect I know what you want to talk about." There was laughter. "As you know, the next phase in our quest for equal rights begins this Friday, with Operation Silent Treatment. In solidarity with my brothers and sisters throughout the state, I, too, will participate. That means no more press conferences until we acquire the six hundred thousand needed signatures to qualify our proposition for the November ballot. If any of you wants to interview me one-on-one, you must show proof that you signed the petition. Us kids will only speak with adults who have signed until the silence is lifted. Now, questions?"

Every hand flew up, including Helen's. Lance pointed to her first.

"Sir Lance, what do you say to your critics who believe you're telling the children of this state to break the law?"

"What law am I telling them to break, Lady Helen?"

"The law regarding school attendance."

"Oh. Well, that law, which was passed by adults without our approval, by the way, just says us kids have to *attend* school Monday through Friday. It doesn't say we gotta talk once we're there. And it doesn't say we hafta actually sit in classrooms, either."

There were gasps, and some laughter, from the crowd.

"We're not telling the kids to ditch, Lady Helen, just not talk. Problem solved. The law isn't broken."

He pointed to another reporter.

"How will you feel, Sir Lance, about the kids whose parents beat them or otherwise punish them for participating?"

Lance looked appalled. "I would feel terrible, sir, just as I felt when I got beaten or locked in closets or raped as a little boy."

There were gasps from the crowd.

"I thought child abuse was already a crime in this state, or do we have to change that, too? Look, we've told every kid through our website and Facebook and Twitter not to take any abuse from bullying parents, but to call the cops or let us know and we'll call them. We're networked to the entire state law enforcement system, thanks to Chief Murphy behind me, and we'll get right on it."

He pointed to someone else.

"Don't you think it's unfair of you to punish good parents by having their children give them the silent treatment?"

"If they're good parents and want what's best for their kids, they'll sign the petition and their kids'll talk to them again. Problem solved. Look, kids don't ask to be born, sir. Parents have a responsibility to take care of the children they create, period. Kids don't have a responsibility to talk to their parents if they don't want to. We're not telling them to disobey their parents, but simply not talk and not verbally participate in school or other adult-created things. We're tired of having no choices out here, that's all."

The other questions were of a similar nature, and Lance deflected each of them with the same dexterity he'd come to display at these gatherings.

The mayor also addressed the reporters, assuring everyone that children who participate in this vow of silence would not be punished by their schools because, as Lance indicated, they would be following the letter of the law. As long as they turned in their written work, their grades could not be penalized because there was no oral participation. Every school board had been notified to get the word out to their individual principals.

"As someone who supports the proposition Sir Lance and his fellow young knights have created, it's my hope that we will hit the needed six hundred thousand signatures sooner, rather than later, and this silence will end that much faster. After that, the ballot box will determine the future of children in this state, and I, for one, am happy to be given a choice in that future. Thank you all for coming."

The reporters began gathering up their stuff and preparing to leave.

The mayor turned to Lance with a smile of admiration. "Please don't run for mayor, Lance, or I don't stand a chance."

Lance laughed, and gave the mayor a high five.

Before Arthur's press conference in Sacramento, the knights held a little birthday party for Lavern, who turned thirteen that day. Enrique and Luis bought a blank birthday cake and painted on it a picture of Lavern in decorative frosting, and he received presents from everyone.

Arthur's was the largest, and upon opening it, Lavern found a brand new bow and quiver of arrows. He gushed excitedly.

"Wow, Arthur, it's awesome," Lavern exclaimed, pulling on the bowstring and taking its measure. "It feels perfect. Where'd you get it?"

Arthur smiled rather smugly. "Amazon."

Everyone laughed.

"You're sure twenty-first century now, Arthur," Esteban chuckled, and the others joined in.

Lavern saw that his name had been engraved on the bow in fancy lettering and grinned all the more. "Wow, it's got my name on it too!" He hugged Arthur. "Thanks so much, Arthur. For everything."

Lavern blew out his candles and they all had fun before getting ready for the conference. As everyone was cleaning up, Arthur noted Lavern looking sad, and approached him.

"What troubles you, my boy? You did not get what you wished for upon blowing out your candles?"

"You wanna know what I wished for?"

Arthur cocked his head to one side.

"That you could adopt me and be my dad," Lavern finished with a sigh. "But I be knowing that can't happen."

Arthur looked down at this boy, already much taller than when first recruited, with broader back and arms from his workouts and archery, and placed a hand to his shoulder. Lavern raised his sad brown eyes.

"I should like nothing better than to adopt you, Lavern, were it possible to do so, for as with the others, I already think of you as my son."

Lavern grinned. "I never had no dad, Arthur. Mine took off 'fore I was born. Do you think maybe, you know, when nobody be around, I could call you Dad sometimes?"

Arthur fought hard to control his emotions. "You may do so whenever and wherever you choose, Lavern. Adoption or no, you are my son."

Fighting back tears, Lavern hugged him tightly and they were standing thus when Enrique entered to announce it was time to go.

Arthur faced similar questions in Sacramento as Lance had taken in L.A. The governor, unlike the Mayor of Los Angeles, was not so keen on the entire plan, since his concerns were primarily financial, and he feared this protest would cost the state extra money if added police presence was required.

Arthur handled the questions adroitly, and the crowd seemed satisfied. Esteban, Lavern, and the other knights affirmed that they too, would only speak with adults who had signed their petition until the six hundred thousand were attained.

One reporter pointed out Lavern, clearly the youngest of the kids, and asked, "How old are you, young man?"

Lavern stepped to the microphone. "Thirteen today, sir."

The reporters chuckled at his politeness.

"This prop doesn't even affect you for another year, if it passes. What are you getting out of all this?"

Lavern looked to Arthur, who smiled and nodded his support, and then turned back to the crowd. "First off, I got me a family now, which I never done had before. Where I lived, the grown-ups wasn't doin' their jobs with us kids, they wasn't takin' care 'a us like they's supposed to. So I figure when I turn fourteen, I can at least vote for people that might help us, and for laws that might protect us, ya know?"

The man nodded and that was the end of the press conference.

Arthur grinned broadly at Lavern.

The remainder of the week was more of the same. At both ends of the state, Lance and Arthur made public appearances. Arthur met privately with the governor, while Lance met once more with the mayor and City Council. Everyone seemed prepared for Friday, no matter what the outcome. Lance and Ricky texted and Skyped their girls, but did not invite them over. Michael neither appeared, nor texted Lance, which bothered him, though he knew it shouldn't. He had kicked Michael out, after all.

On Friday morning, rather than traditional school, those knights who took their classes with Jenny and the other home teachers gathered in the Throne Room in front of the large screen television to watch the news feeds from all over the state. CNN, FOX, MSNBC and other national news outlets were on hand, as this had quickly become a nationally followed story. Cameras were set up outside schools throughout the state to gauge the extent of the protest.

Everyone watched, enthralled, at the sight of school busses disgorging scores of silent children, ignoring the "Good mornings" of their teachers and filing out onto fields, or into parking lots, and sitting down. At high schools, kids parked their own cars, or entered school grounds on foot, in silence, for the most part. Some, who weren't participating, attempted to engage their silent peers, but were rebuffed. Scenes quickly piled upon each other of football fields filled with hundreds or thousands of kids sitting, texting, reading, doing assigned homework.

But all in silence.

It reminded Lance of those zombie apocalypse movies where the world was dead, and silence ruled the earth. He and Ricky eyed each other, and grinned.

Thus began nearly two months of silence for the children of California, as more and more of them joined the cause. As he'd promised, Lance refused to speak with any media personnel about the protest unless they showed proof of their signature. National pundits like Anderson Cooper, who was not a California resident, did get interviews with him and Ricky together, and both boys expressed hope that soon they would have the necessary signatures so that all would get back to normal.

At least until the election.

There were, sadly, incidents where parents beat their kids for not speaking, and these New Camelot instantly reported to the appropriate authorities, and after a few weeks, a rising number of school teachers, frustrated with their inability to teach effectively, and defying union edicts, signed the petitions so they could actually dialogue with their students.

Esteban and Reyna Skyped every night, each trying not to be too gushy, but longing for the day they'd be reunited.

Arthur's group traveled to cities and towns throughout Northern California, intending to spend a week or two in San Francisco before returning home.

Bridget and Ariel dropped by New Camelot whenever they were invited, which became less frequent as time went on. Lance and Ricky always kissed the girls upon arrival, but not again until it was time for them to leave. Otherwise, they played video games or listened to music. But always, each time Lance kissed Bridget, he thought back to his one and only kiss with Jack, and struggled to ascertain how and why it was different.

The emotion was different.

Was it because he thought that first kiss would be his last? Was it because Jack was... gone... and there could be no more sweet kisses to compare to that first one? Or maybe it was because he felt Bridget expected more from him than Jack had?

He shared these thoughts with Ricky, who'd had no experience kissing anyone before Ariel, and didn't have any answers. Both boys knew they loved their girls, at least on some level – both girls were fun and beautiful. But were they *in love* with them? Neither boy knew.

There were protests by adults everywhere Arthur's signature gatherers were stationed, both in Northern and Southern California. They carried picket signs displaying slogans such as "We don't need kids in the Workforce" and "Kids need to stay Kids." There were a few violent scuffles as some attempted to physically prevent people from signing the petitions, and police had become a regular presence wherever signature gatherers were working, thus adding a financial burden to the cities. These added costs encouraged mayors and other public officials to urge their people to sign quickly, if it was their intent to do so anyway, so life could get back to normal.

The New Camelot website, Twitter and Facebook pages were inundated with anonymous threats of violence against Arthur and Lance, even threats to blow up New Camelot itself. Justin sent every one of these to his father, and both Gibson and Ryan spent the lion's share of their time investigating them. Neither was present within the hotel very often, yet both were only a phone call away if needed.

Lance, Ricky, Jenny, and Reyna took a couple of trips down to San Diego during this period to assess progress there. Volunteers had downloaded the petitions and were working feverishly to gather the signatures. In front of the San Diego City Hall, the mayor welcomed Lance and the others, but only Jenny spoke. The only time Lance spoke at all was when he met with a group of kids who were prepared for knighthood. They recited the oath and Lance knighted them, presenting each with a ceremonial sword.

Techie became so embroiled in keeping facts and statistics on the signature gathering that he'd forgotten about searching out Michael's identity. And since Michael didn't show up once during this time, Techie didn't think to look for nearly the full two months.

Lance found he missed Michael during this time, knowing that he shouldn't. His conflicted feelings for the older boy continued to haunt him. He considered his feelings for Bridget, and how, in many ways, he felt more drawn to Michael. He knew he shouldn't have anything to do with him after all that had happened, but he couldn't resist the temptation to Skype Michael one night when Ricky was in the shower.

"How you doing, Michael?"

"Just peachy, Lance. How about you?"

"Good. I'm sure you know we're doing good on the signatures."

"I'm like, so thrilled." Michael yawned.

"Why don't you visit anymore, Michael?"

"Do you miss me?"

"Kinda."

"Then invite me, Lance."

"You ready to apologize to Ricky?"

"No."

"Michael, he's my—"

"I know what he is to you, Lance," Michael interrupted, "better than you do. And the answer is still no. You wanna see me, we can party together."

"Hell, no, Michael. I'd ruin everything."

"Well, then, there's always that key."

And then he hung up.

Sir John kept in regular contact with Lance and Ricky and assured them that he too, wasn't speaking whenever he attended school. His cancer was worsening and he often had to stay home. His mom, he told Lance, had signed the petition immediately. Lance Skyped with her, too, on a weekly basis, and she looked sadder each successive week.

"I don't think he has much time left," she told them one night, her teary face filled with intense sadness.

Lance and Ricky didn't know what to say except that they would do anything they could for John.

She responded with deep gratitude before ending the call. Lance held Ricky's hand for a long while after that, sorrow overwhelming them both.

Finally, on May 1st, the needed six hundred thousand mark was reached. High school teachers were ecstatic because AP exams loomed, as did state-mandated testing. There were still protests featured on the news, but the number of signatures was announced and press conferences were called for Los Angeles and San Francisco, where Arthur was now situated.

The night before those press conferences, Techie called Reyna into the Computer Lab, explaining that it was urgent. She'd been preparing the next day's hectic schedule, and getting ready for the weekend when Este returned, and looked more frazzled than usual.

"What's up, Techie? I'm, like, super busy."

"I finally got around to getting info on our boy."

Her eyebrows shot up questioningly.

"Michael Maitland," Techie said.

"Crap!" she whispered. "I'd forgotten about him since he hasn't been around. Whadda'd you find out?"

Techie punched in a few keys and pulled up a Certificate of Live Birth.

"Birth certificate. So?"

"He was adopted out to the Maitlands. Mr. Maitland is a super hotshot entertainment lawyer. Represents tons of big stars and stuff."

"Okay. I figured he was a spoiled rich kid like me. So?"

Techie pointed at the computer screen. "Check it out."

Reyna bent and squinted at the fine print on the scratchy, poorly rendered copy before her. Then she gasped. "Oh, no!"

She stood and gazed at Techie in horror.

He eyed her uncertainly. "Whadda you gonna do?"

"I gotta talk to Lady Jenny about this."

Still in shock, she patted Techie on the shoulder and hurried from the room.

CHAPTER THIRTEEN
IS IT TERRIBLE OR BEAUTIFUL?

THE PRESS CONFERENCE IN Los Angeles was scheduled for five- thirty p.m., and the one in San Francisco for seven, to maximize exposure and TV coverage. Children throughout the state had resumed talking and daily life seemed to be getting back to normal. Mayor Soto and the City Council members were once again in attendance, and the crowd around the staging area seemed casual and relaxed. People chatted amiably, sharing stories among themselves about the silent treatment they'd received from their kids or grandkids, and there was much laughter and rejoicing at having things back the way they used to be.

Ryan and Gibson drove Lance, Ricky, Jenny, Chris and Reyna downtown, and once more escorted them through the vast, animated crowd.

Lance heard some nasty comments hurled their way along the lines of "Punk ass kid" and "Somebody should've silenced him for good," but mostly there was applause. The detectives glowered in the direction of any verbal threats, but couldn't determine actual speakers in such a massive throng. Overall, people seemed so happy to have the silence lifted that the reality of the looming prop wasn't even an issue.

The Mayor and council members greeted Lance warmly. They expressed their joy in the success of the signature gathering and assured Lance of their support as the election loomed in November. Not all were in favor of the amendment, but they supported Lance and Arthur's efforts to better the lives of children statewide. They realized the absolute need in that area.

Just before the conference was set to begin, Lance got a call on his phone.

"Hey, Lance, it's me, Sir John."

Lance smiled, always happy to hear from the ten-year old. "Hey, little brother, how goes the battle?"

"Not so good," John said, and Lance could hear strain in his voice. "Can you come see me now? There's something I gotta ask you. I know where you are 'cause I have it on TV, but this is real important." The voice sounded tired and lifeless.

Lance knew John wouldn't intrude unless it was important. "Well, they kind of want me to speak here. Where are you, Sir John? Home?"

"Hospital."

Lance's breath hitched in his chest.

Just then a text popped up from John's mom. 'Hurry, Lance. There isn't much time.'

Lance's heart began thumping, and his face must've gone ashen because Ricky hurried to his side.

"What's up, man?"

"What hospital?" Lance said into the phone, and Ricky sucked in a breath.

"Children's," John's voice answered quietly, weak and breathy.

"Okay. I'm coming. Can I bring Ricky?"

"You better," John said, and Lance could almost see him smiling.

He ended the call.

"John?" Ricky asked, his voice cracking.

Lance nodded gravely. He quickly explained the situation to Jenny and said she would have to handle the questions after he told the crowd he had to leave.

Hurrying to the microphone, Lance tapped it loudly to get everyone's attention.

When the crowd had settled down, Lance said, "Thank you all for coming out today, and thanks to all of you who supported our campaign. Especially you, Lady Helen. I'm pleased to announce that we have met our goal and the signatures have been sent to the state for verification. We're on track for November!"

There was some excited clapping and cheers from the crowd, accompanied by boos from a substantial enough contingent to be noticeable.

"I wish I could stay and answer more questions, but Ricky and me have a family emergency that just came up." He held up his phone. "We gotta go, but our mom, Lady Jenny, will answer the rest of your questions. Sorry."

Then, to shouted and ad-libbed questions, Lance hurried behind Jenny as she made her way to the podium. Lance rushed to Ryan and explained the situation. They hurried off the stage to Ryan's car.

Children's Hospital was located on Sunset Boulevard in Hollywood, near to the 101 freeway, and Ryan had to use his siren to navigate his way through the Friday rush hour traffic. Lance and Ricky sat in the back seat, silent and somber. Ricky reached out his hand, and Lance grasped it gratefully. He thought back to the day he'd knighted John into the Table. That had been, what, barely two months ago?

Mrs. Aragon had told him during subsequent phone calls that John had never been able to stand again. That single effort had sapped all his strength, and it seemed he'd begun failing more rapidly afterwards.

Lance had felt badly, fearing he'd hastened the boy's death, but she had repeatedly assured him that the one day at New Camelot, and his knighting, was John's most treasured memory. Alas, Lance had not had time to visit John since that day. Though they'd Skyped often, tonight would mark their first physical contact in two months.

Upon arriving at the hospital, the three were given visitor's badges and directed to the oncology ward, where they hurried to John's room. Mrs. Aragon hovered just outside the door, talking with a doctor.

The doctor flashed a tired smile toward Lance and Ricky. "So, here are the two boys who made John's last few months so special. Thank you both." He shook their hands and then hurried off to complete his rounds.

Lance and Ricky looked after him, stunned. John's mom had been crying, but the tears had dried.

"How is he?" Lance asked, almost a whisper.

She shook her head, her soft brown eyes bleeding sadness. "Thank you for coming."

She hugged them both, squeezing with desperation. A somber Ryan waited outside the door while she led the boys inside.

The first sight of John shocked them both. He looked almost skeletal. His head lolled to one side as he slept. Surrounding him were beeping machines monitoring every vital function. His arms looked like pincushions, with tubes and I.V's snaking into and out of them. Lying beside him on the bed was his sheathed sword. Mrs. Aragon urged the boys forward.

Lance stepped up to one side, Ricky the other. Lance felt an overwhelming urge to cry, but fought it back for John's sake. He gently took John's hand and squeezed.

The boy opened his eyes, and his face lit up when he saw Lance. "Thanks, Lance, for coming." He glanced over at Ricky. "You too, Ricky."

Ricky nodded, and John turned back to Lance.

"Hang in there, Sir John," Lance said quietly. "You'll be swinging that sword again soon."

John smiled, but shook his head. "No. It's time for me to go."

Lance choked back a sob and looked at Ricky, who reached out a hand to clasp Lance's, and with his other hand he gently took John's. Now they formed a circle, one that Lance desperately wished could stop death from entering. But he knew that wasn't possible.

"Lance," John whispered, "what was it like?"

Lance looked at him quizzically.

"Death," John clarified, and Lance almost lost it. Ricky squeezed his hand harder. "Is it terrible, or beautiful?"

Lance lowered his head to collect his thoughts, and control the pounding of his heart.

"It's peaceful," he said quietly. "I saw this field of grass and the sky was blue and the whole horizon was this bright light that looked so warm and amazing that I wanted to go there." He paused a moment, watching John's intent face. He described seeing Mark and Jack together, how happy the two boys looked as they held hands and smiled at him. "As they walked into the light, that's when I came back. It wasn't terrible, John. It was beautiful."

He sighed heavily and tried for the best smile he could muster.

"Cool," John said. "See, Mom, I told you Lance would know."

Lance heard her gentle crying behind him. But his gaze remained fixed on John's relaxed face. Gone were any traces of worry or fear.

"Don't be sad," John said. "The only thing that sucks is I'll never grow up to be an awesome man like you guys."

"Thanks, Sir John," Ricky said, his voice quavering. Lance squeezed his hand, and John squeezed both of theirs.

"I like seeing you guys hold hands," John said. "You two are so cool together."

Lance chuckled, and so did Ricky. "You know what's cool beyond cool, John?" Lance said.

John shook his head.

"You. You're the bravest kid I ever knew. After I came back, and with everything that happened to me since, I've thought a few times how it would've been better if I'd stayed dead."

"Hell, no," John said with a grin.

"Hell, no, is right. I never would've met you, Sir John, or had the honor of knighting you. And you made me realize what a gift life really is. Thank you, my brother."

He bent down. John released his grip on both hands so he could encircle Lance's neck. The hug was weak, but Lance held the boy gently.

"You too, Ricky," John whispered. "Group hug."

Ricky leaned in and wrapped his arms around Lance and John and they remained thus for a time.

Finally pulling away, Lance looked down at the boy, tears in his eyes. "God is *so* lucky to be getting you, Sir John of the Round Table."

John grinned. "Damn straight."

Lance and Ricky laughed, and even Mrs. Aragon chuckled.

John's face darkened slightly. "Can you guys stay here with me?"

Lance looked back at John's mom, and she nodded.

"You got it, bro," Lance assured him.

"Up on the bed next to me?" John added, his eyes hopeful and filled with need. Mom nodded again.

Lance and Ricky crawled under the tubing and IV's and lay on either side of John, each holding a hand while Mrs. Aragon stood and watched her son quietly slip away.

"I love you guys," John whispered after a while.

"We love you, too, little brother," Lance whispered back.

John smiled before drifting off to sleep. He never woke up. It took about an hour. Lance and Ricky shed more tears of grief, feeling the boy's breathing become shallower and weaker. Finally, around seven-thirty, John was gone.

Lance and Ricky climbed carefully off the bed and held Mrs. Aragon while all three cried. The doctor came in and declared John dead at seven thirty-three p.m., and then the boy they all loved was covered with a sheet and removed from the room.

While Lance and Ricky spent John's final hours with him, Arthur and his crew had their own press conference that was supposed to begin at seven, but due to traffic snarls didn't actually start until almost seven forty-five. Because Operation Silent Treatment had ended, the mayor of San Francisco pulled off most of the security detail. There were uniformed officers around for crowd control, but no real security against possible violence.

Thus, no one noticed when earlier in the day someone slipped a backpack underneath the raised dais upon which Arthur was to speak, and slid it directly beneath the podium from which the king and his knights would answer questions.

At seven forty-five, Arthur and his crew arrived and stepped onto a raised platform near the historic City Hall building with its colonnades and capitol dome. Traffic along Polk Street had been diverted for this event, and the street swelled with onlookers. Most cheered when Arthur approached the microphone, but some extremely loud heckling was unmistakable. Esteban and Arthur exchanged worried looks, and Arthur nodded to Lavern, who kept his hands on his bow, just in case.

Thus far, their stops in San Francisco had shown mixed results. More than in any other city, there were loud protesters everywhere they had appeared. It looked like tonight would be no different.

"Thank you all for coming out tonight," Arthur began, his bold, confident voice booming out of the speakers over the crowd. "Alas, traffic was heavy, perhaps because the children are asking their parents to drive them some place or other."

There was scattered laughter and quite a few boos.

Arthur noted the booing, but kept on with his positive tone. "As you know, we have met our goal of six hundred thousand signatures and these have been sent to your state government for verification. If it is God's will, all will be accepted and our proposition will be on the ballot in November."

There was more applause, but also more boos and heckling. The children seemed to be the ones cheering the loudest. Arthur noted several he had knighted earlier in the week gathered right in front of the stage, waving their plastic swords at him in support. He grinned in response.

"Why don't you go back to England or wherever your ass came from!" somebody shouted.

"We don't need no kids taking jobs from qualified workers!" someone else shouted.

Arthur scanned the crowd for the hecklers, but could not pinpoint them. He leaned into the microphone and faced the phalanx of reporters. "Do any of you have questions?"

Hands flew up, and Arthur pointed to one man.

"King Arthur, while your petition drive has proven successful, how do you answer your critics who claim your goal is to undermine parental authority?"

"How does this initiative undermine parents?" Arthur asked politely and calmly. "Our goal is simply to give voters a choice. A yes vote will make children adults in a number of ways, not merely for criminality purposes as the laws stand now, but a no vote will return childhood to all children beneath the age of eighteen. Those who feel their authority would be undermined by voting yes can simply vote no. There is a real choice to be made."

There was strong applause from the crowd, but the boos and heckles continued.

Suddenly, something big and heavy, like a full plastic grocery bag, came sailing through the air above the crowd toward Arthur. Lavern leapt forward, shoved the king back and away from the podium, raised his bow and arrow and shot at the object.

When his arrow struck the thing, it erupted, scattering fruits and vegetables everywhere and sending the panicked crowd ducking for cover.

At the edge of the stage, where Lavern's shove had landed him, Arthur called out, "Knights, take cover!" even as Esteban pelted forward like an NFL lineman and plowed into Arthur, shielding his body and shoving the king further away from the podium. Enrique and Luis leapt from the stage into the crowd as Darnell and the others scattered.

The timer within the backpack beneath the stage struck eight.

Lavern stood by the podium grinning, his young face filled with pride at his expert marksmanship, when the platform beneath his feet exploded upward in a brilliant, obscene flash of light.

Lance and Ricky bade Mrs. Aragon a sad goodbye. She promised to let them know the date of John's funeral.

They both hugged her.

"I'm so glad John had you for a mom, Mrs. Aragon," Lance said through his tears.

"You can be our mom any time you want," Ricky told her, sniffling and wiping the tears from his eyes.

She hugged them even harder, and then Ryan escorted them back to his car.

"I'm sorry, boys," Ryan said sadly, his craggy old face looking miserable. "He seemed like a good kid."

Lance nodded. "Yeah."

"Why do we always lose the good ones?" Ricky asked forlornly. No one had an answer.

They drove home in silence. Even though he wasn't supposed to, Ryan switched off his radio because he didn't want to bother the boys. His job was to guard them, so there was no point listening to calls he couldn't respond to. None of them thought to even turn their phones back on after leaving the hospital.

Upon reaching New Camelot, they were greeted by Reyna and Jenny, who hugged both boys and let them cry some more. Ricky took Lance upstairs because he said he needed to be alone.

Up in his room, Lance lay on his bed and Ricky sat with him. Lance began to cry again. Ricky held his hand, and that felt comforting.

"Why, Ricky? Why did he have to die, and I—"

"Don't go there, Lance!" Ricky said sharply, cutting him off. "You have to stop doing that, man! I mean it!"

"Doing what?"

"Acting like it don't matter if you live or die!" Ricky shot back, wiping away his own tears. "Damn it, Lance, I can't keep hearing you... Hell, don't you know how...?"

"How what?" Lance asked innocently.

"How much you matter to people?" Ricky finished. "Like me. Like John."

"I'm sorry man, I'm just super down right now. I'm feeling death coming for me again. I need some time alone, I guess."

Ricky let go of his hand. "Call if you need anything."

Lance nodded, and turned his head away to face the window.

Ricky moved to the door.

"Ricky!" Lance called out, turning his head, a look of desperate abandon on his face.

"Yeah, Lance?"

"Don't ever leave me. Please."

"I won't," he said, and left the room.

Lance gazed at the brocaded drapes in front of his eyes and cried.

When Ricky got downstairs, he found Ryan in shock and Jenny, Reyna and Chris crying. All stood within the Throne Room gazing in horror at a live news feed from San Francisco, and the words 'Terrorist Attack on King Arthur?' His blood ran cold and he lurched over to Jenny, almost numb with fear.

"What's going on?"

Jenny turned and wrapped her arms around him. "Oh, honey, there's been an attack on your dad. They think it was a bomb, but it just happened and everything's chaotic."

Ricky gasped in fear and stared dumbfounded up at the screen.

A reporter was saying that the entire platform on which Arthur and his knights had been standing had blown up. In the smoke and chaos, no one knew who had been hurt and who'd escaped. Flashing lights moved in the background and sirens blasted from the television speakers. Paramedic vehicles roared into the shot behind the reporter, and police officers fought to control the panicking crowd.

Reyna stood paralyzed with fear.

Jenny looked terrified, but eyed Ricky with concern. "Where's Lance?"

"Upstairs in his room," Ricky said tonelessly, his eyes searching every inch of that screen for some sign of his father. "He needed to be alone. I'll go get him."

"No," Jenny said quickly. "Wait until we know something. He's already been through too much tonight. You have, too."

She threw her arms around him again and, despite his best efforts not to, Ricky began to cry. "Oh, Mom, what if..."

He couldn't even say it. No, it couldn't be possible. His dad was alive. He had to be!

Chris ran to Jenny and Ricky, and all huddled together, watching the story unfold, awaiting perhaps the worst news any of them had ever gotten in their lives.

Lance continued to cry softly. Even knowing this day had been inevitable, the loss of John struck at his heart and pierced his soul. Reaching out to turn off the light, Lance knocked his copy of *The Neverending Story* off the night table onto the floor.

A key fell out of it.

Michael's key.

Lance gazed uncertainly down at that key, glinting in the moonlight peeking through his drapes. He didn't know why, but Michael was what he needed right then, more than anyone else.

Lance made a spur of the moment decision to stuff pillows under his blankets so Ricky would think he was asleep, a spur of the moment decision to slip out of the house unnoticed and go to Michael's, a spur of the moment decision that would change everything for him and the entire crusade.

By the time Lance skated all the way up into the hills to Michael's house, it was already after eleven thirty, and with it being a Friday night, he wasn't surprised to find the house dark. Michael always partied on Fridays. Lance used the key to enter the back yard gate, and made his way past the pool and through the darkened jungle to Michael's back house. It sat lonely and dark beneath a bored, listless moon. He let himself in and figured he'd just lie down on Michael's bed until the other boy got home.

His eye caught sight of the wet bar beside the kitchen, the cabinet door ajar. He wandered over and looked in. There were numerous bottles of liquor. Michael kept his place well stocked. Lance's despondency over John, coupled with that feeling of death reaching out for him, overwhelmed him. He grabbed a full bottle of vodka before starting toward Michael's room. Then he paused, and went back for a second bottle.

Gripping both as though his life depended upon them, he used the key to enter Michael's darkened bedroom. The silence was almost oppressive, deepening his loneliness. He set the bottles on the computer desk and slipped out his phone. He would text Michael and let him know to come home. But the dual computer screens caught his eye. Curious, Lance put down his phone and sat before the two screens.

He moved the mouse and the screens came to life, but access required a password. Lance frowned. What would Michael's password be? He considered the possibilities. It could be almost anything. A thought occurred to him. He typed in 'Frankenstein'. Not correct. Thinking some more, he took a big swig from the vodka bottle. He recalled Michael praising *The Neverending Story*. He tried that. Nothing. Taking another big swallow, he realized the painfully harsh liquor was already beginning to relax him. He typed in 'The Ivory Tower'. Wrong again.

Another huge swig, and more relaxing warmth coursed through him as he thought back on the Michael of the past few months. Then he had it, or at least felt pretty sure he did. He typed in 'Lancey Boy'.

Bingo.

He was in.

Lance drank more vodka and stared aimlessly at Michael's dual desktops. Like everything else about Michael, they were neat, ordered and in control. He saw a folder with his name on it, and opened it. Nearly gagging in the middle of swallowing, he set the bottle down beside the keyboard.

There were subfolders within, a lot of subfolders. One was labeled Lance and Bridget, another Lance and Bodyguard, another Lance and Michael, another Throne Room, another Computer Lab. He had folders that seemed to cover every aspect of Lance's life, including press conferences, public appearances, et cetera.

Lance opened the folder labeled Lance and Bridget. Within were audio files and texting files – every conversation, verbal or text or Skype – that Lance had had with Bridget since meeting her. Lance opened one. He heard Bridget say, "Promise never to be alone with him," and he answered, "I promise."

Lance gazed dimly at the screen as he closed that file. "What the hell..." he murmured, as he stared in shock. He polished off the first bottle of vodka, the alcohol warming his entire body and starting to dull the pain of John's death.

He opened the folder labeled Lance and Michael. As expected, he found pictures of the two of them. There was that infamous video of them dancing, even video of the first time he and Ricky came here and Michael made them change shirts.

Hidden cameras, Lance realized with a jolt. *Am I being filmed now?*

He didn't care. He wanted to see more. He closed that one and opened 'Throne Room'.

Within that folder, he found Skype videos when Arthur or someone spoke to the assembled knights. One of these was his knighting of John.

So that's how you knew about it. You've been tapping into our communications!

Feeling more despondent from the alcohol, Lance clicked open that video and watched it play out, shedding more tears as John rose so painfully on his weakened, unsteady legs and proudly held his cherished sword aloft. He couldn't watch anymore and shut it down.

There was another subfolder filled with pictures and videos of Lance throughout the crusade, including his death and rebirth. Michael seemed to have everything there was to have on him.

Bridget was right, Lance understood in the dullness of his brain. *Michael is obsessed with me. But why?*

Closing that folder, he spotted an entirely separate folder in the lower left corner of the screen, not part of the Lance folder, but separate and distinct. It was labeled simply 'Creating the Monster'. Curious, Lance closed the folder he had been looking in, and opened that one.

Within was a single video, a long video, if the file size was any indication. Lance opened the second bottle of vodka and took a big swig. He was already very drunk and knew if he kept on, he'd pass out long before Michael arrived. He set the bottle down and clicked the video to 'play'.

When the video began, there were a bunch of guys in a bedroom somewhere, dressed in Halloween costumes and wearing masks. Music blasted from an unseen stereo. Everyone appeared to be college age. All except one. There was a smaller form, clearly a kid, wearing a Scream mask and black cloak. The college guys, swigging beer and other drinks through their masks, were obviously drunk as they pushed the smaller one around and mocked him.

"Think you can crash our party and hang with the big boys, huh?" one said with a shove. His voice was nearly lost beneath the pounding beats of the music.

"Little rich boy thinks he's a man," mocked another, who spun the kid around to face him.

There was laughter as three of the big guys grabbed the boy, who struggled, but was too small to get away. A fourth grabbed the Scream mask and yanked it off the boy's head.

Lance gasped.

The boy was Michael.

Younger. Twelve, maybe thirteen, but definitely Michael. Surfer blond hair and thinner, way before hitting the weights, but Michael nonetheless. That same haughty expression masked the obvious fear he must've been feeling.

"You better leave me alone," Michael threatened, though his boyish voice made the threat sound hollow.

"Or what?" a fifth guy sneered. "Nobody gonna know what we did, 'cause you, ya little turd, don't even know who we are."

Michael's eyes went fearful now, the haughtiness gone. "What're you going to do?"

"You came to party, little boy, so let's party," the first guy said, his arm around Michael's throat. He threw him down on the bed, face first.

Lance watched in horror as the struggling Michael had his wrists bound and tied to the headboard, lying face down on the bed. Michael begged them to let him go.

Lance watched in open-mouthed horror. The camera was behind the man, so Lance could not see exactly what he did. But suddenly Michael shrieked like a fire bell, eliciting another round of laughter.

That scream sent waves of nausea through Lance, taking him back in time to his own horrified, pain-soaked cries for mercy. His own deep well of hurt suddenly mixed in with that of Michael on screen, and Lance's gorge rose.

Leaping from the chair, he staggered into the bathroom, lurching toward the toilet, with the seat standing up as though awaiting him. He nearly made it too, but the vomit spewed forth just inches from the rim as he fell hard to his knees, sending pain shooting up into his brain. Puke reeking of vodka splashed across the side of the toilet, onto the floor by the tub, into his long hair, and down his shirt.

Gagging on the smell, more came up, this time into the bowl as he lowered his vomit splattered face over the water and lurched, his body heaving and heaving until there was nothing left.

Turning, he lay weakly up against the bathtub, hearing from the other room, "Now it's my turn."

There were more screams from Michael. Lance lay in a daze, lost in those horrific sounds, reliving his own violation, too weak and traumatized to even stagger back into the other room and shut off the computer.

Finally, Lance could take no more, and he passed out.

The Throne Room of New Camelot was silent and expectant, as everyone stood in anxious anticipation, watching the scene unfold from San Francisco. Gibson called Ryan, and Justin took the phone to assure his dad the hotel was secure in case anyone planned an attack.

"Don't worry, Dad, I got everything covered. Just like you taught me."

"I know you do, Justin." There was a pause. "Be careful, son. I love you."

"Love you too, Dad."

He handed the phone back to Ryan, and the older man spoke wearily into it. "We're solid here, Gib. No worries."

Ryan ended the call and informed Jenny that there were police cars surrounding the perimeter of the hotel, just in case.

Ricky held Chris tightly, clinging to him in solace and fear. There was still no word on Arthur or his knights. The crowd had scattered in all directions, and shrapnel from the explosion had been flung into the crowd. It appeared, according to the reporters, that the bomb had been filled with small nails and other sharp bits of metal.

The camera seemed to be roving everywhere, as paramedics treated people who'd been struck by flying pieces of the stage, or by the nails encased within the bomb. Blood had splattered over the asphalt. The wildly swinging news cameras picked up bloodied children being laid onto gurneys, rushing paramedics who flew into and out of camera range, people of all ages having their faces or arms or legs treated for cuts and gashes. The camera zoomed in on two of Arthur's replica swords lying on the asphalt amidst debris from the stage, the swords he'd been presenting to newly knighted children. Both were covered in crimson blood.

Everyone in the Throne Room stared at the carnage with horror and fear. Reyna looked panicked. She held Jenny's hand desperately. "Where are they, Lady Jenny?" she whispered. "Oh God, what if…"

Jenny tried for a reassuring smile. "You know Este and Arthur. Not much stops them."

The reporter was saying into the camera, "Thus far, there's been no sign of King Arthur or any of his knights. We're hoping he—"

Just then Jenny's phone rang, startling them all. She snatched it from her pocket and saw the name: Arthur.

"Thank God," she whispered, and opened up the Skype line. Almost at once, Arthur replaced the newscaster on the screen.

His face was blackened and dirty, there was blood from scratches to his face, but he otherwise looked unharmed.

"Dad!" Ricky and Chris cried out at once.

"Oh, Arthur, thank God," Jenny said, fighting back tears. "Are you all right?"

Arthur nodded, looking grave. "Yes, is everything well there? I feared perhaps—"

"Everything's secure here, Arthur," Ryan said. "Everybody's fine."

Arthur nodded. "Ricky, all of my sons are well?"

Ricky produced Chris so Arthur could see. "We're okay, Dad."

Arthur suddenly looked scared. "Lance, where is Lance?"

"He's okay, Dad," Ricky quickly added. "It's just, well, John died tonight and Lance was really depressed. He's in his room, sleeping, I think. You want me to get him?"

"No, let him sleep."

"Where's Este, Arthur?" Reyna said, unable to hide her fear. "Is he–"

"He's alive, Reyna," Arthur assured her, coughing as the residual smoke choked his lungs and eyes. "He took several nails to the back, but remains undaunted in searching for his fellow knights within the rubble."

"Oh, God," Jenny whispered. "What happened, Arthur?"

"We do not know as yet. An explosive device, placed beneath the platform."

"Where are Enrique and the rest?" Chris asked uncertainly.

"Unaccounted for, Chris," Arthur replied, his voice heavy with guilt and remorse. "Luis and Darnell were injured by flying metal, but are unharmed. They are helping Sir Este in the search."

A chill ran down Ricky's back. "Lavern? Dad, what about Lavern?"

Arthur dropped his gaze, struggling to find his voice. "Unaccounted for, as well. He… he pushed me aside, just as the bomb went off beneath him."

Ricky gasped. "Oh, God, no…"

"He saved my life," Arthur went on, his voice barely a whisper. "I was not grasping Excalibur at the time."

"Oh, Arthur," Jenny began, fighting her tears. "Do you think he…?"

"I don't know. I must go now, Jenny. I must find him."

"Be careful, Arthur," Jenny said. "I love you."

"I love you more." He turned to Ricky and Chris. "And you, my sons, I love you with all my heart. I shall return to thee. Tell that to Lance, Ricky. Assure him of my love and my safety."

Tearfully, Ricky nodded. "I will, Dad. Watch your back."

"I shall."

He vanished from the screen and Fox News returned with its live coverage of the attack. Ricky took the remote from Jenny and muted the sound. Everyone turned to look at him.

"I think," he said, "we should all pray." He looked around at their faces.

"I think you're right," Reyna affirmed.

With that, all fell to their knees and began to pray.

Michael arrived home around twelve-thirty, instantly realizing the door had been opened in his absence. He cautiously glanced around the living room as he worked his way through the darkened house. He stopped at the wet bar, noticing the door hanging ajar. He opened it and his eyes narrowed at the missing vodka bottles. Then he heard crying from his bedroom.

He quickly pushed opened the bedroom door, and stopped. The video still played. His face was expressionless as he saw and heard his younger self crying out in pain, still blubbering helplessly. That's when he smelled the vomit. Seeing the bathroom door ajar, Michael stepped over and opened it, recoiling in revulsion.

Lance sat spread eagled up against the tub, covered in vomit, clearly drunk and confused, awake and sobbing.

"Oh, hell, Lance!" Michael spat. "Why are you here?"

Lance looked up at him, sadder than Michael had ever seen him look. "Oh, Michael, why didn't you tell me..."

Michael stiffened and stood there, rigid as a statue, his features hard and expressionless. "Tell you what, Lance? That a bunch of drunken frat boys raped my ass when I was barely thirteen? Why would I tell you that?"

Lance wiped tears and snot from his face with a dirty, vomit-stained sleeve. "Cause I care about you," he whispered. "And I can understand. I *do* understand."

Michael's look was cold. "You understand what, Lance? How it feels to be gang raped?"

Lance looked at him, his own violation plastered across his face and brimming outward from his sad green eyes.

Michael stepped forward. "Yeah, I guess you do. Except you were six years old! That bastard! A little kid like you!"

"Oh, Michael," Lance said sadly. "I'm so sorry."

"Don't be," Michael affirmed, his face hard, his eyes narrow and flinty. "I took care of it."

Lance began to cry again.

Michael gazed down at him a moment. "Oh, hell!" He hesitantly sat on the floor beside Lance, careful to avoid the vomit. Cradling Lance against him, he gently wiped Lance's mouth and face with his clean sleeve.

"I can't believe they did that to you, Michael," Lance choked through hitching breaths. "You were just a boy."

Michael just grunted. "That's when I stopped being a boy." He paused, and shook his head. "You wanna know the worst part?"

Lance nodded.

"They dumped me in some park and I had to call my dad to come get me. Hell, Lance, I was bleeding from my ass and could barely walk! He came, but was pissed as hell that I got him away from some *important clients.*" He hesitated a moment, as though taking another breath. "I told him what happened on the way home, and you know what he said?"

Lance looked up at him, but Michael turned face toward the open door. The sounds of his violation still drifted in from the bedroom.

"He said it was my own fault for thinking I could hang around adults and act like a little queer boy."

Lance sucked in a breath of shock.

"I told him I wasn't gay, and you know what he said back? 'You are now'."

His eyes never left the door, his voice never even quavered. It remained solid and steady and cold. "And that was that. He dropped me at home, told me to clean myself up and not tell anyone what happened. He wasn't gonna have his good name dragged through the mud because of his stupid, faggot son. Then he went back to his party."

"Oh, my God, Michael!" Lance pressed his head up against Michael and tried to wrap his arms around him, but Michael rebuffed the move.

"I took care of it myself, Lance," Michael said again, eyes still boring straight ahead.

"How?"

"Never mind."

"Did you give that video to the cops?"

"I told you, I took care of it."

Michael felt Lance staring at him, and against his will, he shivered.

"Why do you keep it? It's horrible."

Michael's lower jaw twitched, but he kept his eyes fixed on the far wall. "Because sometimes I can't remember."

"Remember what?"

"Who I used to be," Michael answered flatly, without emotion, without pain.

"Oh, Michael, I'm so sorry."

Michael pushed him away and glowered. "Stop saying you're sorry, Lance. I don't want your sympathy! I never wanted you to know in the first place. What the hell are you doing here, anyway?"

Lance looked at him, teary eyed. "John died tonight."

Michael looked at him soberly. "The cancer kid."

"I just needed someone, Michael. I felt so alone." He reached up and turned Michael's face toward his. "I think I love you, Michael."

Michael pushed Lance's hands from his face. "That's the booze talking. We both know who you love."

Lance looked up in surprise, his eyes as wide as dinner plates.

"C'mon, Lance, let's get you cleaned up and back home."

He reached out and grabbed the bottom of Lance's vomit soaked shirt and slipped it up and over his head, tossing it to one side.

Lance looked into his eyes. "You're good, Michael. You're still that little boy."

"Keep telling yourself that, Lance, and maybe one day you'll believe it."

Lance eyed him uncertainly, and then passed out again.

Michael caught him before he hit the floor, gently laying his head down on the expensive marble tiles.

"Oh, hell, Lance," he muttered, listening a moment to his little-boy-self begging and pleading for mercy. He sighed and began removing Lance's pants.

Finally at two in the morning, Ricky told Jenny he wanted to check on Lance. They were still awaiting official word on Arthur's knights. Nails had struck so many people, there were literally hundreds of injured and maimed.

Ricky trudged up to Lance's room and crept in. He saw a bundle at the far end of the bed, and tiptoed over. He'd never tell Lance this, but Ricky loved watching him sleep. Lance always looked so peaceful, so perfectly beautiful, so like the miracle boy everyone wanted him to be.

As Ricky inched around the bed, something about the shape looked wrong. He lightly touched it, and felt it cave in. He grabbed the blankets and pulled them back.

Pillows.

"Oh, crap!" he cursed, frantically thinking about where Lance might have gone.

"Bridget!" He slipped out his phone as he made his way out of the room and called Bridget. She groggily answered the phone. "Bridget, it's Ricky. Is Lance there?"

Her voice became clearer. "No, why?"

"He's gone, and all hell broke loose in San Francisco with our dad. Check the news. I gotta go!" He ended the call and took off running down the stairs.

322

Ricky burst into the Throne Room. "Mom, Lance is gone!"

Jenny whipped her head around. "What?"

"He snuck out."

Ryan hurried over. "Where would he have gone? The girlfriend's?"

Ricky shook his head. "Already called her." Then he knew. The handoff up in the hallway. Now Ricky knew what it was Michael had given Lance. "Oh, no! He went to Michael's."

Reyna turned, clearly frightened. "How do you know?"

"Michael gave him a key," Ricky explained. "I just realized that now."

Reyna cursed.

"Do you know where he lives?" Ryan asked urgently.

Suddenly, Ricky realized that he didn't. "Damn! I've been there, but Michael drove and I didn't pay attention!"

Reyna put an arm around him. "It's okay, baby, you didn't know."

"What if Michael hurts him, Reyna?" Ricky said desperately. "I couldn't forgive my—"

At that moment, the doorbell rang, startling them all. Ryan led the way out into the lobby, almost sprinting, Ricky right on his heels. Ryan pulled his gun and pointed at the inside of the front doors. He nodded his head toward Ricky. Ricky pulled open the door.

Michael stood outside, carrying an unconscious Lance in his arms. Lance wore a tee shirt and workout shorts and no shoes.

"The hell!" Ricky roared. "What did you do to him, Michael? Gimme!"

He lurched forward and snatched Lance's unmoving form from Michael, cradling him in his arms, surprised at how easy it was to hold him.

Michael looked solemnly at Ricky, not even with his usual swagger. "Found him at my house. Drunk. Threw up all over. I cleaned him up, that's all. Gave him a bath."

Ricky blanched. "You took his clothes off?"

"Baths usually work better when the guy is naked, bodyguard."

"You bastard!"

Ryan stepped between them, gun still in hand. "Is there a problem, Michael?"

Michael eyed the detective with disdain. "No problem, Sergeant. Ricky boy here seems to think I did something improper to his... boy."

"If you did..." Reyna spat, glaring at him.

Michael held up both hands. "This is what I get for doing Lance a favor. I'm outta here." He turned back down the cobbled walkway.

"And don't come back," Ricky whispered harshly.

Michael whirled to face him, eyes pinned to Ricky like lasers. "Bottom line, Ricky boy? He was hurting tonight, and he came to me. Stick that down your throat and choke on it!"

He turned to strut angrily down the walkway.

Ricky felt a twinge of guilt. Michael *had* brought Lance back, after all.

"Michael!"

Michael turned back, glaring through the dark, his white-blond hair looking almost angelic beneath the front yard lights.

"Thanks, for, you know, bringing him home," Ricky said, his face turning red with shame.

Michael nodded and headed off to the parking lot.

Ryan closed the door and holstered his gun. "You need help with him, Ricky?"

"No. I got him." He carried Lance past Jenny and Reyna.

Chris stood at the foot of the stairs. "Is Lance okay, Ricky?"

"He'll be fine, Chris. Just needs to sleep."

He trudged up the stairs, cradling Lance to his body, feeling his boy's gentle breathing, and entered Lance's room. He lay him down tenderly onto the bed, feeling the strain in his arms, but realizing he'd carried someone his own weight up all those stairs without even struggling. Adrenalin, he supposed.

He carefully pulled the blankets and comforter up over Lance and stood for a time, watching him sleep.

His face doesn't look peaceful tonight.

The perfect features were taut, almost drawn in with pain, as though he'd gone through a traumatic event, even more traumatic than John's death. Ricky wondered if Michael had done something to him, after all.

Ricky slipped off his boots and crawled onto the bed. He lay down beside Lance and held him in his arms, much as the two of them had held John the previous night.

"Why'd you have to go to *him*?"

Lance's even breathing was his only answer. His heart heavy with the night's events, Ricky drifted off to sleep.

Lance awoke in the morning to find arms wrapped around him and a fully clothed Ricky sound asleep. His head pounded beyond belief, and his heart began to thud with sorrow as the events of the previous night flooded back in.

First John, and then Michael.

Oh, God, he thought, *how could you have let that happen to a child? To both children?*

Ricky began to stir, and Lance looked over at his face. Ricky looked so peaceful, so beautiful, yet so sad. Lance gently jostled him, and Ricky's eyes opened. When he found himself wrapped around Lance, he quickly disentangled himself.

Lance sat up and looked around the room, confused. "How'd I get here? Where's Michael?"

Ricky sat up too, and scowled, though he tried not to show it. "He brought you home and left."

"You stayed with me all night?"

"Course." He said it in that tone which really meant, "Who else would stay with you when you were hurting?"

Lance eyed him shyly. "Thanks."

Ricky nodded.

"We lost John, didn't we?" Lance almost whispered, and Ricky sadly lowered his eyes. "My mind is so confused." Then his face darkened. "And Michael, oh God, Ricky, Michael..."

"Michael what? Did he hurt you?"

Lance's eyes welled with tears and he shook his head. Then he noticed his clothes. "Where'd I get these clothes?"

"Michael," Ricky said with a sigh, leading up to the news about Arthur. "He said he had to undress you 'cause you blew chunks. He, uh, he gave you a bath."

Lance looked at him quickly, the realization of what that meant turning him red with embarrassment.

"Listen, Lance," Ricky began, clearing his throat and shifting uncomfortably. "Something else happened last night, besides John."

"What?"

"Somebody attacked Dad and the others in San Francisco."

Lance gagged. Tears instantly burned his eyes. "Is he...?"

Ricky put both hands on his shoulders. "He's okay. So's Este, but we're...well, they weren't sure about the others, especially..."

"Who?"

"Lavern."

"Oh, no..."

"C'mon, throw on some clothes and let's get down there," Ricky said, leaping off the bed. "There's gotta be more news by now."

Despite the pounding in his head, Lance leaped after him and snatched a shirt and pants from his dresser drawer. Slipping into both, he followed Ricky from the room at a run.

They found Jenny and Reyna still in the Throne Room, still wearing the same clothes from the night before.

The TV was now tuned to CNN and the cameras were live at the cleanup sight. Updates scrawled across the bottom of the screen:

'Four confirmed dead in San Francisco explosion'.

Jenny turned when the boys entered. She hurried to Lance and engulfed him in a hug. "Oh, Lance, honey, you had us so worried last night."

Reyna came over. "We were afraid somebody might come after you, too."

Lance pulled away from Jenny to see Reyna's fearful look. "I'm sorry. I was just so depressed about..." He stopped, his gaze pulled back to the screen. "What's the latest? It says people died..."

Jenny looked exhausted. "It looks like Enrique and Luis and most of the others are okay. Some kids up front by the stage..."

"They got caught in the explosion," Reyna finished. "And died."

"Lavern?" Lance whispered breathily.

Jenny shook her head. "I'm sorry, Lance."

Tears sprang to Lance's eyes. Ricky's too.

Reyna stepped forward to hug them both. "He was right over the bomb. They're still trying to..." She trailed off, unable to continue.

"To what?" Lance choked out.

Jenny put a hand to his arm soothingly. "To find all of him, Lance."

Lance gagged, his face ghastly white, his stomach lurching. His gorge rose and he clamped a hand to his mouth as he tried to bolt from the room. He only made it as far as the lobby before he vomited all over the marble floor, dropping to his knees in sorrow.

Ricky was beside him, head on his shoulder, both of them crying tears of loss and horror, not quite believing what had happened.

Jenny told Reyna to find someone to clean up the mess and then knelt beside the boys, holding them in place, sharing their pain. She pulled some tissue from her pocket and gently wiped Lance's soiled lips, and then handed some tissue to both boys and allowed them to grieve.

They remained together until a maid arrived to clean up the vomit. Jenny gently led the boys back to the Throne Room and sat them down.

As though somehow knowing, Arthur chose that moment to call Jenny's phone. She pulled it out and opened Skype. The news broadcast switched to an image of

Arthur and Esteban. Esteban wore a tank top and his shoulder was wrapped all around and under the arm by thick, white bandages. Reyna gasped when she saw him bound like that.

"Este," she almost cried out, but managed to control her voice. "Are you okay? Arthur said you weren't badly hurt!"

Este didn't smile. In fact, he looked lost and forlorn. "I'm fine, baby. Took a few nails to the back, but I'm good."

Arthur looked grave. "Is Lance there?"

Jenny handed off the phone to Lance. Ricky hovered at his right shoulder. "I'm here, Dad."

Arthur breathed a heavy sigh. "Thank the Lord! The moment we were attacked, my thoughts were upon you and Ricky. I feared they would strike at you."

"We're fine, Dad," Lance said, his eyes welling up again. "But Lavern, oh, Dad..."

"I know, son," Arthur replied, his eyes brimming with tears. "Such an amazing boy, such a brave knight."

"How are the others, Arthur?" Jenny asked, leaning in to the phone.

"All sustained some injuries, Jenny," he answered, sounding old and worn out. "Mostly nails or metal striking them. They have been treated, as has Sir Este, and released."

"When're you coming home, Dad?" Ricky asked, his voice filled with desperate need.

"In a few days," Arthur replied. "The police are investigating. An agency called the FBI is also present. I must help all I can, especially with the families of those murdered children." He paused. "And I must wait to bring Lavern home."

He paused again, his eyes wide with pain and loss. "Alas, more knights to bury, though I thank God above that Sir John went peacefully."

Jenny could hear the guilt in his voice. "It wasn't your fault, Arthur."

Arthur nodded, though his face didn't seem to agree with her. "I must speak with the press today. Lance and Ricky?"

"We're here, Dad," Lance said, making sure his and Ricky's faces were in front of the phone.

"Jenny has told me the press down there has been calling all morning, wishing a statement from you. Are you able to comply? I understand if you cannot."

The boys exchanged a look, and both nodded. "We can do it, Dad."

"Thank you, my sons," Arthur said, obvious pride in his voice. "I do not wish either of you to leave New Camelot for any reason. The press will be cleared by

Sergeants Ryan and Gibson and you may answer questions on the front steps only. We do not know how far these people may yet go to stop us."

"We got it, Dad," Lance affirmed. "Don't worry about us."

Arthur tried for a slight smile. "I cannot help but worry, Lance. You are my sons, and I love you."

"I love you too," both boys said in unison, not even noticing the synchronicity.

"Keep in touch, Arthur," Jenny said. "I love you."

"And I you."

Esteban now filled the screen as he took Arthur's phone. "Be safe, Reyna," he said. "Keep the others safe till I come back to you."

"I will. Nobody hurts my family!"

"That's the girl I fell in love with. Badass to the core."

Reyna offered a smile. "I got me a pretty badass boy, myself. You be careful up there."

"Always. I'm too tough to take down."

Arthur's face returned then. "We shall speak later."

The boys bobbed their faces in front of the phone. "Love you, Dad, be careful!"

Arthur smiled sadly and the call ended.

Jenny turned to Lance and Ricky. "You boys really all right to talk to the press?"

"Long as Helen's there," Lance said.

"I'll let them know," Jenny said and left the room.

Reyna said, "I'm gonna check on Chris. You guys good?"

They nodded and she left the room.

Lance sat in a chair, suddenly overwhelmed with fatigue that had nothing to do with his hangover. "How many more, Ricky?"

Ricky sat beside him. "How many more what?"

Lance looked at him sadly. "How many more kids are we gonna have to lose?"

Ricky sighed, and grasped Lance's hand firmly. "We'll make it through. We'll always have each other."

Lance eyed him uncertainly. "Will it be, though?"

Ricky cocked his head. "Will it be what?"

"Will it be for always?"

Ricky looked resolute. "For always."

Lance threw an arm over Ricky's shoulders and the boys sat in silence watching the aftermath coverage on TV, silently grieving the loss of their two brothers, and contemplating a very ambiguous future.

The TV coverage continued all morning, as the number of injured kept rising, with reports flooding into the news outlets from local emergency rooms. Literally hundreds had to be treated for shrapnel or nails striking somewhere on their bodies. San Francisco was stunned by the violence. Theories from right wing militia groups to left wing union thugs, to extremist terrorist groups abounded, but thus far no one had claimed responsibility.

Lance and Ricky got a call from John's mother, who expressed her condolences on the death of Lavern. Lance asked her if the two boys could be part of the same funeral service, and she agreed.

Finally, noon rolled around and it was time for Lance and Ricky to step outside and face more reporters.

"Everybody's credentials have been checked out, Lance," Gibson assured him.

"Helen is right up front for moral support," Ryan offered.

Lance nodded. Accompanying he and Ricky out to the front stoop were Jenny, her hand firmly grasping Chris's, Reyna, Justin, Gibson, and Ryan.

As they stepped outside, cameras began rolling and questions flew at them from all directions. The entire front yard was filled with reporters and cameras, and everybody tried to speak at once. There was a microphone set up on the top step, and Helen pointed it out to Lance. With Ricky beside him, he stepped up to it and cleared his throat.

"Hello, everyone. I guess you all know what happened." He paused to catch his breath. "My dad, our dad," he put his arm around Ricky and pulled him in, "was attacked last night, and one of the best kids I'll ever know... died." Pausing, he bowed his head and squeezed Ricky's shoulder.

Ricky leaned in to the mic. "We're all sick over what happened. Lavern was an awesome kid, an amazing brother, and I don't know why anyone would... I mean, it makes no sense."

Lance fought to compose himself. "I know whenever you all look at that mural downtown, you think of me, and what happened before. From now on, I want you to think of Lavern, because his beautiful hands painted that face that looks so real it scares me sometimes. That boy was a gift from God and I don't want him ever forgotten."

He stopped again, and glanced at Ricky. Both boys pulled each other in for a hug and paused, allowing the silence to surround them. After a moment, they separated, wiped tears from their eyes and looked back at the crowd of expectant faces.

"Are there any questions?" Ricky asked.

Hands flew up.

Lance pointed to one reporter.

"Sir Lance, do you see this attack as possibly the beginning of a war against you and King Arthur?"

"A war for what?"

"A war to maintain the status quo."

"Are you saying that we started this by trying to make things better for kids?" Lance felt his temper begin to rise. Ricky grabbed his arm and squeezed.

"Not at all, Sir Lance," the reporter went on. "But you do realize that if your initiative passes, the adults of this state will be giving up a lot of power. People don't like to do that."

Lance finally understood the drift of the man's question. "If you're asking are we gonna quit, the answer is hell no!"

"We got the signatures we needed," Ricky said, "and now we're gonna get people out to vote. If these people, whoever they are, think they can stop what we started, they're wrong."

"What if there are more attacks?" another reporter called out.

Lance glanced back at Sergeants Ryan and Gibson. "That's their job. But we're not quitting, no matter what."

"Can we quote you on that, Sir Lance?" Helen asked.

""Damn straight," he replied with conviction, and there were scattered murmurs from the crowd.

In San Francisco, Arthur and Esteban were giving a similar press conference. This time, there was a considerable police presence surrounding Arthur and the crowd.

"What are your plans now, King Arthur?" asked a youngish woman reporter.

"The same as they were yesterday," Arthur replied simply. "We have our signatures, and now we move forward to the vote in November."

He pointed to another raised hand.

"Has this attack made you in any way rethink what you're doing?"

Arthur looked puzzled a moment. "If I and my knights were to quit now when we are so close to victory, Lavern's death and that of the others last night would be for naught."

Another hand went up, and Arthur pointed.

"But is what you're seeking worth the deaths of children, perhaps even more children, if these attacks on you continue?"

Arthur looked at Esteban, and he stepped up to the mic, glaring angrily out at the crowd. "Get this through your heads, and that includes you cowards who killed Lavern – I'm not lettin' my boy die for nothing! We're gonna win this fight and we're gonna get choices for kids, and when we get those choices, we're comin' after all of you who been pushin' us around!"

Arthur put a hand to Esteban's shoulder to calm him.

Esteban's eyes welled with tears of pain and sorrow. "Lavern was a good kid, and somebody's gonna pay for killing him."

Arthur gently led him back away from the microphone, and he stepped up again.

"Sir Esteban is understandably emotional over what hath happened. We trust your law enforcement officials will find those responsible and bring them to justice. In the meantime, my knights and I will be leaving your city as soon as Lavern's…as soon as Lavern is released to me. We shall return home and bury our dead."

He bowed and led Esteban off the stage to shouted questions, which both men ignored.

CHAPTER FOURTEEN

WHO SAYS YOU FASCINATE ME?

THE NEXT FEW DAYS WERE spent preparing for the funerals of Lavern and John, and awaiting Arthur's return to New Camelot. Lance and Ricky never left each other's side except to shower, and even then one stood outside the door until the other was finished. There were no new attacks or any claim of responsibility for the first one, but the boys weren't taking any chances.

During all the drama and worrying, Reyna forgot to share with Jenny the information Techie had unearthed on Michael's background. It didn't seem important with everyone focused on the impending funerals, picking up the pieces of the crusade, and pushing forward toward the election in November.

Helen informed Lance that the funerals for Lavern and John would be another media circus because of the bombing, and Lance told her he wanted everyone to stay outside the church except her and Charlie, her cameraman. All she could do was record the event. Unless somebody wanted to talk with her, she wasn't to intrude on anyone's grief. She readily agreed.

Bridget and Ariel texted or Skyped the boys every day, but now, even more than before, they were too busy to chat and couldn't even consider going out anywhere. Lance knew both girls were feeling left out, but it didn't really bother him not to see Bridget. He knew Ricky felt the same way about Ariel. They'd find time to hang out after the funerals were over.

Finally, on the Tuesday following the attack, Arthur and his knights returned to New Camelot. As happy as everyone was to be back together, their joy was tempered with sorrow. Reyna flung herself at Esteban and threw her arms wildly about him in a tight hug, causing him to wince with pain.

"Oh, I'm sorry, Este," she said, mortified as she pulled back. "I forgot. I'm just so happy to see you."

He offered his cocky grin and they kissed, long and deeply.

Jenny threw her own arms around Arthur and they kissed as well, seemingly pressed together forever.

Then Lance, Ricky, and Chris stood before Arthur. The king had shrapnel cuts and residual scrapes on his face.

"I've never been so happy to see all of you in my life."

Lance smiled shyly. "Welcome home, Dad." He paused, feeling oddly tentative, and threw his arms around his father. "I missed you so much."

"And I missed you, my son," Arthur replied, returning the hug. Then he opened his arms and the other two boys were enveloped, as well. They stood that way for some moments, just relishing the physical touch of each other.

Chris lost his joyful look and lowered his eyes, which welled with tears. "I never even got to tell Lavern how cool he was for teaching me to shoot good."

Arthur scooped the small boy into his arms and made eye contact. "He knew you loved him, Chris," Arthur assured him with a tousle of the boy's shaggy blond hair. "He knew."

With that, everyone settled back into life at New Camelot and the funeral arrangements were finalized.

The following weekend the funerals took place at John's parish, St. Monica's Catholic Church in Santa Monica. Lavern's mother didn't care because she had no church of her own. Helen hadn't been joking – every media outlet in the world seemed to be there, no doubt hoping for a statement from Arthur or Lance or even another attack on them during the service. When Lance had called them voyeurs, he wasn't far wrong.

John had many family members and admirers in attendance, including some of the nurses from Children's Hospital. Lavern, of course, had Arthur and a large contingent of his knights. Only his mother and one adult friend attended from his neighborhood.

St. Monica's, a large, oblong-shaped church, was packed. Bridget and Ariel sat together, offering a shy little wave to Lance and Ricky as they entered. The boys nodded in reply before stepping into the second pew from the front. The entire first row quickly filled with John's extended family.

The celebrant, Father Tim, presided over the funeral mass, speaking in glowing terms about John and his heroic struggle. He'd never met Lavern, but he expressed his opinion from all he'd seen of the boy on television that Lavern was every bit as heroic and brave, and had clearly died a hero in saving Arthur's life.

Lavern's mother sat stoically with her friend, but did not stand up to speak about her son.

Arthur stood and spoke on Lavern's behalf. "I did not know John, to my great misfortune, but my sons will speak of him, and of Lavern, when I am finished. It saddens me deeply to stand here and speak about a thirteen-year-old boy so cruelly and unnecessarily taken from us."

Arthur held up a bow and quiver of arrows, blackened and broken. "This was the gift I presented to Lavern when he turned thirteen just a few weeks past. I purchased it from Amazon, which Lavern seemed to find very amusing. But he loved it, nonetheless, not because it was the coolest bow he'd ever seen, but rather because I had taken the time to find it for him, and to have his name engraved upon it."

He held up the bow and those in front could clearly see the name 'Sir Lavern' engraved in Old English script across its face atop the cracked wood. Arthur paused, his voice catching.

"Lavern was a good boy, a boy of gentle nature and a level head, a boy of extraordinary talents and abilities. He was a boy whom I loved, a boy who is irreplaceable, a boy I considered a son to me. May he rest for eternity beside our Lord God, painting magnificent murals upon Heaven's gates."

Arthur stepped down and Father Tim asked if anyone else wished to speak about either or both boys. Lance and Ricky stood, dressed once more in their somber black suits, faces tear-stained, but steadfast. They made their way to the podium. Lance waved Ricky forward first. Ricky stood behind the microphone, looking out at the huge crowd, cleared his throat, and began.

"I didn't know Lavern as long as some of the others, but he taught me some cool moves with the bow and, even though I'm older, I looked up to him for those moves."

He paused, and swallowed hard. "He was my brother, and I loved him like a brother. As for John, well, he was just amazing. He came to New Camelot to spend the day with Lance, but he grabbed onto me too, and included me in everything."

His breath caught in his throat, and he fought the tears. "I don't think I'll ever meet anybody else that brave. *He* made *me* feel better 'cause he was gonna die and I couldn't handle it. Amazing. They were both just... amazing."

Ricky stepped back and swiped at his eyes with his sleeve. Lance placed a hand on his shoulder, and stepped up to the microphone.

"I remember the night my Dad and me met Lavern," he began. "That seems so long ago now." Stopping a moment to compose himself, he sighed sadly. "When he saw me and Arthur on Llamrei right there on his street, I thought his eyes would fall out of his head."

A few chuckles could be heard from the assembled.

"But as soon as he heard about our crusade, he wanted in. And he was in all the way. He wouldn't let me alone till I taught him how to shoot that bow in pitch darkness."

Lance smiled, a tear trickling down his cheek. "He was an awesome little brother, and I'll never forget him. I know him well enough to know that if he were here he'd tell you all that him dying to save my Dad was worth it. He loved my Dad more than anybody in this world. I know that 'cause he told me. If you're listening, Lavern, thank you for saving him. I'll never forget you."

He paused, looked down, and then up at John's mother, seated in the front row.

"Then there was John," he continued in a tremulous voice. "Sir John. The first person I ever knighted. I think that boy had more wisdom at ten than I do now. He brushed off all the embarrassing things I'd done by saying every kid does stupid stuff.

He made me realize that no matter how badly I might see myself, he saw in me somebody to look up to, to want to be like."

His voice caught, and he couldn't go on. He started to cry, tears rolling unheeded down his cheeks.

"He was the one dying and he made me feel better about living. He was incredible. But then, he had an incredible mom." He looked straight at her. "I'd have been so lucky and blessed to have a mom like you, Mrs. Aragon, and I'm so happy John did."

She nodded in acknowledgment, and he continued. "When I came back... from death... I didn't know what to make of it all. I... I kept falling into these depressions, really dark, scary places that I told Ricky made me think of those Final Destination movies. I thought maybe it was all a big mistake and death still wanted me back. But John, who, like, slept right next to death every single day, loved life and lived it more than me. Because 'a him I don't question God anymore. God brought me back, so I guess I need to be back. And he took John, so I guess he needed to do that too."

More tears trickled down his cheeks. "But John taught me a lesson I'll never forget. Life is a gift and we need to make the best we can out of every minute we got."

He nodded to Ricky, and the two boys stepped down to stand behind the two caskets. Both had their sheathed swords attached to their belts. They pulled out their swords and raised them over their heads. Every one of Arthur's knights in the congregation stood as a single unit and did the same.

"Sir Lavern!" Lance called out.

"Sir John!" Ricky boomed right after.

All the knights shouted in unison, "Sir Lavern! Sir John!"

With that, Lance and Ricky sheathed their swords and returned to their pew. Lance noted Reyna cradling a somber Sylvia against her shoulder and his heart lurched again, recalling how the young girl had been sweet on Lavern.

Father Tim turned to John's mom. "Karen."

Slowly, her faced streaked with tears, she rose to her feet and shuffled forward to Father Tim. She wore a black dress with a string of white pearls around her neck, her black hair tied up and back. The priest took her hand and squeezed it gently before moving out of the way so she could take her place at the podium.

"Thank you all for coming today to celebrate the lives of these two magnificent boys." She looked at Lavern's mom. "My condolences on the death of your son."

Lavern's mother nodded in reply, silent and without tears.

Mrs. Aragon looked over the assembled. "John wrote something he wanted me to read, and he asked that Lance and Ricky stand up here when I do."

The boys looked at each other in surprise, but rose and returned to the altar to stand beside her. She suddenly looked self- conscious.

"I know this may embarrass you because I know how fifteen-year-old boys are about things like this, but for some reason he wouldn't tell me, John asked that you boys hold each other's hand while I read this."

Both boys looked startled, and flushed red.

"Something about 'basic human contact'," she went on apologetically. "He said you would know."

Lance and Ricky couldn't help but smile.

"We do," they murmured, and gently grasped each other's hand, keeping their eyes fixed on the floor.

Mrs. Aragon pulled out a piece of paper, written in a child's script, and began to read.

"I know you're all sad to be here and I guess I am, too, 'cause I don't get to see how many people showed up. LOL It don't matter. I had a good life. I had the best big brother. Yeah, he did something stupid and got to heaven before me, but he always took care of me. I guess I'm with you now, bro, since mom is reading this in church. And mom? Don't ever think you could 'a done more for me 'cause you couldn't. You were the best mom a kid could ask for. I especially wanna thank you in front of all these people for the best thing you done for me, letting me hang out with Lance and Ricky. I know you didn't want to 'cause of the stupid stuff they did, but it was the best day of my entire life, mom. Thank you."

She paused, new tears welling and streaming down her cheeks. "'To Lance and Ricky – you guys are the best. You made me feel like part of the team in just one day. You made me feel what it would be like to be grown up like you, almost a man. You made me want to grow up because I wanted to be like you when I did. I knew I wouldn't, but it was a cool fantasy, anyway. I love you guys, and I know you love each other. Whatever happens, don't ever leave each other. You guys are like two parts of a toy that have to be together or the toy won't work. Remember me, Lance and Ricky, because I'll never forget you. Your brother, Sir John the Bold, Knight of the Table Round. PS Thank you, Lance, for not letting my mother help me stand during the knighting ceremony. That would've been *so* embarrassing.'"

She stopped reading and put the paper away. Lance and Ricky once more had tears in their eyes and they couldn't look at each other for fear of bawling.

She looked over at them. "I love you boys for what you did for my son, and for me. Consider me for now, and always, your second mom."

She stepped from the podium and enveloped them in a hug. Still clasping hands, they used their free arms to encircle her and they stood in silence for a time, shedding the last of their tears, soaking up their mutual love and loss. Finally, John's mom released them, the boys shyly unclasped their hands, and the three returned to their pews.

As they did, Lance happened to glance up toward the back of the church. Standing by a pillar, dressed in a suit, eyes pinned to him, was Michael. Their eyes locked a moment before Lance was swept into his pew and Michael vanished from his line of sight.

After the funerals were over, and with the signature gathering at an end, a somber calm fell over New Camelot in the ensuing days and weeks. Lance and Ricky still wrestled and sparred and joked with each other, but not quite as much, and always with a touch of sadness at the loss of two more of their brothers. Yet they could not get John's words out of their minds – that they were two parts of the same toy and neither part could work completely without the other. They didn't openly discuss it, but each could tell it was not far from the other's thoughts.

Lance presented Lavern's mother with his original bow and arrows at the funeral and she gratefully accepted them. It wasn't a week later that Sir Techie called Lance and Ricky into the Computer Lab to show them that Lavern's mother had put the items up on eBay and sold them for five thousand dollars. The boys were shocked and saddened, but not surprised, given what they knew about the mercenary nature of the woman.

The big event looming on the horizon was Reyna's graduation from Granite Hills Charter High School at the end of May, and her eighteenth birthday the week before. And Esteban would turn eighteen the day of her graduation, as well. Unknown to Reyna, or even to Arthur, Esteban had been working extra hard, even while on the road, often Skyping Jenny for more lessons or feedback on his work. He wanted to surprise everyone, especially Reyna, by earning his diploma.

His would be issued from the state, rather than a specific school, due to finishing his studies in the home schooled environment, but he wanted to show Reyna and her parents, and himself, that he could finish something he started. He knew he was smart and that school had always just bored him, but he also wanted the younger boys and former homies who looked up to him to know they could, and should, earn that diploma. It was an important rite of passage in life, even if they didn't think so right now.

Since Jenny was the only one who knew Esteban would graduate, it fell to her to organize everything. It was decided that on Reyna's actual birthday, there would be a small celebration at New Camelot, since her parents insisted she go to dinner with them. Then, for graduation day, rather than go to Grad Nite with her class, Reyna chose to have her big graduation/birthday bash at New Camelot, after the obligatory dinner with her parents.

Jenny insisted she invite her mom and dad to the big bash. She was mortified, at first, by the idea, but then realized she wanted them to see a real family in action, and real love between siblings and parents, though none of them at New Camelot were even related. She figured her parents would thumb their noses at the invite, but promised to extend it, nonetheless.

Bridget and Ariel continued to come by New Camelot as often as possible, and seemed to have a good time with the boys, and the boys with them. Arthur and Jenny watched over the couples rather hawkishly, not wanting anything to get out of hand. The boys, however, never tried to take the girls to private spots, like their rooms, as they'd done on previous visits. Jenny noted this and, based on her experience with teenagers, thought it rather odd behavior. She didn't complain, however, as it saved her the trouble of monitoring them so closely.

Rather, the boys sparred with each other, showing off for the girls. They wrestled, laughingly trying to pin the other while the girls cheered them on. They played around on the computers, Googling Lance's pictures and stories and making comments or even laughing at some of the sites devoted to him, especially the ones speculating about his inherent demonic abilities. The boys seemed happiest when all four were together, which Jenny was glad about, but it still made her curious.

Esteban and the others recovered from their wounds and there were no more attacks on New Camelot or any of her people. The bomb fragments left no clues as to who had made it, and no group claimed responsibility. Anti-Prop 51 groups picketed daily outside of New Camelot, joining the ever-present doomsayers who still believed Lance's return marked the end of the world.

The signatures were on track to be verified by June, in plenty of time to make the November ballot. Sam and his fellow attorneys were monitoring the process to make certain the state didn't drag its feet, and then claim Arthur failed to meet the appropriate deadlines. Also scheduled for June was the final hearing on Arthur's adoption plans. The due diligence had uncovered no claims on the boys and DCFS appeared willing to drop its opposition.

Reyna finally remembered about Michael one day when Jenny mentioned that he hadn't been around since the night of the attack. Reyna told Jenny what she'd found out, and the information shocked her. They shared these revelations with Arthur, and he agreed with Jenny - Lance needed to know, but it might be best for Reyna to tell him, since she and Sir Techie had uncovered the information.

Not sure how Lance might respond to the news, Reyna felt nervous as she sought him out, running over and over in her mind how best to share this knowledge.

She finally found him in the Training Center practicing his archery. She was surprised to find him alone.

"Where's Ricky?"

"Upstairs, finishing Frankenstein," Lance said, as he took aim and scored a perfect bulls eye. He turned to her and grinned. "Here to take me on again? I can still beat you, big sister."

She scowled. "You're the only one who can, so don't rub it in."

He grinned even more.

How beautiful he looks, she thought, *how innocent and perfect, despite all he's been through*.

"I, uh, I wanted to talk with you about... Michael."

Lance lost the grin. In fact, his brightness instantly turned into a darkness more profound than any Reyna had ever seen cross his face.

"What about him?"

She shuffled her feet nervously. "Techie and I did some checking on him."

Lance's eyes went wide. "Why?"

"Because we think he might be, you know, dangerous, and we didn't know anything about his background."

Lance stood there, blank-faced, gazing off past her head, seeing something other than her.

"We found out something shocking, Lance," Reyna resumed, but stopped when his mouth dropped open.

"You know?" he blurted in stunned surprise, turning back to face her.

Now Reyna looked uncertain. "Well, yeah, but I didn't know *you* knew."

"Michael told me, the night John died."

Reyna saw how upset Lance was and enveloped him in a hug. "Oh, baby boy, I'm sorry. I know it must've been a shock to you." He nodded silently into her shoulder. "I just wanted you to know, in case he tried to use it to make you like him more, or something."

Lance pulled away. "He wouldn't do that, Reyna. I know you and Ricky and everybody else think Michael's some kind of monster. He's not, just like the creature in *Frankenstein* wasn't, either. I'm gonna find a way to prove it to you."

He handed her the bow and quiver and left the room before she could reply.

Reyna went to Jenny and Arthur and told them how Lance had responded. Merlin was present as well, and offered the opinion that so long as Lance knew the truth, it might be best to trust him.

"His instincts are much like my abilities, Arthur – a gift from on high."

Arthur nodded, and they agreed not to say anything more to Lance on the matter of Michael's past.

After leaving the Training Center, Lance headed straight to Ricky's room and found him sitting back against his headboard, deep in thought.

"Can I come in?"

Ricky smiled. "Like you gotta ask?"

Lance sat on the bed. He noted *Frankenstein* lying beside Ricky and picked it up. "So, finish this yet?"

Ricky nodded.

"And?"

"I think you're right, that it's Victor's fault, and the other people, for turning that poor thing into a monster. But I still don't get what it has to do with Michael."

His gaze hardened. "He's got everything, Lance. Money, girls, power, cool car. He's a monster just because he gets off on it."

"You're wrong, Ricky."

Fighting back the horrific images he'd seen in that video, Lance told Ricky what had happened to Michael. He left out the part about Michael recording his calls and tapping into their computer system. He felt dirty withholding anything from Ricky, but still he wanted to talk with Michael about that stuff first.

When he'd finished his narrative, the color drained from Ricky's face.

"Hell, Lance," was all he could say, and that was barely a whisper. "No wonder he's a monster." He looked apologetic. "I'm sorry for hating on him. I didn't know."

"None of us did." He looked soberly at his brother. "He's not all bad, Ricky. That little boy is in there and he's still got good in him."

Ricky looked dubious. "I'm sorry, Lance, but I still can't trust him, 'specially with you."

"Thanks. What would I do without my trusty bodyguard?"

"Probably be a lot less cool, much weaker, and a lot less insecure than you are around hotness like me."

Lance shook his head. "If you're the definition of hotness, we're in trouble."

Ricky punched him.

The next day, Lance felt another urge to Skype Michael. The memory of that night in Michael's bathroom haunted him, what he'd seen, what he'd said, what it all meant.

"How you been?" he asked, when Michael's face appeared on his iPad.

"Good, Lance," Michael replied, tossing off a grin. "I'm always good."

"I saw you at the funeral."

"I was bored. And death fascinates me."

That threw Lance for a loop. He paused. An idea came to him. "Is that why I fascinate you, Michael? Because I died?"

"Who says you fascinate me, Lance? You need to keep that ego in check."

"It is in check, Michael, you know that." He lowered his eyes in embarrassment. "I told you I thought I loved you, didn't I?" he whispered. "That night in your bathroom?"

Michael hesitated before replying. "Yeah, but you were drunk as a skunk, Lance. Don't worry about it."

Lance looked shyly into his phone and blew out a nervous breath. "But what if…maybe it's true? Even when I'm not drunk?"

Michael gazed at him long and hard. "Trust me, Lance. It's not true. If you looked far enough into yourself, you'd know it too."

Lance felt confused. "I wish you'd come visit. I can't really go anywhere 'cause, you know, some nut might attack me or something."

Michael sneered. "Wouldn't your beloved bodyguard be pissed if I came over?"

"I told him what happened to you."

Michael's face contorted into something monstrous. "Screw you, Lance, you had no right! I didn't even want *you* to know, and certainly not that little bitch who hates my guts!"

Lance almost pulled back from the phone, stung by Michael's venom. "I just wanted him to understand."

"Look, Lance, get this through your thick head – I don't want your sympathy and I sure as hell don't want his. Do not tell my business to anyone else or there'll be hell to pay!"

He ended the call and left Lance shaken and unnerved by the encounter. And he'd never even got to ask about Michael's spying on him. Michael really was Jekyll and Hyde, wasn't he?

The next few weeks were uneventful—somber, but routine. Now that all the signature gatherers were done, the protests ceased, except those outside New Camelot. Vitriol via the Internet was a constant, but there was far more support than hate.

Gradually, the pain of losing Lavern and John lifted slightly from everyone's heart, though it was never far from their minds. A new shrine to both had been erected beside those of Mark and Jack, and Lance and Ricky saw to its completion themselves.

John's mom had returned John's sword, and since they'd never given Lavern's sword to his mother, it hadn't ended up on eBay.

Mrs. Aragon came for the dedication of the memorial, but nobody from Lavern's family attended. It was sad, and the boys shed more tears with their surrogate mother, but all accepted that John was better now than suffering constant pain. Lance reaffirmed the vows he'd made at the funeral to not let life, or death, drag him down anymore, to live life the way John did, and to never lose Ricky. Ricky affirmed the same.

Reyna finally managed to finagle some extra tickets to graduation, but not enough for everyone in her family. Her parents hit the roof when she told them she wanted Arthur and the others to attend, rather than blood relatives. However, she stood firm and wouldn't budge.

She also extended to them Jenny's invite to her party, but they balked at that idea.

"Imagine us," her mother had said, "associating with gang members and street trash!"

Reyna shook her head in disgust, though secretly she was happy they wouldn't be there. Her actual birthday passed rather sedately. There was a cake and congratulations at New Camelot before dinner with her parents. She knew the real party would be on graduation night.

She proudly announced, "First thing after school tomorrow I'm gonna register to vote."

Everyone cheered and clapped.

"I'm not a kid anymore who can benefit from our prop, but I can sure as hell do my part to vote it in."

Lance caught her eye and grinned.

Graduation day arrived all too quickly near the end of May, and everyone was excited for Reyna. Justin, Darnell, and Merlin were left in charge of New Camelot. Arthur, Jenny, Esteban, Lance and Ricky rode to the venue with Ryan and Gibson in two cars, along with a black and white escort.

Jenny wore a lovely floral-patterned dress, while the men sported their finest tunics, pants, and boots. They made quite a sight entering the grounds of Granite Hills High. Media swarmed over the parking lot, hoping to get footage of Arthur and his knights, much to the chagrin of the principal.

He greeted Arthur as the group entered, scowling as pictures were snapped, and expressed his opinion that while "Your campaign against the school system is misguided, I can't keep invited guests out." He requested that they depart as soon as the ceremony was concluded and to "Not make a scene."

Arthur assured him they would not make a scene, turning on the charm in his assurance that the system as a whole was failing kids, not this particular school. From all Reyna had told him, it was one of the better ones. The principal warmed considerably after that and personally led them to their seats.

The ceremony bored Lance and Ricky, who kept elbowing each other and giggling at the girls checking them out. Reyna looked stunning in her cap and gown and exquisite hair, her looping curls, trailing out from beneath the cap down her back.

When the ceremony ended, everyone filed out to meet their graduates in the parking lot. Arthur and Jenny spotted Reyna laughing with some friends, while a tiny thirty-something woman snapped her picture as a much older man looked on almost with disinterest.

"Uh, oh," Lance whispered, elbowing Ricky. "Time to meet the parents."

Ricky nodded.

"Get ready to be insulted," Lance whispered, as they followed Arthur and Jenny forward.

For his part, Arthur didn't look worried at all, though Jenny did. The others trailed behind as Arthur approached. Reyna burst into a huge smile upon seeing the group and rushed to Arthur, hugging him first.

"Thanks so much for coming, Arthur," she gushed, so excited she lost her stoic demeanor.

"I wouldn't have missed it," Arthur replied sincerely.

Reyna grabbed Jenny and hugged her tight. "Thanks so much for all your help and tutoring," she said.

"Ah, you didn't need much."

Esteban stepped forward with a grin and Reyna couldn't resist. She grabbed him and kissed him right on the lips, in front of her obviously embarrassed parents. The media loved it. Pictures were snapped and video captured.

"Okay, you two," Ricky chided. "Break it up. There's impressionable youngsters here."

Reyna released Esteban and turned her eyes on the boys, smiling and smirking at the same time. "My two favorite bookends." She enveloped both in a hug that pushed them against each other, making them squirm with embarrassment.

"Jeez, Reyna, embarrass us why don't you," Lance whispered, looking around to see if anyone was watching.

Unfortunately, everyone was, with great interest.

She grinned all the more as he and Ricky exchanged a self-conscious look. "Sir John was right – you two are part of the same toy."

"Congratulations, Reyna," Ricky offered, shaking off his awkwardness.

Lance smiled. "Way to go, sis."

Arthur cleared his throat, indicating to Reyna the Latino couple with the camera, standing awkwardly to one side.

Her father was in his sixties with silver hair, jowly cheeks, a slight paunch, and a face embedded with deep frown lines. Her mother, by contrast, was in her late thirties with a shapely figure and well-styled, luxurious shoulder-length hair, surrounding a round face with scarcely a wrinkle. Jessica Hernandez had clearly had a lot of work done to retain her youthful beauty.

Reyna stepped up to her parents, boldly presenting Esteban first. "Mom, Dad, this is Este."

Neither parent said anything, and Esteban looked uncertain. He no longer looked the fierce gang member of his youth, and cut a rather imposing figure in his tunic and leather pants. His hair had lengthened, but he kept it trimmed short on the sides to keep the natural waves at bay and, and though he still seldom smiled, he'd lost the perpetual street sneer he'd perfected growing up. He stuck out his hand to Reyna's dad, but the older man ignored it.

Arthur stepped forward with a very disarming smile. "I am Arthur, Mr. and Mrs. Hernandez." Rather than extend his hand, he bowed in that courtly way of his. When he raised his head he looked warmly at Reyna's mom. "I can clearly see where Reyna acquired her beauty and poise, Mrs. Hernandez."

Reyna's mom blushed and, despite herself, said, "Why, thank you Mr., uh, Arthur."

She glanced uneasily at her husband, but he still glared at Arthur.

"And I presume she acquired her strength of will from you, sir," Arthur offered in as friendly a tone as any of his knights had ever heard.

Oscar Hernandez was clearly flummoxed by Arthur's disarming manner. "Well, yes, I suppose that's true," he said. "However, we raised her to associate with a better class of people than your sort," he went on, quickly adding, "No disrespect intended."

"None taken. These are my sons, Lance and Ricky." Arthur indicated the boys. "Reyna has passed on many of your teachings to them and they are most grateful, are you not, lads?"

Lance almost smiled, knowing exactly what Reyna had taught them about her parents. "Yeah, Dad, we are. Reyna is an awesome big sister, sir. Thank you for sharing her with us." He bowed, elbowing Ricky, who quickly followed suit.

Reyna and Esteban exchanged a confused look, but Jenny had obviously picked up on the game because she eyed Mrs. Hernandez's dress admiringly. "That's a lovely dress you're wearing, Mrs. Hernandez. It brings out your eyes beautifully."

Mrs. Hernandez clearly enjoyed the flattery. "Why, thank you, uh–"

"Jenny," Jenny said, extending her hand. Mrs. Hernandez reached out and shook it. The two women locked eyes a moment, and Jenny smiled. That seemed to disarm Mrs. Hernandez, who pulled back her hand and eyed Esteban appraisingly.

She reached out a hand. "I'm Reyna's mother," she offered, stating the obvious. "It's... nice to meet you, finally. Reyna talks of nothing else. When she talks to us, that is."

"Mom," Reyna chided under her breath. "Not now."

Her mother nodded, eyes still on Esteban. "And what high school will you be graduating from, Esteban?"

Reyna flushed with embarrassment. "Mom!"

Esteban just smiled. "As a matter of fact, Mrs. Hernandez, I just got my diploma yesterday. I been home schooled."

Reyna's mouth dropped open like a fish, and her mother's mimicked hers. Jenny reached into her purse and pulled out a diploma, enclosed within a cloth cover, and handed it to Esteban. He proudly opened the cover and flashed it at Reyna and her parents like an I.D. badge.

Everyone was speechless, even Lance and Ricky, who had no idea.

"I been working extra hard on getting all my work done so Reyna and me, sorry, so Reyna and I, could graduate together."

Lance didn't think he'd ever seen the boy look so proud. Reyna gaped at him, while Jenny and Arthur grinned. Reyna screamed so loud everyone around them turned to stare. She threw her arms around Esteban so hard she shoved him back against Lance, who laughed.

"Hey, chill, Reyna, 'fore you kill somebody," Lance said.

He and Ricky elbowed each other as Reyna kissed Esteban again in front of her embarrassed parents.

"Why didn't you tell me, Este?" she asked excitedly, after pulling back from him.

He beamed and shrugged. "Cause I wanted that reaction from you."

She punched him in the chest, but then smiled that lovely smile she didn't use often enough. "I'm so proud of you, baby."

Esteban looked almost shy as he glanced awkwardly down at the ground. "Thanks. I hoped you would be."

Arthur stepped forward and extended his hand. "And I, as well, Sir Este. You are a man of strong character and will."

Esteban shook Arthur's hand. "Thanks, Arthur. You're like a dad to me and I wanted to make you proud, too."

"I could not be prouder, Este. You went from a troubled, angry boy to a fine, decent man. What's not to be proud of?"

Impulsively, Esteban hugged Arthur before pulling away and hugging Jenny as well.

"Thank you, Lady Jenny, for everything you did for me."

"My pleasure," Jenny replied, releasing him.

Reyna instantly grabbed his hand and squeezed.

"Mom, Dad, I told you before and I'll tell you again, you're invited to my graduation party at New Camelot tonight after we finish dinner. All of my knightly family will be there and I'd *really* like you to meet them."

She stunned herself because she actually meant that. She *did* want her parents to see what she considered her real life, and to partake of it. Mrs. Hernandez looked a moment at her husband, who still stood there looking uncomfortable.

"We'll see, darling," was all she offered. "After dinner is over."

With that, Reyna excused herself to leave with her parents and Arthur and his group set off for New Camelot, paparazzi and media in tow.

Reyna arrived about eight o'clock, and that's when the party really started, though the knights and some of her friends had already arrived and were milling around the Throne Room chatting. Jaime and Sonia were there, too, with baby Arturo, showing him off to everyone.

Ricky and Lance had invited Ariel and Bridget, and were chatting with them near the stage when Reyna finally swept into the room with a flourish.

The boys were stunned to see her parents behind her. Even Jenny was surprised, but Arthur smiled like he'd known all along they would show. He greeted them warmly and suggested Reyna introduce them to the entire company. He and Reyna led them up to the dais. Arthur had the D.J., Sir Khom, silence the music and then he picked up the microphone.

"As you all know, tonight we celebrate three significant events – our own Lady Reyna's graduation from high school, as well as turning eighteen last week."

There were applause, whistles and catcalls.

"Our own Sir Esteban's graduation from high school," Arthur continued, his voice filled with obvious pride.

More applause and some startled gasps from former gang members, mostly Jaime, who grinned and held up little Arturo in salute to Este. They all gazed up at former homeboy Esteban standing on stage beside Reyna, looking both proud and humbled by the recognition.

"And today is also Sir Esteban's eighteenth birth year. He is now, in your culture, legally a man."

More applause and stomping and whooping. Despite his distaste for smiling, Esteban found himself beaming foolishly.

Arthur handed the microphone to Reyna. She looked radiant.

"I don't think anybody out there, including my friends from Granite Hills, know my parents, but here they are and I'm so happy for them to meet you, my fantastic family."

The room burst once more into applause and more whooping. The couple stood uncertainly on the stage beside their daughter,

Jessica flashing her attractive smile and Oscar attempting to not grimace with discomfort.

"Let's hear it for Reyna's parents," Lance called out, and the crowd cheered louder, causing Reyna to grin broadly at Lance.

Arthur took back the microphone and looked out over the throng, easily the largest yet at any of their functions.

"Before we begin this celebration, I'd like to take a moment to reflect on the vast distance both Reyna and Esteban have traveled in the past year, not in your miles or feet, but on the road from children to adults who make me proud to know them and to call them family."

There was great applause and more whooping from the crowd. "It has been a year of extraordinary triumph, and agonizing tragedy. Alas, I suppose life cannot give us the one without the other. I ask all of you present to pause a moment and bow your heads in remembrance of those we have lost along this journey."

Complete silence reigned as every head dropped reverently, even those of Reyna's parents.

"Father God," Arthur went on, "We thank you for our blessings and your continued guidance throughout our noble crusade. Please gather our fallen – Sir Mark, Sir Jack, Sir Lavern, and Sir John – close to your heart. They were the very best this world has to offer, and I trust you will keep them in your care until such time as we can all be together again."

He paused and everyone lifted their eyes.

"Tonight, my noble knights and honored guests, is a night to celebrate triumph, not tragedy. We move forward in our crusade and in life, as we join together to honor these two remarkable young adults – Lady Reyna and Sir Esteban. Let the festivities begin!"

That set the room to thunderous clapping and whooping and foot stomping.

The party commenced and everyone had a blast. Lance danced with Bridget and

Ariel danced with Ricky. The adults, even Reyna's parents, enjoyed themselves, but didn't allow any inappropriate dancing among the youth.

Sir Khom had been given specific music to play, including Reyna's favorite party song, "The Cha Cha Slide." She got everyone into it, including her parents, who actually laughed at their own ineptitude. Lance and Ricky, neither of whom danced well, did these big numbers side by side and paid more attention to each other than their dates, laughing and shoving and bagging on each other's horrible moves. The girls thought it was cute and joined in the fun.

There were presents for Reyna, and for Esteban, who was visibly surprised, since he hadn't thought anyone knew about his birthday. He learned later that Jenny had instructed Sir Techie to message everyone that the party was in honor of him, too.

The biggest surprise of the night came when Michael unexpectedly showed up. He wore the black tunic Arthur had given him along with his designer pants and fancy Nikes. Bridget and Ariel instantly grew nervous, and Reyna ruffled her own feathers a bit, looking like a cobra about to lash out. But then Michael approached her and held out a wrapped gift, causing Esteban to scowl.

"Congratulations, Lady Reyna," Michael said smoothly, knowing he'd brought the entire party to a standstill, but ignoring the whispers and stares from the other kids.

Hesitantly, as though fearing it was a bomb, Reyna took the package from Michael.

"Open it," he said.

Gingerly, she did, slipping off the top of the box and pulling out half a heart on a gold chain. The half heart was also made of glittery gold, and looked expensive.

Esteban saw that and pushed his way to her side. "What the hell, Michael!" He looked furious.

But Reyna held it up, one hand to her mouth in astonishment. She and Esteban read what had been engraved within the half-heart: "Este."

Esteban's face dissolved into disbelief.

Michael chuckled and held out another small box to him. "Happy birthday and whatever."

Esteban hesitantly took the box, eyeing Michael cautiously before opening it. He pulled out the other half of the heart, gazing in amazement at the name "Reyna" engraved within it.

He suddenly looked very embarrassed. "I don't know what to say, man."

Michael shrugged, and Reyna gazed at him appraisingly, like she now saw possibilities within him she'd never seen before. "I don't know what to make of you, Michael, but thank you."

She leaned in and gave him a light hug. Esteban flinched. But Michael didn't try anything rude. He didn't even raise his arms to hug her back.

She pulled away and his gaze roved the room, settling on Lance, like he'd known exactly where to look the entire time.

He wanted to look away, but Lance found he could not. Michael's eyes held him, much to the displeasure of Bridget and Ricky, and then Michael turned back to Reyna and Esteban.

Reyna put the chain around Esteban's neck and he did the same for her. Then Esteban locked eyes with Michael, who seemed amused and disinterested, all at the same time.

"Thanks, man," said Esteban, holding out his hand, but Michael ignored it and turned to walk across the room in Lance's direction.

Reyna and Esteban exchanged a bewildered look, and Reyna shrugged. "This is a party, people!" she called out, and the music resumed. It was a slow dance this time, and Reyna pressed herself into Esteban for a kiss as they began to slowly move to the music.

Michael stopped in front of Lance. Bridget stood to his side, Ricky and Ariel nearby, Ricky eyeing Michael with suspicion.

Michael looked directly at Lance and said, "So who in this romantic little group will dance with me?"

Lance squirmed and wanted to turn away. He knew Michael meant him, but he couldn't dance something like this with Michael. Not here. Not in front of Ricky and Arthur and Jenny.

Why didn't I put Bridget first on that list? She's my girlfriend, isn't she?

He barely had a moment to process that thought before Bridget stepped forward. She glanced into his eyes and must've seen the indecision in them because she eased herself into Michael's arms. "I will."

Michael grinned and they began to slowly move to the music, his gaze over her shoulder never leaving Lance for a moment.

Ricky moved in front of Lance, cutting off his view of Michael and breaking the spell. "You okay, man?"

"I'm gonna sit this one out, Ricky. Dance with your lady."

He moved off to the side where all the chairs sat resting along the perimeter of the room. Unsteadily, he sat and raised his eyes. Michael's head was turned away, but Ricky still gazed long and hard at him. Lance tried to fathom the meaning of that look. Their eyes locked a moment before Ariel cut off his view by taking Ricky in her arms and swaying to the music.

Lance watched everyone dance, suddenly filled with that melancholy he'd sworn he would fight, for John's sake, if for no other reason. He watched Ricky and Ariel dancing, seemingly happy together, even though Ricky's eyes sought him out each time he turned in his direction.

He watched Reyna and Esteban, cradled within each other's arms as though the rest of the world didn't exist. Even his dad and mom danced slowly, intimately, lost within each other's embrace. Loneliness covered him in darkness, and death seemed once more to call his name.

His mind wandered. He saw Mark and Jack holding hands in that beautiful green field that spread outward to infinity. They smiled and waved, but then did something they never had before, in any of his recurring dreams of that final moment. They beckoned him to follow. Jack extended one hand toward him, and Lance reached out to take it.

He felt a hand take his gently, and found himself gazing up into Michael's unreadable face, his hand within Michael's. He yanked it back and looked around.

"What happened?" He felt lost and bewildered.

"You tell me, Lance. I walked over to talk and you gave me your hand. Change your mind about that dance, after all?"

"You know I can't." He lowered his eyes to the floor.

Michael sat beside him, but kept his hands to himself. "Truth or dare."

Lance looked shyly at him. "Truth."

"If we weren't with all these people who know you, would you have danced with me?"

Lance looked down again. "Probably."

"I knew it."

Lance looked up, his face twisted with confusion. "I don't know what it is, Michael, but every time I look in your eyes, I…"

"What?"

"I get confused. There's something in your eyes that, I don't know, brings me back in time to… I don't know, Michael. Maybe dying made me crazy, after all."

"And maybe it *didn't*, after all," Michael said with calm assurance.

Lance eyed him. "I know you been spying on me, Michael, my calls and texts. I seen it on your computer."

"I don't like surprises, Lance. I always like to know what's up."

"If I asked you to stop, would you?"

"Don't know. It's a control thing with me. You know why I trust no one."

"I get that, Michael. But how do you even know how to do all that stuff, hacking and phone tapping? You like James Bond or something?"

Michael pointed to his head. "Walking Wikipedia, Lance, remember? As for hacking, that's easy to learn. If I wanted to, I could hack into the Pentagon without being detected." He sounded proud and haughty, as usual.

"You don't have to spy on me, Michael. We could hang out more this summer, since you have no more school."

Michael sneered. "Hang out? Like a couple of queer boyfriends, Lance? Go to the movies?"

Lance squirmed with discomfort. "No, Michael. I mean we can just hang out… as friends."

Michael snorted. "I don't have friends, Lance."

"What?" Lance exclaimed, shocked. "What about all the people who party with you?"

Michael shrugged. "Jay Gatsby."

Lance pulled a face. "Huh?"

"You'll read about him in eleventh grade."

Still confused, Lance said, "What about school friends? Didn't you go to your prom?"

"Hell, no!" Michael spat. "I didn't do any of that school crap. Of course, I could've asked you to prom."

Lance sighed with impatience. "Michael!"

"Wouldn't that have stuck one up the butt of all those narrow-minded idiots who run my school?" He laughed. "Me, showing up with the most beautiful boy in the world. Emphasis on the word 'boy'. Ha!"

"I *am* a boy, Michael. A real boy, and you don't call boys beautiful."

Michael gazed at him with that annoyingly steady calm. "Okay, the *hottest* boy in the world." At Lance's exasperated look, he grinned broadly to let him know he was kidding.

"What about your graduation next week?" Lance asked. "Can I come?"

"I was already given my diploma, Lance, a week early, on the condition that I do not put in an appearance at the ceremony or at Grad Nite." He laughed hollowly.

Appalled, Lance's mouth hung open in shock. "Why?"

Michael fixed this steely brown eyes on Lance's green ones. "Because I scare them, Lance."

Lance nodded, but didn't break eye contact.

"I scare everybody," Michael went on in that quiet, monotone voice. "But despite all the crap I've pulled, I don't scare you, do I?"

Lance held those eyes. "No."

"Why not?"

"Because I read Frankenstein."

A smile slowly crept across Michael's handsome features and Lance knew his response was exactly what the other boy wanted to hear.

Michael broke eye contact, glancing back out onto the dance floor.

Bridget was making a beeline toward them.

"Uh, oh, Lance, here comes the girlfriend," Michael whispered conspiratorially. "And she's bringing the leash. Ha!"

Bridget stopped and glared down at them both. "You gonna dance with me some more, Lance, or what? I thought *I* was your girlfriend."

Lance glanced once more at Michael, who looked amused. He stood to take her extended hand, but before she could drag him away he turned back to Michael. "You were wrong before, Michael."

Michael's eyebrows shot up. "Me? Wrong? How?"

"When you said you had no friends."

He turned and followed the obviously annoyed Bridget out onto the dance floor.

CHAPTER FIFTEEN
THAT WAS JUST AN ACCIDENT, WASN'T IT?

ON THE FOLLOWING TUESDAY, ARTHUR, Jenny and the boys headed back to Children and Family Court to finalize Arthur's adoption proceedings. As had become procedure since the attack, the family was driven to the courthouse by Ryan with a police escort. Gibson drove Reyna, Esteban and Justin, who wished to witness the event.

Sam, dressed in a stunning royal blue suit and very loud tie, greeted the boys warmly in the hall outside the courtroom, exchanging a private wink with them when Arthur's back was turned. All three boys gave him a little grin before following the big man into the courtroom. They again sat beside Sam and Arthur and anxiously awaited the appearance of Judge Baker.

Ms. Hanson and Ms. Kelly were once more in attendance, but were quietly discussing something and didn't acknowledge Sam or Arthur.

Lance smiled at Ricky, giving him a little low five under the table. He so hoped the surprise they had planned for Arthur would make the man they loved happy, especially given the guilt they both knew he carried over Lavern's as-yet unsolved murder.

"All rise for the Honorable Judge Harold Baker," intoned the bailiff.

Once seated in his perch behind the large wooden bench, the judge said, "We are on record in the adoption proceedings for Mr. Arthur Pendragon and three minors, Lance Sepulveda, Ricky Delgado, and Christopher Wallis. According to the report submitted to me by Department of Children and Family Services, due diligence has been completed and no parents have been located, nor come forth to claim these minors. Is that correct, Ms. Kelly?"

Kelly stood and addressed the court. "Yes, Your Honor. However, in light of the recent death of young Lavern Harris, we wish to once again raise the issue of safety for these minors."

Lance couldn't believe she would use Lavern's death against them. Like it was their fault. He leaped to his feet to say something, but Ricky quickly pulled him back down, and Arthur nodded for of them to remain silent.

The judge eyed Kelly coolly, without emotion. "Do you mean to imply, Ms. Kelly, that the terrorist attack on this man that resulted in the death of a child under his care, was a result of his negligence and therefore he is unfit to be a parent? Is that what you're saying?"

"No, Your Honor, we didn't mean to suggest it was his fault," she replied quickly. "Our concern is with the safety of these children. The attack indicates the very real possibility that Mr. Pendragon may not be able to keep them safe."

The judge removed his glasses, setting them onto the bench. "Ms. Kelly, I could drive away from this courthouse today and get struck by a drunk driver and killed. Does that make me unfit to be a parent?"

"No, Your Honor, of course not."

"Life is risk, Ms. Kelly," the judge went on soberly, "and there are no guarantees for any of us. The court appreciates your concerns, and those of Ms. Hanson, but I have made my decision."

He asked Arthur and the boys to stand, which they immediately did.

"Mr. Pendragon, Arthur, if I may, I should like to preface my decision by expressing deep condolences on the death of your boy. Having said that, I dismiss the DCFS argument that because of this incident you would make an unfit parent. Your boys obviously love you and you love them. That is evident even in the brief time we've been together in this courtroom. Therefore, by the power vested in me by the State of California, I hereby grant this adoption and make it permanent. You are now officially a family."

Chris jumped out of his chair and grabbed Arthur, while Lance and Ricky hugged.

The judge cleared his throat, causing the celebrating to cease. Lance and Sam exchanged a smile, but Arthur looked confused.

"Is there something wrong, Your Honor?" the king asked hesitantly.

"No. Just one more piece of business to complete. Please be seated."

Uncertainly, Arthur resumed his seat, flicking a worried glance at Jenny in the gallery. The three boys smiled behind Arthur's back.

"Through their attorney, Mr. McMullen," the judge went on formally, "Lance Sepulveda, Ricky Delgado and Christopher Wallis have requested of this court that their last names be permanently changed to that of their new father. This court grants that request. Within thirty days, all official documents for the three boys shall reflect their surname as Pendragon. Congratulations, boys."

Arthur's mouth dropped open in shock, and Lance heard Jenny gasp somewhere behind him.

Lance looked at Arthur's face and almost laughed. "Surprise, Dad."

Arthur turned to the three of them, all grinning with amusement. "I am honored and blessed to call you my sons."

He opened his arms and they group hugged.

The judge's gavel slammed down. "This court is adjourned."

Baker sat on his bench and grinned as the new family hugged and high-fived, with Sam joining in, as well.

"Sir Lance," the judge said, pulling Lance out of a hug with Ricky and Chris.

"Yes, Your Honor?"

"Approach the bench, please."

Uncertainly, Lance eyed Arthur, who nodded him forward.

Releasing his brothers, he stepped up and stood before the bench. "Come up into the witness box, please."

Still confused, Lance climbed up into the box and eyed the judge uncertainly.

"I have two requests."

Lance's eyebrows shot up questioningly.

"I would like to shake the hand of The Boy Who Came Back," the judge said with a smile.

Grinning with relief, Lance extended his hand and they shook. "And what's the other?"

The judge, looking embarrassed, slid an 8x10 photo of Lance across the bench toward him, along with a Sharpie. "My, uh, daughter, is quite a fan. I promised her an autograph."

Lance blew out that breathy laugh of his, and Ricky guffawed from the floor, causing Lance to look over sheepishly. Ricky grinned and shook his head with amusement. Lance turned back to the judge.

"Sure, Your Honor. What's her name?"

"Leslie."

Lance wrote: 'To Leslie, may all your crusades be won. All the best, Sir Lance of the Round Table'. He slid the photo and pen back across to the judge.

"Good luck to you, Sir Lance," said the judge, gazing out at the entire family. "To all of you."

Ecstatic, Arthur and his new family, along with Jenny and the others, hurried joyfully from the courtroom.

The arrival of June, normally the best month of the year for kids, because it signaled the beginning of summer vacation and the end of school for two months, did not put an end to school for those at New Camelot. Their home-school status, and shorter hours, ensured that their instruction continued year round, with only a month off in August.

Due to the summer, however, Jenny reduced their hours by one, so now school began at nine and ended at noon. With Arthur's adoption of the boys complete, and the proposition on track for the November ballot, Arthur and Jenny decided that re-igniting the neighborhood beautification campaign was in order. Groups could go out each afternoon to different areas, after taking requests on the website. This way the knights could keep busy and in the public eye. They'd be connecting with people, encouraging them to vote in November, and reminding them of the importance of the crusade. The weekends would belong to the kids to enjoy the pool or just hang out and have fun.

To that end, Lance and Ricky felt compelled to invite Bridget and Ariel over to swim on any Saturday and Sunday afternoon they wanted. Of course, the girls were delighted. Reyna also showed up every weekend so she and Esteban could hang out and swim, and both participated in the clean-up campaigns. Unlike before, however, Chief Murphy and Mayor Soto insisted on police protection in every neighborhood the knights and Arthur visited – they did not want a repeat of San Francisco.

The first few weeks of June passed very smoothly. There were no issues in any of the neighborhoods, and the populace welcomed Arthur and his knights with open arms. Some of the police officers appeared disgruntled with their "babysitting" duties, as Lance overheard one of them say to another, but there were no problems or concerns. Never far from Lance's mind was Richard lurking somewhere in the shadows, stalking him. But other than at that one press conference months before, Lance had not seen him anywhere, and the police had come to a dead end.

Bridget and Ariel did, indeed, come by most weekends to swim and hang out. They obviously enjoyed seeing Lance and Ricky wearing only swim trunks and wrestling in the water, because Lance saw them giggling and pointing. In truth, the boys enjoyed showing off for the girls, working extra hard to gain an advantage over the other in their tussling matches.

However, whenever the girls suggested going to the boys' rooms to listen to music, Lance and Ricky explained that their mom didn't want them in their rooms alone with girls.

"She's overprotective," Lance said with a hollow laugh, when Bridget frowned at the edict.

"Really overprotective," Ricky confirmed.

Jenny was exiting the hotel into the back pool area with iced tea, and frowned at the boys.

Lance looked up and caught her confused look. He lowered his eyes shamefully, because she'd never said that, had only told them to keep their doors open, and she'd clearly overheard his lie. Jenny set the carafe of iced tea onto the table and watched the boys a moment before returning to the hotel.

After the 4th of July, Lance and Ricky went to Arthur and Jenny with a request. The girls wanted to spend the day with them at Manic Mountain in Valencia, a large amusement park filled with thrill rides. Jenny had to explain the concept of an amusement park to Arthur, who thought it sounded much like a festival in his own time.

As always, Sergeants Ryan and Gibson cautioned against the idea.

"C'mon, guys," Lance said. "Nothing bad's happened in two months, and we haven't had any drama at any of the neighborhood clean ups."

"Doesn't mean whoever tried to kill you and your dad has given up, Lance," Gibson suggested.

"Might just be biding their time," Ryan said, clearly not liking the idea.

"Besides," Gibson went on soberly, "an amusement park like that is a big place and easy to get ambushed if that was someone's intent."

"But Dad, and Mom," Ricky implored, "the girls are mad 'cause we never take 'em anywhere."

"That's not really fair of them, Ricky," Jenny put in with a frown. "They should understand your situation. Do they want to put you in danger?"

"No, Mom," Lance insisted. "They just wanna go out with us." And he liked the idea because Manic Mountain was a public place, so he wouldn't be alone with Bridget.

"Maybe they just want to be seen in public with the two best-looking and most famous boys in the world," Jenny put in, with a rueful smile. "I was a teenaged girl not all that long ago, Lance."

Lance looked embarrassed, but didn't reply.

Could that be Bridget's reason? Did she now want the world to know who she was dating, at the risk of losing her privacy?

He knew kids were obsessed with making themselves "famous" on social media, and thought Jenny's idea a strong possibility.

Jenny turned to Arthur. "What do you think?"

Arthur eyed Merlin. "Do your senses indicate any danger with this venture, Merlin?"

Lance studied the wizard, who sported a Megadeth shirt, and wondered for a brief moment when the guy went shopping for all of those shirts.

"No, but then my powers aren't what they were, Arthur."

Arthur considered the situation. "Sergeants Ryan and Gibson, can you protect the boys in such a vast place?"

"We can make certain they never leave our sight, Arthur, but that's not to say we can protect them if a sniper wants to take a shot," Gibson answered honestly. "We're not Secret Service. There's no way to secure that park."

"But nobody'll know what day we're gonna go, right Sergeant?" Ricky said. "The girls won't tell and if nobody knows, and we wear, like, regular clothes with big-ass—sorry, Dad—big sunglasses and beanies, nobody'll even know who we are."

"Yeah, we'll go incog—." Lance struggled to remember. "What's that word, Mom?"

Jenny smiled. "Incognito?"

"Yeah, that's it," Lance affirmed hopefully. "Like the big-time actors do."

Arthur and Jenny exchanged a look.

A worried look.

"Please," Lance implored. "We never get to feel like, you know, real boys and just do fun stuff. I've never even been to Manic Mountain, and everybody says it's lit."

Jenny looked at Arthur, and nodded.

Arthur turned to the boys. "Under no circumstances are you to leave the line of sight of Sergeant Ryan or Sergeant Gibson. I fully recall the desire of boys your age to sneak off privately with their ladies, however—"

"Dad," Lance cut him off, "we wouldn't do that, okay? I promise."

And I don't want to.

"Me too," Ricky affirmed.

"And if the girls want to?" Jenny put in with a slight smile.

Lance grinned. "I'll tell 'em the Pendragon lady will get 'em if they try anything."

That drew a laugh from both Jenny and Arthur, and so it was agreed.

They would go on Saturday next, driven by Sergeant Ryan in his unmarked sedan. They would ask Reyna to shop for the boys to buy jean shorts and band t-shirts or tank tops, more beanies and big sunglasses.

The boys were ecstatic. They high-fived and ran from the room.

The adults gazed gravely at each other.

"Keep them safe," Arthur told the officers. "I implore you."

"We're on it." Then they left the room as well.

Jenny and Arthur looked at each other, and Jenny smiled.

"They're growing up, Arthur," she said plainly. "We can't keep them cooped up forever, and we may not always be able to keep them safe."

"I know, Jenny," he said with a heavy sigh. "But until we determine who has been behind the attacks on us, I wish to keep them close."

She agreed, and they kissed.

The girls were thrilled about Manic Mountain and swore they would tell no one. The boys hammered this point home repeatedly. If the girls wanted to tell their friends after the fact and share pictures they'd take with their phones, that would be fine. But no one could know beforehand. And zero posts on social media, before or after. The girls promised.

When Reyna handed over the jean shorts and tank tops she'd bought, she told them, "Have a great time, but be careful. Try not to be noticed by anyone *but* your girls."

Lance nodded. "We promise."

The weather was hot, but not sweltering, and the park was jam- packed. Of course, everyone had to pass through metal detectors upon entering. Lance, Ricky and the girls passed through with no trouble. The boys kept their beanies pulled down low and didn't take off their sunglasses, which were plastic. No one entering the park gave them a second look – they were just four random teenagers. That feeling of anonymity delighted the boys.

To avoid drawing attention to them, Ryan and Gibson told Lance and Ricky to wait just inside while they cleared security because they were armed and needed to show proper identification. The girls suggested they ditch the cops, but Lance and Ricky said simultaneously, "Hell, no," which offended them, but the boys didn't care. They would not break any more promises to Arthur.

They waited until the two sergeants joined them, and as a group they wandered into the park, the adults a few paces behind the kids to give them some space.

To Lance, it was funny seeing Ryan and Gibson wearing regular clothes. Gibson always wore a stylish coat and tie, and Ryan his ten-year-old jackets and rumpled collared shirts. Today, Ryan sported a tacky Hawaiian shirt and large reflective sunglasses. Gibson wore an ordinary sports jersey, jeans and Nikes. The intent was to blend in and not attract attention. So far it seemed to be working.

They went on ride after ride, holding hands and laughing and screaming. Lance felt a sense of freedom unknown to him for so long that it almost seemed foreign. He knew Ricky felt the same way. Today, they were just two teen boys having a fun day with their girls.

That was before they boarded a roller coaster called Apocalypse, and the ride lived up to its name.

Everything started out fine. The line was horrendous, but the girls didn't mind waiting because they could steal kisses from the boys. After a few, however, Lance suggested they stop for fear of drawing too much attention to them. Bridget looked disappointed, but Gibson gave Lance a nod of approval. The boys wanted to sit in the very front, but the girls saw the much longer line and nixed the idea.

Finally, they boarded the ride, ending up somewhere in the middle of a single train that carried twenty-two screaming, excited teens. Lance and Bridget sat together, and just behind them sat Ricky and Ariel. The ride began, and everyone whooped with excitement. As always, Ryan and Gibson waited until the boys boarded and then exited to the waiting area where the ride would disgorge its passengers.

The coaster chain pulled the train straight up to its ninety-five foot height with a loud *clackety clack* sound, up and up and up. Lance felt like he was heading for the sun, the angle was so steep, and the height jaw droppingly far. The train slowed near the top, giving everyone a birds-eye view of surrounding Valencia before plummeting straight down at fifty-miles-per-hour. Hands flew up, screams filled the air. Lance and Ricky threw up their arms bravely, while the girls clung to the restraining bar in joyful terror.

As the train hit bottom after a rocketing descent, Lance heard an odd sound, like air seeping instantly and loudly from an oxygen tank.

When it didn't come again, he thought nothing of it. At least until the train hit the first curve at teeth-rattling speed, seeming not to have braked at all. Then the train accelerated, or seemed to, racing at a breakneck pace toward the first tunnel. Bridget gripped Lance's hand tightly as a cold feeling enveloped him.

Something was wrong.

The train barreled through the tunnel and flew out the other side. Lance spotted park employees running toward the ride, and saw for a split second Ryan and Gibson pelting after them.

"Oh, hell," he mumbled, drawing a look from Bridget. He turned to her soberly. "Hold on."

Uncertain, she let go his hand and gripped the restraining bar.

Lance whipped his head back. "Hold on, Ricky, to the coaster!"

He didn't know if Ricky heard him or not because the train spun into a whiplash-inducing turn that threw him hard against the side of the car and sent pain lancing through his shoulder. Then they were flung into and out of another darkened tunnel, their speed increasing, the screams of the passengers becoming more real as everyone seemed to realize there was a problem.

Lance caught a split-second sight of workers frantically racing into the control booth, but then the train whipped past and hurled itself into a bone-crunching turn that whipped around into yet another. The car tilted inward, making Lance feel it might topple right off the track. The train swung to the left and began its final—extremely sharp—turn before heading back toward the station.

He gripped his retaining bar with knuckle-whitening intensity. The train pounded forward, shaking and rattling with a deafening cacophony of noise, and spun into the turn at a much greater speed than it was clearly supposed to. Its tail end hit the wooden railing and sent pieces flying outward. Just ahead was the final curve before the straightaway leading back into the station.

Lance had no idea how fast they were traveling, but it was mad fast and his blood froze as he watched the last, extreme curve looming ever closer. No brakes kicked in, as he expected, and the train slammed into the wooden railing, knocking it loose and just barely holding onto the track as it plowed forward into the station.

The next train, ordinarily on its way by now, sat empty before them, the crowds pulled far back away from the impact zone, park workers and fire fighters already awaiting the collision. What looked like a giant airbag had been placed on the track just behind the dormant train.

Someone with a bullhorn bellowed to the riders, "Brace for impact!"

The train slammed into the airbag with neck-snapping intensity, and bounced back. Lance flew forward, the bar digging into his midsection with excruciating pain. His neck whipped back and forth and almost made him bite his tongue.

Bridget cried out as she was flung hard into the bar and back, her head striking the padded seat. The train beneath them buckled and writhed a moment, like an angry snake, and then everything settled into a sudden peaceful quiet, as though everyone was frozen in place. The emergency personnel moved fast. They ran to the train, followed by park workers, and security guards. Behind them came Ryan and Gibson.

The medics went to the front seat, the one Lance and Ricky had so wanted to sit in. It had sustained the greatest damage, looking, despite the airbag, scrunched up like a tiny vehicle that had been struck by an SUV. The two boys within that front car seemed to be unconscious or… no, Lance didn't even want to think that! Hell, all he could think of were those Final Destination movies again. Was this his fault? Was death still stalking him?

Everyone on the train was stunned and shaken, some crying, others clutching elbows or heads. Lance realized too late he should've checked on Bridget first, but the second his lap bar released him, he leaped up and looked back at Ricky. Ricky was clutching his own arm and grimacing with pain, but smiled shyly and gave Lance a thumbs up.

Only then did Lance turn to check on Bridget, to find her looking at him in amazement.

"You okay?"

She nodded, the pain on her face clearly having nothing to do with her bruised shoulder.

Then the park workers and medics were all over them, helping ease everyone from the damaged train, checking for injuries that needed immediate care.

Lance, Ricky, Bridget, and Ariel were banged up a little, mostly bruises and aches, and stiffness in their necks, but they had sustained no serious injuries. Ryan and Gibson flashed their badges to park personnel, who quickly ushered them through.

Gibson stepped to the medic tending to the foursome. "These kids okay to travel?"

"Yes, sir," the medic said, "but best get them checked out by a doctor. Could be whiplash, or even a concussion."

Gibson nodded. "C'mon, kids, we're out of here. Now!"

With Ryan bringing up the rear, Gibson led the stunned quartet down from the platform. People were running in the direction of Apocalypse, obviously wanting to find out what happened, so the group had to force its way against the tide of bodies until they reached the exit. The two officers carefully scanned each face as they walked to the parking lot and moved to Ryan's car, always with one hand on the guns hidden beneath their shirts.

Once they were in the car and heading out of the parking lot, Lance finally found his voice.

"You really okay?" he asked.

Bridget clearly thought he was talking to her, but lost her slight smile when she realized he was talking to Ricky.

Ricky nodded. "Yeah. Banged my arm on the side when we hit is all."

Lance looked relieved, and then smiled at Bridget beside him, not noticing the look she was giving him. He was too caught up in the notion that death still wanted him back, and was willing to take everyone else with him.

"Sergeant Gibson," Lance asked, "that *was* just an accident, wasn't it?"

Gibson turned his head and gave Lance a sober look. "That remains to be seen. You sure no one knew you guys'd be here today?"

"No, we only told the girls and they didn't tell anyone, right?"

He looked at the girls and they shook their heads, still shaken by the ordeal.

Gibson grunted. "Let's see what the investigation shows." Then he turned forward again.

Lance hadn't even heard that last comment because his mind just recalled something, something about tapping into his cell phone calls.

Something about hacking into the Pentagon. Not something.

Someone.

Michael.

Ricky must've seen something in his face because he put a hand to Lance's arm. "You okay, Lance?"

Lance offered a slight smile. But he was far from okay. He couldn't believe Michael would do something like this, but he also knew if anyone was smart enough to pull it off, that person was Michael.

The remainder of the ride to New Camelot was made in uncertain silence.

By the time they returned home, Sergeant Gibson had already called ahead and informed Arthur of the incident, so he wouldn't worry when the story hit the news. They dropped the girls off at Bridget's house, and headed straight home.

When Lance and Ricky entered New Camelot, Arthur and Jenny were there, sweeping both boys into their arms and just holding them. Reyna and Esteban appeared, and so did Chris.

Everyone was so relieved they couldn't talk for a few moments.

Arthur pulled away and examined the boys for injuries. "Are you hurt, either of you?"

Lance shook his head. "We just got banged around, Dad. We're too tough to get hurt, right, Ricky?"

Ricky nodded, but didn't grin. He was clearly shaken up by their close call.

"Banged up is an understatement, Lance," Jenny said, pointing down the hall toward the Throne Room. "People were recording with their cell phones and I almost had a heart attack watching the footage. Thank God, you're all right!"

They wandered into the Throne Room where a local news man was reporting from Manic Mountain. All that the park would confirm was "unexplained brake failure" and several kids in the very front of the train sustained severe injuries and had been sent to the hospital. No cause for the brake failure was speculated on at this time.

Arthur turned to the two police officers. "Coincidence, do you think?"

Ryan said, "My gut tells me no."

"I agree," Gibson put in before turning to Lance and Ricky. "Think carefully about this boys – could anyone have found out about your trip today?"

Lance's mind instantly went to Michael, but he just couldn't believe Michael capable of something like that. And what would be the point when Michael seemed to want Lance alive for whatever reason?

Lance realized he must've had some look on his face because Ryan said, "Lance, do you know something?"

Ricky eyed him with suspicion.

Lance lowered his eyes to the floor. "No, Sergeant, I don't." Then he looked up. "Unless the girls told somebody, and I believe them when they said they didn't. Nobody could've found out we were going today."

He turned to find Ricky pinning him with an intense, questioning look. Lance could see it on Ricky's face – the other boy knew he was lying.

"Okay, here's the deal," Gibson said sternly, "and I don't wanna hear any complaints from you boys. From here on out, you are restricted to this house unless out cleaning a neighborhood with your dad and the rest of us for protection. No more dates with your girls, not until we figure out what happened."

He obviously expected a protest, and Lance noted visible surprise in the man's face when he said, "I understand."

Ricky echoed the sentiment.

"Of course," Arthur added, "the girls may still visit here as often as they like."

Jenny dropped into her mother mode. "Okay, boys, you've had a traumatic day.

I want you upstairs and soaking in a hot bath. That should soothe some of the aches and pains."

Again, neither boy argued. Lance was still mulling over the Michael possibility, and Ricky eyed him questionably. They hugged Arthur and Jenny again, thanked the two sergeants for getting them safely home, and headed upstairs.

As soon as they entered Lance's room, Ricky shut the door.

"Why did you lie down there?"

Lance turned, shocked. "What?"

"You and me practically finish each other's thoughts, Lance, and I can tell when you lie. What do you know?"

Lance looked away in shame. He hated keeping anything from Ricky. "I don't know anything, Ricky."

"But you have an idea."

Lance said nothing, and didn't meet Ricky's eye.

"This has to do with Michael, doesn't it?" Ricky finally said with obvious distaste.

Lance looked up, again startled that Ricky knew him so well. Still, he said nothing.

"Hell, Lance, why're you always protecting him?"

"I'm not," Lance said, but not as firmly as he'd have liked. "It's just something I thought of downstairs, but I don't know anything yet. I gotta talk to Michael, first."

He sat down on the bed, his gaze fixed on the floor.

Ricky crossed the room in three strides. "Look at me, Lance."

Lance slowly tilted his head up and made eye contact.

"Tell me." Ricky's arms were thrown across his chest, his eyes wide and demanding.

Lance sighed, knowing exactly how Ricky would react. "Michael's been tapping into my phone."

Ricky looked aghast. "What?!"

Lance explained what else he'd found on Michael's computer that night, and by the time he finished, Ricky was livid.

"And you didn't think you should tell me about this?" he asked, his voice laced with equal measures of anger and hurt.

"He said he wouldn't do it anymore."

Ricky almost laughed. "He said he wouldn't do it anymore?"

Lance nodded, knowing how feeble it sounded. "He does do what I tell him, Ricky. You just haven't noticed."

366

Ricky stared at Lance as though seeing him for the first time. "I'm telling Dad, now." He made for the door.

Lance leaped off the bed and blocked Ricky's exit. "You can't, Ricky."

"I can, and I'm going to. Now get out of my way before I push you out."

Lance stood his ground. "Ricky, listen to me."

Ricky stared silently, agitated and looking like he was prepared to wrestle him away from the door.

"Look, we don't even know if what happened was an accident, okay? We need to find out, first. Then, if it looks like somebody messed with the ride, I'll talk to Michael."

Ricky still glared. "You'll talk to Michael. And he'll just admit trying to kill us?"

Lance locked eyes with Ricky. "You and me, Ricky, well, what you said before, it's true. We do think the same thoughts. John was right about us. You know I'm not BSing you. There's no reason Michael would want to kill us."

"How 'bout he hates my guts and he's jealous of Bridget?"

Lance turned red, despite every effort not to. "He's not, either. And I was on that ride too. He wouldn't hurt me."

Ricky stared in open-mouthed amazement.

"Give me some time, Ricky," Lance implored. "If it turns out the ride was messed with, I'll confront Michael. You can go with me. If you don't believe what he says, then we'll tell Dad. Deal?"

Ricky stared a moment longer. "Okay. But you don't see him on your own."

Lance smiled. "I won't. I might need these guns of yours."

He lightly squeezed Ricky's taut arms dangling at his side, finding his eyes drawn to the prominent bicep veins.

"Damn straight, you do."

Lance raised his eyes. "Thanks, Ricky."

"For what? Trusting your dumb ass?"

Lance laughed. "Yeah. And just for, I don' know, for caring."

Ricky nodded, his face reddening as they uneasily broke eye contact. Then he returned to his room and both boys took long, hot baths to ease the soreness from their stressful ordeal.

Of course, the roller coaster near-disaster was front-page news and the top story on all TV broadcasts for several days. Lance and Ricky, as well as Arthur and everyone at New Camelot, were happy that no one knew the boys had been on the ride. But two days later, after park officials examined all the ride pictures of passengers, some eagle-eyed worker, who obviously recognized Lance and Ricky, sent those pictures to the media. They had been outed.

Speculation ran rampant: *Was it An Accident, or Sabotage?; Was This an Attack on Sir Lance and Sir Ricky?; Another Terror Attack on New Camelot?*

The initial investigation had proven inconclusive, though closer examination of the ride was still ongoing. The official word for now was "accidental brake failure," but the cause remained under investigation. If the brakes had been tampered with, Sergeant Gibson told everyone, the person had to be a park employee with intimate knowledge of the coaster workings, or somebody insanely smart enough to rig the brakes to fail and leave no evidence behind.

Ricky eyed Lance when Gibson said that last part, but Lance refused to meet his gaze. For now, the question of "deliberate" or "accidental" was open-ended, and the boys were restricted to the premises unless out with Arthur and full police escort.

Lance texted Michael a few times to invite him over, but Michael always begged off without a reason, fueling Ricky's notion that Michael had something to do with the roller coaster incident. This pattern lasted several weeks.

Lance needed to see Michael – there was no other way. He'd promised to confront Michael with Ricky present, but he knew Michael would never tell the truth with Ricky there. So he texted Michael and asked him to meet at De Longpre Park at midnight because there was something important they needed to talk about.

Michael sent back his usual snarky response: "Finally realize you can't live without me, Lance?"

Lance signed off. The next challenge would be to sneak out without Ricky catching him.

When they went to bed that night, each on his own side, Lance made sure not to make direct eye contact even in the dark because he knew Ricky would pick up that he was hiding something. He felt guilty for putting one over on this boy who would do anything for him. They chatted about everything except the girls and the roller coaster incident, for some reason skirting both issues without even consciously willing it to be so. Again, that bond just kicked in.

"You ever wonder why you and me'r so much alike, Lance?" Ricky asked after a long pause which made Lance think he'd fallen asleep.

Lance sighed. He'd asked himself that question a hundred times already and sometimes didn't like the answers he came up with because they scared him. "Not any more. Just happy we are."

Lance could feel Ricky look over at him in the dark. "Me too," he answered, and then there was silence.

Lance lay awake listening and watching the clock on his night table. After a while, he heard Ricky's steady breathing and knew the other boy was asleep. Since it was already eleven o'clock, Lance slithered cautiously out of bed and slipped the extra pillows he'd stashed on the floor up and under the blankets in case Ricky awoke later and glanced over.

Lance tiptoed around the bed and into Ricky's room, where he'd secreted some clothes, shoes, a big hoodie and his skateboard. Then he was down the back stairs and out through the kitchen before anyone could wander around and find him. Justin had gotten some of the older knights for patrol duties, and organized an around-the-clock rotation, but Lance had quickly memorized their schedule and knew when to slip through without being noticed.

He skated to De Longpre Park with ease, and enjoyed the simple freedom of just him and his board under cover of starlight. The park was located on the corner of De Longpre and Cherokee in Hollywood, one of those pocket parks a block south of Sunset Blvd.

Lance arrived at eleven forty-five and entered the dark, somewhat creepy locale, rolling quietly along the tree-lined path to a bench he knew to be just ahead. He stopped and looked around, ever wary of a possible sneak attack after everything that had been happening. Seeing and hearing nothing, he sat on the bench, awaiting Michael and rehearsing what he wanted to say.

Suddenly, from behind him he heard a whispered voice from the past, "Well if it isn't my little fag boy."

Lance leaped to his feet and whirled, knife already out of its sheath and pointing in front of him. From around the tree directly behind the bench stepped the one person who could always reduce him to jelly—the boogeyman.

"The hell'r you doing here?" Lance gasped, his heart already thudding in his chest.

Richard stepped into the light from the street lamp a few feet away, and Lance saw that face in close-up for the first time in six years. He was older, thinner, the yellow hair had been dyed light red, but the evil look remained in those black eyes of his.

"Now is that any way to greet your favorite foster dad, eh?"

Lance glanced around, desperately hoping Michael would arrive. "How'd you find me?"

Richard chuckled, the almost-giggle that haunted Lance's nightmares, and held up his cell phone. "It was pretty easy once I got hired by your cellular carrier, Little Lance."

Lance shivered, his breath becoming shallow, his heart pounding with fear. "Don't call me that."

Richard stepped closer, and Lance backed up.

"How are you, son?" Richard asked, inching closer.

Lance leapt back and swung the blade threateningly before him. "Stay back, Richard, or I'll cut your balls off!"

Richard didn't look the least bit fazed. "Is that any way to talk to the man who loved you?"

Lance cowered, but still waved the knife. "You raped me, Richard, that's what you did, and I hate your guts! I swear I'll kill you if you touch me again!"

Richard stepped closer still, grinning, and reached out a hand to touch Lance's face. Lance froze, knife arm dropping uncertainly, as Richard's fingers lightly caressed his cheek.

"Still soft as a baby's behind, Lance, just like I remember."

Lance went weak in the knees, and almost blacked out with terror.

Then he heard, "Hey, Lance, where are you?"

Richard whipped his hand back. "We're not finished...son." He turned and vanished into the darkness.

Lance stood frozen and shaking, arm at his side, knife blade protruding from his hand, his heart rate frenetic.

That was how Michael found him.

"What's going on, Lance?" Michael asked as he jogged over, casting his gaze toward the distant retreating figure. "Who was that?"

His face beaded with sweat, Lance turned his wide green eyes onto Michael's suspicious face.

"An old... an old foster parent," he croaked, almost gasping for breath.

Michael's eyes narrowed. "Yeah? From when?"

"From... when I was six," Lance murmured, shaking visibly and feeling like a petrified little boy.

Michael's eyes narrowed even further, descending into that murderous glare Lance had seen on more than one occasion. Michael gave Lance a cursory once over, shaking his head in disgust. "Well, he sure as hell did a number on you, Lance. You're shaking like a leaf."

Lance looked helplessly at him, but said nothing. He felt like a cornered rat that knew it was about to die.

Michael placed one hand on his shoulder, and Lance lurched away in terror.

"Look, man," Michael said soberly, "You're spooked as hell. Come back to my place. We'll have a few drinks. That'll relax you."

Lance recoiled. "No, Michael. I don' wanna get drunk, okay?"

Michael just stared at him.

Lance lowered his eyes. "Okay, yeah, I do want to, but I can't. I need to go home. Can you drive me?"

"You called me out here, Lance. What for?"

"Huh?" Lance felt confused, his head filled with cotton.

Did I call him?

"You said you needed to talk to me. What about?"

"It doesn't matter now. I can't think right. Can you drive me or what?"

Michael snorted. "Why should I? You don't want to spend time with me."

Lance's temper rose. "Okay, fine. I'm outta here." He turned with his board and prepared to skate away.

"You're a little girl, Lance, you know that?"

Lance whirled, board in hand, both rattled and furious. "The hell did you call me?"

"A girl, that's what." Michael sneered. "Look at you, the great badass Sir Lance quivering like a baby during a lightning storm. Pathetic!"

Rage engulfed Lance and he strode forward, raising his board to swing at Michael's head.

Michael didn't even flinch. He merely stared with icy, dead eyes. "You hit me with that and I'll break you, Lance. And then I'll kill you."

Lance stopped up short, his mouth hanging open, the board suspended in midair at shoulder height.

Michael's gaze was so venomous that Lance slowly lowered the board and gazed at him in horror.

"Drop dead, Michael," he said, and then turned to walk away, half expecting Michael to jump him. When no sound followed him, Lance called back, "I'm changing my cell number, so don't bother texting me anymore."

Michael tossed off a hollow laugh that made Lance think of a serial killer. "Like

I can't figure out your new one?" He tapped the side of his head. "The Pentagon, remember?"

Lance ignored him. He pelted forward and jumped onto his skateboard, barreling rapidly away from the park.

By the time he got back to New Camelot, Lance had almost been struck by someone running a red light at Cherokee and Hollywood Blvd. He had traveled up Seward to Sunset, in case Richard was still loitering anywhere near the park, cut over to Schrader, then up to Hollywood, taking that to Highland and on up to Franklin.

When he arrived, he was dripping with sweat, and shaking, both from his encounter with Richard, and the one with Michael. He snuck back into the house and slipped quietly into his room, stashing the board in his closet and stripping off his sweaty shirt and hoodie. Slipping into the usual workout shorts he always wore to bed, Lance climbed onto his side of the bed and gazed longingly at Ricky slumbering peacefully on the other side.

He couldn't stop shaking. He kept seeing Richard's face, kept hearing that sibilant, creepy voice. He knew he couldn't deal with this alone. Shivering with fear, he crept over to Ricky and lightly shook his shoulder. Ricky stirred, and then opened his eyes. Something in Lance's face must've alarmed him because he instantly sat up.

"What's wrong, Lance?"

Lance fought to control his voice. "I did something stupid, Ricky. I'm sorry."

Ricky's face crumpled with fear. "What did you do?"

"I snuck out to see Michael."

"Hell!" Ricky spat. "Did he hurt you?"

"No. I mean, yes, but not like you think." He saw the confused look on Ricky's face, and took a deep breath. "Richard found me."

Ricky gasped, and placed his hand into Lance's. "Tell me."

Lance told Ricky everything about the encounter with Richard, and the fight with Michael.

Ricky grew more alarmed by the moment. "We gotta call Sergeant Ryan. Now."

He let go Lance's hand and started out of the bed, but Lance grabbed his hand and pulled him back. "No, Ricky, not now. There's nothing he can do right now."

Ricky looked at him and must've seen how desperate and frightened he was, because he crawled back onto the bed.

"I'm scared, Ricky," Lance whispered. "Richard makes me feel like a frightened little kid. I hate his ass, Ricky, I hate him so much! I want him dead!"

The terror in Lance's eyes, the desperate despair in his voice, caused Ricky to reach over and pull him into a hug.

"It's okay, Lance," he said soothingly. "I'm here now. I got you. He'll never hurt you again. Not so long as I'm here."

Lance fought back the tears that threatened to engulf him. "Oh, God, Ricky, I wanna be so badass and then that bastard turns me into a baby, just like Michael said!"

"You're not a baby, Lance," Ricky assured him. "You're the most badass boy I ever knew. What he did to you was so horrible, you can't help but feel scared. But I got you now."

Lance pulled away and looked Ricky in the face. Their eyes locked. Uncertainty overwhelmed Lance, and he felt the same insecurity emanating from Ricky.

Despite his skittishness, he asked, "Can you hold me tonight, while we sleep, Ricky? Like that other time? I'm just so scared and... I don' wanna be alone."

Even in the dark, Lance felt Ricky hesitate, and feared he'd say no. But Ricky nodded. They lay down side-by-side, and Lance wrapped Ricky's arms around him and rested his head against Ricky's chest.

"Hey, Ricky," Lance said quietly after a long stretch of silence. "Hey, what?"

"Michael *is* a jerkbag, and I'm done with him. Changing my phone number tomorrow."

"Sounds like a plan. Night, Lance."

"Night, Ricky."

Gradually, the two boys grew more relaxed and eventually Lance's shivering ceased, sleep finally overcoming him.

The following morning, the housekeeper called Arthur to the front door. Jenny joined him as he descended the stairs.

"What's wrong, Arthur?"

Arthur looked concerned. "I don't know. The police are downstairs."

She frowned. "Does Sergeant Ryan know anything about this?"

He shrugged.

When they reached the bottom of the stairs, Ryan was already there, dressed and looking almost nauseous with disgust and anger. The front door stood open and police officers were streaming into the house, spreading out and searching the premises.

"What is happening, Sergeant?" Arthur asked with worry.

Ryan's face looked more weathered than ever as he held up a document to Arthur. "They have a warrant to search the premises, Arthur," he said wearily, "especially the armory. They're going to confiscate all knives and short-bladed weapons you have."

"Why?"

Another man stepped forward, African-American, burly, barrel-chested, wearing a suit and flashing a police badge.

"I'm Sergeant Wallace, Homicide, King Arthur," he said in a flat, emotionless voice. "I need your key to the armory."

Arthur looked worriedly from him to Ryan. Ryan nodded. Reluctantly, Arthur pulled his keys from his belt and slipped the armory key from its ring, handing it to Sergeant Wallace.

"Thank you," Wallace said curtly, and handed the key off to a uniformed cop by his side. "Where is the armory?"

"Within the training center," Arthur replied, pointing out the proper direction, and the uniformed cop set off down the hall.

Ryan looked almost tragically sad. "They also need Lance." He could barely meet the king's wide, questioning eyes.

Jenny sucked in a breath.

Arthur's face paled. "Why?"

Wallace remained stone-faced. "Please ask him to come down, King Arthur, or we'll have to go find him."

Deep fear enveloped Arthur as he looked at Jenny and gripped her shaking hand softly. "Jenny, if you would, please ask Lance to join us."

Terrified questions dancing across her blue eyes, Jenny nodded and retreated up the stairs.

She knocked lightly on Lance's door, then pushed it open, startled to see the two boys wrapped in each other's arms, fast asleep. Not knowing what might have gone on between them, her fear for Lance took precedence. She walked to the bed and gently shook them awake.

The boys opened their eyes, saw Jenny's concerned face floating above them, and then realized how she'd found them. Burning with embarrassment, they quickly disentangled themselves.

"It's not what you think, Mom," Lance hurriedly said, his voice filled with self-conscious fear.

She tried for a smile. "It's okay, Lance. Um, I need you boys to dress and come downstairs right away."

Her trembling voice and fearful expression must've been obvious because both boys sat upright with concern.

"What's wrong, Mom?" Ricky asked.

She tried to appear calm. "The police are here, Lance. They want to talk to you."

Lance blanched. "Uh, ok. We'll be right down."

She nodded and left them alone, closing the door with a finality that scared Lance even more. The two boys eyed each other with worry, and then jumped from the bed to get dressed.

Arthur and Jenny, along with Chris, Justin and the other patrol-duty knights, watched as uniformed cops swarmed about them into and out of every room, including the upper floors. Cops carried off all the knives and dirks, as well as any sharp kitchen knives, in sealed plastic bags.

Ryan and Wallace stood in the lobby with Arthur and Jenny.

"You gonna tell me what this is about, Mitch?" Ryan asked Wallace.

The bigger man looked stoically at his colleague. "This is a homicide investigation, Ryan. You know I can't say anything in front of possible witnesses."

"Is Lance under suspicion for something?" Jenny asked, her voice more unsteady than she would've liked.

Wallace just looked at her. "I can't say, ma'am."

A sound drew her attention to the stairs, and all heads turned to see Lance and Ricky standing at the top, dressed casually in jeans and t-shirts, eying the group with worry.

Arthur cleared his throat. "Come down, my sons," he said as casually as he could. "This officer must speak with you, Lance."

As Lance and Ricky began their descent, Wallace nodded to several uniformed officers who waited at the bottom of the stairs for the boys to descend. The moment Lance stepped in front of them to approach Arthur, one of the cops grabbed him and yanked his hands back behind him, almost wrenching his shoulders.

"Ow!" Lance cried out in pain, as the other cop slipped handcuffs around his wrists and snapped them in place, hard and tight. "That hurts!" he bellowed as Ricky moved forward to help him.

"Don't interfere, young man, or you'll be arrested as well," Wallace intoned sternly.

Ricky stopped and glared at the man before turning his terrified eyes onto Lance, who grimaced with pain at the tightness of the cuffs.

"What's going on?" Lance almost shouted.

Arthur stepped forward toward Wallace. "This is outrageous!"

"Don't come any closer, King Arthur, or I'll arrest you too."

"What is this about?" Jenny asked. "You have no right."

Wallace held up another document. "An arrest warrant for one Lance Pendragon."

"On what charge?" Ryan asked, his fury clearly on the rise.

"Attempted murder."

There was a moment of stunned disbelief as Arthur and Jenny exchanged a look.

Lance glanced over at Ricky in astonishment.

Wallace nodded to the officers on either side of Lance, and they led him toward the open front door.

"Dad, help me!" Lance called out, and Arthur stepped forward again.

Two more officers blocked his path.

"Don't," Wallace intoned firmly.

But that didn't stop Ricky from ducking away from the cops and darting around the two holding Lance. He blocked the door, locking eyes on Lance's desperately fearful green ones.

One of the cops holding Lance growled, "Outta the way, kid, or you'll be under arrest for obstruction of justice."

Ricky mad dogged him and looked again at Lance. "Lance, I..."

Though terrified, Lance affected the badass demeanor he always used whenever he felt threatened. "It's okay, Ricky," he said with as much assurance as he could muster. "I need you here."

"Lance, I..."

Lance tried for a little grin. "No worries."

More reluctantly than he'd ever done anything in his life, Ricky stepped aside and watched Lance dragged from the house like a common criminal.

Ricky, Arthur and Jenny, her hand in Chris's, hurried outside. They were followed by Justin and the others as Lance was led toward a waiting police cruiser.

The media was already out in force. Cameras captured images of Lance, his hair flying and hands cuffed behind his back, looking lost and desperate as he was dragged to the police car.

As the two cops neared the car with Lance, the older one leaned in to the boy's ear. "Hope those cuffs are snug enough, *Sir* Lance," he sneered, his voice laced with sarcasm. "I've been waitin' to slap those on you ever since you torched my car at Round Table!"

Lance turned his head to eye the self-satisfied expression, careful not to reveal the pain cutting into his wrists.

The cop snorted. "Uppity ass little Mexican punk, trying to change things that shouldn't be changed. Should've stayed in your own country."

Lance met his gaze. "This is my country."

The cop scowled and unobtrusively shoved Lance toward the open back door of his cruiser, causing him to stumble and bang his head on the top of the car, momentarily leaving him dazed.

"Back off," the cop's young partner said, but the other one ignored the admonition, roughly pushing Lance into the back seat and slamming the door. He glowered a moment at his partner before heading around to the driver's side. The partner got into the passenger side and the siren came on. The gate was flung open by the security guards and the car moved forward through the crowd of reporters and spectators pooled outside.

Arthur despondently watched his son dragged away. His heart broke almost as much as on that long ago night when he felt Lance's life slipping away from him. Jenny took his hand, and a crying Chris threw his arms around the devastated Ricky, who stared in helpless abandon long after the police car bearing Lance was lost to sight.

Ryan stepped up to Arthur. "Wallace said they're taking him to the Hollywood station for questioning." He turned to Jenny. "Get Sam on the phone and get him down there pronto. Arthur, you're with me."

Arthur nodded, squeezing Jenny's hand before she ran back into the house to make the call.

Ricky looked desperately at Arthur, fighting back tears, his wide brown eyes filled with desperation. "Oh, Dad…"

Arthur drew Ricky and Chris into a tight hug. "We'll get him back. This is all a misunderstanding."

He released them, patted Ricky on the shoulder, and followed Ryan hurriedly to the detective's car.

Ricky held the tearful Chris tightly, his heart and soul numb with sorrow. They stood holding each other until Jenny came out to bring them inside, away from the prying eyes of the media.

Once upon a time in the City of Angels, a boy came back, and hope endured.

The Lance Chronicles Continue in Book III:

THERE IS NO FEAR

THE LANCE CHRONICLES

Book I:

CHILDREN OF THE KNIGHT

Book II:

RUNNING THROUGH A DARK PLACE

Book III:

THERE IS NO FEAR

Book IV:

AND THE CHILDREN SHALL LEAD

Book V:

ONCE UPON A TIME IN AMERICA

Michael J. Bowler is an award-winning author of nine novels—*A Boy and His Dragon*, *A Matter of Time*, *Children of the Knight*, *Running Through A Dark Place*, *There Is No Fear*, *And The Children Shall Lead*, *Once Upon A Time In America*, *Spinner*, and *Warrior Kids: A Tale of New Camelot*.

His screenplay, "THE GOD MACHINE," won First Place in the 2017 Scriptapalooza competition.

He grew up in San Rafael, California, and majored in English and Theatre at Santa Clara University. He went on to earn a master's in film production from Loyola Marymount University, a teaching credential in English from LMU, and another master's in Special Education from Cal State University Dominguez Hills.

He worked producer, writer, and/or director on several ultra-low-budget horror films, including "Hell Spa," "Fatal Images," "Club Dead," and "Things II."

He taught high school in Hawthorne, California—both in general education and to students with learning disabilities—in subjects ranging from English and Strength Training to Algebra, Biology, and Yearbook.

He has been a volunteer Big Brother to eight different boys with the Catholic Big Brothers Big Sisters program, and a decades-long volunteer within the juvenile justice system in Los Angeles.

He has been honored as Probation Volunteer of the Year, YMCA Volunteer of the Year, California Big Brother of the Year, and 2000 National Big Brother of the Year. The "National" honor allowed him and three of his Little Brothers to visit the White House and meet the president in the Oval Office.

He has completed three new novels aimed at the teen market, and one for middle grade.

His goal as an author is for teens and middle schoolers to experience empowerment and hope; to see themselves in his diverse characters; to read about kids who face real-life challenges; and to see how kids like them can remain decent people in an indecent world. The most prevalent theme in his writing is this: as a society, and as individuals, we're better off when we do what's right, not what's easy.

Website: www.michaeljbowler.com

FB: michaeljbowlerauthor

Twitter: https://twitter.com/MichaelJBowler

tumblr: http://michaeljbowler.tumblr.com/

Pinterest: http://www.pinterest.com/michaelbowler/pins/

Amazon: http://www.amazon.com/Michael-J.-Bowler/e/B0075ML4M4

YouTube: https://www.youtube.com/channel/UC2NXCPry4DDgJZOVDUxVtMw

Google+: https://plus.google.com/u/0/+MichaelJBowler

Instagram: michaeljbowler

PRAISE FOR CHILDREN OF THE KNIGHT
(BOOK 1 OF THE LANCE CHRONICLES):

"This novel was stunning. As a nation, we are making our children disposable, writing them off as nothing worth saving and treating them like adults in a judicial system riddled with corruption and, worse, a simple lack of caring."

— Sammy on *Goodreads/Amazon*

"I think there is every human emotion packed into this story. This is the first in a series and it is amazingly powerful."

— Jerry on *Goodreads*

"Growing up, I knew far too many kids just like the ones in this book. I was one of them. These characters are real and heart-rending."

—Giovanni, former foster child

"Who, but the children, fight FOR the children! If I could make this required reading in all schools, colleges, book clubs, etc.. I would in a heartbeat. My 15 year old son is reading this now and it had raised so many questions from him, questions I am so happy he has asked."

— JoAnn on *Goodreads*

"*Children of the Knight* is one of those stories where you start reading saying to yourself "that'll never work" and then 6 hours later you put it down sobbing, having read one of the best young adult books currently in publication."

— Josh at *Greedy Bug Book Reviews*

"I loved the way characters were brought to life and allowed to experience all emotions, including uncertainty, jealousy, shame, anger, happiness, and love. All of them, especially Lance, made an impression on me and I'm not likely to forget them anytime soon."

– E. Summers on Goodreads/Amazon

"Children of the Knight is one of the most emotional books I have ever read. I am not usually overly emotional when reading, yet at various times during the novel I found myself laughing, cheering, feeling terrified for the characters, and even almost crying. This is one of the few books I would recommend to anyone and everyone."

– The Broken Bookshelf

"I laughed. I cried. I felt. Simply put, this is easily one of the best books I've read in the past five years. Bowler's writing invites readers to truly hear water dripping and shots going off, truly feel sneers and snarky comments from peers, truly witness and experience injustice in its most disturbing form - one involving children. This book will call you to action on behalf of our society's "optional children." If you read anything this year, read this book."

– Nora at Only God Writes Trees